D0047069

Forever Amish

—

A NOVEL

KATE LLOYD

David C Cook®

transforming lives together

FOREVER AMISH
Published by David C Cook
4050 Lee Vance View
Colorado Springs, CO 80918 U.S.A.

David C Cook Distribution Canada
55 Woodslee Avenue, Paris, Ontario, Canada N3L 3E5

David C Cook U.K., Kingsway Communications
Eastbourne, East Sussex BN23 6NT, England

The graphic circle C logo is a registered trademark of David C Cook.

All rights reserved. Except for brief excerpts for review purposes,
no part of this book may be reproduced or used in any form
without written permission from the publisher.

This story is a work of fiction. Characters and events are the product of the author's
imagination. Any resemblance to any person, living or dead, is coincidental.

Unless otherwise noted, all Scripture quotations are taken from the
King James Version of the Bible. (Public Domain.) Scripture quotations
marked NIV are taken from the Holy Bible, New International Version®,
NIV®. Copyright © 1973, 2011 by Biblica, Inc.™ Used by permission of
Zondervan. All rights reserved worldwide. www.zondervan.com.

LCCN 2014933824
ISBN 978-0-7814-0874-5
eISBN 978-1-4347-0791-8

© 2014 Kate Lloyd
The author is represented by MacGregor Literary, Inc. of Hillsboro, OR.

The Team: Don Pape, Traci DePree, Nick Lee, Ingrid
Beck, Tonya Osterhouse, Karen Athen
Cover Design: Amy Konyndyk
Cover Photo: Steve Gardner, Pixelworks Studios

Printed in the United States of America
First Edition 2014

2 3 4 5 6 7 8 9 10

061014

To my dearest sister, Margaret Coppock

Note to Readers

Thank you for joining my fictional characters in magnificent Lancaster County, Pennsylvania. Any resemblance to real members of the Amish or Mennonite communities is unintended. I ask your forgiveness for any inaccuracies.

Above all else, guard your heart, for everything you do flows from it.

—Proverbs 4:23 NIV

PROLOGUE

Lizzie Zook was on a mission of a most urgent nature. Ignoring Bishop Troyer's stern voice nagging inside her ear, warning her that her shenanigans would land her in a wagonload of misery, she logged onto the Internet.

Lizzie's heart fluttered with excitement as she typed her email, then—whilst she wondered what other enticements she could use—her gaze drifted around the shop with its multitude of vintage fancy and plain items for sale. Nothing was new or quite old enough to be an antique, she thought, much like she herself at age twenty. She'd soon be an *alte Maedel*—old maid—stuck at home helping Mamm with the chores all day and listening to her younger brothers arguing and teasing—never having any fun. Never getting married.

The brass bell above the shop's door jingled, and she felt brisk March air waft into the room, followed by the sound of a woman clearing her throat. Ach! Out of her peripheral vision she saw the bishop's wife. Lizzie ignored the portly woman and pushed the Send button before she lost her nerve. If Lizzie didn't take drastic action, who else would mend her fractured family?

CHAPTER 1

"Hold on, Sally. Where ya headed?" I heard my father say as he shuffled across his lot, Honest Ed's Used Cars. Yup, my dad was Honest Ed. I didn't care what quips people made about car salesmen; Pops was the most trustworthy man on earth—except in one area.

I shoved the nagging thought aside. "I'm taking a weekend getaway," I said. "I need to clear my head."

He had the hiccups again. "You'd leave without saying good-bye or asking permission to borrow a car?"

"I was about to." I opened the trunk of a '67 Mustang, an automobile my father coveted but my fiancé, Donald, wouldn't be caught dead driving. "I didn't think you'd mind."

"I suppose not." Pops indulged in an extensive yawn. The early spring sunshine radiated from the asphalt beneath my feet, but he wore a wool jacket buttoned to his chin. "Where you going?"

"Lancaster County, land of the Amish. To a place called Bird-in-Hand."

His features contorted. "Why there, of all ridiculous places?"

"When I was young, I begged you to take me, but you never would. And Donald flat out laughed in my face when I suggested it for our honeymoon." I stowed my overnight bag and shut the trunk. "For a couple of months, someone named Lizzie has been emailing me through the Contact Page on my website, asking me to visit her."

Pops scratched the side of his nose. "Lizzie who? What does she want?"

"She's hinted she wants to buy a dog." And she'd also implied she was in a jam and needed my help. Why me? Maybe she was trying to start a kennel of her own.

"Did you tell her you don't have any for sale?" He blinked several times.

"Yes, but ..." I wouldn't divulge how persistent she'd been or how artfully she'd dodged my queries. She hadn't even given me her address. "Maybe I can find a corgi kennel in her area for her."

His voice turned gruff. "Can't you locate one on the Internet and then write her an email?"

"She claims she isn't allowed to use the Internet anymore." A pewter-gray cloud moved in, hogging the sunlight, leaving us in the shade, the temperature dipping. I should have brought a warmer jacket but didn't want to delay my departure by racing back to the house—a three-minute walk.

"Huh?" He frowned. "Or speak on the phone?"

"She didn't give me a number." I eyeballed the Mustang's tires, trying to determine if they had sufficient pressure. "She said she works in a secondhand store—a consignment shop in a town called Intercourse, near Bird-in-Hand."

"It's got to be a prank."

"Yeah, I can't find the Sunflower Secondhand Store's website. But there actually is an Intercourse, Pennsylvania, and I want to see it. What a hoot." I needed a distraction—something to make me forget my whole world was on the verge of collapse.

"Sally, I don't want you going there." The corners of his mouth stabbed down. "It isn't safe for women to meet people through the Internet. I wish you'd never built that website."

"In retrospect I agree. Now that Mr. Big's gone, I'm ready to give up the dog-show world."

"Then stick around, kiddo." He covered his mouth to yawn again, his fingers puffy—a fact he blamed on consuming too much salt. "I'll keep you busy. On a Friday afternoon I can't spare you or the car."

"Sure you can. Ralph wheels and deals ten times better than I do. He'll fill in if you get swamped. And you know this Mustang's priced too high." I figured he kept the fire-engine–red coupe on the lot to attract customers.

He massaged his back, below his rib cage.

"Are you okay, Pops? If you're too sick, I'll stay home."

"I'm fine." But at five foot nine, he seemed to be shrinking. "Shouldn't you be planning your wedding?"

"My future mother-in-law's marriage extravaganza?"

"Hey, if she wants to pay for it."

"Attempting to influence Darlene Montgomery is like trying to stop the rising tide." I edged toward the driver's door. "Now, about this weekend …," I said, not wanting to burden Pop with Donald's and my stalemate. After our snarly clash—our worst skirmish in the year we'd dated—I wondered if I still wanted to marry him, even with the invitations printed. I wasn't sure I loved him—or ever had.

"I'm against your going, and that's that." Pops crossed his arms, tucked his hands out of sight.

"Please? I need a getaway. Unless you don't feel good enough, in which case I'll take you to the doctor's." I'd offered to for weeks.

"I'm fine and dandy. Never felt better. Case closed."

"Okay. So will you lend me this car?" I usually got my pick from his inventory of about three dozen. Some were clunkers, but others were sleek beauties—their chrome polished and their tires replaced. "I'm twenty-seven, if you've forgotten." I stood tall, not easy for a woman of five feet four inches. "When you were my age, you were already married."

"But no good came of it."

"What do you mean? You had me, didn't you?"

"Yeah, but your mother—"

"What about her? Come on; spill the beans." I felt the weight of sadness and resentment I'd carried all my life.

"Nah, I don't want you wasting your time and money trying to track her down." His breathing seemed labored. "She knows where to find us."

"She does?"

"Probably not, but she could. If she wanted to."

No use pursuing this figure-eight conversation. I couldn't wrangle the information out of him. Pleading, cajoling, and bribery had never worked.

"I'm going away for the weekend, even if it means riding the bus." I was behaving like a brat. And running away from my problems. "Or I could hitchhike—"

"That's downright stupid talk. What's gotten into you?"

"Guess I'm having a midlife crisis."

"Give me a break. Have you prayed about it?"

He had me there. I believed in God—a nebulous entity who'd created the universe then seemed to step back to let us screwed-up humans inadequately run the show.

A battered Subaru Forester coasted off congested Highway 7 and into Pops's lot; I knew Pops was already evaluating the vehicle as a trade-in. A couple emerged to inspect a two-year-old silver Toyota Highlander SUV.

"I won't hitchhike if you lend me this car." I removed the price from the windshield, opened the coupe's wide door, and tossed the placard on the floor behind the passenger seat. Then I settled into the cushy driver's seat to check the gas gauge. Almost full—surprise! I clamped my GPS to the windshield, then hopped out again. "I already entered the B&B's address."

"I don't have the time or energy to argue." His face turned pale, like the blood was draining out; perspiration moistened his cheeks. "You'll drive carefully?"

"Yes. What's the problem? Pretend I'm going to a dog show. It's not as if I've never driven anywhere by myself." I hugged him and felt his ribs, little muscle. "You'll look after Ginger, won't you?" My remaining corgi; I'd recently sold my other female to a Canadian couple who planned to breed her.

"I won't let her starve." He watched the couple circling the Highlander. "They don't call me Honest Ed for nothing."

Yeah, well, if he were so honest, why wouldn't he fess up about my mother?

"I've got an idea," he said, his hiccups increasing. "Instead of Pennsylvania, why not head to Cape Cod? I have a buddy and his wife you could stay with. I'll give him a call."

"You took me to visit them yourself last fall. I want to go somewhere new."

"But the weather could turn cold. The groundhog saw his shadow last month, meaning a late spring."

"No, he didn't. It was foggy that day."

"As I recall, it was slightly overcast. There was some dispute." Gnawing his lower lip, he looked perplexed. "Do you realize this car is older than you are?"

"But in mint condition. Isn't that what I heard you tell a customer? Didn't you nickname me Mustang Sally when I was little?" He used to belt out the song, but his lungs didn't have the oomph for singing anymore. When I was a girl, I'd heard his baritone voice next to me at church as he'd held the hymnal. But he'd stopped attending a couple years ago. He said sitting in one position so long gave him what he called the heebie-jeebies because his skin itched. I had no excuse; my faith lay as shallow as a streambed at the end of summer. And my fiancé wouldn't come with me—not even once. He'd plan outings on Sundays and take off without me if I weren't ready.

As I watched Pops amble across the lot to approach the man and woman, I second-guessed the wisdom in leaving him. Why exactly was I taking this excursion? I doubted I'd meet up with this Lizzie person.

I admired a stand of maples on the other side of the lot. Nothing outshone Connecticut's glorious chartreuse new-growth foliage first sprouting through bare branches in the springtime. I'd only been to

Pennsylvania to attend dog shows in Philadelphia. But the idea of meeting people conveyed by horse and buggies intrigued me, something else Donald would abhor. And he despised farmland smells like manure. Once we got married, my chance to play tourist among the Amish would vanish.

On the other hand, had Lizzie's incessant emails turned me bonkers? Was I so lonely I'd drive hours in search of a fictitious friend? Women engaged to men like Donald Montgomery shouldn't be without close acquaintances. But I was. Two girlfriends had moved from the area and one homeschooled her children and spent weekends with her husband and kids. And most of the competitors I'd met at dog shows weren't really friends. They'd probably breathed a sigh of relief when Mr. Big died.

Minutes later, the looky-loo couple took off. My father sauntered back my way. I got in the Mustang and started the engine; it rumbled to life the way new cars don't anymore. The opposite of the 2001 Prius sedan we sold last week.

I lowered the Mustang's window, and my father said, "That car's speeding-ticket red."

I loved that he felt protective, but his hovering bordered on suffocation. "When I get home, I'll wash and polish this baby," I said. "I won't scratch the mag wheels or scuff the white-walls." I scrounged in my purse for my cell phone and held it up. "Call me if you need me. I'll dash right home."

He ran his palm across his mouth. I took his silence as my cue to skedaddle before he changed his mind and made me drive the red Dodge minivan in the next parking space, the type of vehicle I'd used for dog shows. And someday for children, I hoped.

I waved. "Bye-bye, Pops. I'll be fine." I was acting impulsively but felt a tug from deep inside, like a trout that had swallowed a lure and was being reeled in. I nosed the Mustang onto busy Highway 7. Following a stream of traffic toward Danbury, I felt so giddy I started singing "Mustang Sally"—the few lyrics I could remember.

Adhering to the GPS's directions, I merged onto I-84 W, then zigged and zagged, crossing New Jersey until finally entering Pennsylvania. As I drove, the sun seemed to grow in size, a giant salmon-colored orb beckoning me to continue. I covered twenty-some more miles and exited. The sun was sinking, lowering itself into a cushion of cumulous clouds and casting a bronze sheen across the valley below, where I was going according to my GPS.

On a two-lane road, I cracked the window and breathed in the heady aroma of fertile soil and a trace of smoke, different from any fabric of scent my nostrils had ever embraced. I felt a shift inside, a stirring deep in my chest, like descending into Pops's cellar and inhaling the musty odor that transported me to a long-forgotten but beloved time and place.

I considered checking in at the B&B, but my empty stomach demanded immediate attention. I decided to find a restaurant on my way to Bird-in-Hand. When I'd spoken to the woman at the B&B, she'd mentioned she was just down the road from Intercourse; she didn't even chortle when saying the name. Tomorrow, I might catch a glimpse of the Sunflower Secondhand Store. If it existed.

Steering the car south, my gaze swept the panorama of the boun-teous valley: softly rolling recently seeded fields—unlike the wooded hills north and east of New Milford, Connecticut—rock fences meandering through them. I loved New Milford and Litchfield

County's red barns and dense deciduous woodlands, but now I stared in awe at Lancaster County's majestic white farms and silos, and the windmills, their blades revolving in the breeze, glinting in the early evening light.

I hugged the side of the road as a horse and gray covered buggy driven by a bearded man approached from the other direction. My heart leaped for joy—the only way to describe my elated reaction—surprising me. Sally Bingham, who rarely got wowed, was fascinated. I'd always wanted to learn to ride a horse, but Pops hadn't been able to afford the lessons. "Half the intelligence of a dog," he'd said, then wouldn't tell me how or why he knew.

My cell phone rang. The screen lit up: a photo of Mr. Big. I'd change the image when I got home. No use reminding myself of what I'd lost due to my own carelessness. I checked the caller ID and recognized a Pennsylvania prefix: 717.

CHAPTER 2

I answered my cell phone to hear the B&B's proprietress say, "Thank goodness I caught you before you arrived." Her voice was aflutter. "We had a storm last night—we needed the rain, that's for sure—but our roof leaked. I just discovered your room was hit the hardest. The bed's soaked."

Ah, my chance to get upgraded. "Do you have other rooms available?"

"Nothing, I regret to say. And we have a waiting list. I called around and couldn't find another vacant room closer than the city of Lancaster. I'm afraid it's a good drive from here and not in the best part of town. I'm sorry, miss, really I am."

I was tired and grumpy when I said good-bye to her. Good riddance, I felt like saying, all the time recalling Pops's disapproval of my coming here. I was tempted to make a U-turn and slink back home. Or find a cheap motel on the highway.

Why hadn't Donald called?

I reminded myself I usually came groveling to him. But not this time. We needed to start our marriage on an even footing or I'd always be the underdog. Yesterday, when I'd told Donald that Pops's kidneys were in trouble and I might offer one of mine should my father need it, Donald said, "No way; no how. That would ruin our honeymoon." His words made me feel prickly inside. He'd shown no sympathy for Pops. Did I want to marry a man who'd let my ailing father die without a fight?

I lowered my window farther and the fragrances of moist sod, mowed grass, and farm animals inundated the car, luring me into the valley. For late March, the air felt coolish, in the forties. Cars zipped along, as they did back home. But with buggies on the road, I slowed for fear of hitting one. Sure enough, I spotted a gray carriage in front of me—an orange-red reflective triangle affixed to its back—and told myself to be content following it.

A blanket of clouds enveloped the sun and the road darkened, yet few street lamps shone and most of the houses remained relatively dim. I'd heard the Amish didn't use electricity, so how did they light their homes?

Motoring south on the two-lane road, life moved in slow motion. I followed the buggy until it rolled off onto the shoulder. I seized the opportunity to speak to the driver. I scooted up next to it to see an Amish youth at the reins. We both stopped. Leaving my car idling in Park, I lowered my passenger-side window. The young man, around age eighteen and wearing a straw hat, eyed the Mustang with what appeared to be envy.

"Hey there," I called. "You know of any motels or bed-and-breakfasts around here?" I doubted the woman at the B&B had called every single hotel in the county on my behalf.

"*Nee*, but I'm meeting up with a couple friends. One of them might." He tipped his head toward two buggies at the side of the road ahead of us. One of the drivers, dressed Amish and about the same age, stood outside.

I rolled the Mustang forward and asked the same question. The young man ambled over to admire my car and removed his wide-brimmed hat, revealing longish straw-colored hair, flattened on top and cut like someone had placed a mixing bowl over his head, following the rim.

"My parents rent out a room at our farmhouse and it's vacant." His voice carried a sing-songy accent. He seemed harmless enough, but out of habit I locked my car with my elbow.

"'Tis true," he said, and replaced his hat, pushing his bangs to his eyebrows and over the tops of his ears. "My mamm will fix ya supper if you're hungry."

"I could do with a snack." An understatement. My stomach was gurgling.

"I'm Jeremy." He grasped his horse's reins when the brown mare lowered her head to munch scrub grass.

I didn't give my name—none of his business, Pops would say. He'd drilled into me when I was a child: never talk to strangers. "Sure, I'll swing by and take a look." What other options did I have?

"If you'd care to follow me, I need to head home—after I pick up *mei Schweschder*—my sister. Won't take long."

"Okay, thanks."

He hopped into his buggy and slapped the reins. The reluctant mare grabbed another mouthful of grass before clopping back onto the road. I put on the headlights and trailed behind him, watching the reflective triangle. Keeping near the shoulder, I ignored the cars and trucks stacking up behind us, let them zoom past. People on their way to join their families.

I pictured Pops eating alone tonight and felt apprehension flood my chest, dampening my spirits. When I got married and moved to Brewster, New York, with Donald—where his parents lived—I wouldn't be around to care for Pops. Unless I called off the wedding. The invitations were addressed and stamped, set to go in the mail Monday, in three days. Would Donald's mother have a fit if I told her not to send them? Or maybe Darlene would be relieved. She was probably worried spitless about what Pops would wear to the rehearsal dinner and how he'd act during the ceremony.

Ten minutes later, I saw the regal sign for the town of Intercourse, founded in 1754. The small village seemed sparse, nothing like New Milford with its neatly manicured green and white gazebo surrounded by shops and restaurants. This town's streets were devoid of pedestrians and most of its stores already closed. I raised my windows. Why had I driven this gas-guzzling flashy car, a cinch to break into? I was glad I'd packed my overnight bag in the trunk, out of sight.

Jeremy drew to a halt off to the right on the other side of town, about a half mile farther. Thankfully, the triangle reflector caught my eye. I stopped behind him, glanced off to the left, and saw a sign: Sunflower Secondhand Store.

"Land o' Goshen," my father might sputter. The store really existed.

A young Amish woman in her early twenties at most, wearing a mid-calf dress, an apron, a cape, and a white heart-shaped head covering, stood struggling to lock its front door.

Jeremy yelled, "Hurry up or you're walking!" impatience grating his voice. "Someone's following me home."

The young woman blasted him with a volley of words in another language, what I presumed was Pennsylvania Dutch, because I understood bits and pieces from high school and college German classes. "I can't leave it open, now, can I?" She tried another key.

I called out my window. "You closing shop for the day?" What time was it? The clock on the forty-plus-year-old car's dash didn't work and I'd neglected to wear a watch.

She turned to me. "Yah, and I'm running late."

"You need help locking up?" Between Pops's old house—where I lived—and his compilation of vehicles, I doubted a lock existed I couldn't finagle. And I wanted to get moving.

"Yah, I do or I'll be out here all night."

Ignoring Pops's lectures to mind my own business and not speak to strangers, I drove into the gravel parking lot at the side of the two-story building and got out.

"I ain't got much time," Jeremy said. "Our dat needs me."

As I approached the flustered young woman, I inspected her pretty face—the set of her pale blue eyes, her high cheekbones, her sandy-blonde hair tucked into a bun and straggling out from under the delicate white organza head covering. No makeup.

"I usually don't close," she said, her pale complexion blotchy, "but the owner went home early." She handed me a key ring. Why would she trust a complete stranger who drove a car? But on the other hand, why was I trusting her Hicksville brother in a buggy? Pops would have a fit.

"Let me try." I extended my palm. Without hesitation she handed me the key ring. "You're using the wrong one." I slid a stainless steel key into the lock and with a little prodding turned it, then heard the bolt click into place. The store was faintly illuminated by an overhead look-alike Tiffany lamp. I glanced through the store's wide windows and saw a plethora of secondhand items: tea cups, quilts, clocks, old-fashioned dolls, and a case of reading material off to the left. I should have thought to bring a novel and take a break from TV.

I gave her the keys, and she dropped them into her apron pocket. "You're ever so kind," she said, with the same accent as Jeremy.

"I'd better hurry," I said, still unnerved to be standing in front of the Sunflower Secondhand Store. "My mission is to find a place to spend the night. Jeremy said your parents rent out a room."

"Yah, you come home with us. We're used ta havin' *Englischers* staying with us."

"I'm not English."

"Sorry, I meant anyone who isn't Amish. Although my dat— my father—may insist you park your car at the side of the house so neighbors don't see it. It sure is red, like a cardinal. We mostly use the back door, anyways."

"All right, I'll follow you and Jeremy." I couldn't resist asking, "Say, do you have someone working at the store named Lizzie?"

"Yah, that would be me."

"You're Lizzie?"

She bobbed her head. "Yah, Lizzie Zook."

I felt what Pop would call bamboozled, like last winter when my tires skidded on a patch of black ice. Out of control, I'd fishtailed, pulled a one-eighty, and ended up headed in the opposite direction.

"Are there many Zooks in Lancaster County?" I asked.

"Oh, yah, 'tis a common name." Her gaze took in my skinny jeans and suede loafers.

"And probably a good many Lizzies, too," I said.

"Yah, my aunt on my dat's side and two cousins. Why do you ask?"

"Because I'm Sally Bingham." I held my breath, half-hoping her face would remain placid because she'd never heard of me. She must be in some kind of trouble, because she didn't look like any pedigreed dog fancier I'd ever met.

"Sally!" Her hands flew up to cover her cheeks. "Ya came? I can't believe it."

"That makes two of us." I didn't put faith in coincidences and happenstance. I felt disoriented, my world rotating in the wrong direction. This couldn't be the person who'd emailed me because I didn't believe in flukes. I refused to.

"'Tis an answer to prayer." Lizzie's voice rippled with elation.

I was stunned to find her standing before me. Knock me over with a feather, Pops might say. He'd also caution me to beware. "Things are seldom as they seem," he'd occasionally sung, a line from an old Gilbert and Sullivan musical.

"*Willkumm!*" Lizzie said, harpooning me to the present. "I can't tell ya what this means to me." Her oval face beamed like a kid opening a birthday present.

"So you're Lizzie?" I tried to make light of it, when in fact I felt as if I might topple over a cliff. I was tempted to dive into my car and take off. But how could this young woman do me any harm? Yet she seemed to possess enough gumption for both of us.

"I'm that Lizzie Zook," she said. "Ever so glad ta finally meetcha."

"Happy to meet you, too." No, I wasn't. I didn't like surprises. My words marbled out. "So you're in some kind of trouble or what?"

She put a finger to her lips. "I can't talk in front of mei *Bruder*—my brother—Jeremy."

The sky was fading, the world turning monotone. The temperature was dropping. Chilly air traveled up my jacket sleeves. What alternatives did I have? I'd at least check out their accommodations.

As I watched Jeremy adjust his hat, I formulated a plan to exhume Lizzie's scheme—my hunch was she'd devised one. "Is it okay for you to ride in my car?" I asked.

"Yah." She bounced on her toes. "That would be ever so nice." She spoke to Jeremy in Pennsylvania Dutch. He jiggled the reins and the horse lugged the buggy forward.

"I told him to go ahead," she said. "We'll probably pass him."

I stood for a moment, marveling at Lizzie's lack of sophistication—or was it a theatrical act for my benefit?—before opening the passenger door for her.

"You ready?" I was glad she couldn't decipher what lay behind my cheerful facade.

"*Denki,*" she said as she got in. "Thank you."

"Sure, no problem." I bopped around the hood, slid behind the wheel, and started the engine while she buckled her seat belt. The tires bit into the gravel parking lot as I backed up, then maneuvered the car toward the road. Jeremy and the buggy were nowhere in sight.

"Okay, Lizzie. Where to?" I switched on the headlights and rolled forward.

At that moment, a horse pulling a carriage came cantering in our direction. A spike of fear shot through me. I slammed on the brakes and skidded. The horse stopped short and reared, its front legs pawing the air. The driver, a bearded gent I guessed to be in his sixties, settled the animal, then gave me a less-than-cordial look, his lips drawn back.

I mouthed the words I'm sorry, but his expression remained severe as he glared at Lizzie and me.

Lizzie sank down in her seat. "Ach, 'tis Bishop Troyer," she said, wringing her hands.

My mind floundered with uncertainties. Recalling Pops's admonishment not to come, a shiver ran through me. What was I getting myself in to?

CHAPTER 3

As I watched the bishop's horse and buggy recede from sight, I envisioned the car slamming into the horse, and the buggy toppling to its side, injuring, if not killing, the man.

The near accident was my fault. Distracted, I hadn't given driving top priority. I felt a wedge of shame for my negligence. I wasn't normally impetuous or strong-willed. Why had I ignored Pops? Why did I insist on borrowing this pretentious car that didn't even have headrests?

"Thank the *gut* Lord you didn't crash into Bishop Troyer." Lizzie craned her neck to gawk out the window. "I hope he doesn't tell my parents he saw me in your car."

"What's the problem? Is riding in a car against your rules?"

"I can be a passenger. But ..." She resecured her seat belt. "He appeared in a hurry. He must have been needed somewhere."

"Unless he just robbed a bank," I said, hoping to make light of the situation.

"Nee—he never would."

"I'm joking." I coasted onto the road. "Who'd use a horse and buggy as a getaway car?"

An automobile honked, startling me, urging me forward. I was so shaken I was tempted to renege on my offer to drive Lizzie home. But Jeremy had taken off; I couldn't leave her stranded. Anyway, I needed to talk to her alone so she'd explain her emails.

My right foot pressed too hard on the accelerator and the Mustang jolted forward, as if to prove I was an irresponsible driver. The car's chilly interior evoked goose bumps on my legs. I turned up the heat but kept the fan on low. I wanted to hear every word this young woman had to say. I'd regather my courage and filter her explanation as if through my father's ears. I admired his built-in radar; he could detect a tire-kicker from a genuine buyer across his lot.

I hugged the side of the asphalt road, allowing the car on my rear bumper to zip past me. Then I swerved to a stop on a wide patch of dirt alongside a plowed field. "Before we go anywhere, I insist on an explanation," I said, trying to sound parental, when in fact only six or seven years separated us. "Why did you keep emailing? Are you in trouble or not?"

"Nee, I was searchin' for a dog," Lizzie said, all innocence, her face angelic. "For a Welsh corgi, in particular."

"Is that right? A Pembroke or Cardigan Welsh corgi?"

"Uh … the kind you have." She tucked rogue tendrils of hair under her cap, its strings dangling. "I get them mixed up. The one without a tail."

"I don't believe for a second you're in the market for a show-quality corgi." My words came out angrily—what I called my "bad-dog voice," which I saved for our neighbor's German shepherd when it heckled my Ginger through the chain-link fencing.

"Well?" Swiveling in my bucket seat, I saw her worrying her lower lip with her front teeth. "I'm not moving until I get a straight answer."

"You're right. I don't need a show dog." She laced her fingers. "Bishop Troyer would frown upon dog shows. Prideful is what he'd call them."

The hair on my arms bristled. "I have every right to be proud of my dogs' blue ribbons, particularly those earned in the Bred-by-Exhibitor class. Not to mention placing First in Group several times." I'd hoped for a Best in Show with Mr. Big, but too late now. My Best of Breed and group-winning Pembroke Welsh corgi, my sweetie-pie favorite dog ever, had died last month.

"'Tis not our way to make others feel unworthy," she said.

A brown-and-white pinto and an open buggy carrying a couple in their late teens glided toward us from the other direction. "Look at that horse," I said. "Wouldn't owning such a showy animal make others feel jealous? Wouldn't the owner feel proud?"

"Ya might be right. Not a display of humility, for sure. But 'tis not my business to be judging others. That in itself is a sin."

She was dodging my questions like a pro. So far I'd learned nothing, and my stomach was churning with hunger. Enough already, with playing Twenty Questions. I'd drop Lizzie at her farmhouse, gobble down a quick meal, and scram.

"Want to give me the directions?" I said, my impatience expanding with my hunger.

"Yah. Follow this road, then take the next left." She gestured with a sweep of her arm.

I waited for two cars and a van to cruise by, then tucked in behind them.

Lizzie gazed up at the visor. "I was lookin' through a book at the store on my break—not when I should have been working, mind you. Yah, a book about dogs. Did you know corgis can be used for herding ducks, not to mention sheep and cattle?"

"Yes, I'm aware of that fact." I'd once brought Mr. Big to an unofficial fun trial; he took to herding sheep as though he'd been rounding them up his whole life. "Why didn't you simply come out and ask me in your emails?" I said. "Why did you want me to come here? I could have found you the name of a local kennel."

"But then I wouldn't have met you." She gave me a coy look, her chin dipped. "Isn't this nice, getting to know each other and all?"

Was she pulling my leg? I appraised her simple attire and recalled her using the wrong key; maybe she was—how to put it kindly?—a bumpkin. I began fretting about her parents' house. Was it a log cabin?

"I don't believe anyone would contact my kennel for a herding dog," I said. "As stated on my website, I'm down to one female adult, an American/Canadian champion, but her show career is over." With Donald's distaste of dogs, I felt as though I'd have to find a good home for her eventually. Unless Pops wanted Ginger. No, he was already buried in responsibilities and his future was unclear.

"My time's running out working at the Sunflower Secondhand Store, so I won't have access to the Internet," Lizzie said, as if that made one wit of sense. "I gave notice to Mrs. Martin, the Englisch lady who owns it. Tomorrow is my last day."

"Where was she just now?"

"The poor lady—she's getting on in years—twisted her ankle this morning. Her *Dokder*—doctor—told her to elevate her foot and use an ice compress. I doubt she'll be able to put weight on her leg for a week. She opened the store just last fall and now this misfortune."

"Can't you fill in for her?"

"Nee, I mustn't."

"Something wrong with the job? You get fired?"

"No, I enjoy workin' there ever so much. But my dat—my father—says I've taken my running around—what we call *Rumspringa*—too far. 'Tis time I prepare for baptism classes and settle down." Her rosebud mouth drooped at the corners. "My brothers Jeremy and Peter are also running around. Dat put his foot down and says we must shoulder our load on the farm."

"If I were running around, as you call it, I'd be exploring the world somewhere exciting like Paris or Rome." A huge exaggeration—I'd never left North America.

"You travel a lot?" she asked.

"Not really. Air travel is such a hassle these days." I still had no clue where Donald and I would spend our honeymoon. He'd insisted he'd chosen a fabulous romantic location as a wedding present and told me to pack for warm weather and bring my passport. I'd begged for a hint, but he refused. Once we married, I had to wonder if he'd make all the decisions.

The heater blew dusty warmth at my legs.

Lizzie patted her knees, smoothing her apron skirt. "That feels *wunderbaar*. Take the next left," she said, and I turned onto a smaller road. We passed expansive farms, plowed fields, dots of green I

assumed were baby alfalfa, and every now and then a brightly illuminated house with cars or a pickup parked out front.

"Those homes belong to Englischers," she said, answering my
inquiry before I could verbalize it. And yet she hadn't come clean
with the biggest question: why and how she'd tracked me down.

I glanced at her outfit. Lizzie dressed as if she were living in
another century. Even though we shared a few common features, she
and I couldn't be more different. She wasn't wearing makeup and her
hands were bare, her nails clipped short. My unruly, sandy-colored
hair was loosening from its ponytail, long bangs straggling over my
forehead. Not to mention my one-carat engagement ring, which—
for the first time—seemed out of place. Gaudy.

"If you're running around, as you call it, why are you wearing
Amish clothing?" Not polite, but no time to dillydally. I figured we
were almost at her house.

"I tried dressing Englisch for a couple days, but Dat hated it.
Anyways, I'm used to these and our customers like them." Pulling
down the visor, she glanced at herself in the mirror, then flipped it
shut. "I'm ever so sorry."

"Can't you look at yourself? I've heard Amish don't like to be photo-
graphed, but surely they must see their reflection every now and then."

"We're allowed, as long as it's to part our hair, not ogle at ourselves. We have enough tourists doin' that."

"Like me?"

"No, I didn't mean to insinuate—here, take the next right. We're
close now."

A dozen starlings landing on a row of poplars caught my sight.
With no one behind us, I let up on the gas again, slowing to ten

miles per hour. "Let's start at the beginning, Lizzie. How did you find my name?"

"My Mrs. Martin showed me how to Google Welsh corgis. Your kennel's name popped up, so pretty, like it was calling to me."

I was proud of my website, one reason I hadn't closed it down. But I'd promised Donald I would as soon as we got married.

I flicked on the radio—no CD player in this out-of-date car. Bad reception, but I could make out the words to "Help!" a Beatles song from the sixties that seemed to suit the Mustang. And me. The vocalist—John Lennon?—was begging for support, needing to get his feet planted on the ground. I could relate.

Lizzie squirmed in her seat, crossing and uncrossing her legs, and biting at her fingernail. Seeing her discomfort made me feel more in control. I sped up and tailgated a van. "What's wrong?" I asked her.

"Our bishop don't like us listenin' to the radio."

"You've got to be kidding." I tapped my fingers on the steering wheel as if I hadn't a care in the world. "What about classical music?"

"He forbids radios in the home. But I enjoy music and I'm not baptized yet." Lizzie stroked the Mustang's black vinyl upholstery. "My brother was practically drooling over your car." She giggled—a girlish titter reminding me of a mockingbird. "Such a fine comfy seat. I like it ever so much."

Was she trying to distract me or was she just ditzy?

"Here we are!" she said with exhilaration. "Ya see the next house?"

Up ahead stood a two-story clapboard home with a trio of gables and a smaller house oddly attached to one corner, a wraparound front porch with a railing, a sizable barn, and several outbuildings. "Spanking white," Pops would label them. A lovely and impeccable property with a manicured lawn. Not like the houses in the movies *Psycho* and *The Addams Family*. Maybe my misgivings were for naught. At twenty-seven, had I turned into a paranoid, suspicious worrywart?

No. Meeting up with Lizzie was downright bizarre. I hadn't emailed that I was coming or agreed to visit her. Nor had she sent her home address.

"If ya wouldn't mind, continue into the driveway," she said.

As I motored up the narrow lane, I caught sight of a cylindrical tin-roofed corncrib. On the other side of the barn stood a silo and a windmill.

"Would ya please park over there?" She pointed to a couple of low buildings near the barn. "Right there, behind that shed, if ya don't mind. We all use the back door. 'Tis no slight on you."

I could see gangly Jeremy ahead in the barnyard, unhitching the mare from the buggy. The animal stretched its neck, shook its head.

"Get a move on it," Jeremy said to Lizzie as we exited the car. "Dat's finished milking. Everyone's waitin' on us for supper." He took the horse by its bridle and guided her into the barn.

I spoke over the car's roof. "What about me?"

"'Tis fine." Lizzie slammed the door too hard, making the car sound tinny. Pops would cringe. "Come inside," Lizzie said.

"With such short notice? I need to know how much this is going to cost." A startling thought came to mind. "Do you accept credit cards?"

"No. But you can talk it out over dinner." Lizzie ushered me to the back stoop. "We always have room. Wait 'til you taste Mamm's *appeditlich*—delicious—cooking."

A dog-show term, *faultfinder*, came to mind: a spectator who sees a dog's faults instead of its good qualities. Blinded by a less-than-perfect muzzle width or tail carriage, the viewer missed the dog's flawless gait. I'd become one, all right: focusing on negatives, momentarily ignoring this unique chance to stay in a real Amish home. Even though Pops wouldn't approve.

I inhaled the farm's sweet scent knowing Donald would hate it. Thank goodness he wasn't here.

Above me the blackened sky displayed a glamorous near-full moon. With only a lantern on the house's back porch and a light of some kind in the barn, I stood gazing up. Glittering stars populated the luminous heavens, mapping out constellations.

I'd take a chance, I decided, jump on this carousel, and enjoy the ride. Maybe I'd stumbled into a sliver of heaven. I deserved a weekend retreat.

Using prudence—my father's words of warning niggling at me—I left my overnight bag in the trunk, then followed Lizzie up the stairs. She entered a dimly lit back room laden with clunky work boots—lined up like a battalion—heavy jackets on pegs, an archaic washing machine with a hand-wringer, and a small sink near a door that must lead to the kitchen.

Ahead, I heard raised jagged voices—both male and female— squabbling in what I deduced was Pennsylvania Dutch, reminding me of a dogfight I'd once witnessed—a gruesome sight.

An Amish brawl? I wanted to turn around and run for cover.

CHAPTER 4

I inched away from the voices blasting through the door.

"Wait, Sally." Lizzie reached out to grab my arm, but I retreated toward the back stoop. She tailed me through the utility room. "You've traveled so far," she said. "Please don't go."

I was relieved I'd left my overnight bag in the trunk. I'd find a diner and a cheap motel room along the highway. Or just grit my teeth and drive straight home.

My iPhone rang, shattering the air, causing both Lizzie and me to start. The racket in the kitchen fell silent, as if someone had flicked off a TV set, which I figured they didn't own, since I'd seen no electric wires running to the house.

Clutching my purse, I trotted down the stairs, dug out my phone, and saw our home number on the screen. "What's up, Pops?" I tried to sound nonchalant while my thoughts ricocheted with worries about my father's health.

Lizzie hovered nearby. I turned away from her.

"I wanted to see how my favorite girl is doing." Pops had the hiccups again.

Could I answer Honest Ed without lying? "I was about to check in." A half-truth. "How about you?"

"I'd feel better if I knew you were safe."

"I am. Need me to come home?" I zeroed in on my car, several yards away. "I don't mind, not in the least."

I glanced up at the sky to see clouds drifting across the moon, darkening the landscape. My thoughts twirled back to my childhood. I recalled Pops sitting on the end of my quilt-covered bed reading my favorite book, *Goodnight Moon*. Then he tucked me in as if I were the most precious child in the world. But I hadn't felt cherished by my mother. Had Mom ever read to me at bedtime? Not that I could remember. If we bumped into each other on the street, would she and I recognize each other? I liked to think she kept my photo in a frame on her bureau. As a child I'd toyed with this crazy notion: I'd locate my mom, she and Pops would reunite, and we'd live happily ever after. But fairy-tale endings never happen.

"You know I didn't want you traveling alone," he said. "But I have good news. I sold the red minivan and the Ford Explorer, and there's a couple interested in the yellow Cadi."

I heard the wind stirring the bare branches of the hickory tree growing at the side of the Zooks' house and felt the breeze playing across my cheeks. "That's good, but you sound tired. I could kick myself for leaving." What had gotten into me? Should I admit to Pops that I'd called his doctor's office a few days ago to pry privileged information from an office assistant, an older woman I'd known since childhood who was about to retire? No, I'd get her in trouble, put a blemish on her record.

"If I could redo this day, I'd be lounging in the living room with you and Ginger," I said.

"Everything okay?" Tension strained his voice. "Is the Mustang still purring like a pussy cat?"

"With that exhaust system? Rumbling like a lioness is more like it."

He laughed. I enjoyed the sound of it.

As I said good-bye and slipped the phone into my handbag, I heard an owl's raspy screech in a distant stand of trees, giving me the shivers. I noticed movement out of my peripheral vision. Lizzie tugged at my jacket sleeve, startling me. My purse flew out of my hand.

"Won't ya please come inside?" She scooped up the purse and dusted it with her apron. Inhaling the earthy smell of manure, I dreaded to think where my bag had landed.

"Here ya go. Good as new." She gave it to me, then her arms hung at her sides. "I'll bet Mamm and Dat were discussing chores, is what they were doing. We have two-dozen Holsteins ..." Her eyes had lost their luster and her voice its vivacity.

Was their argument a dispute about Jeremy's not doing his share of the milking? Or had I piloted the Mustang too quickly on their dirt driveway? Perhaps they'd heard my tires and beefy exhaust. Or had I walked into an episode of *Family Feud*?

"I heard a woman's voice in the fray, and what sounded like an elderly man's," I said.

"My *Mudder*'s parents join us for dinner every evening. They live in the *Daadi Haus*." Lizzie pointed to what appeared to be a smaller house attached to the corner of her parents' spacious home. "They'll be sorely disappointed if you don't come in."

"How would they know anything about me?"

"Jeremy will have told them."

"But he's still in the barn."

A pretty woman in her early fifties stepped outside, bringing with her a cloud of tantalizing scents: warm biscuits, stewing beef, and steaming vegetables.

"Good evening." The woman, clad in a mid-calf–length navy-blue dress and black apron, descended the steps. "*Kumm rei*—come in," she said. A white, heart-shaped cap like Lizzie's covered her sable-brown hair. "We were just talking—well, we were discussing something a little too loudly, I regret to say."

"Don't let her leave, Mamm." Lizzie's eyes pleaded with the woman. "She's been on the road all afternoon."

The woman nodded at Lizzie, then turned her attention to me. "I'm Rhoda Zook, Lizzie's mamm." Her voice was kind and gentle, the way a mother's should sound. "Since you're here, please won't ya join us?"

"How much does dinner cost?" I asked, stalling. I couldn't take any more surprises.

"No charge, after our *rilpsich*—foolish—behavior." Rhoda examined me with what seemed to be curiosity. Her gaze settled on my face, my blue eyes that played chameleon depending what color I was wearing. Today, a khaki-colored safari jacket and a long-sleeved powder-pink T-shirt.

"Please, the supper's getting cold," she said, moving closer. "My husband, he's been workin' hard since sunup."

Voracious hunger edged out what Pops would call good sense. "Okay, thank you," I said. "Since I'm here—"

"Yah, you're here, aren't ya?" Lizzie lightly clapped her hands.

With Lizzie mincing at my heels, I followed Rhoda up the back stairs, through the utility room into the large kitchen. Lizzie opened the door, and I was embraced by the warm air, the temperature inside spiking twenty degrees. A myriad of delectable aromas, including cooking blackberries, filled my nostrils. The heat urged me to discard my jacket.

A group of half a dozen Amish people—all gawking at me and spanning several generations—hemmed the perimeter of a rectangular table, plates and napkins set before them. At the head hunched a brown-haired man tugging on his bushy beard. Next to him stood an empty seat; Jeremy plunked onto it.

"Sorry, Dat."

No answer from the man, whose hair was flattened on top and fashioned like Jeremy's. I guessed he was Pops's age, but this husky guy owned wide shoulders and muscled forearms. His hands were large, like a boxer's, and his nails chipped.

I dropped the Mustang's key in my jacket pocket and Rhoda hung it on a peg by the back door alongside several wide-brimmed straw hats. As Lizzie settled onto a bench, Rhoda directed me to a chair on the other side of the table, then sat at my side. Next to Lizzie perched an ancient-looking lady wearing wire-rimmed spectacles and the same white cap as the other women.

Farther down the table sat two clean-shaven men—one younger than Jeremy, one maybe ten years older than I was, and a grizzly bearded gent. The men wore collared shirts and suspenders and had the same funky bowl-on-the-head haircuts.

The man dominating the end of the table, who still hadn't acknowledged me, let out a guttural sound and all heads bowed, as if choreographed, for an extended minute. While they prayed in silence, I scanned the sparsely decorated room and saw a calendar, a woodland scene gracing its top, but no other decorative touches. Drab linoleum covered the floor. A refrigerator—powered by what, I couldn't imagine—stood against the wall next to a stove. A sink and wide counter with a window overlooking a field. No dishwasher, toaster, or Cuisinart. A cloth-lined wicker basket of corn muffins—the perfect vehicle for butter—and several jams and jellies sat in the center of the table, causing my mouth to salivate.

The head honcho grunted and all said, "Amen," then raised their heads.

I echoed, "Amen." I'd sat at many dinner tables and said grace, but never in silence. There was nothing normal about this family. Or my afternoon.

For a moment, we sat like statues; the kitchen teemed with a peculiar energy.

"Our main meal is usually at noon, but we've got a hearty supper for ya tonight," Rhoda told me. "Leftover beef stew from yesterday." She served the man, then ladled stew and noodles onto my plate. "Sally, eat yourself full," she said.

Hey, wait a minute, Lizzie hadn't mentioned my name. Maybe Jeremy had. No, I hadn't given it to him. Perhaps he'd been eavesdropping on Lizzie and my conversation back in town.

"Sally was such a gut help for me lockin' up the store," Lizzie said, paying no heed to the splendid meal. "I don't know what I would have done without her."

Rhoda tipped her head toward the sourpuss at the end of the table. "Sally, this is my husband, Reuben Zook."

The big guy sneered at me as if I were a nuisance—a flea on a dog—then dug into his stew with gusto. Was he this rude to all their lodgers? No wonder they had a vacant room.

My mouth watered so much I could barely say, "Hello." Then I plunged a fork into a cube of beef. The meat, laced with glazed onions, melted in my mouth.

"Dat," Lizzie said. "Please won'tcha greet our guest?" Even when raising her eyebrows, her smooth forehead didn't crease. No crow's-feet around her eyes or a blemish on her creamy skin.

He swallowed a mouthful. "*Himmel*, yous made me wait twenty minutes for dinner."

"I'm sorry, Dat. It couldn't be helped. Mrs. Martin hurt her leg."

Jeremy belted out a hoot. "When I'm late, you're all over me, Liz. Like it's the end of the world."

"We've had enough bickering for one evening, " Rhoda said. She turned to me. "I hope you'll like your room. 'Tis all fixed up."

Which I took to mean a bed was made with fresh sheets.

"I'm sorry to bring this up at the dinner table, but how much do you charge?" Having played the car trade-in game, I suspected I was being set up for a backroom closing, when a car salesman pretends to negotiate with the manager on behalf of the buyer. A "kitchen closing" instead. I'd joke about it with Pops when I got home.

"There'll be no fee," Rhoda said, passing me the muffins.

"For tonight," Reuben said, and shoveled in another mouthful. I noticed his upper lip was cleanly shaven, as was the old gentleman's across from me. But Jeremy and the two other younger men's chins were clean, save a day's worth of stubble. They stared at me as they chewed their food. If the family took in lodgers, what was so odd about me, other than I wasn't paying? My citified clothes, compared to their antiquated apparel? My glitzy engagement ring? I noticed neither Rhoda, Reuben, nor the older couple—whom I guessed to be around eighty—wore wedding bands.

"Sally can stay for the whole weekend, if she likes," Rhoda said, her fist on the plastic checked tablecloth as if signaling her husband. "I hope she does."

"*Ich bedank mich*, Mamm—thank you." Lizzie's face came to life, and she clapped her hands. "It will be wonderful to have her staying right here with us, yah?"

Reuben let out a belch, but Rhoda didn't seem insulted. I wondered if bad manners were commonplace. If anything, she looked pleased, her lips spreading into a smile.

I split a muffin, browned to perfection. A puff of steam escaped, filling my nose with ambrosia. I lathered it with butter, took a bite, and savored the taste while my gaze drifted around the table. I wasn't usually shy, but I'd never felt so out of my element. Why had I been invited to be their guest? Maybe they really did want a corgi and expected me to give them one in return for their hospitality.

"Then it's all settled." Lizzie took the freckled hand of the elderly woman, whose face was crinkled and hair almost as white as her cap. "These are Mamm's parents," Lizzie said. The old, bearded fellow smiled, revealing crooked teeth.

"And that hooligan over there is my baby Bruder, Peter. He's sixteen."

"Hullo," said the young man, then looked away. His hair and complexion were darker than Jeremy's, and he seemed to favor his father in looks—I hoped not in temperament.

"No need ta be *naerfich*," Lizzie said. "She ain't gonna bite ya."

"I'm not nervous." His round cheeks blushing, Peter scowled at her. "Some of us have been up since four thirty, not lounging in a fancy shop all day chatting with Englischers."

"I hear tell you've got an Englisch girl you're mighty fond of." Lizzie tossed him a wry smile.

"Mind your own business. You should talk." He wiggled in his chair.

"Ow!" Lizzie yelped. "Dat, he kicked me under the table."

She and Peter glanced toward Reuben, who seemed to be concentrating on consuming his meal.

Reuben swallowed a forkful of beef. "Too much running around," he said. "You young folk think this farm's going to take care of itself?" Then he lapsed into Pennsylvania Dutch for a sentence or two, for what sounded like a reprimand.

Rhoda inclined her head toward the broad-shouldered man in his late thirties near the far end of the table. "Sally, this here is Armin King, who's staying with us." Clean-shaven and—if not for his haircut and suspenders—what I'd call a hunk. He appeared to have broken his nose in the past, which only added to his ruggedly handsome features. His gaze was unabashed and penetrating; I couldn't help staring back as he gave my face a thorough looking over in a way Donald hadn't for months—if ever. I sensed Armin appreciated what he saw. And so did I.

His brown eyes held onto mine, and he said, "Hullo, Sally." Then his stare glommed on to my ring and he seemed to lose interest, as if I'd turned invisible.

"Hi," I said, but he stabbed his fork into a stalk of broccoli. Which was just as well; I was engaged and had no business flirting with a stranger, even if I were on the verge of a breakup. I had to smile as I envisioned Donald sitting at this table. What was I thinking? He'd refuse to enter the barnyard let alone the home.

"Armin could be living a couple doors down in a fine big house belonging to his Bruder Nathaniel," Jeremy said. "If he'd just—"

Armin's eyes narrowed, and he set his napkin on the table as if ready to leave.

"Armin's welcome to stay with us as long as he likes," Reuben said, not looking up from his plate. "He does twice the labor as my sons." He nodded to Armin, who placed the napkin back in his lap and took a bite of pickled beets.

The older lady, Lizzie's granny, leaned forward. "What brings you this way, dear?" she asked me.

I contemplated describing Lizzie's barrage of emails but figured her father would be furious. He held not a shred of good humor on his craggy, bearded face.

"Someone seemed quite determined I should come," I said, but the old woman didn't respond.

"*Grossmommy* can't hear very well," Lizzie said, smearing a muffin with butter. But I had to wonder. My hunch was the old woman caught every word.

"Leah is my mother," Rhoda said. "Sorry, I was so *verhoodled* when you arrived I clean forgot to introduce my parents properly.

And this is my father, Leonard. We go by first names around here."

From across the table, the aged gent who made me think of Rip Van Winkle said, "Gut ta meet ya." I recognized the man's gravelly voice as one in the vocal ruckus only minutes ago, but he seemed tame enough now. Maybe I hadn't been the topic after all. Yet I couldn't shake my feeling of unease, like I was standing under the spotlight onstage of a Broadway flop, curtains about to swing close. No applause.

Except Rhoda and Lizzie seemed delighted to have me here, as if I were the guest of honor. Rhoda passed me strawberry jam, a similar red hue staining her cheeks—maybe from hurrying around the kitchen preparing this meal, then coming outside to fetch me.

I heard a jet—no, thunder—rumbling in the distance and was glad to be in a snug kitchen, even if an unconventional one. No need to worry about the lights going off; a gas lamp hung above the table and another, its base housed in a wooden cabinet, stood in the corner next to a rocking chair.

I sampled tasty items I'd never heard of before. According to Rhoda, all the preserves—beets, pickles, and a tasty relish called chow-chow—were jarred in this kitchen or at a neighbor's. I should get the recipes; Pops would love them. But not Donald. He'd described himself as having a discerning, sophisticated palate and boasted he'd never eaten at McDonald's.

"Down in our cellar, we had enough to last us through the winter and longer should we need it," Leah said, wrinkles fanning around her eyes. "Until our garden and trees ripen this summer." Aha, Lizzie's grandma could hear when she wanted to.

After I'd finished eating, Rhoda stood and motioned to a lattice-topped pie resting on a cooling rack on a side counter. "May I serve you blackberry pie or butterscotch pudding?" she asked me.

"Sounds delish, but I'm about to burst. I can't eat another bite." I watched the others accept dessert. How did they manage to stay so trim? I thought about Pops, who'd dropped ten or twenty pounds over the last few months. He claimed nothing tasted good to him anymore. I'd looked up kidney disease online and found both weight loss and a nasty metallic taste were common symptoms. I recalled the old saying, "You can lead a horse to water but you can't make him drink." More and more, Pops acted ornery.

I spoke to Rhoda. "I feel rude for asking, but I'd like to see my room when you're done eating."

"Of course you would." Rhoda folded her napkin and set it aside. "Let's get that out of the way right now, then you can rest easy knowing where you're gonna spend the night."

"Before after-dinner prayer?" Reuben said in a harsh tone and rapped his fork's handle on the table.

"We can pray when we get back," Rhoda said.

"You pray twice?" I had to wonder what they'd pray about. I should be concentrating my prayers on Pops's health. Why did he have to become sick, of all people? He'd centered his life on raising me, tried to be two parents in one.

"Yah," she said. "It never hurts to thank the Lord too often." She got to her feet, then spoke to Lizzie. "In the meantime, offer the men more dessert and then start cleaning up."

"I was planning to." A pout formed on Lizzie's lips. "I did last night, didn't I? And this morning I helped with breakfast. And brought in the eggs."

"Doesn't make up for your bein' gone most of the time, hurrying off to that store or tending to Nathaniel's vacant house." Reuben let out another belch.

"Glad ya liked the meal," Rhoda said to Reuben. Guess I wouldn't give Pops such a bad time about his less-than-stellar table manners in the future.

"This way, Sally." Rhoda led me out of the kitchen and across the living room's wooden floor, past a couch, a low coffee table, a recliner, and an assortment of other chairs. Embers glowed in a stone fireplace. She stopped for a moment to toss in a chunk of split timber, then led me up a steep, uncarpeted staircase. The temperature dropped as we ascended. I couldn't rid myself of the prickly feeling I shouldn't be here. But a rumbling storm was brewing closer. I heard rain rattling against windowpanes and branches scritching the side of the house.

Rhoda tipped her head to the first door on the right. "This is our Lizzie's bedroom." She continued a few yards and opened the second door. "Here ya go." She lit a lamp with a Bic lighter, illuminating a double bed covered with a vibrantly hued quilt. The buttermilk-yellow walls looked recently scrubbed. An unadorned bureau, a straight-backed chair, wooden pegs on the wall, and a small closet with a couple hangers. Sparse but clean. Not so bad.

"The bathroom's across the hall," she said, snagging my attention. "Recently installed, so now we have two."

"Thank you," I said. "For everything."

"You're more than welcome. We're glad you're here."

What was the catch? Nothing came without a price—as Pops would say. I didn't carry much cash.

"How much does the room usually cost?" I asked.

"Nothing for you to worry about, Sally. You're our guest."

"Thanks. That's generous of you." I'd be gone in the morning anyway. First thing.

CHAPTER 5

Rhoda moved to the bed and folded the quilt's corner down to expose white sheets with a sweet fresh-off-the-line fragrance. She fluffed the pillows, a welcoming invitation to burrow into dreamland. Exhaustion blanketed me, but I couldn't go to bed yet. The battery-operated clock on the bureau informed me the time was only seven thirty.

"I thought it was later." I stifled a yawn.

"Seems that way tonight to me, too. Reuben and I usually turn in early, but our schedule's off." She let out a weary sigh. "I got a late start preparing dinner. We had a couple of unexpected visitors. First a Mennonite neighbor we often hire to drive us and then our bishop. Perhaps you'll meet them while you're here."

"I might have run into the bishop already." I recalled the man's piercing glare.

"Ya met him?"

"Not exactly." My throat tightened at the thought of seeing him up close, then I assured myself he wouldn't recognize me—unless he spotted the Mustang. "We passed him on the road." No need to reveal the hair-raising circumstance.

A flash of lightning brightened the bedroom, casting stark shadows. Thunder snapped like a lion tamer's whip slashing the air. My skin prickled. Electrical storms often clambered through New Milford, but I'd never felt so exposed, as if standing on a golf course toting a metal club. Did Amish erect lightning rods? I was afraid to ask for fear the answer would be no. Between the brewing storm and the bickering family, I'd suffer from nightmares all night.

"Did ya bring luggage?" Rhoda asked, corralling my thoughts.

"Yes, a small carry-on—still in my trunk, unfortunately." Rain pelted against the bedroom windows. "I'll wait until the storm lets up so I don't get soaked."

"Nee, we'll send one of the men to fetch it." Her gaze searched my face. "Come downstairs and have hot apple cider or *Kaffi*—coffee. If the pie doesn't suit you, I made snickerdoodles and peanut butter cookies this afternoon."

When had I met a more gracious woman?

Thoughts of my mom permeated my mind—as they often did. As a little girl, I'd been headstrong and sassy, according to Pops. Had I whined and scared Mom away? She'd left when I'd turned one. The image of a brunette in a flowered apron coagulated in my brain; she'd stood in our basement where Pops and I stored canned food and extras. Was I remembering a neighbor? An elementary teacher? I owned no photograph of my mother. Had Pops burned them or ripped them to shreds? I only knew her first name: Mavis.

Well, I refused to allow the woman who'd deserted me like rotten week-old sardines disrupt my day. I had enough worries.

"A cookie sounds yummy." I gave my stomach a pat, glad I was wearing jeans with a bit of stretch in them. "Lizzie was right about your cooking. Dinner was delicious."

"Thank you, but every woman in the county cooks as well. It's the least we can do for the men who work hard all day. And to feed our guests, like you."

She was humble too. I wondered if Lizzie appreciated her good fortune. They shared the same oval face, high forehead, and pale skin, although Rhoda stood taller—my height plus a couple inches—but the two women owned opposite personalities. And Rhoda's movements were methodical and graceful while Lizzie flitted.

I didn't yet have a handle on the purpose of Lizzie's emails and was more mystified by her contacting me than ever. Tonight the occasion to pry the truth from her would present itself even if it meant knocking on her bedroom door at midnight.

I followed Rhoda into the long hallway and glanced to my right to see a polished wooden floor smelling of wax, several closed doors, no ornaments on the walls. "The size of your home makes my father's and my house look like a cottage," I said, envisioning our weathered shingled saltbox: two stories in the front, a pitched roof to the one-story in the back of the house, a central chimney. "You get many lodgers staying with you?" I asked.

"Now and then. We need a big house to hold Sunday service once or twice a year. And maybe someday a wedding."

"For Lizzie? She has a boyfriend?"

"Not that we know of. We pray if she has a beau he's one of us." She shifted her weight, as if hesitating to descend to the first floor. I figured she was used to serving patrons, but she seemed anxious.

"Should we get back to the kitchen?" I asked.

"Yah. When he's done with his meal, Reuben reads Scripture to the family. Some evenings he works in his shop after supper, but as I said, we're behind on our schedule."

I could hear Jeremy and Peter chuckling in the room below. Jeremy sounded like a full-grown man, but Peter's voice hadn't yet completely dropped to a man's octave.

"Lizzie and the boys often play board games. My *Kinner*—children—would enjoy it should you care to join them." She moved to the top step. "And we have books checked out of the library if you prefer reading."

"I'm a slowpoke. I'd never have time to finish a whole book." I couldn't imagine what type of literature this family liked reading. About agriculture and milking cows? "Do you have magazines?" I asked.

"Yah, *Family Life* and *The Connection*, and a newspaper—*The Budget*." Rhoda's eyes were much the same color as Lizzie's, a pale blue like faded denim. "You're welcome to stay two nights." The corners of her mouth lifted. "Like I said, no charge."

"You're kind, but I couldn't accept." I wanted to ask why she was acting so charitably but didn't wish to be disrespectful. "Is there somewhere I could plug my cell phone in to recharge the battery?"

"Yah, but not in the house."

"Oh, yeah." I chided myself, recalling I hadn't seen electric appliances or lightbulbs. "I don't dare turn it off. My father's ill."

Her hand wrapped the bottom of her throat. "Nothing serious, I hope."

"Most likely his kidneys, although he's being stubborn and delaying treatment." Why was I blathering? Not like me to reveal private information. But I figured Rhoda would never meet Pops.

"How long has he been ailing?" she asked.

"I'm not sure. A steady decline for a couple of years. He ignored his symptoms until I insisted he see his physician, who ran a battery of tests, then referred him to a specialist. Pops shrugged off his fatigue, swollen ankles and fingers, and lack of appetite as age related, but I've reminded him forty-eight isn't old." I couldn't afford to lose another parent, I'd teased. But I wasn't joking. Since graduating from college—well, most of my life—I'd felt disconnected, even when at the car lot or showing and grooming my dogs. I needed him.

"I have a cousin who had kidney disease," she said, moving closer. "He's doing fine again, working his farm."

"That's wonderful. So far I've only heard about years of costly and timely dialysis followed by a transplant."

Pops and I had reversed roles—when it came to his health, I was acting like the parent. Maybe my absence would spur him into taking action. I'd never known him to be so apathetic. Except when it came to my mom.

"And your mother?" Rhoda said, her voice strained. "Does she take gut care of him?"

My molars clamped and my chest sank, but I slogged along with the least offensive version of the truth. "Mom split when I was a one-year-old." Always painful for me to admit: my mother didn't love or want me.

Rhoda took a quick breath, more a gasp. "Ya don't mean it."

"You think I'd make something like that up?"

"No. I'm sorry, truly. I didn't mean anything." She leaned against the wall.

"I'm the one who's sorry, Rhoda. I shouldn't be so defensive." When would apathy be my first reaction?

"Did your father remarry?" she asked.

"No, he's single."

"All those years, a single man. I'll keep both of you in my prayers, if ya don't mind."

"Okay, if you like. His name's Ed Bingham."

Sucking in her lips, she looked disappointed. It struck me as odd. Why would she care?

"Honest Ed, everyone calls him." I fabricated my fake perky facade. "He owns a used car lot. No horses and buggies in Connecticut that I know of."

"I see." But I could detect confusion on her face, her gaze lowering to the floor.

Rhoda pivoted toward the staircase. "I must get back to Reuben," she said. I tailed her down the steps.

Jeremy and Peter sat playing checkers in front of the fireplace—Jeremy on a couch, Peter on a chair, a low coffee table between them.

"Ya want to join us?" Jeremy said to me. "I'm beatin' the pants off my little brother."

Peter coughed a laugh. "You are not, you braggart."

"Maybe later," I said. With nothing else to occupy my time, I wouldn't mind playing a board game.

I entered the kitchen and saw Lizzie bending to kiss her father's hairy cheek—evoking a toothy grin. "You're the best dat ever," she said.

I expected the grouchy coot to swat her away, but his grin widened. Moving behind him, she draped her slender arms across his chest and gave him a hug. It appeared Lizzie's infectious good humor had rubbed off on Reuben. I shouldn't have felt a round of envy, but I did. Or was she conning all of us? I needed to keep up my guard.

"Yah, okay, you can work at the store tomorrow," he said. "But don't think of workin' on Sunday or any other day after that, no matter what. I already have the bishop on my back."

"Yah, for more things than one."

He stiffened and she stepped away.

"Dat, the store isn't even open on Sundays." She straightened her cap and tossed its strings over her shoulders. "No need to be *naerfich* about that or anything else."

"I ain't nervous," he said. She served him another wedge of blackberry pie. "Doesn't your Mrs. Martin have any Englisch girls working for her?" he asked.

"She did, but Peggy moved with her family to Maryland." Lizzie let out a wistful sigh. "I'll miss her ever so much."

"Ain't our problem your Mrs. Martin didn't think to hire a replacement." He forked into the pie. "You did tell her you were quitting, didn't you?"

"Yah, but she didn't know she was going to fall off the stepping stool this morning and hurt her ankle, now, did she?"

I noticed Armin was gone, as was the sweet older couple, Rhoda's parents. Lizzie darted about the room gathering plates, flatware, and glasses, and slid them into sudsy water. My first impulse was to offer to help since I wasn't paying for my room.

As if hearing my thoughts, Rhoda said, "Sally, please have a seat and try one of my cookies, won't ya?" She steered me toward a rocking chair near a black, four-legged, cast-iron cook stove not in use.

"You have two stoves?" I said.

"I couldn't bear to give my Mudder's up when we replaced it with our new gas oven." She stroked its cool surface. "We use it when cooking for large groups, like church service and work frolics and barn raisings. And it warms this room in winter."

No central heating? Great, I'd freeze tonight. I noticed a stack of split wood sitting at its side.

"Kumm right here." She straightened the cushioned seat.

As I lowered myself onto the rocker, I felt comforted and swathed in warmth, like a baby being lulled to sleep. My father and I didn't own a rocking chair. I should buy him one for his birthday, I decided. I set my purse at my feet and pushed myself into motion with my toes.

I wondered if Mom had cradled me in her arms when I was a newborn. My past was as blurry as fog hovering above a swamp. No memories of my parents hugging or kissing each other. But they'd had me. An act of love, or was I an accident conceived in the backseat of a car? Mom was out there somewhere—or had she died? Did Pops harbor a dream she'd return to us—as I did? And she'd love me, her darling, dearest daughter. Or had she birthed five other children and forgotten I existed? Why wouldn't Pops give me the real scoop?

Lizzie set a cup of coffee on a small table at my elbow.

"No, thanks. I don't dare drink caffeine before bedtime." Especially tonight while my mind squirmed with troubling thoughts.

Lizzie removed the coffee cup and slurped down the brown liquid. "I'll make you herbal tea." She flushed water into a kettle and placed it on the stovetop. "Mommy Leah's special blend for a good night's sleep."

"Yah," Rhoda said. She laid a peanut butter cookie atop a plate, on the small table. "My mamm drinks it every evening. You can stay put while Reuben reads the Bible, if you like, or come join us when we go in the living room. You're most welcome."

I felt another sliver of jealousy as I watched Lizzie and Rhoda exchange loving glances. And Lizzie had grandparents practically living with them somewhere in this sprawling house. I'd never met my grandparents. I'd asked Pops about his folks, but he said they'd died years ago—which didn't explain why he never visited their graves. When I got home, I'd demand he tell me where the cemetery was; I should be more persistent.

"If you worked all day, you'd have no trouble with sleep," Reuben said to me. He licked his fork, then bellowed out a yawn. "Jeremy and Peter, get in here and thank the Lord." The two young men strode into the kitchen.

After a throaty noise, Reuben initiated a quick silent prayer. Rhoda, Lizzie, Jeremy, and Peter sat with him, their heads bowed. I had to wonder what was weighing on their minds, then reminded myself farming was an exhausting occupation. The wind and rain could be flattening their newly planted alfalfa or removing the chicken coop's roof.

When finished, Reuben aimed his voice at me again. "I'll be reading the Bible in German," he said.

Was he trying to humiliate me? I smothered a chuckle. German was the one foreign language I halfway understood. Not that I wanted to listen to him pontificate.

"I could ask Dat to read the Bible in English." Lizzie stood and moved to the sink. She rinsed the dishes and flatware with vigor and arranged them on the drying rack. "You'd do that, Dat, wouldn't you?"

He yanked his scraggly beard. "I 'spose."

"Ich bedank mich, Dat."

"Please join us," Rhoda said to me as she stowed leftovers into the refrigerator. "Then you can play checkers with Jeremy and Peter."

"Or Scrabble," Lizzie said. "That's my favorite."

Scrabble was my favorite board game, too, but I wondered what language they'd use. And the spelling?

"I'm comfy right here for now." I sank my teeth into the best peanut butter cookie I'd ever tasted, then pushed the back of my head against the rocking chair as if there were nowhere I'd rather be. After all, how would I entertain myself if I were at home? Would I be waiting for Donald's call? No, I would have broken down by now and crawled to him, when, in fact, he owed me an apology for being selfish and not considering Pops's welfare.

The back door shuddered open and Armin trudged in, lugging my dripping wet canvas bag. He'd removed his jacket. I found myself admiring his brawny physique and his damp curling hair.

"Thank you." I stood up, hoping no one had noticed my ogling. Rhoda rushed over with a towel to wipe my bag and mop the puddle.

Reuben got to his feet. "*Kumm shnell*—come quick—Lizzie and Rhodie." Then he left the room. Although cantankerous, he'd given Rhoda a pet name, telling me he loved her.

"You want me to help?" I asked Lizzie as I sent Armin a sideways glance, watching him pat his hair with a towel. No two ways about it;

he was more interesting than he should have been. I had no business getting to know him. We might as well be from opposite ends of the globe. And I was engaged to be married. Had I turned fickle? No, I wouldn't allow myself to be.

"Dat wouldn't like it, Sally." Standing at the sink, Lizzie scrubbed a pan and rinsed it. "I need to pull my weight around here."

I contained a smile. She couldn't weigh much more than one hundred pounds. "I don't mind," I said.

"Nee, I'm used to it."

"You're our guest, so please relax." Rhoda dabbed the floor around my bag and handed the damp towel to Armin. "Thank you," she said to him.

"*Gern gschehne*—you're welcome." Armin took the towels into the darkened back room and hung them by the small sink.

"Thanks for getting my things," I said, but he didn't answer or return.

"Is he shy?" I felt disappointed he hadn't given me eye contact again.

Lizzie chuckled. "Our Armin shy? Nee. Every *Maedel*—young unmarried woman—in the district has her eyes set on him."

"Are you one of them?" I figured no subject was off-limits between us after the emails she'd sent to lure me here. Or had she? Pops had remarked I had an overly active imagination. But I wasn't imagining his opposition to this sojourn.

"Armin is like a Bruder to me," Lizzie said. "And he's too old. Thirty-seven."

"He's not so old," Rhoda said, then turned to me. "He could be living in his own house and farm. Unfortunately, he and his older brother, Nathaniel, have been at odds ever since Armin wouldn't get baptized then moved to New York State, leaving Nathaniel to work the family farm."

"He could be courting someone for all I know. Around here, we often keep things hush-hush until the minister announces it." Lizzie scoured the bottom of another pan.

"Weddings take place in late fall, after the harvesting's done," Rhoda said.

"There will be many a wedding this next year, starting in November," Lizzie said. "I can't wait. 'Tis such a gut time."

"To those baptized in the Amish church." Rhoda's voice turned serious. "So we don't have to worry about our Lizzie getting married yet."

"But she's so young," I said.

"Not around here I'm not." Lizzie spoke over her shoulder. "Two of my friends are married and already have children. Such cute little fellas."

Meaning she thought I was over the hill? "Do you wish you had grandchildren?" I asked Rhoda as she poured me tea.

"Between Lizzie's two older sisters, who live in Indiana with their husbands, I have seven grandchildren."

I halted my rocking. "I assumed Lizzie was the eldest." She was bossy enough.

Lizzie lifted her chin. "They treat me like I'm the youngest, because I've waited to get baptized until I tried my hand working in the Englisch world for a while."

"You've had four years to join the church," Rhoda said. "This summer—please tell me you're planning to take baptism classes."

Lizzie gave her hands a quick dry on her apron. "I will. Most likely." She moved to my side. "I'll come back to finish the kitchen after Dat is done reading. Don't ya lift a finger." Her skirt swaying, she followed Rhoda into the living room.

Here I was, closing in on thirty and unwed. What must they think of me? Who cared? I did, or I wouldn't be seeing myself through their eyes.

I propelled the chair again. I envisioned Lizzie's grandma sitting here doing embroidery or quilting, two womanly tasks I never learned. I was struck by the fact I didn't even have an aunt or uncle, let alone a grandmother. Pops and I were a dynamic duo, we'd always joked. Maybe I should get online and search for our relatives. But Pops claimed he'd tried without success, and he was adamant I not waste my money or energy. And Donald's mother was ecstatic she'd be our kids' only grandmother. She'd never once asked me about my parents' families.

Through the kitchen door, I heard Reuben's somber voice reading the Bible in High German. Was he using Scripture to rebuke Lizzie for working rather than saddling herself with a husband and children at her young age? She seemed immature, but apparently not around here.

Reuben switched to English, for my benefit no doubt, his volume expanding, quoting from Romans 12:2. He cautioned believers not to conform to the world, which I supposed included me. Had he chosen the passage for Lizzie or his whole family, so none would get too chummy with this outsider? An explanation of why he hadn't welcomed me as Rhoda had.

CHAPTER 6

Nestled on the rocking chair in the kitchen, my toes tapped a comforting rhythm. The swaying motion lulled me to a dreamy state. I ignored Reuben's booming voice in the other room and the rain blipping against the windowpanes.

I reminded myself I'd longed for a space of time to sort through the complicated situation I'd left in New Milford. I mulled over my priorities, Pops at the pinnacle. He wouldn't like Donald and my arguing over his health. He certainly wouldn't want us delaying our wedding for him. If my father's health plummeted, who knew if he would accept one of my kidneys should he need one. He was used to calling the shots, but his choices were dwindling.

A dog howled in the distance. My thoughts drifted to Mr. Big. A weight of guilt still bogged me down, shackling me to the moment my favorite Welsh corgi leaped from the parked minivan's back hatch and injured his spine last month. If only I'd looked after him more carefully. Stroking his silky coat had grounded and soothed me. Exercising him, grooming, and showing him had brought me purpose. Now I had none. I recalled the joy of standing in the ring exhibiting his attributes.

I stretched out my hand, took hold of the teacup, and swallowed a mouthful of tea. What herbs were blended into this concoction that reminded me of dried dandelions? I noticed Lizzie had also placed a sugar bowl, honey, and a spoon on the small table. This family certainly liked their sweets.

My thoughts sidestepped to Donald—"the love of my life" I'd called him until days ago. I'd thought we'd spend a lifetime together but now held serious doubts. His convictions—his core beliefs—and mine didn't coincide, not when it came to Pops. And I had to wonder if I'd fit into his parents' hoity-toity community in Brewster, New York.

Years ago, my only steady high school boyfriend had launched off to college in Southern California and I'd never heard from him again, not even at my high school's five-year reunion. I'd dated over the years, but nothing serious until I met Donald Montgomery through a mutual acquaintance on Lake Candlewood. I was the only single woman not drooling over his ski boat and over him. He was drop-dead gorgeous, but as a salesman's daughter, I'd learned not to slobber over hot merchandise; interest in a vehicle only made the price skyrocket. Apparently Donald had found my standoffish attitude refreshing at the time. But since getting engaged, he didn't seem to respect me anymore. Had I considered what kind of a husband and father he'd make if his universe revolved around him?

From the sound of the pattering rain, the storm was subsiding—at a lull, anyway. I decided to dash outside and lock the car.

With the Mustang's key in hand, I pushed myself to my feet and shoved my arms into my jacket sleeves. No one would miss me.

Snapping my jacket, I stepped into the dank utility room and walked right into Armin. I came at his broad chest with such force I almost lost my balance. He took hold of my upper arms, steadying me, and held on to me for what seemed a beat too long.

I felt a curious current pass between us, like a pull of magnetism. No matter, I told myself. Any woman would find him attractive. I'd simply ignore him for the short amount of time I'd be here.

"Where are you going?" he said, his face inches from mine. "I got your bag."

"But my car's still unlocked. Or did you lock it?"

"I left it as I found it. It's safe. We've never had anything stolen."

"Are you kidding? Someone could go for a joyride, no sweat. That car belongs to my father."

"Then I'll lock it."

"No, I have to make sure it's done correctly." My fingers tightened around the key. "That's a vintage Mustang."

"I know how to lock a car, I can assure you."

"You've driven a car?" I asked him.

"Yes, many times while buying and selling horses. It doesn't take a PhD to lock an automobile."

"I wasn't inferring you're ignorant."

A swirl of clouds must have blustered into the valley; the rain increased, pounding the roof.

"Better take this." He handed me a flashlight. "The Zooks have a *Schaerm*—an umbrella—somewhere around here." He rummaged through a bin of tools and handed me a black umbrella with a hooked handle.

"Thanks." I stuffed the key and flashlight into my jacket pockets, stepped onto the back porch, and struggled to open the contraption. Then I picked my way down the steps. At the bottom, a gust of wind whipped the bat-like umbrella inside out, yanking it from my hands and tossing it several yards.

Armin loped down the steps, not bothering to put on a jacket, and grabbed the scuttling umbrella. He gave it a shake, then came over to shield me from the escalating downpour. I didn't deserve his kindness after speaking to him so harshly.

I grabbed the handle, my hand partway covering Armin's. I heard a tree branch creak in the forested area beyond the field, followed by a thud.

"I'll walk you out there," he said, still grasping the umbrella's handle.

"Thanks." I couldn't help but notice the warmth of his large hand, a workingman's skin, the opposite of Donald's, who made his living sitting behind a desk.

Nearing the car, I heard a rustling noise and sloshing footsteps, barely audible above the spattering rain. "Did you hear that?" I said. Glad to have Armin at my side, I clung to his elbow.

"Probably a barn cat," he said.

"No way. What feline's dumb enough to venture out in this storm?"

His mouth widened into a smile. "A tomcat?"

I halted, held my breath, and heard what sounded like footsteps crushing leaves. A chill ran through me. "That's no cat."

"A *Hund*—a dog?"

I could see into the car: a dim glow, the steering wheel and dash-board. "Hey, the car's interior lights are on."

A gust stretched the umbrella's fabric. Armin reached up with his other hand to keep it from flapping away. He repositioned the umbrella over me as I brought out the flashlight and rounded the car. I wondered: Would Donald venture out here with me? He was a prep-school city boy, a Yalie snob teeming with qualities I'd admired until recently. How could I have fallen for a guy who looked down his nose at my father, the finest man I knew? And I figured Donald's parents deemed he was marrying beneath his potential, anchoring his family to the middle class when he could wed an uptown society girl.

I flicked on the flashlight. "Look." I pointed to a couple foot-prints near the driver's door. "Someone's been out here. A man, judging by the size of the soles. Are these yours?"

"No. Too small. They're probably Jeremy's before he came inside."

"Jeremy didn't have time. And his prints would have washed away by now. These are fresh. Someone's been in the car. See, the door isn't closed properly."

"Well, I shut it just fine when I got your bag."

I wondered if he'd slammed the door instead of using both hands to produce a substantial thud—a trick Pops taught me to make a car sound solid.

"Ach, what difference does it make now?" He peered down at me.

"None, I guess." I felt moisture soaking my suede shoes—ruined; I didn't even need to look. "My fault. I should have locked it immediately."

"We don't lock the house and have never had a break-in. Was anything stolen?"

I flashed the light on the AM/FM radio: still there. And so was the GPS, which I usually stored out of sight. "No, I don't think so."

"No mud on the carpet," he said over my shoulder.

"We might have scared the prowler away." I turned the flashlight's beam into the darkness alongside the barn and smaller buildings. Reuben owned an impressive farm, but my gaze settled on the elongated shadows where a stalker might be lurking.

"After all this fussing, aren't ya going to lock it?" Armin said, in what seemed a mocking tone.

I glared at him. "In a minute."

With damp hands, I leaned into the car, detached the GPS from the windshield, and stowed it under the front seat. Then I locked the Mustang, double-checking both doors and the trunk.

Minutes later, I plodded up the steps and into the back room with Armin following. Rain saturated his hair, rivulets snaking down his shoulders. He collapsed the umbrella and leaned it by the door.

I felt like a badger tunneling into its den after sighting a coyote. Someone had been casing my car and neglected to close the door; I was sure of it.

"Oh, look at ya!" Lizzie said as I entered the kitchen. "What were you doing out in that storm? You're soaked through and through." She handed me a clean dish towel, and I patted my face and neck.

Reuben eyed me with suspicion. "What were yous two doing out there?" His stare cut into me like a serrated knife, as if Armin and I had been indulging in a scandalous rendezvous.

"I was locking my car." I set the flashlight on the counter, then struggled out of my jacket, its shoulders darker from the rain. "I heard someone out there."

I glanced behind me and saw Armin's tousled hair, beads of water hanging from the ends. He was in better shape than any man at my health club, muscles apparently earned from toiling in the fields.

"It was most likely a Hund," Armin said. Reuben nodded in agreement, their camaraderie annoying. No two ways around it: they were poking fun at me. Yet Armin's gaze latched on to mine again—shutting out the rest of the world. Maybe he thought I looked like a drowned rat, as Pops would say. No doubt I did.

"Sometimes the neighbor's dog tries digging into the chicken coop," Reuben said, his thumbs hooking his suspenders.

"I guarantee you that wasn't a dog," I said, and Reuben snickered. "Listen." I planted my hands on my hips. "I know what sounds a dog makes. And I certainly recognize their footprints, unless dogs in these parts wear boots."

"You're an authority on dogs?" Reuben asked.

"As a matter of fact—" I sandwiched my lips together to keep from revealing more.

"The car door wasn't closed right," I said, switching tactics. "I doubt even your neighbor's clever dog would open and close my door."

Reuben huffed. "You probably didn't shut it properly to begin with."

A canine down the road let out a succession of throaty barks, as if to emphasize his point.

"Who'd want ta steal your car?" Armin said, taking a towel from Lizzie and patting his hair.

"Plenty of people."

"Not around here." Reuben rubbed his eye. "Although the car's red color could be a temptation, luring a young lad like the devil."

"I hope Bishop Troyer doesn't see it," Rhoda said.

"He'd never forget a car like mine," I said, but Lizzie kept mum, as if she hadn't heard my remark. Or been in the car when I'd almost run into the bishop's horse and buggy.

"Please, Reuben, Sally's our guest." Rhoda took my jacket. "The bishop knows we accommodate boarders when the Lord sees fit. We talked about it with him this very day."

"Hush," Reuben said, his voice severe. Rhoda slipped into the utility room to hang up my drenched jacket.

"Bishop Jonathan Troyer was here in this house?" Lizzie's pale face and pencil-thin lips told me she was worried. Or afraid? When she noticed my stare, Lizzie's mouth formed a meager smile, and she said, "Sally, let me help you."

Armin was sock-footed, and I realized I should have deposited my grime-covered shoes in the back room. I stepped out of them and peeled off my socks.

"Here, I can take those." Lizzie placed them on a mat just inside the kitchen. "You can go barefoot if you like. Or I'll lend you slippers."

My soaked jeans plastered my calves and ankles like a second skin. "Thank you. I didn't think to bring extra shoes, other than for running." When packing today, I'd envisioned sprinting out of my cozy B&B in the morning before breakfast and taking a jog under sunny skies.

"Ya never drank your tea, and it's gone cold." Lizzie examined my cup. "And your cookie's only half eaten."

"I'll run upstairs, change into dry clothes, and be right back." I looked for my bag. "I didn't bring much."

"Mamm put your belongings in your room," Lizzie said. "I'll have hot water waiting for you when you return."

"Great. Then you and I can sit down and talk."

"Yah. We can chat."

Reuben frowned at Lizzie's enthusiasm. I was evidently an unwelcome influence on his daughter. He had yet to acknowledge me for helping Lizzie lock the store, then giving her a ride home. Jeremy had threatened to ditch her in town; she could still be walking if I hadn't. Did Reuben hold me responsible for the gruesome weather like a woman jinxing a boat at sea?

As I left the room, Armin said, "I'd best be turning in," before I could thank him for escorting me to the car. Even if he'd razzed me, I was grateful he'd braved the storm. Not many men would. Certainly not Donald. I turned to reenter the kitchen and heard the door shut.

Then Rhoda said, "What got ya in such a foul mood tonight, Reuben?" To give them privacy, I closed the door but could still hear their voices.

"Besides the bishop's harping at me and his accusations?" he said. "And the whole district is privy to Lizzie's tomfoolery."

"Ya know, Dat?" Lizzie said.

"I told him last week," Rhoda said. "As soon as Arthur spilled the beans. You should show your dat the same respect."

"I'm afraid our Arthur likes to gossip with his riders," Lizzie said. I heard someone stacking dishes, placing them in a cupboard, its door swinging shut.

"When you're riding with him, sit in the backseat and button your lips," Reuben said.

"It's not as if I haven't known Arthur my whole life," Lizzie said.

"And ya can't blame the bishop's visit on our Lizzie," Rhoda said. "That was partly your doing."

They fell silent, although I guessed Reuben had plenty on his mind.

I felt a wave of relief relax my shoulders. Their argument had nothing to do with me. The family was engulfed in a personal spat. Bad timing on my part. I would ignore their dispute—something to do with a prying bishop and a guy named Arthur.

CHAPTER 7

I headed for the staircase leading to the second floor. I passed Lizzie's brothers, Jeremy and Peter, in the living room. Seeing them seated before the stone fireplace clad in trousers and suspenders, their shaggy hair dusting the tops of their ears, I felt transported back a century.

Jeremy stared at my soaked jeans and bare feet. "What happened?" he asked.

"Were ya outside on this brutal night?" Peter gaped at my damp legs. Then he looked away, his cheeks blushing. Embarrassed by my revealing silhouette?

"I was checking on my car." At least my long-sleeved T-shirt remained unscathed and wasn't sticking to me. Comparing myself to Rhoda's and Lizzie's modest dress, I questioned my motives for exposing my shape to the whole world. No wonder Reuben had been put off when I'd first entered the kitchen. Or was there more to his crabby attitude toward me? He couldn't treat all outsiders with such animosity unless they only took in Amish boarders.

Pops's words, like a fish out of water, reverberated in my ears.

"Kumm join us when you get dried off," Jeremy said. Their game over, he repositioned the checkers on the board atop the knee-high coffee table.

The crackling fire welcomed me. "I might, after I drink the tea Lizzie's fixing."

"Bring your tea in here," Peter said. As we spoke, the two got into their game, their checkers gliding diagonally on the dark squares.

"Lizzie won't stick around for long." Peter peeked up from behind his bangs. "She'll sneak out the moment Dat and Mamm turn in."

"Hush, blabbermouth," Jeremy said to him. "Keep your voice down."

"She'd go out tonight?" I looked through the window into the bleakness. A car motored past on the road; I heard rain spraying up from its tires.

"Ya don't know our Lizzie." Peter lowered his volume and glanced toward the kitchen door. "But don't tell her I said anything."

Jeremy reached across the coffee table and socked Peter's arm. "Lizzie will give you what for for spouting off," he said, a notch above a whisper.

"I'm so scared of my sister."

"Well, ya should be."

I watched Jeremy jump his red checker over Peter's black disc and snatch it off the board. "Gotcha."

"Pride cometh before a fall," Peter said, and jumped his checker over two of Jeremy's. "Ya may be older but not wiser."

"I bet Lizzie won't go anywhere in this storm," I said, but neither responded. They were either immersed in their game or not willing to argue what they knew to be true—or perhaps they didn't wish to be overheard. Why would Lizzie leave the comfort of this house, I had to wonder, especially when her father insisted she rise at dawn to do chores?

As I trotted up the stairs, I heard Peter speak. I stopped to listen. "Come on, tell me what our *Schweschder's* up to."

"Our sister ain't up to nothin'."

"You can trust me," Peter said.

"What are ya talking about? You're the last person I'd trust."

"Bruder, I know a thing or two about you, so don't ya give me your I'm-so-innocent look. And I know about Dat—"

"Ya don't know the half of it," Jeremy murmured. "Sounds like the bishop's found out even if Mamm don't guess a thing," he said.

"Are ya kidding me?" Peter's voice rose in pitch. "You should have been in the kitchen before supper tonight."

I felt goose bumps erupting on my legs but waited until Peter finally said, "That's why Dat got passed over for minister again. Only one nomination."

"Must have been Mommy Leah. Mamm wouldn't want him buried with a lifetime of extra responsibilities."

"'Tis God who does the choosing through the lot, anyway."

"Yah, but first a man must be in good standing and nominated."

As I padded up the stairs and into the hallway a brief lull ensued. I stood with my hand on the doorknob and tried to untangle their words. Reuben wanted to be a minister? Was he trying to get into divinity school? I couldn't think of a poorer candidate. Was Lizzie Reuben's stumbling block because she was working at a store?

Peter raised his volume and asked, "What were you thinking when you took Sally to see Lizzie?"

"How was I ta know who Sally might be? And think about it, how would she know who I was, let alone recognize our buggy?" He must have been creaming Peter at checkers, because he snorted with laughter and said, "King me!"

After a pause he said, "Truly, I don't think Sally was looking for Liz. You should have seen the verhoodled expression on Sally's face when they met, like she was seein' a ghost."

That was how I'd felt—as if running into a phantom, a figment of my imagination. I'd hoped I'd done a better job concealing my shock upon meeting her. Evidently not. And now I was eavesdropping. What if their father caught me? He might boot me out into the night, storm and all.

I turned the knob as quietly as I could, entered my room, and found my sweatpants and zip-up hoodie hanging on wooden pegs on the wall. I hadn't packed much. I pulled open a bureau drawer and found my lingerie, running shorts, and socks neatly folded. Instead of my slinky pink nightie, a white cotton ankle-length nightgown and an aqua-green robe lay across the end of the bed. I hadn't thought I'd needed a bathrobe at the B&B and was glad to have use of one to dodge across the hall to the bathroom.

I noticed a small hand mirror on the bureau and shuddered to think what I looked like. I brought the reflective surface to my face. Not so awful, considering the wind and rain. But my hair was a different story. I raked the shoulder-length sandy-colored strands with my fingers to no avail. Then I wriggled out of my jeans, and I dove into my heather-gray sweatpants and matching hoodie. Thankfully, while bringing in my overnight bag, Armin had kept my belongings dry. But where was the bag?

Once dressed, I rolled my jeans into a wad and carried them downstairs to find Jeremy and Peter still playing checkers and chattering in Pennsylvania Dutch. In the kitchen, I spotted Rhoda speaking to Lizzie and to Reuben, who was sitting at the head of the table, his shoulders hunched.

"Excuse me, is there a place to hang these to dry out?" I asked Rhoda.

"Yah, sure." She took the soggy jeans. "I'll wash them. No trouble."

"I could do it right now," Lizzie said, her hands reaching out.

"I thought you were going to bed early," Rhoda said.

"I'm planning to."

"I'll hold ya to it." Reuben tugged his untrimmed beard. "Did ya hear me?"

"I haven't gone deaf, Dat."

Reuben pushed his chair away from the table and got to his feet. He looked weary, wrung out. His gaze met Rhoda's, then he turned to Lizzie. *"Gut Nacht."* Not giving me a glance, Reuben trod out of the room.

"Good night, Dat," Lizzie said to his departing form. Jeremy and Peter's laughter in the living room came to a halt.

Lizzie emptied my cold tea into the sink. "Mamm, I could wash those jeans right now," she said to Rhoda again.

"You just agreed to go ta bed early, ain't so?"

"Tomorrow will be fine," I said. "Do you have a dryer?" I hadn't seen one, only that relic of a washing machine with a ringer that would probably mangle my favorite jeans.

"Nee, but it won't take long for the sun to dry them tomorrow."

"Mamm will be gentle on them," Lizzie said, seeming to pick up on my angst. "Don't ya worry. See how nice she launders my *Kapp*?" She smoothed her hand over her delicate white head covering.

"Must all Amish women cover their heads?" I asked.

"Yah," Rhoda said. "In case we wish to pray, as instructed in the Bible, 1 Corinthians 11:6."

I persisted. "Even in the heat of summer?"

"Yah, always covered with something." She carried my jeans into the utility room and returned a minute later. "Well, Sally, see you in the morning. You can talk while Lizzie finishes cleaning the kitchen. Unless there's anything else you need."

"No, not a thing. Thanks for bringing my clothes upstairs." I sank onto the rocking chair. I was beginning to feel at ease in this kitchen. Twice the size of mine, but already familiar.

"Glad to help." Rhoda backed out of the kitchen. "Gut Nacht."

"Go to bed, Mamm," Lizzie said. "I want to speak to Sally." Lizzie's demeanor lightened the instant Rhoda left. Lizzie tossed aside her damp rag and said, "Think I'll make us hot chocolate with whipped cream instead of tea. How does that sound?" She strode to the refrigerator, poured milk into a pan, and set it on the stovetop to warm. "You like our Armin, don't ya?" she said. "I could see the way you two were looking at each other."

Oh, dear. "You didn't lure me all the way to Lancaster County to meet Armin, did you?"

"Nee, but now that you're here, you admit he's a fine man."

"Then why is he still single and working for your father?"

"By choice, believe me." She stood at the counter, whipping cream using a whisk. "The single women bring him baked goodies—sticky buns, whoopie pies, apple crisp, pineapple cake—trying to snag his attention, hoping to get him to drive them home from Sunday Singings or take them out on a date. And they invite him for dinner, but he usually declines, not wanting to lead them on."

She stirred squares of chocolate into the hot milk—I doubted it was pasteurized—added sugar, and poured the cocoa into two mugs, then plopped a dollop of whipped cream atop each. She gave me one mug, pulled up a chair, and settled close to me.

Finally, my chance to get some straight talk. But before I started my interrogation, I couldn't resist taking a sip. Steam rose from the cocoa's surface. My taste buds embraced the frothy beverage. Never had I enjoyed a creamier hot chocolate.

"Sally, tell me about your family," she said, dominating our conversation while my mouth was full.

No way would I mention Mom. Thinking of her made my throat constrict. I chomped into the cookie but had trouble swallowing the buttery crumbs, so I took another sip. "I live with my father, but you already know that."

"How would I?"

"Good question. How did you know about my dog kennel?"

"A few months back, a Mennonite neighbor who makes his living driving us Plain people spotted a used passenger van at a car lot named Honest Ed's in Connecticut. And he saw your kennel's name on a nearby sign. When he got home—Arthur lives down the road a spell—he told me about your dog kennel, right next to the car lot. And like I said, Mrs. Martin Googled it for me."

"I've since removed the sign." I felt a pang of defeat as I recalled tossing it into Pops's Dumpster. "But why would this driver give two cents about Welsh corgis?"

"I must have mentioned my idea of buying a dog to Arthur. He drives me to go shopping and such when I can't use our buggy." She swigged a gulp of cocoa. "Now here's an odd twist to his tale. Arthur thought the owner of the lot looked the spitting image of someone he knew as a lad. But when Arthur introduced himself, the car-lot fellow shooed him away saying he'd changed his mind and refused to sell him the van." She stared into my eyes awaiting my reaction, but I wore a poker face while my mind whirled with questions and inconsistencies.

"That doesn't sound like my father. He wouldn't pass up a genuine sale," I said, realizing too late what I'd divulged. I lay the cookie aside. "The driver—Arthur—must have spoken to Ralph, my father's assistant."

"No, the man claimed he was the owner."

"I know my father. Arthur must have been lowballing him, trying to wheel and deal on the van, or backing out at the last minute. Selling cars isn't an easy game."

"No, I 'spect not."

I'd come here to escape the world, not discuss my father and automobiles. But my curiosity was screaming for answers. Scrutinizing her features and finding her face pinched, I asked, "Did Arthur know the car salesman or not?"

"The fellow Arthur knew as a youth had a different name altogether."

I recalled my conversation with Rhoda, who seemed overly inquisitive about Pops. "My father's always been Ed Bingham, and he's from New Jersey, not Pennsylvania. So that mystery is solved."

"Yah, I guess—" Her squinty eyes indicated she wasn't convinced. "Are ya married?" she asked, her gaze moving to my ring.

"No. I'm engaged—I guess." I twisted the band, hiding the sparkly stone in my palm.

She tasted her drink, licked her upper lip. "Tell me about your beau, Sally."

"Tell me about yours," I said. Lizzie was way too nosy; time for her to do the talking.

She glanced at a clock above the stove. She jumped to her feet. "I didn't realize it was so late. Ach, I need to run out to the barn and make sure Jeremy turned off the lantern. We don't want the barn burning down." She chugged her hot chocolate. "You're welcome to stay up as long as you like, but I should warn ya the rooster crows mighty early. Dat rousing Jeremy and Peter for milking will wake you for sure. And Mamm will be rummaging in the kitchen preparing breakfast."

"I should have brought earplugs."

"Not such a bad idea around here." She jaunted toward the back door, found a hooded jacket and a flashlight.

"I can't believe you're going out in that rain," I said.

Jeremy swaggered into the kitchen. "Caught ya, Liz."

Hands on hips, she spun around to face him. "Caught you, my dearest Bruder."

"I'm using Taffy tonight." I assumed he was referring to a horse.

"Nee, I was about to—"

He raised his freshly shaven chin. "Take the buggy without telling Dat and Mamm?"

"I have permission."

"You do not." He positioned a straw hat on his head, pushing down hard, and dove into a jacket. "I'll drive ya to Sunday Singing in a couple days. Surely some poor chump will give you a lift home."

"I can't wait that long." She smuggled the flashlight into her apron pocket and slipped her feet into ankle boots. "Don't your Englisch friends drive automobiles? Can't one of them come fetch you?"

"I could ask you the same question."

They lapsed into Pennsylvania Dutch, but I could make out several words my father occasionally used, like *Dummkopp*—what he called an aggravating customer when he and I were alone. I'd always assumed my father was attempting to speak German but never corrected his pronunciation.

I got to my feet. "Hey, you two, if you need a ride I can help out," I said, and they both stiffened—as I expected they would.

"Uh—never mind," Lizzie told me. "I couldn't impose on you again tonight. But thank you ever so much for the kind offer."

The rain continued drumming against the ground outside the kitchen window. I didn't relish venturing into the storm, but I wanted to see their drama unfold—enacted for me, I figured. In my teens, I'd sneaked out at midnight while Pops snoozed. Looking back, I wondered if he knew about my forays. As a single parent, he'd let a lot slide, bringing the incidents up later in the form of offhand wisecracks. Rarely a punishment.

"I don't mind." I wondered if their parents would act as leniently. Doubtful. Not Reuben, anyway. "Could you lend me a pair of boots? My shoes are shot."

"Never mind." She slithered out of her jacket and draped it over a hook. "Armin will shut off the lantern in the barn like he always does."

"The storm's too fierce for either of us." Jeremy wrenched off his hat and pitched it onto a peg by the back door. His hair lay flat on his forehead. "I made sure the livestock was secure before I came in for supper, so there's no reason for us to go out to the barn. And like ya said, Armin is sure to turn off the barn light." He narrowed his eyes at her. "Liz, stick around and keep Sally company. Have another cookie."

"*Leib* Bruder, you have one." She held out the plate of cookies, but he shook his head.

"I've had my fill," he said. "Whip up more hot chocolate for Sally." He turned to me. "Liz makes the best hot chocolate in the district."

"Ain't you generous? I'll make you a cup too."

"Nee, denki." He covered his yawning mouth, his fingers curled into a ball. "Dat will be rapping on my door before sunup. I'm betting Peter's already in bed."

"Then I'll turn in too." Lizzie blinked and rubbed her eyes. "Why, I'm so tired I can barely keep my lids open."

"Me, too. Gut Nacht." Jeremy plodded out of the room.

I was sure those two were up to mischief. But what could they possibly conjure up on a tempestuous night in the middle of nowhere? Unlikely either of them would coerce a horse into leaving the safety of the barn. I could imagine the animal refusing to budge from the dry structure, which made me wonder how they coped during winter.

I sat on the rocker again and set it in motion. "Where's Armin?"

Lizzie's eyebrows raised—one crease on her otherwise blemish-free forehead.

"Just curious," I said, wishing I hadn't asked.

"Out in his cabin most likely." Lizzie kicked off her boots and moved toward the front room. Noticing she'd left her boots conveniently near the back door, I wondered if she would traipse out as soon as I turned in.

She fiddled with her cap strings. "He makes himself morning Kaffi but eats his breakfast with us after milking. You can see his place tomorrow if you want."

"No, thanks, if it means getting up at milking time." Realizing I wouldn't speak to him again, I felt an unexpected twinge in my stomach, which I chalked up to indigestion. I doubted our paths would cross again. Except for a little ribbing, he'd been my hero out in the storm. But what would be the point in looking for more? In fact, I was so miffed at Donald I might give up men forever.

No, not if I wanted a family and children: to feel a baby maturing in my womb and dedicate the rest of my life to caring for him or her. A roomful would suit me fine. My father was an only child. Both his parents died when he was young. I had no siblings, aunts, uncles, or cousins. What would I do if Pops died from kidney failure? How would I survive?

"I'll say good night, Sally." Lizzie eased toward the door to the living room. "Leave your cup and plate. I'll wash them in the morning."

"But wait, you and I haven't had our talk. You never explained your emails."

"We can chat after breakfast." She backed into the front room
and closed the door. I heard Jeremy and her half-whispering to each
other as they passed through the living room, then movement on
the staircase. Maybe I'd been wrong after all and they were going to
bed. What I should do as well. But I felt wired—wide awake—and
didn't want to be alone, how I'd felt most of my life, even when
surrounded by bustling crowds at dog shows: saying hi and good
luck to acquaintances who knew me by name but who didn't know
the real me. Bottom line: I longed for my mother's eyes watching
from the sidelines. I'd often scanned the many faces, hoping she was
there. Every time I received a trophy, I'd clung to the dream she'd run
forward to congratulate me. Pathetic.

A newspaper—*The Budget*—lay folded on the floor. I opened
it, but I couldn't concentrate on the articles, mostly concerning an
unexpected cold front moving in, notices for auctions, and mention
of a Mennonite nonprofit fund-raiser, a big to-do I wouldn't mind
attending if it meant buying a new quilt. What was I thinking about?
I didn't have spare money and doubted any of Donald's or Pops's
friends intended to give us an Amish quilt as a wedding gift. If we
got married.

Feeling glum, I finished my cocoa and washed the cup and plate
in the sink. No need to leave Rhoda a mess. She was bound to be the
first person in this kitchen in the morning.

The back doorknob rattled and heavy footsteps crossed the utility room.

I wasn't usually jumpy, but I felt adrenaline surge through me.
At home, Ginger warned me when a stranger was approaching. And
Pops was close by to protect me.

I watched the knob to the kitchen door turn, and Armin entered wearing slippers. He placed his damp hat on the peg next to Jeremy's, then rotated and stared at me, his eyes round, like I didn't belong here. Did he expect to find a young beauty named Lizzie?

"Looking for Lizzie?" I asked before thinking, then wished I hadn't.

Armin's jaw flexed. "I have permission to come and go as I please." He reached out and filched a cookie off the plate on the counter, bit into it.

He hadn't denied he was searching for Lizzie. I couldn't imagine why this fact made my chest tighten. More than ever, I wished I could restart the day. No, I didn't. I wouldn't have met Rhoda, my hospitable hostess. What I'd hoped my own mother would be like should I ever meet her—if she were still alive. She could have passed away years ago. My life would almost be easier if Mom were dead and buried securely under a marble tombstone in a graveyard I could visit. Instead, I lived with the prospect she might unexpectedly appear in 3-D and flip my life into an ocean of chaos. Or fulfill my childish dreams.

Donald's mother, Darlene, my future mother-in-law, wouldn't plug the void left by Mom's abandonment. I recalled the day Darlene chauffeured me to Manhattan to Bergdorf Goodman to pick out a wedding dress. "My treat," she'd insisted, not permitting the saleswoman to reveal the price tags on the opulent gowns with plunging necklines and elaborate skirts—when I'd hoped for an understated sheath. Why hadn't I spoken up? I usually didn't play the underdog. Probably because I wanted Darlene to accept me, to grow to love me as her own daughter. I should be grateful, I'd told myself. Most young women would be ecstatic to receive such a lavish gift. Would I ever wear that wedding dress? Or was I destined to never marry? I pondered what having Rhoda for a mother-in-law would be like. Or a mother. Lizzie probably didn't appreciate her good fortune.

Armin moved toward the back door, snagging my thoughts. "I suppose I'll be on my way," he said, but seemed to be vacillating, not putting on his hat.

"Already?" He'd obviously not come in to speak to me.

"Yah, I was hoping to find … Reuben."

Armin's explanation struck me as false; he must know Reuben turned in early. "I think he's in bed. But if you wouldn't mind, I could use help." I got to my feet and pulled my cell phone out of my sweats pocket. "My phone's low on juice. Is there anywhere to charge my battery?"

"Can't you place your calls, then turn it off?"

"My father might need me," I said in my defense. "And someone else could call, although he probably won't. I should have told him I was going away for the weekend hours ago." But Donald hadn't contacted me to apologize for his bullying behavior.

Only feet away, Armin gave me his full attention. He had the most beautiful brown eyes. I wondered what he saw. A foreigner wearing smudged makeup or an attractive woman? Not that I should care.

I brought out my left hand to expose my engagement ring. Armin probably found diamond rings pretentious since no one around here seemed to wear jewelry. Not even a wristwatch. "The man I'm engaged to could call me. We had a disagreement—" As my mind explored the enormity of our differences, a lump in my throat closed off my words.

"I don't wish to be nosy." Armin ran a hand through his thick espresso-brown hair. "But if he doesn't know where you are, it seems an unusual way to carry on a courtship. Can you not call him yourself?"

"I could, but I have my reasons." I was tempted to spill the entire story but decided not to.

"Where's your phone charger?" he asked.

"In my overnight bag, zipped into a side pocket." I was glad I hadn't brought my laptop computer, Pops's Christmas present to me. The rain might have ruined it.

"Rhoda set your bag in the utility room to dry off." Armin swallowed the remaining cookie, then put out his hand. "Give me your phone, and I'll grab the charger on my way out. I'll plug it in next to Reuben's fax machine in his shop."

"He has electricity?"

"Only in his workshop next to the barn. For now, anyway."

I recalled Rhoda's comments about a bishop's visit. "What kind of a business does Reuben run?"

"He builds—well, I'd best let him tell you himself."

"No hints?" I handed him the phone. "Something illegal?" I joked, but Armin didn't smile.

He stuffed the phone into his pocket. "I better keep my mouth shut. Reuben will tell you should he wish you to know."

I recalled what Pops asserted about loose tongues sinking ships. "Fine. Okay," I said.

"How did ya come to be here, anyway?" He stared at the closed door leading to the front room, as if expecting someone.

"Lizzie emailed me several times. Although how I ended up in this kitchen still boggles me."

He shot me a look of disbelief.

"It's true." My hands moved to my hips. "If I had my laptop with me, I could show you the proof." Or had I deleted her emails?

"Was Lizzie advertising rooms for rent over the Internet?" he asked. "Her parents could use the money, but they wouldn't approve of that method."

"No, she told me she had a problem but wouldn't be specific. And now she denies the whole thing. And she had questions about my dogs." Lizzie's emails had never mentioned renting rooms, but maybe detaining me as a tenant was her goal, though I couldn't imagine inviting the kennel owner for a visit and then demanding rent. But what did I know about Lizzie other than I'd stopped her from sneaking out of the house against her parents' wishes? The word *conniving* came to mind. She was a trickster.

"Why isn't Rhoda billing me?" I recalled the sumptuous meal, the large portions, and desserts aplenty. Pops and I had scrimped over the years as the economy fluctuated. "Should I have insisted on paying for dinner? If she and Reuben are low on cash, I'll leave something on the bedroom dresser when I go. Not that I carry much money."

Standing at about six foot—an inch taller than Donald—Armin's face revealed bafflement. "But you drive a fancy car that must burn gasoline like a schoolkid sipping soda through a straw."

"Don't you all use gas, propane, or diesel to run the refrigerator and stove?"

"Yah, in small quantities." He took a step away from me—not that I blamed him. I sounded snappish. What was wrong with me? Why take out my anger about Donald's and my spat, for the storm, for everything spiraling out of control on Armin?

"In many ways, your lifestyle sounds superior to mine. Fact is, I'd love to be part of a big family." Except I preferred Pops to Reuben ten times over. "How many siblings do you have?"

"Two. A sister who moved to Ohio years ago, right after our parents died, and an older brother, Nathaniel, who lives next door."

"Why don't you stay with him?"

"I tried, but we've never seen eye to eye. I lived up in New York State for several years. Then when I returned, I lived with Nathaniel until he remarried. His new wife, Esther, said I could stay on, but I felt like a third wheel."

"Ever been married?" I asked him.

"Nee, not with this shaved chin." He smoothed his hand across it. "Once an Old Order Amishman's been married, he wears a beard—not that I've been baptized into the church." I tried to visualize him with a tuft on his chin. He'd look cute anyway with those puppy-dog eyes.

"I courted a woman once …" He frowned as if recalling bad memories. "Are you always this inquisitive?"

"Sorry. I'm being rude. I already scared Lizzie and Jeremy up to their beds a few minutes ago." I wasn't ready to be alone.

The corner of his mouth lifted. "Then you did both a favor."

"What do you know about their monkey business? They weren't planning a joyride in the Mustang, were they?" I checked my empty pockets, then remembered I'd stashed the key in my purse on the floor by the rocking chair.

"I can't imagine they'd do something that outlandish." Armin half-filled a glass with apple cider from the refrigerator. As he took a sip, Rhoda opened the door to the living room and entered.

Her shoulders stiffened. "Sally, I thought I heard you and Lizzie turn in. Your door was shut." She seemed edgy. Because I was here instead of Lizzie? Because I was here, period?

Then what Pops would call "a doozy of an idea" inundated my brain: Rhoda and Armin had planned a meeting—a clandestine get-together.

No, I refused to believe anything bad about Rhoda. Without makeup I couldn't be sure of her age, but I figured she was older than Armin by ten or fifteen years. Not that younger men weren't sometimes attracted to older women. I'd recently seen a movie about such an improbable couple. Rhoda and Armin saw each other every day … and Reuben was as surly as the neighbor's German shepherd back home.

"Lizzie and Jeremy went upstairs," I said.

Rhoda's gaze homed in on Armin's face, as if she were trying to convey a message, and he stared back at her with intensity, his lips together. Pops and I spoke what we laughingly called "silent pig Latin" on the car lot. With a lift of one brow, he'd tell me he'd hooked a hot prospect, or a slight shake of his head meant he had looky-loos and wanted help getting rid of them so he could make a bona fide sale. But these two were communicating a mixture of anxiety and fear. That I'd caught them together?

Rhoda broke eye contact with Armin and turned to me. "Are you sure our Lizzie and Jeremy went to bed?" she asked. I was struck by the notion she wasn't being straight with me. Was she jealous, finding me alone with Armin? Ridiculous, I told myself.

"I heard footsteps on the stairs and figured they were Lizzie's and Jeremy's," I said. "Where would they go on a miserable night like this?"

Rhoda sent Armin a sideways glance.

"I haven't seen them since supper," he said, but I didn't believe he was addressing her real question. No, something secretive was unfolding before my eyes. "You want me to go look for her?" he asked.

"Nee, I'll check her bed. We don't pay you to babysit. That girl of mine—well, no need to burden Sally with our problems."

"I'd say there is, when you think about it," I said. "If it weren't for her, I wouldn't be here." The rain and wind grew in velocity, filling the world with a whooshing sound, air compressing through the cracks around the windowpanes.

"Sally claims our Lizzie sent her emails." Armin's mouth curved into a smile, but Rhoda's face remained solemn.

As Armin sipped his drink, my cell phone rang. Armin set his glass on the counter. I watched helplessly as he fished my phone out of his pocket and answered it. "Hullo?" he said much to my horror. He bobbed his head. "Yah, she's right here. Hey, wait just a minute. No need to get hostile." He passed the phone to my outstretched hand like it had turned to a hot coal. "For you, Sally."

"What did you expect? How dare you answer it!"

"Since when is it a crime to answer a phone entrusted to your care?"

I snatched it away from him.

"Who was that?" Pops said. "You okay?"

"Sure. Couldn't be better." I felt like a teenager, lying to Honest Ed, who could usually detect deceit in my voice. "Someone was about to charge my phone's battery," I said. "I can't imagine why he answered it with me standing right here."

"At the bed and breakfast? Don't lie to me, Sally. I called them and the receptionist said you weren't staying there. Where are you?"

"Why did you call, Pops? Are you all right?" Out of the corner of my eye, I noticed Armin handing Rhoda a folded scrap of paper as he passed her on the way to the sink to deposit his glass. She kept her gaze on me as she slid the paper into her apron pocket.

"Yeah, yeah, I'm fine," Pops said. "I wanted to let you know Donald stopped by. He was none too pleased to hear you'd taken off. And I'll come out and tell you right now we didn't have a pleasant tête-à-tête. Which got me worrying. I don't get it, the way you flew out of here. Where are you?"

"In someone's lovely home." I glanced around the kitchen at the African violet on the windowsill, the wooden cabinets, the long table that could easily accommodate a dozen if called upon. A room a lot like Pops's and mine in temperament, but double in size and without electric lighting and appliances. And Pops liked to listen to the radio sitting on the shelf above the stove during the World Series or any time the Yankees played, a habit leftover from childhood, he'd told me. Having grown up in New Jersey, he'd always been a Yankees fan. "Not everyone from New Jersey speaks with an accent," he'd informed me more than once.

As I mused about my father, I turned to Rhoda and was surprised to see her mouth working her lower lip. "I'm staying with an Amish family that rents out rooms," I said.

"What the—?" Pops let out a puff of air so loud it rivaled the downpour battering the side of the house. "How did you end up there?"

"I'm not exactly sure. Remember those emails?" I peered out the window and saw the windmill whirling with such velocity that its blades blurred together. Rain slanted against the barn. I shuddered to think Pops's Mustang might leak, but I wouldn't mention my neglecting to lock his prized automobile or stow it under cover. I was still sure someone had prowled around it. Here stood Armin looking so concerned, yet he'd chided me when I'd pointed out the footprints in the mud. Was all his kindness aimed at Rhoda? I felt a prick of jealousy for no logical reason.

"You said Donald came over to see me?" I felt a smattering of hope and dared to wonder if Donald brought flowers as he had on our first few dates or whenever we quarreled. Yellow roses. He'd wooed me like a starlet in a Hollywood movie.

"Maybe he came to set me straight," Pops said, "because the minute I said you were gone, he went ballistic."

"You had an argument?"

"Donald-schmonald," my father said.

My sentiments of only an hour ago. But my world felt topsy-turvy. Maybe I'd overreacted to Donald's criticism of Pops's kidney treatment. No, Donald had acted downright mean-spirited.

"Pops, the bed-and-breakfast's roof leaked and the room was flooded, so I went looking for lodging. I came across this huge Amish home that rents out rooms, only they don't have electricity inside, so one of their farmhands was about to charge my phone. Not a big deal."

I glanced into Rhoda's face and saw apprehension, her features taut. Maybe Reuben didn't allow cell phones in the home. I caught Rhoda and Armin exchanging looks again. Then she gave her head a small shake.

"Is the Mustang all right?" Pops said.

"I'm afraid I had to park it outside, and it's pouring."

"Wish you'd checked the weather report before you left. I heard the mercury's going to plunge. You could have driven the trusty Caravan."

"We could store your car in a shed," Rhoda said, moving closer to me. She could probably hear my father's words.

"Who's that?" Pops demanded.

"My hostess," I said.

CHAPTER 8

"I want you to jump in the Mustang and come home right now," Pops told me.

I cupped my mouth with my spare hand. "Stay up most of the night and drive in pouring rain?"

"Then I'll come get you. I took in a trade-in a few hours ago, a Chrysler that cruises like a dream. Or the Toyota Highlander." Instead of his typical easygoing cadence, he sounded frantic.

"What's gotten into you?"

"You'll always be my little girl, Sally, honey."

"Aren't I safer here? I don't want you on the wet highway." Pops's ritual over the last year was to turn in early. He'd complained of fatigue and fell asleep in front of the TV. And he rarely took a car out for a road trip without first switching tires and checking the brakes.

"I guess you're right." He let out a yawn. "It's raining like crazy, and our lights have been flickering."

"Are you all right, Pops?"

"Sure, Ginger's keeping me company. But you know she hates lightning." My corgi headed for the shower stall during electrical storms, so I figured she was cowering. But Pops could handle her; he never let me down.

The lantern above the table emitted a warm glow. "The lights won't go out where I'm staying. And there's a fire burning in the hearth in the next room."

Rhoda extended her hand, then brought it back, laying it on her chest. Did she want me to turn the phone off so I didn't disturb Reuben, who might awaken like a grizzly bear after spring's first thaw?

I lowered my volume. "I need to say good night. I don't want to wake the whole household."

"But—but, wait." I'd never heard him sound so uptight. His words stammered out in a rush. "Tell me one thing: the last name of the family you're staying with."

"Zook."

"Zook?" He paused so long I assumed we'd lost reception, then he said, "No matter. There must be hundreds of Zooks in Lancaster County."

"What's the big deal? Hey, wait a minute." An extraordinary notion unfurled itself in the back of my mind. "Was my mom's maiden name Zook? Are you saying my mother was from Lancaster County and not New Jersey? Does she still live around here?" The puzzle pieces were beginning to jigsaw together. Pops was terrified I'd run into her.

"That's the last place you'd find Mavis." He sputtered a chuckle. "And Zook wasn't her last name."

"How dare you laugh about her." I felt anger boiling through my chest, strangling my throat, cutting off my air supply like a choke chain. "Did she grow up in Lancaster County or not?" My words turned feeble. I pleaded, "Why won't you tell me?"

Rhoda stepped closer, like the tide inching in. But I wouldn't let this opportunity skid by my elusive father. What if he died before I found my mother?

I turned my back to Rhoda and spoke a skosh above a whisper. "Pops, I've made a decision. I'm going to hire a private detective until I find her."

"Please, Sally, can't you leave well enough alone?"

"No. I can't and I won't."

Rhoda tapped my shoulder. "Excuse me, Sally," she said. "May I speak to him?" Her voice was so gentle that I rotated and gave her my phone with a shaky hand.

"Ich bedank mich—thank you," she told me, then placed the cell phone to her ear as if it were a foreign object. "Hello? This is Rhoda. Your daughter's fine and safe with us. I promise to look after her." Her facial expression changed from one of wide-eyed expectancy to disappointment. She handed the phone back to me. "I'm afraid we've lost him."

I placed the phone to my ear and heard nothing—a canyon of silence. "I'm sorry," I said. "He must have hung up." Rarely had I felt so mortified.

"Maybe he lost reception," Armin said. I assumed he was trying to allay my embarrassment. I felt my cheeks radiating heat.

"The signal was clear a minute ago."

"Perhaps not at his end," he said.

I checked the battery: I had maybe fifteen minutes max left on it. I'd been fretting about keeping the phone charged because of Pops's precarious health. Maybe his illness was impairing his judgment. But why be rude to Rhoda? He didn't even know the woman.

"Yah, I bet Armin's right," she said. Her small hand slid into her apron pocket and she fingered something—the note Armin had given her? Truth was, she might not be the wonderfully perfect woman I'd initially thought. Was there no one in the world I could trust? I felt like I did every Christmas and Mother's Day—like a pitiful, abandoned child. But I held in the tears pressing at the backs of my eyes. I never cried in public, and I wasn't about to start now.

"Do you think he might come to our house?" she asked me.

"How could he possibly know where it is?" I forced a smile while my stomach clenched. "I'm certainly not going to tell him. Not after our conversation."

"Now, please don't be too harsh on him," Rhoda said.

"Yah," Armin cut in, "you should show your father respect."

I glared at him. "Don't you have a brother just down the road?"

Armin opened his mouth, but Rhoda put a finger to her lips as if to shush him.

"I'd appreciate a sibling if I were you," I said to him. "I'd do anything to have one. And as you might have surmised, I'm looking for my mother." I froze as I realized I'd revealed a segment of my personal anguish to another near stranger. What had taken hold of me? I'd never even told Donald how much I longed to find her, only that my parents were divorced—although I had no proof.

"I'm ever so sorry," he said. His words showed empathy, but I doubted he could relate. He had relatives, and from what I'd seen of Reuben, men called the shots in this society. "What kind of a mother would leave her child?" he said, and I cringed. "Was she *ab in Kopp*?" He circled his index finger over his temple as if speaking of a crazy woman. "Or was she kidnapped?"

"That's a new twist I hadn't thought of." I pictured Pops and me sharing a can of beans for dinner one evening when I was about six. "Since my father's never been rich, I highly doubt she was held for ransom."

"You mean he's struggling financially?" Rhoda wrung her hands.

I put on what I called my "artificial happy face" that customers and dog-show judges saw. "My father owns a car lot, and it does pretty well." Yet I knew from doing the books that money was tight.

"Then I guess he wouldn't think much of our horse and buggies," Armin said with a half smile. "Although you come look at my Thunder in the morning. He's a fine animal, fast and feisty. A Thoroughbred stallion who won a few races. Not that I'm boasting, mind you. God made him that way."

Had Armin changed the subject to put me at ease? Whatever his motive, I felt my insides relax and my breathing calm to its normal pace.

"Sure, I'll look at your horse," I said, mostly to be polite. "As long as I don't have to ride him."

"I'm training him to pull my buggy and spring wagon, but every once in a while I jump on his back and we cross my brother's pasture, over the stream, and through the forest. There's no faster horse in the county." He seemed to grow in stature.

"You should take Sally over to see the property," Rhoda said. "Yah, after milkin', you show her the place, and then take her by your brother's. You know he wants to see you."

"No, he doesn't. I'm as good as shunned."

"That just isn't true," she told him.

"I'll be leaving in the morning," I said. But my curiosity was tweaked. Would he offer me a ride in a buggy?

"Nee, please stay longer," Rhoda said. "You must. Please."

"But you'll want to rent out my room, won't you?"

"We have plenty of space. This house is bigger than it looks. Truly." Her fingers traced her dress's neckline. "There'll be no charge, I promise."

"I couldn't let you turn away a paying customer." But staying would give me an added break from my father and Donald. Or was I being selfish? Pops had given up everything for me; I owed him my allegiance. In spite of what I'd told him, I couldn't afford to hire a private detective. I'd do my own sleuthing. I wondered if Pops had kept his old high school annuals; I'd never seen one in our bookshelves. The Internet was where I should have started my search years ago. Maybe Facebook.

"If you stuck around, you'd be doing Rhoda and Reuben a favor," Armin said. "Seems like you kept Lizzie and Jeremy home tonight."

"Then my suspicions were right." Those two imps were ready to hit the trail. "Would they really take a horse and buggy out in the rainstorm?"

Rhoda shrugged one shoulder. "They're in their running-around years, so they have more freedom to do as they please." She sounded aggravated but not surprised. "However on such a perilous night, Reuben would throw a fit."

In the news, I'd heard of trucks and cars colliding with horse and buggies. Any parent would worry, including my father. I was being too hard on him. But his driving me back to Connecticut when I already had an automobile was just silly.

Rhoda glanced at the ceiling. "I'd better check to make sure they're home." She slid her arm through mine. "Before I say good night, Sally, tell me you'll stay another day."

I felt myself teetering with indecision. I still hadn't corralled Lizzie into our private conversation. Having worked at the car lot, I was skilled at reading people's expressions and body gestures, but Lizzie remained an enigma. My best guess was she'd claimed she was in a predicament to lure me here. But why?

"Let's wait and see what tomorrow brings." By then I'd be ready to flee this cockeyed household. Yet the surroundings were quaint and cozy; being stuck here, with the wind howling outside, gave me a sense of comfort and peace I hadn't felt for years. "I'll call my father in the morning and see if he needs me. I'll bet Armin was right. A tree branch fell on a telephone line and cut my dad off." I pulled up my phone's call history and noticed Pops had been using his cell phone. No matter. I refused to believe he'd hang up on Rhoda, a complete stranger. Not like him; he was usually polite to his most difficult customers.

"A nice big breakfast will be waiting for ya in the morning," Rhoda said. "You pay no attention to any noises you hear before sunup. We eat after milking time. Gut Nacht and sweet dreams."

"Good night," I said as she left the room. Then I held my phone out to Armin. "Still willing to charge this culprit?"

"Yah, if you'll help me find the charger." Armin flicked on a flashlight, and I followed him into the utility room. He lifted my canvas bag from the floor where it lay by the back door and carried it into the kitchen. The fabric was almost dry.

"Thanks." I unzipped the side pocket and extracted the device. "Glad I didn't forget this."

"Are you angry at me for answering your phone?" Armin gave his head a slight shake. "I had no right. None at all."

I'd forgotten I was miffed at him. "Not anymore," I said, setting my phone and charger on the counter. "Too bad it was my father calling and not a certain man." I glanced down at my ring. It had lost its luster. "He would have had a fit when you answered."

"You'd like to make the man you're engaged to jealous?"

"It wouldn't hurt him." Donald was a head turner; I figured he wasn't used to anything less than adulation from his girlfriends—if we were still a couple. Had he instructed his mother to hold off sending out the invitations?

"I won't answer again." He raked a hand through his hair. "The Lord admonishes us not to covet. I wouldn't wish to lead a man into temptation, into thinking or doing something he'll regret."

"That's a new one. I'll turn the ringer off for the night. Then no one will be tempted to answer it."

"Gut idea." He scooped up my phone and charger, then propped my bag by the door leading to the utility room. "See you in the morning," he said, and left.

Fatigue encompassed me the way it had when I used to return from a weekend of showing Mr. Big. Would I ever own another stupendous winner? Not only were his confirmation and gait superb, but he'd smile up at the judges as if to say, "Pick me!"

When would I stop blaming myself for his accident? I'd been negligent and couldn't shake my feelings of guilt. I wished I had my Ginger here to keep me company tonight. But the bed and breakfast had stated no pets allowed, and I wouldn't leave Ginger in the car. Anyway, Pops might need her company. I wondered if he'd let her sleep in his room.

I climbed the stairs with heavy feet. Sure enough, Lizzie's door was closed. But was she in bed? None of my business, I told myself.

My room was chilly. I tossed off my clothing and put on the nightgown Rhoda had lent me. I snuggled into bed, the mattress stiff and unforgiving. But the quilts felt like arms around me assuring me everything was okay when nothing was further from the truth. I recalled the dumb saying "Today is the first day of the rest of your life."

Well, tomorrow would be mine.

CHAPTER 9

I awoke with a jolt to a clacking sound. A rock hitting my window? How long had I been asleep? I guessed over an hour by the heaviness of my limbs and my mental confusion. Was someone stealing the Mustang?

No, a thief wouldn't throw a pebble at a window. I swung my legs over the side of the bed and landed on the wooden floor; chill air traveled up my gown. In darkness I peeked around the window shade and saw a male figure and a flashlight's beam.

The rain and wind had eased up; the trees no longer swished like hula dancers, nor were droplets pounding the ground. The moon—with crepe-paper–thin clouds dashing by it—illuminated the property like a fifteen-watt lightbulb, giving the world an eerie appearance.

The young man stood gazing up at the house for a moment, then receded to the base of a tree.

Armin? I wondered, then noticed the guy was hatless, his pale hair short—to his disadvantage if he wished to stay hidden. On closer inspection, this fellow was not as tall as Armin—about Pops's height, but his torso was stocky. No beard. In my foggy half-asleep state, my brain struggled for clarity.

I heard the rustle of fabric in the hallway, then the pitter-patter of movement on the staircase. Below me in the front room and kitchen, the air lay still, but a door creaked open and closed. My nose against the windowpane, I saw Lizzie in a black coat and hat descending the stoop. She looked over her shoulder, then rushed toward the young man, who turned off his flashlight. Together, they disappeared from sight.

The bedroom's icy air spurred me to either get dressed or pounce back into bed. But would I fall asleep again? I reminded myself: I had no control over Lizzie's actions. Obviously. I'd delayed her attempt to leave earlier, so she'd waited until I was in bed. I checked the hands on the battery-run clock on the bureau. Who in their right mind would leave the house at midnight?

Minutes later, a motor started up, but it carried little heft, unlike the Mustang's 390 engine's robust growl. I'd recognize it. I couldn't see the Mustang from this window; the shed stood between us. Other automobiles passed by every now and then on the main road out front. Maybe I'd heard one of them.

If only Pops were here. At home, he always sailed in to save the day. Tonight's phone call infested my mind. I doubted I'd get back to sleep until I checked on the Mustang. I felt foolish for not bringing its key upstairs with me, not that a thief couldn't break in. Even I could, using a coat hanger. And a carjacker could bring the engine to life in a snap.

I flicked on the flashlight Rhoda had left on the bed table, then wriggled into my sweatpants, a long-sleeved T-shirt, and a hoodie. Cracking open the door, I was relieved not to run into Reuben.

Lizzie's door was closed tight, but I knew she wasn't in bed. Unless Rhoda had been the woman leaving earlier. No, the female figure I'd witnessed was petite, her movements spritely. Yet the night was dark; I could have made a mistake.

I made my way through the living room and into the kitchen. I opted to borrow a black woolen coat hanging alongside my jacket. It was long enough to cover my legs and appeared warm. I also grabbed a black hat, the same type Lizzie had worn. I didn't think Rhoda would mind. I'd be back in a few minutes.

I took the liberty of stepping into a pair of work boots, thinking they were Peter's—too small for Reuben and Jeremy—and headed outside. The rain had stopped. Clouds still streaked across the sky, but enough light reflected from the moon's porcelain surface to assist me down the steps and around the corner. The flashlight's beam illuminated the Mustang's sleek fastback and its mag wheels. All my fretting for nothing, I chided myself. I let out a lungful of air. Lizzie might be gallivanting about the county, but she wasn't in Pops's vehicle. Nor were a swarm of teenagers on a joyride at our expense. Pops's words nagged at me. I should have stayed home to look after him.

I breathed in the perfume of moist earth, manure, hay, and a trace of burning wood. I noticed a ribbon of smoke curling from a chimney on the other side of the Mustang. Armin's abode? I stepped around to see a rustic, quaint clapboard cabin with two windows and several steps leading up to a covered porch. Two rocking chairs lounged by a front door that appeared to be newly painted.

Armin was most likely asleep in preparation for tomorrow morning's chores. Or perhaps reading by the fire. Did he even know how to read? I realized I was being a snob.

Years ago, I'd overheard Pops mention to someone that the Pennsylvania Dutch only went through the eighth grade, but were well educated, intelligent, and industrious. I figured he'd gleaned the information from a magazine, since I'd never seen a book about the Amish in our house. Just the opposite. *Road and Track* was Pops's style. And he never uttered the word *Amish*. Pennsylvania Dutch was what he called them on the rare occasions they came up in conversation.

As I turned to go back to the house, I admired the lofty barn and silo under the stippled moonlight. Beside the barn stood a smaller building with what looked like electric wires running to it. The white structure, dwarfed by the barn, appeared recently built. Reuben's workshop, I assumed, and wondered if Armin had remembered to plug in my phone. By now, it might be charged. Had Pops or Donald called and left a message or texted? I was used to keeping my phone close by, and admit I was curious what I'd find in Reuben's shop. I wouldn't be breaking in, because Armin told me they never locked their doors.

As I approached, a dark form scampered past my ankles. A rat! I let out a scream. I hated rats.

In a flash, a cat bolted after it, brushing my shin. I yelped and spun around to retreat to the safety of the house, but I stood for a moment to see if I'd woken anyone, if lights were coming on. I saw none. Not that someone couldn't be watching me from a window.

In my mind, I improvised an explanation should Reuben trundle outside to scold me. The truth: I'd come to check on the car and get my phone. No one told me Reuben's office was off-limits. All very logical. Then why was I trembling?

That stupid rat.

Close up, the building was larger than I'd first thought. Desire to retrieve my phone spurred me forward. My flashlight's beam leading me, I inched toward the door. My free hand went out to grasp the knob.

"Was is letz?" Armin said, and I twirled around to face him. "What's wrong?" he said. "I heard a woman scream."

"Sorry." I steeled myself. I wasn't about to admit I was afraid of crawly, furry rodents. "A cat ran across my path and startled me. I apologize for waking you." In the dim light, I noticed he'd dashed outside wearing a long work jacket and was carrying his hat and a flashlight. I felt a flush of gratitude for his presence, the aura of confidence he exuded.

He positioned his hat on his mussed hair. "Even when asleep, I keep an ear open. Sometimes a dog or coyote gets into the chicken coop."

But Lizzie had escaped without his notice?

I wished Ginger stood at my side. Small in stature but fearless, my corgi could see in the dark far better than I could. No rat would dare dash past her.

"Why doesn't Reuben keep a dog?" I said, stalling, because I didn't want to admit I was sneaking into the man's workshop.

"Reuben doesn't much care for them."

I felt my hackles rising. "Dogs are man's best friend." Mine had been loyal; they'd never have abandoned me like my mother had.

He let out a sigh. "I once had a big collie mix—the prettiest dog you've ever seen—but he took off one day and never returned."

"Sorry for your loss."

"Yah. I haven't had the heart to replace my Rascal." He buttoned his long work jacket. "Rhoda and Lizzie keep telling me I should get another, but I'm not ready. Rascal just might return on his own." He fell silent for a moment, then added, "Only I was living next door when he left."

An idea that would explain Lizzie's emails sprouted like an acorn and took root. Perhaps she was planning to buy him a new dog. A Pembroke Welsh corgi that even Reuben couldn't help but fall in love with. Did Armin have a birthday coming up? Maybe Lizzie had been telling me the truth the whole time.

"My Rascal more or less found me when I was up in New York State," he said glumly. "He might have headed back north to where we used to live."

"I've heard stories of dogs finding their way home."

"I guess I should write the woman—"

"A girlfriend?"

"Yah, but we split up when I didn't join the church and she married another. I feel foolish even mentioning it."

"Lizzie said several women have their eyes set on you." My turn to interrogate him. "In these parts I hear you're quite a catch." I could understand why, but I wouldn't let him know I was attracted in spite of his Beatles haircut. I reminded myself he couldn't compare to suave and sophisticated Donald. But where was Donald tonight? Not pining over me.

Armin gave a one-shouldered shrug. "I'm in my late thirties. I should settle down and start a family of my own. In fact, Rhoda invited a young lady over for dinner next week—some phony excuse. Rhoda likes playing matchmaker."

"Really? I figured she'd want you and Lizzie paired up."

"Nee, Lizzie and I are like sister and brother."

For no reason, I felt a sense of relief, like removing a small pebble from my running shoe.

"Do you know this young woman who's coming over?" I wondered if she were beautiful and clever. I hoped she wasn't. But why? Because I wanted him to remain a bachelor and die childless like I would if I didn't get back with Donald or find someone new? My biological clock was ticking and couldn't be rewound, but men possessed decades of opportunities.

Armin straightened his hat. "I've driven Marjorie home from Sunday Singing a couple of times. But so have other fellas." He scrutinized my borrowed jacket. "What are you doing out here anyway?"

"I came to check my phone. You did plug the charger in, didn't you?"

"Just like I said I would. I was planning to put it in the kitchen when I got up." He was talking down at me, like Reuben had earlier. I felt icy air traveling up my pant legs. The temperature was dipping as quickly as Armin's mood.

"Since I'm here, do you mind if I check on it right now?" I tried to sound nonchalant but heard the tremor in my voice. "My father might have called again."

"Reuben doesn't like strangers in his workshop."

"But you'd be with me." On Pops's car lot I'd learned never to take a customer's first no as their final answer.

"I suppose it's okay." He strode ahead of me, opened the door, and lit a gaslight, illuminating the one-story space, the size of a double-car garage. I shut off my flashlight and followed him inside. The unctuous smell of turpentine and wood stain assaulted my nose. Ahead lay a room jam-packed with tools, plywood, and two-by-fours. Sawdust and scraps of metal and wood littered the floor. Jars of nails, screws and bolts, and a stew of hammers, screwdrivers, and paintbrushes lay scattered across a counter. The opposite of the main house's interior. The word *slovenly* came to mind, but I had no right to be judgmental; Pops's tool bench in his garage wasn't any neater. Still, I bet Rhoda never set foot in here.

I slipped my flashlight in a jacket pocket and zeroed in on my plugged-in phone sitting atop a desk covered with a mishmash of diagrams, papers, pencils, and an old-fashioned typewriter.

My phone was charged, but no messages or texts awaited me. I told myself I didn't care. But I did. Sadness weighed upon my chest as if I were submerged in water. I tried not to let my disappointment show but felt my shoulders slump.

"What does Reuben make here?" I turned the phone's ringer back on, then stuffed it and the charger in my pocket.

"Mostly small wooden items like quilt racks. When he has time. A big farm like this keeps a man working all day spring, summer, and fall. But Reuben likes to keep busy in the winter, too."

I scanned the room searching for anything that might bring a bishop's disapproval. "Where does he sell his merchandise?"

"At a roadside stand, until he runs out of stock."

"What are these?" I pointed to a stack of what appeared to be mahogany boxes with ornate brass hinges cloistered in a corner.

"Well, now, they're jewelry boxes, if you must know. Reuben made them for tourists."

"May I?" I set one on the corner of the desk and admired the cover: an inlaid stem of red roses and fern-colored leaves as lovely as I'd ever seen. "Maybe I could take one home as a souvenir if they're not too expensive."

"They're not for sale." Armin hovered over me as I lifted the cover. A burst of music filled my ears, notes sprinkling around the room. My surprised reflection stared back through a mirror affixed to the inside of the opened lid. Scarlet-red crushed velvet lined the rest of the container. I removed a shallow, partitioned shelf—I assumed for storing earrings—to see more lush red velvet.

"What an exquisite jewelry box." The last thing I expected to find. "And Reuben made it?"

"Yah, he's color-blind," Armin said, flatly.

"There's a problem with the color?"

"He thought he'd bought green fabric. And he sent away for the music box mechanisms not knowing what they played. He'd never heard of the tune before."

"It sounds vaguely familiar."

"The bishop's wife says an Englisch woman told her it's the theme song for a black-and-white TV show named *M*A*S*H*. It elevates war and makes a wicked life seem funny and appealing."

"Oh, yeah, I've seen it on Pops's favorite oldie channel. The show took place during the Korean War." I lowered the lid and the music ceased. "Has Reuben been selling them?"

"Englisch women snapped them right up. But then Bishop Troyer's wife complained to him that Amish women were buying the boxes too and humming the song."

"A problem?" I said.

"*Verboten*. In the first place, we're not to wear jewelry. Even wrist-watches. And the bishop said Reuben chose Satan's favorite color—red. And so fancy." He picked up the jewelry box. "I shouldn't have let you open it. Not that you follow the *Ordnung*—our unwritten rules. But the Bible admonishes us not to cause another to stumble."

"Don't worry. A jewelry box won't lead me into a life of debauchery." I contemplated the trashy magazines for sale back home, right in the grocery store where kids could see them, and the grungy R-rated movies I detested. "Is this why your bishop is on Reuben's back?"

"Mostly. Ya see, Reuben didn't destroy them when the bishop admonished him to. Now everything Reuben does is under scrutiny."

I glanced around and saw several quilt racks waiting to be sanded and stained. "I feel sorry for Reuben. He probably thought he'd found a way to bring in extra income and unwittingly did it all wrong."

"'Tis true. There was no evil intent. But he should have run his idea by our bishop or deacon first and saved himself the money and his reputation. And then heaped them on the burn pile when the bishop demanded it, and repented." Armin stacked the jewelry box with the others and pivoted to me. "Reuben can be a bit bullheaded."

"I don't doubt that, but I can understand why he didn't want to throw them away. He must have put hours and hours into each one. Maybe he could install a new tune."

"Makes no difference. A man must listen to God's Word, not his own. To add to Reuben's problems, someone reported seeing him at a local bar downing a beer." Armin's hand swiped his mouth. "Ach, I shouldn't have told you."

I heard an engine idling and wondered if Lizzie were returning with her young man. I was tempted to sprint out and catch them, then remembered I was in Reuben's workshop, uninvited. Alone with Armin, who didn't seem to hear the car door. But I assumed he'd heard it. Lizzie must be stealing into the house and tiptoeing into her room.

In any case, I'd be close on her heels.

"No worries," I said, "I won't mention our conversation to anyone." I took one last look around. I hoped Armin wouldn't tell Reuben I'd been snooping in here. One more blot against me, when, in fact, Reuben was in the hot seat. But I cared what Rhoda thought of me.

"I'm afraid everyone in the district has already heard. With phone shanties—our Amish grapevine—juicy news purveys the county like the stench of a skunk."

"I know all about gossip," I said. "As a girl, kids ridiculed me behind my back and teased me openly about not having a mom. I invented stories about my sophisticated and glamorous mother, a flight attendant for United Airlines, based in Chicago, who got stuck flying holidays."

Armin stared at me as if waiting for me to continue.

"In other words, I'm against petty gossip, what my father calls tittle-tattle," I said, rather than reveal my thoughts. Not that I hadn't already blathered about my reprehensible mother. What was it about this place that pried me open like bolt cutters snipping through chain-link fencing?

A horse whinnied—more a squeal—the sound emanating from the barn next door. "That's my Thunder," said Armin. "I'd better take a look."

A nanosecond later, I was racing after Armin toward the barn. He yanked the door open and stepped inside the black cavern.

A voice, sounding like Pops's, shouted inside my head: run back to the house and watch from the window! But the vagrant who'd prowled around the Mustang might be lurking in the shadows.

Following Armin, I aimed my flashlight's beam around the barn's spacious interior. A row of stalls contained six massive, statuesque draft horses and several other horses, including the mare that had pulled Jeremy's buggy earlier. Meaning he must be home, although Lizzie had insinuated his friends owned cars.

My flashlight's beam landed on Armin as he sauntered over to a restless horse. He patted its rump. The tall animal bumped the wooden stall, causing the boards to moan.

"What's bothering you, boy?" Armin said, then spoke to it in Pennsylvania Dutch. He stepped into the stall and stroked the horse's arched neck and nose. "I'm here. Everything's okay." A minute later Armin emerged from the stall. "Someone's been in here."

As I strode over to them, the horse's ears pinned back and his head jerked. Armin put a hand up to stop me. "Better keep your distance. My Thunder doesn't take to strangers until he gets to know them."

"Fine. I don't want to get bitten." I inched nearer, still out of the horse's reach. "Maybe he heard my voice next door."

"No, someone's been in the barn, I can tell. One of those stools is at a different angle."

I looked over to a potbelly stove with a couple stools and chairs nearby. "Jeremy was in here after I arrived," I said. "Maybe he moved it."

Armin sniffed the air. "Wearing aftershave?"

I inhaled deeply, my nostrils struggling to decipher the musky layers of dried hay, silage, and manure. "I don't smell anything remotely like a man's aftershave." Then a whiff of a pleasant fragrance drifted into my nose but quickly vanished.

As I scanned the barn's interior again, today's events circled through my brain like a NASCAR race on the verge of a pileup. I expected a bum or rodent to jump out at me. "I wish my dog was here," I said. "She'd ferret out anyone."

"And further agitate the horses."

No use arguing with a man I'd awakened from slumber. But I was nervous about walking back to the house alone. My whole life I'd put up an impervious facade, and I wanted to convince Armin I was braver than I really was. I felt like mentioning I could stand in front of hundreds of spectators demonstrating my dogs' attributes to hard-nosed judges. But why stretch the truth? Deep in my core lay an uncertainty, like a rock tumbling into an endless well. Nothing I could grab hold of. Someday I'd like to hear the *sploosh* as I landed in a tub of warm sudsy water. What I hoped would happen when I married Donald. But now figured was a fantasy.

The longer I was away from him, the less I missed him.

"I saw Lizzie out the window with a young man earlier." I couldn't withhold the information anymore. "I thought I heard a car leaving, but maybe the two came in here first."

"Or someone wanting to keep warm." With ease, Armin clambered up the ladder to the hayloft and shone his flashlight in every corner. "No one up here." As he descended I admired his agility.

"We don't mind a homeless man taking shelter as long as he asks permission and doesn't strike a match," he said.

A horrific vision of the barn catching fire from an itinerant's cigarette made me shudder. As a child I'd watched a two-hundred-year-old barn burn, a ghastly sight I'd hoped to never witness again.

"'Tis been a tetchy night," Armin said. Yet he'd discounted the footprints around the car.

On guard, I kept close to him as he moved to the potbelly stove, its black metal surface still emitting warmth, making me want to huddle close. I felt the security of Armin's presence. No one would dare attack me with him at my side. Or would I have to defend myself? Was he a nonresistant pacifist? I was used to stalwart men like Pops, who would protect me with his life. And my Ginger would too.

"Maybe an animal spooked the horse," I said, listening to bird wings fluttering in the rafters.

"Could be. I've heard tell a bobcat's been seen in the area. Their scream sounds somewhat like a woman's."

I felt heat rising up my neck to my cheeks. "I'm afraid I'm the one who got you up."

"I know." He guffawed. "You think I can't tell the difference between a woman and a wild animal? How thick-headed do you think I am?"

"I didn't mean to infer—"

"Ach." He stepped outside, then aimed his flashlight's beam toward my feet as I exited the barn. "If anyone's ab im Kopp—off in the head—it's you," he said.

"Are you calling me crazy? How dare you!"

"You woke me from the nicest dream." He closed the barn door.

"About the young woman coming over for dinner?" Why did I feel a pinch of jealousy over a man who'd just insulted me?

"I can't see how my dreams are any of your business." He covered his mouth to yawn.

Staring back at him, I tried to ignore his rugged features, his eyes that pulled me right in.

"Ach, I can't stand around chewing the fat." He glanced at the sky as the rain started again. "I've got to get up to milk the cows in a few hours."

A raindrop hit my cheek. "I'm sorry I bothered you." I really was. "I shouldn't have come out here."

"You'll not get an argument from me there. I'll walk ya to the door to make sure you get inside safely—and stay there."

CHAPTER 10

I was so rattled I thought I'd never fall asleep again, but the next morning, when I opened my eyes, sunshine peeked around the green shades. Thank goodness I wouldn't have to attempt lighting the lantern on the bedside table. I checked the clock and saw it was already seven thirty.

The scent of coffee and bacon seeped under the door, beckoning me to arise, even if the room was chilly. When I'd collapsed into bed last night, I'd been so cold, exhausted, and agitated, I'd slept in my clothes. I bet I was a wrinkled mess. But who cared? I'd grab a quick breakfast, say my farewells to Rhoda and Lizzie, drive home, then shower and change in familiar surroundings. Lancaster County had appeared so peaceful when I'd arrived, but Pops had warned me on many occasions that appearances were often deceiving.

Sock-footed, I used the bathroom. No sign of Lizzie. I stood outside her door and rapped lightly. "Lizzie, are you up?"

No answer. I figured she was doing her morning routine: household chores and collecting eggs. Not wanting Reuben to get on her case, I decided to zip my mouth about her antics last night. Although audacious Lizzie seemed to have her father under her coquettish spell, she was capricious: all sweet, acting obediently, then sneaking off into the night with a guy. And like a cunning politician, she'd avoided speaking to me. But I didn't have time to pry the truth from her. Or see Armin again. Just as well. He obviously found me a pest, which made me feel melancholy, like I had in the days following Mr. Big's death.

I heard men speaking Pennsylvania Dutch down in the kitchen. And then Rhoda. If not for her, I might have retreated back to bed to wait for the men to hitch up their horses and hit the fields, which I assumed was today's agenda. Saturday was a workday on a farm; that much I knew. And today was Pops's busiest day on his car lot. I had no right looking down at Lizzie for working at the store instead of on the farm; I'd abandoned Pops on a weekend. Often, when the lot got swamped, I'd help write contracts, entertain the customers' kids, wash and polish cars for delivery, and occasionally sold a few. Thankfully, Ralph was there to assist today, but Pops needed me, his flesh-and-blood daughter, to help with customers.

I felt glum, a lump expanding in the back of my throat.

Pausing on the top step for a moment, I listened to the chatter in the kitchen diminishing. Maybe their mouths were full—or better yet, the men had left the house. Had Armin explained how I'd woken him, then insisted on entering Reuben's workshop? I hoped my scream hadn't torn the whole household from slumber.

I heard the back door close and heavy footsteps descending the porch. But I still detected voices just above a whisper in the kitchen. I ambled down the stairs to see a man sitting at the table, hunched over, his face buried in the crook of his elbow. The homeless fellow from last night, I figured. Rhoda stood with her hand on his back, as if comforting him.

"This is for the best," she said. "All things will work together for gut; you'll see."

I stood in the doorway. "Good morning, Rhoda. Sorry to interrupt."

The man raised his head and hiccupped. I must be losing my vision or my mind, was all I could think, because he resembled an older version of my father.

"Pops? Is that you?"

He wiped his damp cheeks with his shirtsleeve.

"What are you doing here?" I said.

He forced a crooked smile. "Is that any way to greet your father?"

"How did you know where to find me?" A mixture of anger and incredulity roiled inside me. "Did you follow me yesterday? Put a tracking device on the Mustang?" How bizarre would that be? I moved closer to him. "Well?"

His gaze refused to meet mine. "I've been here before," he said.

"That's impossible."

The back door blew open, and Reuben stomped in. "You still here?"

At first I assumed he was talking to me, but the force of his words was directed at my father.

"Please don't send him away." Rhoda stood between Pops and Reuben like a shield.

"Are ya kidding?" Reuben said. "No one ever sent him away. He intentionally left. The man has yet to confess his sins and ask for forgiveness. We're sinning by allowing him in our home."

"That's not entirely true." She pulled out a chair across from my father for me. "Remember, he was never baptized."

Had I stumbled into a parallel world? Was I being set up for some obnoxious reality TV show? A quick glance didn't turn up any camera crews taping us. Reuben's features revealed contempt, and Rhoda's face displayed both fear and expectation—the corners of her mouth quivering.

"What's going on?" I said. "Pops, what are they talking about?"

He rubbed his forehead with the palm of his hand. "I don't know where to start."

"I do," Reuben cut in. "Your father disgraced the whole family."

"He's—" Rhoda's voice was wobbly. "He's my younger Bruder." She swallowed, sniffed. "And I'm mighty glad to see him. I never thought I would again."

"It would have been best for all if you hadn't." Reuben's callused hands gripped the back of his chair at the head of the table. "He's not one of us anymore. He even changed his name."

My knees went weak. I landed on a chair, coming down at an odd angle that twisted my back. "Ed's not your real name?"

Pops stared at the saltshaker on the table. "No."

"He ran off with a floozy." Reuben shoved his chair against the table so hard the salt toppled over.

"But without her, we wouldn't have our Sally," Rhoda said, her voice tentative and pleading.

Reuben huffed. "She's not ours. Sally's Englisch through and through."

"We could ask the bishop what to do," she said, and Reuben scowled, etching crevices across his face.

"Don't you dare speak to him about this. You want us all put under the *Bann*? Don't we have enough problems already?"

"Wait a minute, everyone," I said. "Don't I have any say?"

"Nee." Reuben's voice filled the room like a tidal wave. "This is my house and you're nothing more than a guest. Both of yous, get out!"

"But this was my parents' home, Reuben." Rhoda's fingers intertwined over her stomach. "We should include them in this conversation."

I pictured the older couple, Leah and Leonard Bender, from dinner last night. "Let me get this straight, Rhoda." I ignored Reuben's glower. "That older couple are my father's parents?"

"Yah. Seeing their son would be an answer to prayer." A tear skidded down Rhoda's cheek; she blotted it with her apron. "They'd be ever so happy."

I recalled the verbal battle upon my arrival. "Do they know about me?"

"An inkling, but we weren't sure. Lizzie's been trying to track down my brother and came across your website."

I felt as if I were peeling an orange and finding an onion inside. "So the whole story of looking for a dog was a scam."

"Not completely." Rhoda dipped her hands into her apron's pocket. "Lizzie's been hankering to own one ever since she found out you raised them."

Reuben and Rhoda were my aunt and uncle. And Lizzie was my cousin, as were her two brothers and two older sisters I'd yet to meet. Rhoda's parents were my grandparents! I'd hardly paid them any attention last night.

"Lizzie had no right to interfere." Reuben expanded his chest. "Where is she? Sally must have kept her up late talking."

"Still out in the chicken coop," Rhoda said.

"Don't go blaming my daughter," Pops said in a shaky voice. "She's the best daughter a man could have."

I glared at him, a man I realized I didn't even know. "Why have you lied to me?" Bile rose in my throat as I allowed my rage to unleash itself. Pops shrank in stature, his neck bending forward. "If you're not Ed Bingham, who are you?"

"Ezekiel Bender." Reuben widened his stance. "But that name wasn't good enough for him. Nor were his family and our ways. He was a self-centered *Laus*—louse. All he cared about was cars so he could crisscross the county, then leave. And that hussy Englisch girl friend of his, she let him drive her father's automobile."

"She beguiled him, Reuben," Rhoda said. "Really, she did. He was so young and running around. He got into the wrong gang." Her glance flitted my way. "That's what we call informal youth groups."

"He blatantly broke every rule," Reuben shot back. "Even though his family needed him."

"You grew up here?" I asked my father. The floor beneath me seemed to sway. I hardly knew up from down. "You were Amish?"

Pops bit his lower lip.

"You sat and ate breakfast in this very kitchen?" My words echoed off the walls.

"Yah, he did," Reuben said. "And look how he repaid his parents."

"Ya want me to get them?" Rhoda asked Pops. "They'd be sorely disappointed if they missed you."

"If you wouldn't mind." Pops's taut face seemed racked with pain, his mouth a thin line.

As Rhoda slipped out of the kitchen, I stared at Pops and waited for him to speak up—to make sense of my crumbling world. Honest Ed was a sham and a liar. "Are you even my father?" I asked, fearful of his answer.

"Of course I am."

"Don't believe anything he says." Reuben tugged his earlobe. "He started fibbing when a lad. I know; I was a couple years older and remember when he stole that wallet."

"I didn't steal it," Pops said. "I found it in an alley. Someone had taken the cash and credit cards."

"Then why did you confess to the bishop?"

"Because he wouldn't believe me, and I wanted things back to normal." Pops pressed his palms together. "But I never took the money, I swear before the Lord."

"You're lucky the Almighty doesn't hurl a bolt down and obliterate you for invoking his name." Reuben moved closer, like a coyote stalking a wounded rabbit. "And I suppose you didn't borrow our Englisch neighbor's car and go joyriding."

"Ya got me there." Elbows on the table, Pops's forehead drooped into his hands. "I was lucky they didn't press charges. But I only did it once."

"Because you snagged yourself a fancy girlfriend with a convertible so you could drive all you wanted, yah?"

I felt dizzy, the room spinning as I tried to envision Pops as a young Amishman, dressed like Armin on a date. My dad on a date ...

"My mother?" I got to my feet and grabbed hold of Reuben's elbow. "Was that woman my mom?"

"How would I know who your mother is?" Reuben yanked out of my grasp. "Your father never sent us a wedding invitation."

"Did she look like me?"

He scrutinized me as if I were a mongrel caught rummaging through the garbage. "Her hair was darker than yours and reddish."

"But she could have colored it," Rhoda murmured from behind me.

"Please, I have to know who she is," I persisted. "Would anyone remember her last name?"

Reuben stroked his beard. "What does it matter now?"

"You don't understand. I feel like half a person." At that moment, an orphan.

"Why don't you ask your father?" Reuben said.

Rhoda stepped back into the kitchen. "Ezekiel, Leah was so shocked she near fainted. She's too weak to stand. She and Dat are asking: Would you go speak to them in the Daadi Haus?"

"Okay." Pops rose and shuffled out of the room, his head hanging low as if on his way to prison. What was wrong with him? I'd be thrilled to see my mom.

Stepping into the living room, he appeared to know where he was headed. Everything Reuben said about him was true. My father had chosen to abandon his parents, just as my mother had left me. He'd seen firsthand the anguish I'd lived with, and yet he'd ignored his own mother and father. Had they been pining over him, or had they shut him out of their minds so they didn't go crazy with worry? I hoped Rhoda would tell me about my mother. A younger woman like Rhoda would be more likely to remember a bad influence on her brother. But Rhoda shadowed my father and left me with Reuben.

"The Lord admonishes us to forgive." He curled his weathered, sun-spotted fingers into fists. "But I don't know that I can."

I felt the gulf between us narrowing. "I know what you mean," I said.

"I can't dawdle around here." Reuben massaged the back of his neck. "Not with him in this house. Sally, I feel sorry for ya, having that reprobate for a father."

My first urge was to defend Pops, but I stood in a daze, white noise filling my ears. All that malarkey about honesty he'd drilled into me was rubbish. My life was like a Chutes and Ladders game— I'd landed on the big slide and hurtled to the bottom of the board.

Reuben put on his hat, pulled down hard on the brim, dug his arms into his work jacket, and strode out the back door. Then it hit me; I needed time alone to think without feeling like a target at a shooting range. I'd dive into the Mustang, and return later after Pops had left. Then I'd get acquainted with my grandparents and speak to Rhoda in depth, now that the deplorable truth had been revealed.

But where would I go in the meantime?

CHAPTER 11

My thoughts spiraling, I grabbed my purse and found the Mustang's key.

I laced on my running shoes, jetted through the utility room and out the back door, and descended the steps. As I unlocked the Mustang, I heard a far-off yipping sound, like a dog immersed in a fish bowl. But I dismissed the persistent noise. Relief surrounded me as I sank into the car's cushioned driver's seat. I slid the key into the ignition and turned. The starter clicked, telling me the battery was dead. I tried again. Nothing but gaping emptiness.

The interior light had been on last night when the door was ajar, but most batteries didn't drain that quickly. If I'd been the new buyer, I'd be hopping mad. Well, I was livid. My father had lent me a car with a bum battery and hadn't bothered switching to a new one. If I were in his lot, he'd get me started in a snap. I bet he'd tossed jumper cables in the muddied Toyota Highlander parked at the side of the house. Pops always came prepared. Except the person I'd just seen in the kitchen looked like a shell of the man who'd raised me. Honest Ed. What a laugh and a half.

I could think of only one person to call for help. I brought out my phone, located Donald's number, and tapped Send. The phone rang several times, then switched to his answering service. It was Saturday morning, only eight o'clock, but he rose early and often worked on weekends. Or he might be catching a round of golf.

I tried his number again and a woman answered, "Hello?" in a sultry voice.

"I'm sorry," I said. "I must have gotten the wrong number."

Then I heard Donald's muffled words. "Give me that." He spoke into the phone. "Sally?"

I trembled all over. "Who was that?"

"Uh, somebody. No one important."

"Well, thanks a lot," the woman said.

"Donald, who is that?" I said.

"A woman I dated back in college. I ran into her last night—"

My throat swelled with fiery contempt as I envisioned them fondling each other as they tumbled into his king-size bed.

"And you two happened to wake up together?"

The woman jabbered in the background, followed by Donald's angry voice. "Shut up! Not you, Sally. I don't know what happened. Guess I had a few too many. Anyway, where are you?"

My mind spun like a kid's pinwheel. I opened my mouth, but my tongue felt swollen and didn't work. A ripple of queasiness churning in my stomach, I thought I might vomit, but remembered I hadn't eaten breakfast or even had coffee.

Then a rap on the window startled me. "Sally?" Armin said. "Are you okay?"

"Who's that?" Donald demanded, his voice brusque. Some nerve.

"None of your business. And tell your mother not to send out the invitations."

"What are you talking about?" Donald's voice shouted from my phone before I turned it off and stuck it in my pocket. I gripped the steering wheel and sat frozen in disbelief as I tried to reconstruct my life, but not one piece slid into place. My head fell forward. I was better off without Donald, I told myself. Hadn't I contemplated that very thought only yesterday? He'd just cheated on me—could there be any other explanation? Out of revenge for my sudden departure? Or were his escapades a common routine? I'd once seen lipstick on his shirt collar, but he'd sloughed it off and said it was his mother's.

I opened the car door. "I don't suppose you have a set of jumper cables, do you?"

Armin shook his head.

"Do you even know what they are?" I asked.

"Ya got no cause taking your frustration out on me. As a matter of fact, I lived in the Englisch world and used to own a truck. I got plenty of practice starting that old jalopy." He stepped aside as I got out on shaky legs.

"Sorry." I inhaled as best I could, my chest as tight as a new fan belt.

"I could check with the owner of the SUV or an Englisch neighbor or call the garage in town from the phone shanty." Armin looked down at me with concern in his eyes. "Why are ya in such a hurry?" he said. "Rhoda and Lizzie said you'd be staying for a couple days."

On this cool morning, heat snaked up my legs as if I'd just run a marathon. "I told them I'd decide in the morning. Anyway, that was before my father showed up. Do you know anything about it?"

"No, but I saw that SUV arrive an hour ago and an Englischer went in the back door. That's your father?"

"Sally!" Lizzie hastened across the barnyard from what must have been the chicken coop, judging by the eruption of clucking sounds she left in her wake. "Are you leavin' without saying good-bye?"

"You started this whole ordeal." I spit out my words like poison darts.

"Sally, I thought—"

"That you'd play God? Why didn't you tell me?"

She fiddled with her prayer cap's strings. "Mamm was determined to find her long-lost brother before her parents died. I offered to help."

"How dare you!" She hadn't caused my father to be a lying scumbag or made my mother abandon me. Still, to lead me blindfolded into this three-ring circus.

"Aren't ya happy to know the truth? We're cousins, Sally." Her arms flung out to hug me, but I backed away. Lizzie wasn't my ideal cousin; she was a little sneak like my father. There was no one on earth I could trust.

"Please promise me you won't leave whilst I'm at work," she said. "I have to go in today, what with Mrs. Martin injured. There's no way 'round it."

I felt betrayal squashing me as if I were trapped in a giant car crusher, compacting me to the size of a smashed tin can. Would I have preferred to live in ignorance the rest of my life? I asked myself. Yes, if reality felt as if I were drowning.

I could barely catch a breath.

The plaintive words *Please, Lord, help me* vacillated through my mind, then puttered out. No one was going to come to my aid. I'd never felt so helpless.

"I was going to ask you for a ride to work, Sally," Lizzie said.

I grabbed my purse out of the passenger seat and slammed the car door the way Pops hated. "I can't help you. This old heap isn't going anywhere. The battery's kaput."

Lizzie turned to Armin and batted her lashes. "Please don't make me ride my scooter. It's so cold this morning." She glanced at a blue two-wheeled scooter—like a miniature bicycle with a board between the wheels—leaning up against the barn.

"Yah, I'll give you a lift." His mouth hinted at a grin, as if he'd heard her entreaties and given in often. "I was going to hitch up Thunder and go to the hardware store in a few minutes on an errand for your dat."

"Thank you. I'll hurry and get ready. Please, Sally, say you'll ride into town with us."

"I don't know." By the time we returned, Pops might have left. I figured Reuben would see to Pops's speedy exit. Then I could grill Reuben and Rhoda about my mother. Or would Reuben boot me out too?

As Lizzie dashed into the house, I heard a dog's yipping again and realized the sound was coming from the Toyota.

"Ginger?" I loped over to the vehicle to see my darling corgi, her black nose pressed against the window. I made a quick decision: if the vehicle were locked, I'd break the glass before asking Pops for the key. But when I tried the handle, the door swung open. My father had left my beloved dog in an unlocked vehicle. I was incensed; someone could have taken her. He had no respect for me or my treasured pooch.

"Come to Mama," I said to the frisky mahogany-brown and white corgi, her pint-size body wiggling. She launched herself into my arms. I held her against me as if she were the only tangible reality in my life.

Ginger growled, and I turned to see Armin leading his bridled horse from the barn. In swift maneuvers, Armin attached the gray covered buggy's wooden shafts to Thunder. The horse bent his ears back and his eyes bulged at me and Ginger with what seemed to be suspicion. Thunder's deep molasses-brown coloring was pretty in the daylight, but the horse looked ho-hum compared to some of the high-stepping beauties I'd seen on the road last night.

Ginger barked, but the horse paid no attention. "Shush, girl," I said, then spoke to Armin. "Maybe this isn't a good idea."

"Nah. Thunder isn't afraid of anything. Certainly not a puny dog with no tail."

I leaned into the SUV for Ginger's leash and clipped it on. "I'll have you know she's an American and Canadian champion purebred Pembroke Welsh corgi. A big dog in a small package."

"Don't get bent out of shape." Armin passed the reins through a series of rings on the harness. "I wish you could have seen my Rascal."

I pursed my lips. Now was not the time to become embroiled in the subject of people who carelessly allow their dogs to romp freely where they could get lost or run over by a car.

"Come on, girl." I guided Ginger to a grassy strip so she could relieve herself. Then I led her back into the barnyard as Lizzie emerged from the house and flounced over to us.

"Sally, you brought one of your dogs!" Her soprano voice swooped up an octave.

Ginger wagged her stub of a tail and pulled on her leash.

"I didn't bring her. My father did." I supposed I was glad he hadn't left Ginger at home by herself but wondered if he were using her to soften the blow. He'd proven beyond a shadow of a doubt he was devious; I had to assume anything was possible.

"She's so cute, like in the pictures." Lizzie stooped down and put her hand out to Ginger, who licked her fingers. "She likes me." Lizzie tickled Ginger under the chin. "Yah, you like me, don't ya, little princess?"

Not everyone was a dog-person, so I supposed I should have been pleased. Donald had complained of the white and reddish hairs on his slacks. He didn't have much use for cats, either. I wanted to plug my ears as our recent conversation replayed itself in my mind, but questions about Donald's faithfulness tunneled through my brain anyway. I figured he'd come up with a logical excuse, like the woman passed out or blah, blah, blah. And I might believe him, because my own father had talked me into his fabrications. How could I have been so gullible?

"I best warn ya," Lizzie said, breaking into my cavorting thoughts. "Dat doesn't like pets in the house."

"But you were all set to purchase one?" Another contradiction in her flimflam story.

"I figured once Dat saw a puppy, his heart would melt."

"So where can I keep her?" I glanced around the barnyard, which appeared larger in the sunlight.

"Your dog could stay with me," Armin said. "What's her name?"

"Ginger." Ginger jumped up on his leg, and Armin bent to scratch her between the ears. I felt a wave of fondness for him wash over me. "Thanks for your kind offer, but I may take off at the end of the day."

"Are you sure?" Lizzie steepled her hands under her chin.

I considered my measly options and felt marooned—a woman and her dog with little money and no destination.

"I've got a fine gut idea," Lizzie said. "You come to the store with me. By the time we get home, your father might have left."

"True. This is my dad's busiest day at work." I watched Ginger sniff the ground and hoped she wasn't trying to follow Pops's scent. "I'm surprised he left at all when there's money to be made. His assistant must be manning the ship."

Oh, Pops, why did you have to be a phony? I'd always resented the jokes about conniving automobile salesmen and had defended him. I associated with several fine car salesmen, among them Pops's assistant, Ralph, a good guy with a wife and three late-teenage kids.

"While you're gone, I'll get your car started," Armin said.

"Thank you," I said, meeting his gaze, not sure why he offered. I found the key and handed it to him. "That would be great. If it doesn't get you in trouble."

"Nah, I'll be fine."

"So, then, you're coming to the store for the day?" Lizzie asked me.

"I'd like to bring Ginger."

"Yah, sure. The customers will love her. She's so cute and cuddly."

I scanned my sweatpants and running shoes. "But look at my clothes. And I haven't even washed my face."

"You can freshen up in the back room at the store. No matter about your clothes and shoes. If you like, I'll lend you a dress, apron, and cape." Lizzie twirled and the black apron and dress's plum-colored fabric swished around her calves. "I have extras. Most of our customers would never know the difference, seeing as you haven't applied makeup yet. They'll think you're one of us." She showed me the straight pins holding her apron in the back. "I'd help you pin it on."

I didn't want to insult her by refusing and considered how easily I could slip into anonymity for the day; no one would ever find me. "I'll come to town with you but think I'll skip the clothes."

"If you want a ride, we'd best get going," Armin said. "I told Reuben I'd help him in an hour or so."

Armin assisted me and Ginger into the buggy. Lizzie hurried to the barn and returned with a bulky, quilted shoulder bag. She lugged it into the backseat and perched behind me on a bench.

Armin undid Thunder's tether and the animal came to life, shaking its glossy mane, his front hooves hopping in place as if it had ants in its pants, Pops would say.

I made a vow to never quote my father again. I'd banish him from my mind. At least until he told me why he'd lied all my life.

Armin climbed into the buggy and grasped the reins. Lizzie leaned forward and spoke between Armin's and my shoulders. "Maybe we should use one of Dat's horses."

"Nee, Thunder will be fine." With a staunch grip, Armin worked the leather reins to steady the animal, whose front legs were still prancing in place. Then Armin adjusted one rein, and the horse turned and bolted from the barnyard. "Whoa, now." Armin continued speaking to the spirited animal in Pennsylvania Dutch—I guessed he was trying to soothe the horse or maybe he was making a threat.

I'd always wanted to ride in a real Amish buggy and felt my arms prickle with a rush of adrenaline. "How long have you owned Thunder?" I wanted to keep the conversation light. Even though I barely knew this man, I enjoyed talking to him too much. And I liked the way he looked at me.

"Not long. I have a lot of training to do, but he'll be fine. He'd leave my brother's horse, Galahad, in the dust."

Thunder overtook every buggy on the road. Armin waved at the other drivers, mostly bearded men, and they waved back, although a few looked irritated, their mouths turned down, disapproval stamped on their faces. I enjoyed being transported in the swaying carriage: the gritty sound of the metal wheels on the roadway and the horse kicking up gravel that hit the bottom of the floorboards. We retraced my drive from the night before, passing enormous barns and vast acres of pastureland I hadn't noticed under the evening sky.

Armin handed me a small blanket. "Are ya cold?"

"Not with Ginger on my lap." She felt heavier, which I couldn't blame on one night in Pops's care, although he often fed her table scraps against my wishes. I'd have to put her on a diet.

"I guess that little dog is good for something."

Lizzie's hand reached over the seat back and nabbed the blanket. "Armin, don't ya go insulting our guests. I read all about Welsh corgis, and I can't think of a finer dog."

"If you say so." He clasped the reins as we waited at an intersection, then allowed Thunder to surge ahead.

"Ach, there's the bishop," Lizzie said as the bearded man passed us going the other direction.

CHAPTER 12

I ducked my head for no good reason. Did I expect the bishop to pull a U-turn and come after us to scold me for last night's near collision? I checked over my shoulder and saw Lizzie craning her neck to watch him drive away.

Armin, on the other hand, kept his concentration fastened on Thunder, who tried to challenge every other horse on the road in spite of the blinders affixed to his bridle.

A topsy-turvy image came to mind: my father sitting in Armin's spot just like Jeremy had the night before. I approximated what my father's age had been when he took off. He couldn't have been much older than Lizzie. Pops had no doubt gotten up early, milked cows, worked in the fields alongside his father like all the other young Amishmen in the area. The enormity that he'd hidden his childhood from me made me feel as though I were encapsulated in an episode of *The Twilight Zone*, an old TV program Pops still watched as reruns.

Minutes later, I recognized the Sunflower Secondhand Store. Armin steered us into the parking lot and Thunder halted reluctantly, shaking his head, his beautifully arched neck stretched toward the road.

"Did you remember the key, Lizzie?" Armin said.

Lizzie huffed from the backseat. "Ya think I'm losing my memory?" She dug into her apron pocket for the ring of keys. "But I'm ever so glad I have Sally to help me unlock the door without Mrs. Martin here."

"I'd better help you get out," Armin said to me.

"That's very sweet of you." I was surprised by his chivalry.

Thunder pawed the ground and chewed his bit as Armin tied him to the hitching post. Then Armin strode around to my side of the buggy, scooped up Ginger with one arm and helped me with the other. It seemed Armin once again held on to my hand longer than necessary, but maybe he could tell by my silence I felt confused and defeated, and he was trying to comfort me.

Once on the ground, I made sure Ginger's leash was securely clipped to her collar. She and I followed Lizzie to the store's front door. I turned to say good-bye to Armin, but he was already gathering Thunder's reins, and moments later, he steered the buggy out of the parking lot. Thunder tore off down the road, reminding me of my near collision with the bishop last night. Since the minute I arrived in Lancaster County, disaster had pursued me. Pops's words of caution about coming here haunted me. But now I understood his objective—to keep me buried in his underground cavern of lies.

Lizzie handed me the keys, and I wrangled the one I recognized from the night before into the lock. I read the sign on the door's lower half. "Hey, the store doesn't open till ten." I glanced at my watch. "It's not even nine."

"Yah, we're early, but Armin wasn't going to wait around for us, and you were in a hurry to leave, weren't ya?"

She had me there. Who'd pick up a hitchhiker with a dog?

Lizzie pushed open the door, and a bell jingled overhead. "I know you're going to love the store."

No use arguing with her. And Ginger seemed eager to go inside. She must've smelled an edible tidbit. I hadn't noticed dog food in the SUV and wondered when she'd last eaten. Had my father forgotten to bring her kibble, or had he given her a Big Mac on the way? Human food was not good for dogs and usually upset Ginger's stomach. In any case, she was wide at the girth and skipping a meal wouldn't hurt her one bit. I'd been so consumed with planning my wedding and Pops's illness, I'd neglected exercising her.

Stepping inside, I examined the small store's cluttered but ornate interior and decided there were worse places to be. The air smelled of old things—a pleasant, dusty odor laced with lemon-scented furniture polish.

"Half of the items are here on consignment," Lizzie said, "except the books—but they're used."

To the left, a floor-to-ceiling bookcase displayed rows of paperbacks that seemed to be Amish or historical romances, and also hardback cookbooks. I would thumb through those while biding my time. The rest of the shop was a potpourri of knickknacks—figurines, brass candlestick holders, salt and pepper shakers. A handwritten sign stated that local craftsmen had produced the items displayed on one table: potholders, tea cozies, handmade floppy dolls—most faceless—and small wooden toys. A rack laden with hand-stitched quilts stood behind a cash register and a small computer. All other wall space was adorned with framed prints and paintings, and quilted wall hangings.

Ginger and I followed Lizzie into the back room, where she leaned her quilted bag from home against a couch, then flipped a circuit breaker, which started the sound system—a stringed instrumental piece Lizzie promptly switched to a popular station. Then Lizzie turned on the electric baseboard heat. The back room contained a wooden desk piled high with receipts and papers, a wooden padded chair, a shabby plaid sofa with saggy cushions, a worn oriental carpet, and several filing cabinets.

I wandered into the cramped powder room and splashed water onto my face. Gazing into the mirror, I saw haggard blue eyes and straggly beige hair that verged on mousy brown. I viewed myself through Donald's patronizing eyes and felt small—not petite—and sadly insignificant. I couldn't help wondering about his overnight guest. Donald's bimbo was probably long legged, chic, and voluptuous—everything I wasn't.

I brought out and turned on my phone. Four new texts from Donald popped up: three stated, "Call me!" and one said, "Sugar, it's not what you think!"

I turned the phone off again and stuffed it into my purse. I didn't trust myself to stand up to him. I envisioned his thumbs urgently stabbing at his phone. I'd only seen him fly off the handle once. He'd punched his fist into a wall, then apologized profusely, saying he'd never done anything like that before and never would again. Then he'd taken me out for an extravagant dinner and treated me like a princess.

My jaw clenched; my molars ground together, I needed time to cool down and wrap my brain around something other than Donald. And Pops.

When I exited the bathroom, I noticed Lizzie had spread a towel across the far end of the couch for Ginger, who'd curled into her new nest. She'd dozed off, her head on a pillow. Lizzie filled a ceramic bowl with water and set it on the floor near the back door. I felt a smack of guilt for not thinking of Ginger's welfare ahead of my own.

"I'll need to duck out later to buy dog kibble," I said.

"There's a small market just around the corner," Lizzie said. "Do you want to run over there now? Or would ya like a cup of Kaffi first? Mrs. Martin has a fancy coffee maker you won't believe. Top of the line." She moved to a snazzy espresso machine perched on a counter above a small refrigerator. "It even froths up milk, just like Starbucks." Lizzie set to work preparing a cup. Minutes later Lizzie and I were enjoying the nutty flavor. My hunch was Lizzie would miss this handy device.

"Mrs. Martin keeps fruit and yogurt in the refrigerator and cookies in the cupboard, should you want a bite to eat."

She leaned over the end of the couch, grabbed hold of her quilted bag from home, and set it by her feet. The bag flopped on its side, spilling a cascade of clothing, including jeans and an orange sweater. Too small for me to wear and definitely not Amish. "Ach. These are for a friend." She stuffed the contents back in her bag with rapid movements.

"I wish I could fit into those," I said. "But I won't be waiting on customers, anyway."

"Only if you'd like, to help pass the time. When tourists show up, we get mighty busy and it's fun." She let out a wistful sigh. "I'm going to miss working here something fierce." Then she proceeded to a metal wall safe, spun the dial several times, and extracted a zippered money pouch much like Pops's.

Carrying my coffee and purse, I followed her into the store and watched her empty the pouch's contents of dollar bills and change into the cash register, count the money twice, then close the drawer.

"You need help?" I said.

"Maybe if a shipment arrives. One's late. It should have been here yesterday from New Hampshire." She set about dusting the books and doodads.

Fine, I'd select a fiction book and snuggle up next to Ginger in the back room. On closer inspection, I was surprised how many Amish novels stood shoulder to shoulder on the bookshelves. I'd never thought to read an Amish book, but that was before I was aware I carried Amish blood in my veins. On one or on both sides?

"Almost all the Amish fiction is written by Englischers," Lizzie said, "but I love reading them." She gave me an impish grin. "I sneak them into the house past Dat. He frowns upon us reading romance novels of any kind. He and the bishop agree on that."

I could write a book, but it wouldn't be a romance. If someone had told me last week my engagement to my Prince Charming would splatter over a cliff, I would have laughed them off. I glanced down at my left hand; the sight of the ring that once made my heart sing filled me with revulsion. I wrenched it off and dropped it into my purse where it disappeared beneath the hodgepodge of stuff.

The telephone on the counter rang, and Lizzie reached for it. "Hello, Mrs. Martin. How are you feeling?" Lizzie straightened the pens and pencils in a ceramic cup and a stapler on the counter as she spoke. "I'm so sorry." She glanced to the front door. "I have an Englisch friend here to help me today, so don't ya worry about a thing." Moments later, she returned the receiver to its cradle. "Mrs. Martin wonders if you'd be willing to work for her this next week. Otherwise, without me, she'll have to close the store."

"You're kidding, right?"

"Nee, she's quite serious. Her doctor told her to keep all weight off her sprained ankle for ten days. She's old and wasn't healthy to begin with."

"But she opened this shop?"

"Just last fall. I think partly to empty her house. But the store quickly became popular."

The bell over the front door rang and a blond man in his early twenties entered. Lizzie's countenance elevated to one of giddy expectation. She sashayed out from behind the cash register, her hips swaying. "I wasn't expecting you."

The young man wore corduroy slacks—frayed at the hem and a couple inches too short—a hoodie, and a goofy grin. "I saw the lights were on." Electricity zinged through the air like fireworks on the Fourth of July.

I figured he wasn't Amish, not with his slicked-back hair and long sideburns. Unless he were running around, as Reuben called it.

"May I help you find something?" Lizzie said, I assumed for my benefit, because she obviously knew him.

"Just driving by and thought—" He reached out and touched her hand.

Her gaze glued to his, she back-stepped. "I'd like you to meet my cousin Sally Bender."

"Bingham," I corrected. "And you are?"

"Joe Miller." He had a long narrow face and appeared scruffy— rough around the edges, as Pops would say. Again, the fact my father's real name was Ezekiel Bender rocked my world. Trying to appear composed, I was once again inundated with incredulity. Outrage. Sadness. I felt a tidal wave of tears building behind my eyes, but I'd have to deal with my new reality at a later time.

Joe looked me up and down. "You must not be from around here."

"Nee," Lizzie said. "Sally and I just met last night. Remember, I told ya—" She covered her mouth with her hand.

"Oh, yeah." His foot rotated toward the front door. "Guess I should go."

"Hey, wait up." I marched over to him and caught a whiff of aftershave. Not that many men didn't splash it on in the morning. "You're the guy who stopped by last night." I tilted my head. "Am I right?"

His spine, suddenly rigid, told me I was correct, even though he shook his head.

So this was Lizzie's secret rendezvous. He stood several inches shorter than Armin and was narrower in the shoulders, making him appear scrawny.

"Were you in the Zooks' barn last night?" I said, not letting him off the hook.

"No," he said in a tinny voice lacking conviction.

"Whoever was in there was wearing aftershave." I stepped nearer to him and inhaled. Sure enough, I recognized the fragrance. And a trace of cigarette smoke. One question answered.

"How about my car?" I said to him. "Were you pawing through that, too?"

"No way," he said. And yet my own father had admitted to stealing an automobile. Pops was a bald-faced liar. Maybe Joe was too.

"Please, Sally, don't tell my dat about last night." She glanced into the back room through the open doorway, then turned to me. "Didn't you say you wanted to buy dog food, Sally?" I was being dismissed so the two of them could have a cozy heart-to-heart. I wasn't the babysitter or chaperone and was tempted to run my errand.

I spotted Ginger stretched out on the couch through the open doorway to the back room. If anything happened to her—I couldn't take a chance. Not after losing Mr. Big.

"I'll keep an eye on her as if she were my own," Lizzie said. "I promise." As if her promises meant anything; I didn't trust her.

"No, thanks. But maybe you could go shopping for me."

"I'd like to help ya out, but I mustn't leave the money in the till." She worked her lower lip.

"I bet your friend here would fetch dog food for me," I said. Joe grimaced.

"He won't know the brand or how much to buy." This little shyster had an answer to everything.

"I'm not leaving Ginger and a grocery store won't let her inside."

"You could tie her out front," Joe said.

"Absolutely not. Someone might walk off with her." I couldn't fathom what Lizzie saw in him.

But I was in a no-win situation. I strode into the back room and found a ten-dollar bill in my wallet. As I returned, he was speaking intently into Lizzie's ear, then he gave her a peck on the cheek and they hugged each other. No wonder Lizzie had been so keen on coming to work today.

At the sound of my footsteps, they hurriedly moved away from each other, like swimmers pushing off from the side of a pool.

"Here you go." I handed the money to Joe. "I only need a couple days' worth." I gave him the name of my favorite brand, made of lamb and rice.

"Don't blame me if I get the wrong kind." He tucked the money into his back pocket.

The bell above the front door jangled. Our heads pivoted to watch a plump, older Amish woman shuffle in. She was dressed like Rhoda and Lizzie, but her elephant-gray hair was parted down the middle with severity and her cap strings were knotted under her chin. "I saw movement through the window." She glared at Lizzie. "Are you open?"

"Not quite," Lizzie said. "I just arrived."

"Then why are people in here?" The woman scoped out the shop and her squinty gaze landed on the books, then she glanced at me and frowned, her wispy brows meeting over beady eyes.

"It's still early." Lizzie scurried to the front window and flipped the sign from Closed to Open. "We usually don't open for a while." She straightened her prayer cap, tucked in errant strands of hair.

"Why are you still working here?" The woman narrowed her eyes at Lizzie, then at Joe, who hustled out the door and closed it, causing the bell to clatter. "My husband said your father told him you'd given notice."

"Yah, 'tis true." Lizzie's face blanched. "But the owner twisted her ankle. I can't leave her high and dry. She'd have to close her shop today. It says in the Bible we're to love our neighbors and respect those in position of authority."

"Don't you go quoting the Bible to me, Lizzie Zook. Didn't you hear the sermon two Sundays ago? The minister warned young folk about dabbling in the outside world when you should be attending baptism classes. You won't find anything but sorrow away from communion with God and the community." The woman reminded me of my snooty English teacher in middle school.

"Yah, I was there," Lizzie said, cowering.

"I hope you were paying attention and not nodding off from staying up too late the night before." The woman glanced over her shoulder to the front door. "Who was that young fella?"

"Just someone looking for a gift."

She pruned up her face. "Don't try pulling the wool over my eyes, Lizzie. I think I recognize him. Amos and Mary Miller's son Joseph?"

Lizzie strolled around behind the counter and began rearranging and stacking papers.

The woman spoke to me. "I'm Bishop Troyer's wife."

"Hello." I put out my hand, but the older woman folded her arms across her chest. I gave her my car-salesman smarmy smile, all the time pitying the man married to the crotchety busybody. And her poor children.

No, I'd rather have an overbearing mother than none. It occurred to me this portly woman might know of my father's escapades. And of my mother.

CHAPTER 13

"I'm Sally, visiting from Connecticut," I said to her. "I'm looking for someone you might remember from many years ago. Her name was Mavis."

Paying me no heed, the bishop's wife scanned the novels. She pulled one out, flipped it over, read the blurb on the back cover, then eased it back into place. She obviously had no intention of helping me.

Lizzie brought out a rag and got busy dusting and rearranging the wooden toys and knickknacks as if the woman and I were any old customers. A moment later the bishop's wife left without a farewell.

Lizzie dropped the cloth on the counter and let out a puff of air. "It wonders me she'd happen to stop by."

"I can't imagine she followed us, not at the speed Armin drove." I watched a horse and buggy trot by and hoped it was Armin returning from the hardware store. My heart missed a beat. Then my shoulders sagged when I saw the driver was a bearded gent.

Lizzie peeked out the window too. "The bishop might have asked his wife to keep an eye on me."

"Do you think he heard my father's at your house? Having Pops there isn't going to help your parents' situation. Your poor mom."

"Yah, but just because Mamm decided to live with her parents forever and ever doesn't mean her children should."

"I'm done living with my father, that's for sure." I strolled to the bookcase and grabbed the first paperback book I saw—a lovely Amish maiden holding a prayer cap graced its cover—then wandered into the back room with my coffee cup. Ginger still lay sacked out on the couch. Pops had probably kept her up all night. To arrive at the Zooks' farm so early, he must have left Connecticut well past midnight. Not only was Pops a liar, but his thinking had gone awry. Or was his erratic behavior also part of an act? My temples throbbed as I tried to brush away the atrocious facts.

I sat next to Ginger and sipped the coffee, now lukewarm. She raised her head for a moment, then her eyes slid shut again. This was going to be a long day, no doubt about it, so I was glad she was in a poky mood. On the other hand, this little town might hold a treasure trove of answers to questions about my mother. I couldn't wait to go back to the house and grill Rhoda. I doubted Reuben would help me. Yet, on the other hand he might if it meant scaring my father away for good.

Minutes later, a bevy of non-Amish—what Lizzie called Englisch—women wearing coats or parkas bustled into the store. I got to my feet to see them poring over the books and telling each other which novelists they liked best. It occurred to me my mother might parade into this very store should she live in the area. Or be visiting relatives. Didn't all women love to read and shop? I scoped out each woman's face, hoping to catch a glimpse of recognition. How old would Mom be?

During the transactions, Lizzie thanked each woman courteously as she rang up their orders, although she asked one to please not take her picture. After the women left, they were replaced by several more women, and a husband and wife. I gazed at every woman's face, a preposterous enterprise, I knew. But I found myself becoming obsessed with meeting my mother through a crazy coincidence.

This store was a thriving enterprise. I wondered about Mrs. Martin, whom Lizzie was so fond of. If Joe was any indication of Lizzie's taste, I shouldn't expect much. Not that I was all that smart when it came to men; I was a pushover if ever there was one.

A rapping on the back door woke Ginger. She let out a bark. I unlocked and opened it to find Joe holding a five-pound sack of kibble. Ginger hopped off the couch, her triangle-shaped ears erect and her face cocked in that adorable fashion that had won her many blue ribbons. I'd always thought my dogs were good judges of character, but perhaps Ginger was being hoodwinked by the smells wafting from the bag.

Joe set the dog food on the floor by the desk and handed me my change. Before I could thank him, he turned and fled out the door, pulling it closed.

Ginger stretched, lifted her nose, and inhaled. I found a plastic bowl in the cupboard above the coffee maker and filled it with kibble. She dove in to it.

"Sally, could you come out and help me?" Lizzie said from the doorway. "The store's so full I can't handle everyone. Not and ring up sales too."

I was used to working all day, not to mention attending hectic dog shows over the weekends, but I felt wiped out and emotionally drained. "Sure, give me a minute." I clicked on Ginger's leash and took her out the back door so she could stretch her legs and find a patch of grass, then we returned. I locked the door and closed Ginger in the back room.

"Must be a tour bus," Lizzie said as I neared her. "We usually aren't this busy until the afternoon. Mrs. Martin will be so pleased when she sees all the business we've done."

The day seemed to fly by. When shoppers asked me to help select books, I followed the bishop's wife's example and scanned the back covers for clues. Fortunately other customers were eager to wade in and give their opinions. Several oohed over the featureless dolls. One woman spoke to Lizzie by name and said she was sorry to hear Lizzie was leaving.

Lizzie showed me how to use the cash register, not much different from Pops's. She seemed awfully naive, allowing me, a near stranger, to handle the money. Not that I'd consider taking any. And she kept calling me her cousin and grinning. I smiled back, but warned myself to be on guard.

Several customers asked me questions about the Amish. I glanced to Lizzie for the answers. She responded a few times, then pointed to the bookshelf and said, "We have nonfiction books about the Amish, Mennonites, and Lancaster County on the bottom shelf."

I grew so hungry thumbing through several illustrated Amish cookbooks with a customer I thought I'd swoon. Then Joe poked his nose through the partially opened front door. He was carrying a brown paper sack that looked like it had come from a café or bakery.

Lizzie beckoned him to enter by flexing her index finger. His gaze darted around the room, then he skulked in and set the bag behind the register. He handed her a small package; she slipped it into her apron pocket. "See ya later," he said to Lizzie in a subdued voice and was out the door.

"I'll be waiting."

Lunchtime had rolled around, and I hadn't even eaten breakfast. Between customers, Lizzie and I dashed into the back room for bites of food and drink. Joe had brought us each a ham-and-cheese sandwich, heavy on the mayo and mustard, and two cans of soda. Maybe I'd underestimated him after all. Who was I to make judgments about Lizzie's boyfriend when I'd done such a horrendous job choosing my own?

"Joe's coming to pick me up after work," Lizzie said, during a period of quiet.

"Will he give me a lift too?"

"Not today. We're going in the opposite direction."

"Then how will I get home?" I was calling Lizzie's house my home? "I mean to your place?"

"Armin will come or send Jeremy."

"What did Joe bring you, other than lunch?" I asked.

Lizzie fingered the parcel in her apron pocket. "I wasn't going to tell anyone, but I can trust you, can't I?"

"You mean the way I've trusted you—blindly?" I arched an eyebrow.

"I've only had your best interest in mind. And my mother's and grandparents'." Her hand dipped into her apron pocket again, and she brought out a parcel wrapped in tissue paper. She opened it enough for me to see a small heart-shaped locket and chain. "If I don't tell someone I'm going to burst."

"Okay, I'll keep it to myself," I said. "Who would I tell?"

"My parents." Lizzie eyed the front door as two English women stood looking in the window. "Promise me ya won't."

"Okay. Hurry up and tell me, while we're still alone."

Her eyes seemed to twinkle. "Joe and I are running away together."

CHAPTER 14

I searched Lizzie's face for signs she was serving me another table-spoon of sugarcoated gobbledygook.

"We're going to elope." The corners of her mouth lifted into a grin. "Ya know, get married."

"But Joe? Can't you find someone—more, well, someone else?"

She placed her hands over her heart. "He's the one I love." The two women entered the store, bringing with them a gust of chill air. The wind had kicked up; hail slanted down. "It appears we're going to have snow tonight," one of the women said to us. "Just heard the weatherman announce it on the radio. The temperature's plunging."

I ambled over to the front window to watch sleet spitting down, pedestrians hunched over, a horse and buggy hurrying by. I hoped Armin would pick me up today, considering the weather. So much for the groundhog not seeing his shadow.

One of the women said, "We'd better come back another time." They scanned the store. "Cute place. Are you open tomorrow?"

"Not on Sundays," Lizzie said. After the two women exited, Lizzie told me, "This shop may never open again unless you come back on Monday."

"I can't believe you'd lay a guilt-trip on me after I've been working here for nothing all day." Anger sharpened my voice, but where that ire was emanating from, I couldn't decipher. A mishmash of paradoxes swirled in the back of my brain .

The telephone by the cash register rang, and Lizzie answered it.

"That was Mrs. Martin," Lizzie explained after a stop-and-go chat. "She said you could stay in her back room. She insists you read any books that catch your fancy."

"Ginger and I live in that cramped little cubicle? It would never work." On the other hand, it was a roof over my head and a quiet hideaway.

Through the window, I noticed the sleet transforming into white pellets, dotting the streets and sidewalks.

"Ach, what happened to our beautiful springtime weather?" Lizzie wrung her hands. "This isn't how I envisioned this afternoon."

"You and me both. Even if Armin gets the Mustang going, that rear-wheel–drive coupe can't handle snow or icy roads. No weight over the rear wheels." I could tell by Lizzie's blank expression she had no clue what I was talking about.

A UPS truck skidded to a stop up front. A uniformed driver lugged in a sizable carton and set it on the floor by the register. "Almost didn't make it," he said. "The roads are getting clogged with traffic." Lizzie signed for the package, and the driver jaunted back to his truck, then sped away, his tires spinning.

I watched Lizzie open the box. "Oh, dear, I've got books to put away," she said. "I mustn't let them sit in the damp carton over the weekend."

I helped her empty the box and carried the books to the shelves. She restocked the fiction by author, nonfiction on the bottom shelf, oversize books on the next, by the cookbooks and magazines.

I heard knocking on the back door, and Ginger barked. I left Lizzie and hustled to check my pooch.

"Who's there?" I said.

"Joe."

I opened the door and a block of frigid air filled the room. His jacket's shoulders were darkened by moisture. His tattered Nikes were soaked, as were his pant legs. Droplets from his jacket landed on the carpet.

"Is Lizzie ready?" he said as I let him in. I noticed a fifteen-year-old blue Chevy Cavalier, a compact with a dent in its rear fender and a missing hubcap, parked outside the building.

"To run off with you?"

"She told ya?" Joe's pale face and round eyes reminded me of a scared rabbit.

"Yes, and you two were so obvious earlier, how could I miss it? But to elope? That's crazy thinking."

I questioned myself about my own rational choices. I was considering marrying Donald. Who knew, I might still do it if I got desperate enough. Then I recalled the feeling of safety as Armin helped me from the buggy, his firm, strong grasp.

CHAPTER 15

"Just how well do you know Lizzie?" I asked Joe, who stood staring at the door to the shop.

"We've known each other most of our lives." His gaze almost met mine, then he looked away.

"You'd sneak off with her without telling her parents?" I understood why Joe wouldn't want to lock horns with surly Reuben. But what about dear Rhoda? Did Lizzie care nothing for her mother's feelings?

"From what I've learned looking through the books in the store, Lizzie could be shunned," I said.

"Nee, neither of us have been baptized." Aha, in spite of the car, clothes, and haircut, he was Amish.

"Couldn't you go back to living among the Amish?" I said.

"We've made up our minds." He stood with a hand on hip. "We can always confess and repent and join the church later." He seemed offhand, bordering on pompous.

"But this is a monumental step. What's your hurry?"

"We have our reasons, that's all I can say."

Lizzie came into the room and a grin flashed across her face. "You're here already?" She unbundled the locket and fastened it around her neck.

"I thought it best I didn't come to the front door." Joe swayed from side to side. "The weather's turning ugly. We should be on our way."

The store's front doorbell jangled, and a man said, "Anyone here?"

Recognizing Pops's voice, I cringed. Not that I didn't love him anymore. I did, but I couldn't bear to hear him lie to me again.

"Want me to go out there?" Lizzie asked me.

"Sure, maybe you can get rid of him."

But too late; Pops strode to the door leading to the back room. Ginger pranced at his feet. "Hi, girlie-girl." Pops bent down and scratched her between the ears. It occurred to me how accepting and faithful dogs were; no matter that he'd left her in the car alone; no matter that he'd lied to me.

Rarely was I tongue-tied, but I felt as if I'd swallowed a mouthful of salt.

"I came to give you a ride, Sally," Pops said. "And you, too, Lizzie."

"Thank you, but I don't need one." She sidled closer to Joe.

"I told your family I'd pick you up, Lizzie, seeing as I've got an SUV with four-wheel-drive."

"Still, I don't need a ride. Thanks all the same."

I stepped to her side. "Lizzie, please don't do anything impetuous that you might regret."

"This is my only chance." She looped her arm into Joe's.

"What's going on here?" Pops said.

"How is Lizzie any of your business?" I asked, then realized she was his niece. Like a flame igniting, heat traveled up my throat. Pops had yet to ask for my forgiveness for lying—not that a simple "I'm sorry" would begin to erase a lifetime of betrayal.

"I've been there," Pops said.

"Where?" I asked. "Where have you been?"

"In their situation. I can see what's going on." He'd never looked so thin and frail. I couldn't help but worry. He was, after all, my dear father, the man who'd raised me and loved me very much. But it didn't feel like true love, which required honesty.

Lizzie inched toward the back door. "We've got to go." She reached into her apron, extracted the store's key ring, and tossed it to me. After years on the car lot, my hand instinctively reached out and nabbed it.

"Hey, you can't leave like this." I fingered the keys.

"Yah, I must, right this minute." She handed me a piece of paper with the name Doreen Martin and a telephone number written on it. "I called Mrs. Martin and told her we were closing early due to the weather. Please lock the front door when you leave."

"But how will she get her keys back?"

"Please, won't ya help me with that and call her?"

"No, tell her yourself."

"I can't." When she opened the door, I saw white snowflakes drifting through the air. She and Joe stepped out into the storm.

CHAPTER 16

Standing in the store's back room, I listened to Joe's tires spinning, then his car rolling away. Ginger circled Pops's legs and leaned against him as if she liked him more than she liked me. Had everyone in the world deserted me?

"Sally, aren't you glad I showed up when I did?" Pops said.

"No, I never want to speak to you again," I said. "Not until you come clean."

"Now, honey, I know you don't mean that. You're my darling Mustang Sally."

"If you think quoting that dumb old song is going to make an ounce of difference you're crazy." I remembered how he used to sing it to me in front of my girlfriends, which embarrassed me to no end. But when he and I were alone, the tune made me giggle and feel loved. "I'm not going with you anywhere ever again until you tell me the truth," I said. "Doesn't it say in the Bible 'Let your yes be yes and your no be no'? Haven't you quoted that verse yourself and used it to make me fess up when I was a teenager?"

Pops fidgeted with his wristwatch band, checked the time. "It's almost five."

"Are you planning to drive home tonight in this storm?" I felt myself being drawn in, feeling sorry for him, because I knew he was a sick man. He hadn't always been sick, but he had always lied to me about who he was, where he was from.

I crossed my arms, widened my stance. "I'm not spending half the night on the road with you."

"Okay, I get it. I'll take you and Ginger to the Zooks' and drop you off there. And I'll switch cars."

"Armin got the Mustang going?"

"No, I did. I bought a new battery at a discount store."

I marveled at his ability to sidestep into a new subject. But did I want to spend the night here? Not particularly. Not when I figured Rhoda was preparing a yummy supper.

I lifted my chin. "I'm waiting, Pops."

"It's a long story."

"So? Spit it out," I said. "I've got the time."

He stuttered his first words. "As—as I guess you've figured out—I grew up Amish. I met Mavis during Rumspringa, when I was running around doing things I had no right doing. I was a bad seed, just like Reuben said." He shut his eyes for a moment. "I never fit in. I always wanted to be like the other kids in town, riding bicycles and going to the movies."

"You couldn't go to the movies? Or even ride a bike?" I felt sorry for him, even though I knew I was falling for a poor-little-me story.

"That's no excuse for my laziness." He ran a hand across his cheek and ear. "I was slothful and thoughtless. And there was a pretty young Amish woman who liked me. Sixteen and baptized. She was so sweet. I could have easily courted her if I'd joined the church. But instead I started seeing Mavis." His sentence tapered off, his words muting.

The mention of my mother's name made my legs go weak and the room spin, as if I'd just gotten off a carnival ride. But I needed to pull myself together; I could not let this opportunity pass. "What was my mother like?" I felt a stirring in my chest. Finally, the theater lights would dim, the screen would light up, and my life would be revealed in fabulous 3-D.

"She was cute. It was so long ago." He sniffed. "And I guess you'd say she had a nice personality. Fun, anyway. Game for anything." Pops rubbed his forehead with the palm of his hand. "But that's not why I went out with her."

"What are you talking about?"

"You're not going to like this, Sally. I wouldn't blame you for hating me, if you don't already."

"Just tell me the truth. I can't take any more rabbit trails." I clamped my lips together to contain my barbed words. I remembered reading in the Bible that the tongue was the most powerful organ in the body; I itched to unleash mine, to jackhammer into him with my wrath.

I waited in vacuous silence for several minutes.

"She had a car," Pops finally said. "And the guys in town—I don't know how else to say it—they said she was easy."

My stomach twisted. Maybe I didn't want to hear the story after all. Maybe knowing the truth would make me feel worse. But not knowing would eat me alive.

"Well, was she?" Sarcasm corrupted my voice.

"Yes." He skimmed his jawline with his knuckles. "We had our fun, then the next thing I knew, she said she was pregnant."

"Are you talking about me? So I was a mistake? If she was such a hussy, how did you know I was yours?" A knot the size of a golf ball expanded in my throat.

"I believed her, that's all I can say. When she said she was going to the city to have an abortion, I promised to marry her and raise the baby. That's you, Sally." His eyes got so watery he looked like he'd break down and cry, but he blinked away the veneer of moisture. "I was doing what was right, and I still believe it."

"You two got married then?"

He pinched between his eyes. "She kept putting me off. One excuse after another. We lived together for over a year. Then one day she said she couldn't stand it anymore."

"Couldn't stand what? Did you treat her badly? Did you fight?"

"Please don't make me tell you, Sally."

"You've gone this far. Spill the beans and be done with it."

"She fed you on a bottle. I did, that is, and changed and bathed you, and I got up and walked you at night. You had colic and you screamed. Poor little thing, you couldn't help yourself. But your mother wanted to put you up for adoption. I couldn't let you go. I wouldn't. Not for anything. One day she packed her bags and left."

"She left because of me? And you two never got married?" I felt light-headed.

"I reckoned she'd be back," he said. "She'd walked out on me before, and she always returned after a week or so, when she was out of money. But she didn't that time, and I got scared. Scared she'd change her mind and go to a court of law to get custody—take you away."

"Why didn't you bring me home to your parents?"

"Because I'd disgraced them. I'd already harmed them enough. And I figured if I came back to my folks, Mavis would hear of my whereabouts through her parents. If they even knew she'd given birth. I think she kept her pregnancy a secret." He took a lengthy breath, let out a dry cough. "She and I had been living down in Danbury. A neighbor said his boss was looking for a salesman in his car lot and that same neighbor's wife let me drop you off for the day while I worked. They had several kids, so his wife said one more was welcome. She was a good Christian woman who no doubt saw right through my story."

I vaguely recalled an older woman—she'd be ancient by now.

"I didn't want to be found so I legally changed my name and eventually opened my own lot."

"Dishonest Ed's." My mind spiraled with doubts, but an inner voice warned me to be cautious. His answers could all be lies. "Mom never came back asking after me?" I said. "Not once?"

Pops gave his head a slight shake. "Sorry."

"And you never contacted her parents?"

"Twice. They had a telephone. Her father told me to never call again and hung up. I don't know what Mavis told them about me, but it must have been bad."

"Or they might have read about you in the local paper. I mean, you did steal a car, right?" I leaned against the desk for support. "But they might want to know they have a grandchild."

"They could have moved or passed away. Rhoda might know."

I needed to go back to the Zooks' house to get my questions answered. But how could I arrive without Lizzie?

I sat in the passenger seat of the Toyota SUV with Ginger in my lap and the bag of kibble at my feet. Pops cranked the engine and turned the windshield wipers to high. They worked feverishly without maintaining our sight of the road through the accumulating snow. Globby flakes landed on the glass as soon as the wipers cleared away the white debris. At only five thirty, the sky was darkening to the color of steel.

"I guess you don't need directions," I said, not that I was sure I could give them. The flurrying snow made it impossible to tell north from south.

"I know the way." Pops gripped the steering wheel as he nosed the SUV onto the road and tucked it in behind a sedan that was fishtailing. A pickup stood abandoned off to the left. We passed barns—their roofs whitened—and sheeted fields. A beautiful sight in any other circumstance. I wondered if the newly planted crops would spring to life again when the snow thawed. And how about me?

From the opposite direction, blinding headlights approached like a locomotive. Pops slowed and moved to the right as a semi barreled past us. I pondered what would happen if we crashed into an out-of-control vehicle and I was killed—not my usual mode of thinking. Still, wouldn't it be easier to have my life snuffed rather than face more intolerable pain?

Bottom line: I was a mistake, never loved or wanted by my mother. And I couldn't foresee a resolution with my father. Or Donald.

Then I considered innocent Ginger. Who would take care of her if something happened to me while Pops was critically ill? Yet, I felt devoid of strength, my will to survive waning. I was tired of being a trouper. The way I'd felt in the dog-show ring: smiling and animated on the outside, my heart racing with panic on the inside. I'd feigned courage many times.

Up ahead, off to the right, I saw red brake lights blinking: a car in the ditch. Only its rear bumper and back tires were visible through tall scrub grass.

"Hold it," I said. "That looks like Joe's Chevy." A white blanket was already camouflaging it.

"If I stop, we might not get going again ourselves. Or someone could run into us."

"You'd leave Lizzie stranded in a ditch? Stop, this instant!"

Pops slowed, sliding to a halt at the side of the road. He switched on the Toyota's emergency flashers and left the windshield wipers going. A layer of ice accumulated on the glass in spite of the defroster blowing on high.

I lowered my window; a blast of wind flung snow against my face. Sure enough, Joe was helping Lizzie trudge through snow-covered grasses toward the road.

"Lizzie, are you okay?" I called. She'd shed her prayer cap, but there was no blood on her forehead—a good sign.

She moved lethargically, like a bird that had flown into a window and was dazed. Maybe she had whiplash.

"We're headed to your parents'," I said.

"I need to take care of my car," Joe said. An expression of panic warped his face. I wondered if his car or Lizzie were his number-one priority. In any case, he appeared younger, like the stray terrier-mix, its ribs showing, that had wandered to our home one winter.

Pops got out, closed his door. "I doubt you'll get a tow truck tonight."

A tree limb yards away from Joe's Chevy cracked and landed with a thud. A car motored by at a crawl on the road, too close for comfort, followed by a pickup.

"I need to get out of here," Pops said, "before I get sideswiped. Or one of you gets hit. This road is as slick as an ice-skating rink."

"But my bag's in the car." Lizzie's breath made small clouds in the chill air.

"Leave it," Pops said, "or send Joe."

Ginger peered out the window. My thoughts cavorted back to Mr. Big's tragic injury. I grabbed Ginger, held her tightly.

The wind howled and the globules of snow hitting my face and ears seemed to distort Lizzie and Joe's conversation. No, they were speaking Pennsylvania Dutch at rapid-fire speed.

Pops said, "You two get in, before someone smacks us."

As Lizzie climbed in the backseat, Joe scampered down the ditch, slipping once onto his keister, and returned lugging Lizzie's bag. Then he slid in next to Lizzie.

I heard metal-clad hooves ringing on the icy road, and spotted a horse and covered gray buggy headed our way. It pulled onto the shoulder on the other side of the roadway, and Armin leaned out the window.

"Everyone okay?" he called.

"I told you not to come," Pops said. "You're crazy being out here."

Armin scanned Lizzie and Joe, then his gaze riveted onto mine. "Sally, are you all right? I'll give ya a ride if you want." His question made me think he'd gotten an earful about Pops from Reuben.

Joe lowered his window. "How about me, Armin? Can you give me a lift home?"

"Nee, you're on your own. Sleep in the bed you've made for yourself."

Thunder jerked his head, his ears back, as a car rolled past. I sat for a moment in indecision, then said, "Sure, I'll take you up on that."

"Sally, have you lost your mind?" Pops said.

Dashing across the snowy thoroughfare would be a reckless act, I knew, but I needed to gain distance from my father. And from Lizzie and Joe.

Without answering Pops, I hopped out with Ginger, my purse, and the bag of dog food in my arms, traversed the road, and climbed into the buggy.

CHAPTER 17

I settled onto the buggy's bench. The interior was frigid, but I didn't care. Armin offered me the blanket from this morning, and I gladly took it now, wrapping my legs.

"Why did you come, Armin?" I hugged Ginger to share my warmth with her—and vice versa. "I can't believe you'd bring Thunder out in a blizzard." The air itself seemed white.

"I wanted to see how he'd do on the slick roads. I doubt any snowplows will be out tonight, seeing as this should melt off tomorrow."

"But still—" He'd obviously risked his life and Thunder's safety to come fetch me. Or maybe he was looking after Lizzie, not me at all. Had he surmised Lizzie was skipping town without telling her folks?

Thunder shook his head and tossed his mane. Snowflakes, illuminated by Pops's headlights, shimmered through the air like iridescent sequins. Armin steered Thunder onto the road and made a U-turn at a wide spot, then passed the SUV. I could imagine Pops coming unglued at the sight of Armin's daredevil maneuver.

I looked over my shoulder and saw Pops easing the SUV onto the road behind us.

"How on earth did the four of you end up there?" Armin said, breaking into my thoughts.

"Are you asking if we were following Joe and saw him swerve off the road? No, Lizzie was in the car with him."

"Ach, I was afraid of that. But I'd hoped they'd both come around."

"Would you have stopped them?" Pops's headlamp beams reflected off the glistening pavement, casting long, distorted shadows of the buggy and Thunder ahead of us.

"Sally, I did much the same thing at their age, so it would be hard for me to give them advice."

"You'd be the perfect person. Unless you're glad you left."

"I don't know." His gloved hands gripped Thunder's reins, keeping the nervous horse at a moderate trot. "If I'd stayed, I'd probably be married and have ten kids. Maybe it would have been for the best." His words lacked enthusiasm, sounding more like a question.

The sky's light was draining. Snowflakes like marshmallows smothered the buggy's glass windshield. Armin turned on a battery-operated windshield wiper. Ginger huddled close to me, as if she could tell we were in a perilous situation. Cars coming from the other direction inched along, their headlamps glaring.

I prayed silently: Please, God, get us home safely.

I realized I'd referred to the Zooks' as home again and amended my prayer. Lord, find me a home where I truly belong. To keep my thoughts from squirreling into the past, I gazed out the side window and watched the snow accumulating. I was struck by the transformation. The whole world could turn on its head and I was helpless to stop it. And yet, with this blanket of snow came tranquility and beauty. The bare trees were turning into elegant works of art. Many of the homes we passed were now illuminated by what must be gas or kerosene lamps, sending beacons of light into their front yards.

Mesmerized by the beauty amid the ashes of my life, I realized I hadn't spoken for ten minutes. I slid a glance at Armin and saw his remarkable profile—a man intent on watching for oncoming traffic and controlling Thunder. And taking care of me.

"What brought you back to the area?" I asked, giving myself an excuse to look at him.

"'Tis a long story. I was making a good living as a horse jockey."

"A jockey?" In spite of the circumstances, a grin widened my mouth. "I can see Thunder running in the Kentucky Derby." I'd watched the race on TV many times and had been wowed by the horses, the daring riders, and the winner's circle. "But, Armin, you're twice the size of a jockey."

"That's what we Amish call men who buy and sell horses. All my life, I've had a keen eye for them, thanks to my dat, although I bet he wished he'd never taken me to horse auctions as a kid."

"I don't get it, why you chose to leave in the first place." My queries circled around my father's departure, but I didn't want to voice them.

"To buy and sell horses I needed to deliver them long distances in a truck. The required driver's license was and still is forbidden by the Ordnung." He tightened up on the reins as Thunder increased his speed. "Whoa, now." The buggy glided for a moment, its back wheels swaying—a toboggan effect.

"I grew up just down the road from the Zooks," he said. "In fact, there's an empty house, it's back door yawning open for me should I want it. It's where mei Bruder Nathaniel's wife and her mamm used to live, making it Nathaniel's."

"Just sitting there, vacant? I don't get it. Why would you prefer Reuben's tiny little cabin?"

"To live in Nathaniel's home, he'd call the shots." His gaze fixed to the road, he leaned forward. "We've never seen eye to eye. He'd be on my case all the time. Once a big brother, always a brother."

"I'm sorry," I said. "It's none of my business. At least you have a place to live." I knew I sounded like a spoiled brat: showing up in a sporty car and having my father come all this way to look for me.

Armin negotiated his way onto the Zooks' lane and the horse increased his speed. Rambunctious Thunder seemed like a homing pigeon, aiming for cover. I was ready to warm up too; my fingers were popsicles. I hadn't thought to bring gloves when I'd left New Milford or asked to borrow a pair from Lizzie this morning.

We passed Pops's Mustang, barely visible under a mattress of snow. The wind had gusted a white bank against the car and the outbuildings.

Armin brought Thunder to a halt in the barnyard. "I'll be back." He jumped out, unhitched Thunder, and led him into the barn, leaving me sitting in the buggy not knowing what to do next.

As I wondered what Rhoda was preparing for supper, my stomach clenched with hunger. But what kind of a reception would Ginger and I receive from Reuben? And Pops? Would he have the gall to come inside again?

My father muscled the SUV alongside the house. I could discern the silhouettes of two people; Pops must have dropped off Joe on the way. It seemed as though Pops and Lizzie were having a serious conversation, the way they sat like statues. The SUV's engine was still running; the heater was probably warming them.

Armin came out of the barn and opened the buggy's door. "Come on, Sally. You'll freeze out here."

I hesitated. "I don't want to talk to my father."

"You come in my place and wait 'til he's gone, if you like. I'll build us a fire. You and your little Ginger can warm yourselves whilst I take care of Thunder."

I had no other option, unless I sprinted to the house. But then, what about Ginger? The last thing I needed was a go-round with Reuben about bringing her inside.

"Sure, thanks," I said. He lifted Ginger from my arms with care, then helped me down onto the snow-covered yard.

"Careful, it's slippery."

He set Ginger on the ground. Her nose rooted into the snow and she snorted.

My first step, I almost lost my balance. Then I picked my way to his cabin with Ginger at my heels. I wondered if my father and Lizzie were watching us, but I refused to look their way.

Carrying the bag of kibble, Armin stomped his feet to loosen the snow from his boots, then opened his front door.

"My shoes are drenched," I said. I could feel the skin on my feet shriveling. I unlaced my shoes and left them on the porch. My socks were soaked so I removed them, too.

"Never mind. I'll lend you socks." He guided us inside. For a moment, all I could see was a black tunnel. Armin set the dog food down, then lit a lantern with the flick of a Bic lighter. The flame undulated up the wick, casting an amber glow across the small room. I saw a La-Z-Boy, a round table with two straight-backed chairs, a threadbare sofa, and in the corner a single bed with a quilt covering it. I had the oddest notion that Rhoda had made the quilt for him. No logical reasoning behind my assumption, and certainly no rationality for me to feel sadness because of it. I'd had a bad day and what was left of the cockeyed optimist in me had evaporated.

Armin reached into a small chest of drawers and handed me a pair of woolen socks that were much too long but comfy. I pulled them on over my stinging toes while he stooped before the hearth, ignited crumpled newspaper and kindling, and added split wood. Minutes later, dancing flames bit into and consumed the timber, sending fingers of smoke up the chimney and emitting glorious heat.

"Why don't ya sit here?" He pulled a chair from the table and set it before the fireplace for me. Then he draped a shawl across my shoulders as Ginger leaned against my legs.

"I've got to feed Thunder," Armin said, stepping outside.

As I relaxed and watched the flames, I hummed, then sang the first stanza of "Amazing Grace," a hymn I recalled from church. I didn't know the other verses, so I repeated the first several times. "I once was lost, but now am found ..." I'd never spontaneously sung it. What was coming over me?

Fifteen minutes later, I heard Armin clomping his boots on his front porch. I felt a tingling rush of anticipation when I saw him.

"Is my father still here?" I asked.

"His vehicle is. And so is yours. He and Lizzie must have gone into the house."

"Do you think Reuben will kick him out?" I recalled the yelling match when I arrived, multiplied by ten.

"Hard to tell. Your father is Rhoda's brother, but Reuben is Reuben." He chuckled as if he had many stories to tell about Reuben's behavior. "But it's such a grizzly night out. Who would send a man away into such a storm?"

"Reuben?" A sputter of laughter erupted from me.

Armin set a pan of water out for Ginger and filled another with dog food. She gobbled a mouthful.

"Your father brought Lizzie home safely," Armin said. "Once Reuben finds out he might cut your dad some slack."

"I wouldn't want to be in the room when and if Lizzie tells her parents what she had planned with Joe. I can't imagine why she's in such a hurry to get married."

The obnoxious and monstrous conversation with Pops about my mother replayed itself in my mind. Tears sprang from my eyes and an unexpected sob erupted from my belly.

"Are ya okay?" Armin pulled up the other chair and sat next to me, our knees touching.

I couldn't hold in the tide of grief. An inner torrent of emotions gnashed through my mind like shards of glass. I spilled out the whole story. "My parents never got married. After I was born, my mother wanted to give me away." I couldn't believe I was babbling on, but I seemed to have no control. "I have doubts Pops is even my father." I voiced hideous facts I'd planned to never share with anyone. I was inundated with shame, as though I should wear a scarlet letter on my chest, when in fact my mother was the wanton woman who'd tossed her own child out like dirty laundry. She and Pops had passed on to me a legacy of humiliation.

Armin offered me a Kleenex. I dabbed my eyes, sniffled, and mulled over Pops's story for a while in silence. Then a thought strafed into me like an attack of wasps.

I blew my nose. "You don't suppose Lizzie's pregnant, do you?"

He stiffened. "Why would you ask?"

"It might explain why she's in such a hurry."

"I surely hope not." He patted his hand on his leg and Ginger wandered over to him. "Now your little dog, that's a different story."

"What are you talking about?"

"Ginger. She's expecting a litter, isn't she?"

CHAPTER 18

"Why would you think Ginger's …," I sputtered. "That's impossible. She can't be pregnant."

He shrugged. "If you say so."

"I do. I do say so. My only male dog died last month and I never let her run loose." My throat closed around itself. "Unless that wretched German shepherd next door climbed the fence. Highly unlikely. I don't know a dog that could scale and enter an eight-foot-high covered chain-link fence." I inspected Ginger's ample tummy and wondered how I could have been so blind to her matronly condition.

The corner of Armin's mouth curved up. "My Rascal could—"

"Are you inferring your dog visited New Milford, Connecticut, last month?" My words bulleted out, then I paused as I realized Armin wasn't at fault. I was. I felt like an idiot.

"Unless it happened before Mr. Big died." My words stumbled over each other. "The day I put him to sleep was the worst day of my life—until today." A tear threatened to seep out. "His death was my fault. I should have tried harder to keep him alive." I wiped under my eye. "I'm sorry; I'm usually not like this. I never cry."

He handed me more Kleenex. "No matter."

I pondered the ramifications of Ginger's being pregnant. A dog's period of gestation was sixty-three days, meaning Ginger could be weeks away from whelping a litter. Maybe she'd just put on weight, as I'd originally thought.

"Why are you so sure Ginger is carrying a litter?" I asked.

"Comes from being around farm animals my whole life." Armin draped my wet socks over the fire screen and set my running shoes against it to dry.

"She's no common farm animal."

"Why are you upset? Would a litter of pups not be a blessing?"

"Not now. I don't have a place to live. I don't feel comfortable staying with my father." But in the recesses of my mind I knew it was a possibility.

I prayed the puppies were the progeny of my beloved Mr. Big. But I reminded myself not to gather expectations: I couldn't take another disappointment.

"We have a vet who stops by every so often." Armin shifted. "Zach's not my favorite man, but he knows his stuff."

"What's wrong with him?"

"A personal matter." Something about his terse answer made me think a woman was involved.

"If I'm still in the area, maybe he'd have a look at her." I tallied up my measly resources. "Never mind, I can't afford to pay a vet for a house call."

"I'll see what I can do. Zach owes me a favor."

"How's that?"

"Boastful though it may sound, I could have stolen his sweetheart if I'd wanted to."

A pounding on the door—what must have been the side of a man's clenched hand—made me start. I sat up straight as the doorknob turned. I expected to see Pops stride in. But instead, Reuben stomped snow off his boots, shook his hat, then entered, and shut the door behind him. His face was beet red, except for his white lips and snow-covered beard. He didn't make a snide remark about my being alone with Armin, but instead he paced back and forth in front of us.

Armin sat exactly as he'd been: relaxed, at ease.

"Rhoda has supper almost ready," Reuben said, "but I'll not sit at the table with the likes of Ezekiel. Yet Rhoda won't let me turn him away. And her parents are frantic to speak to him more. He informed them he's ill, and Rhoda is buying right into it."

"That's my fault," I said. "I told Rhoda my father was sick— before I knew they were related. I'm sorry."

"You have nothing to be sorry for," Armin said.

"Yah, it's not your fault, Sally." Reuben hung his hat on a peg. "In fact, you have my sympathy." Reuben glanced down at Ginger, who lay at my feet, then back to me. "You're not thinking of bringing that Hund in the house, are ya?"

"Ginger's staying with me," Armin said.

"That's gut. Dogs make me sneeze."

"Come on, Reuben. You say everything makes you sneeze."

He rubbed his nose. "Can't a man be the head of his house? And now a human mongrel is sitting at my table." He paced again, shook his head; melting snowflakes fell to the floor.

I felt sorry for him. "Is there any way I can help?" I said to him. "Maybe if I go in there—"

"I'll come in with you, Sally," Armin said, leaning forward, his hands on his knees. "We can put your father down at the far end of the table."

He got to his feet in a slow way that told me he didn't mind sitting by my side one bit. I couldn't imagine a more unlikely pair than us, yet there was no man I trusted more at the moment.

"Come on, Sally." Armin tapped my elbow. "I'll lend ya boots. Then we'd best get in the house so the family can eat. Rhoda has probably been preparing something extra special in your father's honor."

"Certainly not in mine." Reuben sounded peeved. He leaned over and fluffed Ginger's coat; I couldn't help but notice that he didn't sneeze. He straightened his spine and redeposited his hat. "All right, then. I'll not be exiled from my own home."

Leaving Ginger, Armin and I followed Reuben across the snow-covered barnyard, up the back steps, and through the utility room. We removed our boots and entered sock-footed.

I inhaled a mélange of mouthwatering aromas. On the counter sat a platter of stewed meat and onions, squiggly noodles, steaming carrots and broccoli, and biscuits. All of the scrumptious bouquet Pops and my kitchen never produced, because I rarely cooked and had never made bread from scratch. And he recently claimed he wasn't hungry anyway.

"Kumm rei, Sally!" Lizzie said. I figured she was wondering if I'd told Reuben about her escapade. I'd let her ruminate for a while longer.

My grandparents' faces lit up when they saw me. "Sally, dear," Grandma Leah said. "I'm so happy to see ya. I was afraid you'd leave before we got acquainted." She and my grandpa were already seated at the far end of the table. Next to them slouched Pops, who kept his gaze fixed on his plate. Jeremy and Peter were also seated. I assumed the two had worked all day. Lizzie had mentioned that since Sunday was a day of rest, extra chores needed to be accomplished on Saturdays.

"Welcome, Sally." Rhoda floated over to me and gave me a hug, her arms enfolding me. "The roast has been in the oven all afternoon. I hope you like it." She glanced to Pops. "Your dat always did when he was a boy."

Reuben and Armin removed their hats, plunked them on pegs. Reuben parked himself at the head of the table. He skidded his chair in without acknowledging Pops.

Reuben bowed his head, made a guttural sound, and we all sat in silence. I wanted to be thankful. After all, I was at a dinner table with my family, of sorts. If they were my family. If Pops were even my father.

During the silence, I opened my eyes and wondered what Reuben was praying about; maybe that Pops and I would disappear like a poof of steam. I didn't blame Reuben. My father's head was bent, his forehead in his hands. A lifetime of repentance, I wondered, or a show put on for his family's benefit?

The moment Reuben cleared his throat again, all said "Amen" in unison as heads lifted then arms reached out to gather sliced bread, biscuits, and butter. Rhoda served the roast. First to Reuben, then to her parents, then to my father, as if he were an honored guest. Reuben sliced into his meat, his knife grating on the plate.

Rhoda asked Lizzie about her last day at work.

"Nothing special," Lizzie said in a ho-hum manner. "Lots of business, though. Sally was such a fine gut help. I don't know what I would have done without her."

I recalled Joe and Lizzie scaling the snowy bank. I assumed Reuben knew nothing of the incident, or he'd be outraged. I was still confounded by Lizzie's willingness to run off without telling her folks. Exactly what my father had done. Lizzie and Joe's crazy scheme got me thinking: my mother could have been Amish, in her running around years. No, Pops said her parents owned a car. Unless some Amish people owned cars. Maybe she was Mennonite? There was so much I needed to learn, as if I were an oak tree with no taproot, barely grounded.

"Mrs. Martin wants Sally to stay on at least for another week." Lizzie slathered butter and peach jam onto a slice of bread. "Or better yet, a month."

"That would be wonderful." Rhoda passed a dish of pickles around the table. "Sally, are you going to do it?"

"I told her you would," Lizzie informed me.

"Without my permission?"

"You can stay here with us," Rhoda said, ladling out gravy for the meat.

Reuben harrumphed. He dropped his knife, its handle clanking on the plate. "Yah, okay, she can stay. But not your Bruder."

"But surely he can spend at least one night," Rhoda said. "We won't send him out in a snowstorm knowing he's a sick man."

"If he's sick, it must be the Lord's will."

I could see Grandma Leah's face growing tense, her mouth turning inward, hiding her thin lips, probably holding in her words so she didn't antagonize Reuben. She finally said, "Maybe it was God's will that Ezekiel return to us so he can get medical help."

Reuben scarfed down another mouthful. "We don't even know he's really sick."

"Just look at him," Rhoda said. "His cheeks are hollow and his hand's shaking."

She was right, but I'd gotten used to seeing it, so I didn't always notice.

"Maybe that's guilt on his face and fear traveling down his arm." Reuben sent Pops a sneer. "You could never believe him, so why would he suddenly become honest now?"

I was thinking the same thing of Honest Ed. I looked around the room and realized there was no one, not even Armin, whom I could totally trust.

We ate in silence for the most part—I'd never seen Pops so quiet. Just the sound of clattering flatware and an occasional belch, which seemed to satisfy Rhoda. I'd always frowned when Pops belched, but now I realized uncouth manners might be a show of appreciation to the woman who'd prepared the elaborate meal—which I found myself consuming, in spite of my scudding thoughts.

I glanced out the window and saw more snowflakes shimmering to the ground. I wasn't going anywhere tonight.

As if reading my thoughts, Armin said, "Sally, you could spend the night in my cabin with Ginger. I'll sleep in the barn."

"Nee, it's too cold," Rhoda said. "And I want our Sally with us."

I glanced at Lizzie, who sat moving her food around her plate with her fork, nibbling mouthfuls every so often. I had very little doubt what was occupying her mind: Joe. I'd have to ask Armin about him later. Lizzie was so pretty, she must have had her pick of young men. Unless she'd told me the truth, and the young Amish men her age had already selected their brides. No, Armin was proof that wasn't true.

"Lizzie, you're hardly eating a thing." Rhoda tried to serve her more noodles, but Lizzie shook her head.

"She's moping because today was her last day at the store." Reuben aimed his next words at Lizzie. "Don't you think for a minute you're going to change my mind."

"I wasn't, Dat." She sipped her water. "I told you I wouldn't go back, and I won't."

"At least we've got one situation settled." He swabbed butter onto a biscuit and bit into it.

When everyone had finished their meals, Rhoda and Lizzie cleared the table. "Ya want coffee or tea with dessert?" Rhoda asked.

"I've got more chores." Reuben pushed his chair away. "I'm full up to here." He motioned to his throat.

"Aren't you going to say an after-meal prayer?" Rhoda said.

He looked angry enough to spit. "Can't a man have any peace in his own home?"

CHAPTER 19

Reuben bowed his head for an abbreviated minute, then I listened to his footsteps tromp out the back door, followed by a slam.

Armin got to his feet. "I'd better help with the livestock." He swatted Peter's shoulder with the back of his hand. "You two come with me."

"But I haven't had dessert yet," Jeremy said.

"I'm sure your mother will save you a slice of pie." He jostled Jeremy's chair.

"Yah, of course I will," Rhoda said. "And I'll make ya hot spiced cider or cocoa. Be sure to wear your winter coat."

Peter sulked. "Mamm, I ain't a little boy anymore."

"Then, why aren't you out helping your father?" Armin said. I figured he was taking Jeremy and Peter with him for my benefit, so I could talk to Pops and my grandparents with more privacy.

Like a sprite, Lizzie helped Rhoda clear the table, and then the two of them brought out chocolate pie, a plate of cookies, and a stack of dessert plates.

"Please, won't ya sit down here by us?" Grandpa Leonard said to me. His gnarled finger pointed to Peter's now-empty chair. I wanted to speak to him so very much, but my father—just yesterday my beloved Pops—smelled like a stinkbug. And I had to take into consideration: I might not be related to my grandparents. Unless they'd adopt me. Nah, who would adopt a grown woman?

Pops guzzled his glass of water. "Never mind." Practically his first words at the table—not his usual talkative self. Using his arms, he pushed his chair away from the table. "I'd better split, for everyone's sake."

"Nee, please don't leave." Rhoda's voice turned urgent. "You hardly touched your supper."

I almost jumped in to explain that Pops had declared he no longer had an appetite; a metallic taste like a tarnished spoon had pervaded his mouth. But he was a grown man. He could talk for himself. Rhoda brought a bowl of whipped cream from the refrigerator and set it on the table. "You have yet to taste my pie, Ezekiel. Chocolate used to be your favorite when you were a boy. I made it 'specially for you."

"You shouldn't have gone to all that trouble." His eyes were sunken.

"Are ya kidding? You're mei Bruder."

"You're kind, Rhodie, but then you always were." Pops stood, a sluggish process. "I don't deserve your hospitality."

Rhoda's voice rose to a ferocious pitch. "We must forgive those who harm us."

"Yah, 'tis a sin to bear malice," Grandma Leah said, her face a road map of fine lines. "Especially against your own child." Her hand trembled as she reached out to touch Pops's forearm. "Please sit. Reuben won't be in again for at least an hour."

I listened and watched them as if I were in the audience of a movie theater—a spectator. Which was how I wanted to be: in the shadows, unseen. I wondered if they'd be so distracted they wouldn't notice if I left the table. But the moment my knee swung to the side, Rhoda caught sight of me.

"Sally, don't ya want to speak to your father?"

I couldn't even shake my head; my shoulders were as hard as concrete. "I've said all I have to say to him. There's no point."

"But, Sally—" Pops leaned closer to me.

"Ezekiel, we want you to spend the night here," Rhoda said.

"You mustn't disobey your husband, Rhodie." Pops's hands grasped the back of a chair, as if it were a pair of crutches. His complexion was murky—maybe from the dim gas lighting. No, his skin was definitely darker. He looked wobbly, ready to keel over. It took all my willpower to remain seated and not rush over to help him.

"Please," Lizzie said, "don't leave us, Uncle Ed."

"Yah, we can call you anything you like," Rhoda said.

"Ed is fine," my grandfather said, then wagged his finger. "But it's greislich—terrible—for a man to change his last name, to discard his ancestors. Our heritage is very important. We must never forget it."

"But for tonight," my grandma said, "we can accept Ezekiel as he is." She was practically pleading, a pitiful whimper. "We don't want him on the road in this storm."

With everyone talking, I decided this was the opportune moment for me to leave. Rhoda glanced at me for a moment but didn't protest.

Minutes later, wearing the borrowed rubber boots, I practically skated across the frozen snow to Armin's cabin. The sky seemed to be clearing and flakes drifted down lazily. Armin's front porch was dark, but I noticed a dim light inside and heard Ginger's yip. I knocked, then let myself in. When Ginger saw me, she jumped for joy, as only dogs do.

"Looks like you're spending the night in this cabin," I told her. My gaze stole over to Armin's bed, which looked comfy, a refuge, what I'd hoped to find at the bed and breakfast yesterday. If things got too weird around here, when the weekend was over and the tourists returned to the city, I might just drive over to that B&B to see if they had a vacancy.

What was I thinking? I had Ginger with me.

Donald's alligator billfold always bulged with an array of credit cards and hundred-dollar bills. He could afford to stay at a pricey pet-friendly hotel, but I couldn't. I asked myself, frankly, if his financial standing—that sense of security—hadn't played a role in my falling for him. No, he'd sent flowers, opened doors, paid me compliments, wooed me. Except when it came to Pops.

I draped my jacket over the back of a wooden chair. My annoyance and frustration had seemed to warm me from the inside on my walk here, but now I realized the cabin had cooled down. I added wood to the fire and used the poker to nudge the glowing embers toward the center. In a swoosh, the wood ignited. I felt pleased with my accomplishment. Silly that such a minor task brought me joy I so desperately needed.

Armin had left a lantern burning on a side table next to his sofa. I dug into my purse and found the preowned Amish novel I'd borrowed from the store today. With a plaid wool lap blanket covering my legs, I settled onto the couch and opened the paperback and started reading. After spending the day selling books like this, I was surprised to find the story intriguing. I could relate to several of the characters. Yet my lids grew heavy, and I set it aside, rested my head on a pillow, and closed my eyes.

I must have dozed, because the opening door jarred me to consciousness.

"Taking a cat nap?" Armin said.

"Uh, I guess working today was harder than I thought." I didn't know why I was so flustered and embarrassed by his sudden appearance.

"Are you sure you don't want to sleep out here?" He removed his jacket, gave it a shake out the door, then hung it on a peg. He yanked off his boots and stepped into his slippers.

"Thanks for the offer," I said. "But I'd better go back to the house." I could only imagine what Reuben would conclude if I slept out here. Talk about wagging tongues. And this place would be freezing in the morning, not that the big house wouldn't get cold, with no central heating.

The saying about March coming in like a lion and going out like a lamb somersaulted through my mind. Well, not true this year. I recalled a brutal March in Connecticut, as a child. We kids in the neighborhood had thoroughly enjoyed the snow. Or was it February? My past seemed like a hazy morning without a horizon.

"I hate to leave Ginger," I told Armin.

"She'll be fine."

"I worry about if she needs to go out. She's not used to wandering around a farm."

"I'll keep a gut eye on her."

A light rapping on the door caught Ginger's attention. She hurried over to it.

"Coming." Armin opened the door. "Rhoda."

She ducked her head in and spotted me, then turned to Armin and paused. I sat up straighter and lay the blanket aside—not that I was doing anything wrong.

"Sally, your father's staying in the extra bedroom on the first floor." She moved just inside the doorway. "I helped him into bed and was concerned to see how swollen his feet and ankles are."

"I've been concerned about that too. Did he explain what's wrong with him?"

"Nee, he didn't have to. Ach, his foul breath told me everything. My cousin had the same problem. I wonder how long before he goes into renal failure."

"I've tried to get Pops to return to the doctor's, but he won't listen." I felt guilty for my glib reply, but the truth was I had no power to make my father do anything he didn't want to do.

"Please come sleep in your room," Rhoda said. "The men will get up as usual to milk the cows and feed the livestock, then we're off to church service, a day of rest to reflect upon the Lord."

"Leaving me alone with Pops." I recollected the two-headed pushmi-pullyu in the Doctor Dolittle book Pops read to me when I was a kid. Half of me worried about Pops's health while the other half wished to avoid further confrontation with him.

"Could I come to church with you?" I assumed Lizzie wouldn't disappear during the night, not in this weather. "Do you have room in your buggy for everyone?"

"Armin can drive you." She turned to him. "Can you do that for our Sally?"

Armin looked ill at ease, his lower lip tightened. "Yah, I can, even if it means running into my brother."

"Can't you just sit on the other side of the church?" I asked.

"Nee, the men sit on one side, the women on the other." Rhoda gestured with her hands. "Sally, you may sit with Lizzie."

"But I can't go to church dressed like this." I glanced down at my sweats.

"We'll lend you a dress, a long wool coat, and a wool bonnet to cover your head. You'll need it tomorrow. Even if the snow lets up, it'll be a mighty cold ride."

Armin crossed his arms. "I don't think this is such a good idea. No telling what the bishop might do. Your family has troubles enough."

CHAPTER 20

The next morning by seven, I felt as trussed up as a turkey on Thanksgiving, including the long straight pins fastening the back of Rhoda's sapphire-blue dress—as if holding in my stuffing. I also wore a delicate white apron that reminded me of Alice in Wonderland.

How had I allowed Rhoda to talk me into wearing an Amish outfit? Because Lizzie's waist was two inches slimmer than mine, I borrowed a dress and apron from Rhoda, who'd said the dress was too small for her—still on the loose side for me but at least I could breathe. If I wanted to go unnoticed, I'd better don a white prayer cap, Lizzie had informed me. My fault for voicing my concerns about staying home all day with Pops, who still hadn't gotten up. Maybe he'd slept even more fitfully than I had. Or maybe his kidneys had given out, and he'd never wake up again.

A pitchfork seemed to stab into my belly as I considered the possibility, but I dismissed the gruesome image and reminded myself it was time for tough love. I had to get him to agree to see a doctor.

Grandma Leah and Grandpa Leonard opted to stay home and care for him. The poor things; they were clinging on to every moment of seeing their wayward son. I took comfort from it, knowing I wasn't leaving him completely without care.

Shivering in Armin's open buggy fifteen minutes later, I pulled the black wool bonnet down over my ears and held the coat's collar around my neck. Today, the azure-blue sky was as vast as an ocean and hard as polished chrome. The snow from last night—a couple inches—was pristine, cloaking the blemishes of the earth. The sun's intensity reflecting off the snow made me squint. I reached into my purse and found sunglasses, then slid them back away. I hoped I wouldn't stand out too much; I wanted to fade into the woodwork, be anonymous.

"I'll tell everyone you're my cousin visiting from far away," Lizzie called to me as she hurried to the family carriage. "They might think your bishop allows you to wear your hair this away."

She was referring to the fact that I hadn't parted my hair exactly down the center as instructed. But I'd slicked back my bangs, gathered my disorderly locks with a rubber band, and tucked the ends up under the cap. My hair had been such a mess this morning; it needed taming.

Armin climbed into the open buggy, his weight making the rig shift. I couldn't help noticing how good-looking Armin was in his black felt hat and black coat. His boots were polished and he was cleanly shaved. I bet every eligible woman at church would flirt with him. None of my concern, I told myself, but I wondered how he'd escaped matrimony so long.

Minutes later, Reuben drove his covered buggy, carrying Rhoda, Jeremy, Peter, and Lizzie, out of the barnyard, and Armin followed. Thunder wasn't as feisty on the icy ground. I guessed the temperature to be in the mid-thirties. We followed Reuben's buggy for ten minutes to a three-story home standing beside a barn and several outbuildings, their roofs white. Dozens of carriages—carbon copies of Reuben's—were parked outside. Young men in their teens, about Peter's age, unhitched the horses and led them into the barn.

"You're having church here?" I craned my neck and expected to see a spire.

"Yah, in a home with all the wall partitions removed," Armin said. "Unless it's got a sizable basement. Rhoda and Reuben's house is built that away—most of the walls on the first floor come down. Every family is expected to host church service at least once a year. During the warmer months and depending on the size of the home, we often meet in barns."

Ahead, women in black winter coats stood clustered, waiting to enter. I was grateful Rhoda had lent me old-fashioned black leather ankle boots or my feet would've been freezing in the snow. More buggies arrived, mostly driven by bearded men and teeming with children who jumped out and threw snowballs at each other in spite of their parents' admonitions. It was a frolicsome, riotous scene that brought me back to my youth—the sound of their exuberant laughter, their quick movements, all refreshing and endearing.

Oh, I longed for a child of my own, more than I'd realized.

A covered carriage rolled up and I recognized the bishop—his features and copious graying beard were embedded in my brain. As he got out and walked to the front door, the sea of people seemed to part, and several men tailed him inside, followed by the rest of the males, including Reuben and Armin, then Jeremy and Peter.

"Don't ya worry about a thing." Lizzie slipped her hand through the crook of my elbow. She greeted several young women, who spoke to her in Pennsylvania Dutch. *"Gut Mariye,"* she said to them. I could make out a few words: she was telling them she'd brought her cousin. I smiled and bobbed my head. I figured the longer I kept my mouth shut the better.

The bishop's wife passed by and bestowed a brisk nod upon me. I waited for her to call me an imposter, but she moved on. I wondered if she knew about Lizzie's escapades. Lizzie had stood at the side of the road with Joe last night for all the world to see—or at least this little neck of the woods, anyway. And the bishop's wife had recognized Joe in the bookstore.

"Time to go in." Lizzie bumped me with her arm. "No worries; I'll show ya how to act," she told me as we proceeded to the house. "Do everything I do. When we sing—I'll warn you, it's going to move at the speed of a tortoise—you can mouth the words or hum. No one will notice the difference."

But her statement didn't ring true: every Amish woman who glanced my way gave me a wide-eyed look of doubt. And the older women weren't smiling fondly upon Lizzie, although one or two greeted her. I decided that what they thought of me was the least of my troubles. It would be comforting to sit among strangers who knew nothing of me or my nebulous history. Unless they'd heard about me from the bishop's wife.

Once inside the house, after the men had entered, my nostrils were met with the smell of pine oil. This home was immaculately clean and tidy, and rows of backless wooden benches stood in an orderly fashion, filling every inch. Lizzie explained that the benches belonged to the district; they'd been delivered and set up yesterday, as they were every other week and at weddings. The women found seats on the opposite side from the men. Children of all ages, including infants, sat mostly with the women, but a few men held or corralled toddlers. I scanned the room and found Armin—my, he had wide shoulders and good posture—beside Reuben. On Armin's other side sat a tall, bearded man with the same espresso-brown hair as Armin's. Armin seemed to be leaning away from the man, who spoke soberly into his ear.

Armin rotated his head; his eyes scanned the women until he found me. His gaze focused intently on my face and the corners of his mouth lifted. I felt a tingling rush in my chest, like when I drank bubbling 7UP too quickly. I smiled back at him—I couldn't resist. But then I wondered if he found the sight of me, dressed Amish, comical: no makeup, hair hidden under a cap. I hoped not. But then his gaze—like a jolt of electricity—told me he appreciated what he saw.

The other man, seated next to him, seemed to notice Armin and his stare zoomed in on me too. For several moments, both men watched me. I wiped the grin off my face. The other man spoke to Armin soberly, then the man's face lit up as he nodded to a woman sitting somewhere in front of me.

"Who's the guy by Armin?" I asked Lizzie in a subdued voice.

"His older brother, Nathaniel. His wife and mother-in-law are a couple rows in front of us."

I saw the woman she was referring to: nice looking and a few years Rhoda's senior, making her late fifties, sitting by a wrinkly faced oldster who had her neck craned and was inspecting me through thick glasses. When she saw me eyeing her, her mouth bunched together.

"Ach, 'tis a long story." Lizzie tipped her head toward me. "Nathaniel was a widower for many years until he re-met Esther, whose daughter moved here from the other side of the country. The family was hoping Esther's daughter would join the church and settle down with Armin, but she wed a Mennonite, Zach Fleming, our veterinarian."

Several bearded men and Bishop Troyer climbed the home's wooden staircase to the second floor. Lizzie explained the ministers were going upstairs to pray and plan the service while we sang. They didn't even have a sermon in mind? Our pastor back home had mentioned that he prayed, pondered scripture and his sermon all week in preparation.

Hymnbooks appeared and people opened them, but only a few of the adults in the congregation of about two hundred seemed to glance at the words. Lizzie opened a hymnbook and handed it to me. Amid the rustling, a man's baritone voice started a German hymn, then everyone joined in. A cappella: no musical instruments. The song moved slowly, like a rolling ocean wave on a calm day, cresting and falling in a lethargic, comforting manner, the voices blending together, vibrating in my ears and touching me somewhere deep inside. I recalled Pops singing Christmas carols in German and now it made sense. Also why he was so set on my studying German in high school and college. As I picked up some of the lyrics, I felt myself healing from within.

CHAPTER 21

When the singing ended, a bearded middle-aged man with a gentle way about him and who was carrying a Bible stepped to the front of the congregation. All eyes pivoted toward him and my feelings of contentment dissipated, as if I'd emerged from a warm bathtub into the chill air of reality. What was I doing here? How long had we been singing? Thirty minutes on the second song alone. I glanced over at Armin and then to Rhoda, to make sure they were still there, anchoring me.

Then I refocused my vision and thoughts as the bearded man—who must have been a minister—read Romans 3:23 aloud in German. I could loosely translate: We all have sinned and fall short of the glory of God, but we are justified freely by the Lord's grace. Not what I wanted to hear while I stewed over my father's shortcomings—his blatant lies.

Then a second minister read Leviticus 19:18 in German and in English. "Thou shalt not avenge, nor bear any grudge against the

children of thy people, but thou shalt love thy neighbor as thyself."
I could translate most of his German message—sometimes he broke
into Pennsylvania Dutch.

My mind wandered to my father, who must have awoken and
had breakfast by now. To arrest my scuttling thoughts, I inspected
the men's side of the room again. No sign of Lizzie's beau, Joe, who
might have hauled his car out of the ditch by now. I doubted he'd
have the impertinence to drive it to the service or show up wearing
street clothes anyway.

Finally Bishop Troyer moved to the center and all spines
straightened, including Reuben's, who must have nodded off,
the way his head jerked. For a minute, the bishop spoke right to
Reuben, who squirmed on the hard wooden bench. Bishop Troyer
opened the German Bible and read Colossians 3:13. Then he
repeated the verse in Pennsylvania Dutch and in English. For my
sake, or were there others in this room who couldn't understand
German or Pennsylvania Dutch? He admonished everyone to forgive each other for all grievances as the Lord forgives them.

I'd heard the Amish were magnanimous with their determination
to forgive. But I assumed repentance was required. I couldn't imagine Reuben coming to the bishop to ask for forgiveness. Fabricating
jewelry boxes didn't seem such a horrendous crime. Maybe Reuben
had long disobeyed the rules set before him. Or maybe the bishop
wanted Reuben to forgive Pops. Good luck on that one.

When I evaluated Reuben's attitude, he had some nerve putting my father down when he was obviously in the hot seat himself.
But he was here this morning, listening to the words God had commanded, while Pops rarely attended church.

And how about me? My heart was so filled with indignation; it held not an empty spot for forgiveness. Not for Pops and not for my mother, either. My bio mom, a term I'd heard used for surrogate mothers. If I had a precious little girl, I'd never give her up, for anything—especially if her father were willing to care for her. Or would I? Since when did I become Madam Perfect? I only had my father's side of the story, and like Swiss cheese, it could be riddled with fabrications.

My chest tightened as I tried to recall my early childhood. I must have cried and wailed when Mom left. Did she even say good-bye to me, or did she skulk out the back door while I was napping? I wondered if she'd ever had a change of heart and tried to locate me without success. Questions I'd ask Rhoda and Grandma Leah.

At the end of the service, when we were finally excused—what must have been three hours later—I smelled coffee brewing. The men rearranged sets of three benches side by side and elevated them on some sort of trestle to convert into tables, while the women scattered into the kitchen to prepare a meal. I followed them. A plump lady about Rhoda's age, who I assumed to be the mistress of the house, jabbered gaily in Pennsylvania Dutch, using hand motions to direct the girls and women, and pointing out the stacks of plates, multitude of flatware, and napkins. Platters of sliced ham and cheese, bread, pickles, and dishes of macaroni and vegetable salads, mayonnaise and mustard, sat on the counters.

I peeked back out into the expansive living room and was disappointed to see the men sitting around the tables on benches; they were going to eat first, and I was evidently going to help serve them before I got my chance to dig in. The women set the tables in an orderly fashion. Our hostess handed me and another young woman a coffee urn as three others quickly placed cups and water glasses on the tables. Trailing them, I poured coffee. All very ingenious; I admired their dexterity.

I surveyed the sea of heads and located Reuben, Armin, Jeremy, and Peter. I strolled over to them.

"May I serve you gentlemen coffee?" I asked, and they grinned up at me.

"Don't you look nice." Jeremy's cheeks blushed.

"Shush," Reuben said.

"Well, she does." He held out his cup for me to fill.

Their table was as far away from Bishop Troyer's as it could've been. At the other end of the room, Armin's brother, Nathaniel, and Nathaniel's mother-in-law sat dining with the bishop and his wife. Nathaniel's wife must have been helping in the kitchen.

As I strolled among the tables, several men glanced up at me with what appeared to be a look of confusion, but none refused my offering of coffee. "Ich bedank mich," one said, which I assumed meant thank you.

Then other women brought out the platters of cold cuts and cheese, salads and sliced bread.

When we women were finished serving, the others chattered, but again I kept my mouth closed for fear of the reaction I'd get at uttering English words. Or was the fact I wasn't Amish as obvious as a tail feather on a fish?

Where was Lizzie? I finally located her with Rhoda in the kitchen slicing bread.

"What did ya think?" Rhoda said as I moved toward her. "Could you understand the sermon? A fine gut message, yah?"

"Yes, it was thought provoking." I'd avoided seeing Pops all morning and was suddenly inundated with guilt and sadness.

"I'll have to hurry home so I can see our Ezekiel," Rhoda said. "Sally, you may stay and eat. Armin can give you and Lizzie a ride home."

"Thank you, Mamm." Lizzie smooched Rhoda's cheek.

I directed my words to Rhoda. "Lizzie said the man sitting next to Armin during the service is his brother," I said.

"Yah, Nathaniel King." Rhoda scanned the crowd as women cleared dirty dishes and then brought the men dessert. "As far as I know, it's the first time the two brothers have sat together in months."

"We saw Armin at Nathaniel's wedding last December," Lizzie said. "But not at his daughter-in-law's. I bet Nathaniel was none too pleased."

"If ever there were a man who'd forgive Armin, it's Nathaniel," Rhoda said. "Even after all the sadness Armin brought his parents."

"My father says there are two ways of looking at everything." I smooshed my lips together; I was quoting Pops again. I couldn't get him out of my head.

"Yah, we have an Amish saying—'tis almost the same," Lizzie said.

"But in the eyes of God, there is only one way to live one's life." Rhoda delivered Lizzie a stern look. "Maybe you'd better come home with your dat and me, and I don't want you going to the Singing tonight, have I made myself clear?"

"But, Mamm, please, please don't make me come home so soon." Lizzie snaked an arm around Rhoda's waist.

Rhoda's mouth grew hard. "If you leave the house without permission tonight, I'll send your father after you."

It occurred to me that by covering for Lizzie, I'd become a liar, like Pops. Yet, did I have the right to tell Lizzie whom she should marry when my own parents never bothered to make me legitimate? A repulsive thought rippled through me like sludge down a drainpipe. Had Mom really refused to marry Pops or was he lying about that, too?

Rhoda turned to me, her countenance relaxing. "You should go to the Singing with Armin later tonight. It would be good for both of you. He's turning into a hermit."

"I don't think so." The old movie and TV program *The Odd Couple* came to mind.

"You'd be doing Armin a favor, getting him out of the house," Lizzie said. "I should go too. All the girls sit on one side of the long table and the boys on the other. You'd have someone to talk to, Sally." I suspected she'd arranged a rendezvous with her lover boy. I couldn't see the locket Joe had given her, but it was probably hidden under her violet-colored dress, placed over her heart.

Reuben sauntered over to us. "Hurry up and eat," he said to Rhoda and Lizzie. "It's started snowing again."

"But I'm starvin'," Lizzie said, "and I want to talk to my friends and then play volleyball."

"Dressed like that?" I said. "In the snow?"

"Yah, I can play just fine this away."

"I suppose if Sally and Armin promise to look after you this afternoon, it might be okay until supper," Rhoda said. "Then I want you home."

"The less our Lizzie is around Sally's father the better," Reuben said. "How about our sons?"

"Peter and Jeremy can find their own way," Lizzie said. "They won't want to leave yet, either."

Reuben tugged on his beard. "I'll get the horse hitched up and be back in fifteen minutes for you, Rhodie."

I didn't want to find myself in the same horrible position as yesterday, but Lizzie was begging me with her eyes to keep quiet. Finally, she said, "Mamm, I'll come home after we eat. Surely, it won't snow as much again, will it?"

"I'll have a quick snack too," Rhoda said.

"Gut." Lizzie looped her arm in Rhoda's and said, "You'll see. Everything is just fine. Come on, Sally."

I lagged behind them, hoping to run in to Armin. But the first man I came face-to-face with was Bishop Troyer. He wore a sober expression, but his eyes were friendly, crinkled at the corners in a way that told me he might be containing a smile under his thick beard.

"You look familiar." He peered down his nose. "But I can't quite place you." His hat in hand, he scratched his head. "Unless you drive a red car."

"Guilty."

"Of leading one of the flock away?"

"No." I was tempted to enlighten him on Lizzie's mischief: how she'd lured me here under false pretenses, how she'd nearly eloped last night. But I was not a snitch. The Zook family was already under the bishop's microscope.

"I'm Bishop Troyer," he said, "and you are?"

"Sally Bingham. I could be Reuben and Rhoda's niece. Or maybe not." I sounded like an idiot; a woman my age not knowing who her relatives were. In this tight-knit, closed community, everyone knew everyone.

"Are you Ezekiel's daughter? I hear tell he's in town."

"Yes, he came looking for me." I saw myself through the bishop's eyes and realized how ridiculous I looked dressed Amish. I'd left my wool bonnet with my coat and wondered how I'd ever find the right one without Rhoda's help.

But before I could continue my explanation, he said, "Are you contemplating joining the church?"

"No, but I wanted to come to the service, and I didn't have the appropriate clothing. I enjoyed the sermons and the singing. Although—no offense meant—three hours was a long time." I reached up and felt my prayer cap: flattened and sitting at a tilt, allowing strands of hair to spill out.

"Even members who understand every word sometimes nod off." He chuckled under his breath. "I was once young. I recall how difficult it was to keep awake. Old people get drowsy too."

"I could understand a little," I said. "And I know enough of the Bible to recognize the verses the ministers were referring to."

"I hope you'll ponder the lessons taught." He couldn't be alluding to my father, could he? I contemplated asking him about Pops and my mother, but after his poignant sermon decided better of it.

"Were those other men ministers?" I found the cap's strings tangled behind my neck.

"Yes, chosen by God. As I was. Every man must agree to serve

as a minister or deacon when he is baptized, and possibly bishop, for
the remainder of his life."

I speculated about Reuben, who'd apparently not been nominated to become a minister and was in some kind of trouble. I
figured if Lizzie took off, her elopement would be the final nail in
Reuben's reputation. I couldn't imagine him standing before the
congregation in humility preaching the Lord's Word. But who was
I to judge?

I saw Armin meandering through the crowd, headed in our
direction. Among all these Amish men, he appeared ordinary. Well,
better than ordinary—he was the most handsome man here. The
bishop turned his head and acknowledged Armin's arrival. Armin's
posture grew taller and his stride more determined, unlike the reaction of most of the other men when they saw the bishop. I figured
Armin had come over to save me from an embarrassing interaction.
Yet, I felt secure talking to the bishop. He seemed a fine man.

Armin and the bishop greeted each other in Pennsylvania Dutch
and spoke briefly, then switched to English.

"I want to speak to you, Armin," Bishop Troyer said.

Armin's gaze remained level, and he stared at the bishop as if
they were equals, which I figured was not in Armin's favor, because
Bishop Troyer's brows lowered.

"I'd be remiss if I didn't tell you your name was brought up at the
last bishop's meeting a few days ago," he told Armin. "Almost every
bishop in the county had some complaint."

The way his tongue was working the inside of his mouth, Armin
appeared to have something stuck between his teeth. But he didn't
answer the bishop's question.

"Your brother has been more than generous," the bishop said. "He could've turned around and sold Anna's house, just like that." He snapped his fingers. "Nathaniel has more than enough acreage, what with his two daughters married and living elsewhere."

Armin shifted his weight to one leg. "Yah, mei Bruder is a generous man. I won't say a word against him." But I got the feeling Armin had plenty on his mind: evidence that Nathaniel had treated him unfairly.

I wondered why Bishop Troyer chose to continue this conversation with me as a witness. Was his message meant for my ears too? Did he think that because I'd worn this getup I was ready to turn my back on the modern world? I sifted through all the luxuries I'd miss if I lived on an Amish farm. Cars came to the top of the list, not to mention my cell phone, computer, and electricity. I couldn't live without them. Well, maybe for a couple weeks or months.

I ruminated over my upbringing, my father's infatuation with automobiles, which had rubbed off on me. I could recognize almost every make and model, and I was good at appraising their value even without a Kelley Blue Book in hand. Yet, the idea that my father would abandon his parents just so he could drive a car sickened me. That he'd dated my mother because her parents let her use their coupe. No, he'd admitted that he'd mostly spend time with her because she was loose. Some DNA I carried.

Bishop Troyer kept his gaze fixed on Armin. "How can it be that you'd rather live in a cabin and work for Reuben instead of living in the fine house your brother bought for you?"

"He didn't buy it for me."

"I know all about Nathaniel's letting Esther and her mother live there, but now that they live in Nathaniel's home, and he's built a beautiful new Daadi Haus for Anna, there's no need. Esther's daughter is happily married and living in Gordonville. Anna's home sits vacant except for when people need a place to stay."

"Yah, like I said my brother's a generous man, in most areas." Armin pivoted toward the kitchen.

"It's wrong for one man to have so much. He should put the house on the market," the bishop said. "At least rent the acreage to someone wanting to farm it." He glanced my way. "Our farmland is shrinking, making men seek employment in factories or move to other parts of the country."

"Sally," Armin said, stroking his jawline, "you should get yourself something to eat. Go sit with Liz."

I noticed Lizzie at a table among a group of young women, their plates piled high with food. I was famished, but I didn't want to leave Armin's side or miss what the bishop said next.

As if anticipating my thoughts, Bishop Troyer said, "I hope to see you again, Sally. It's never too late to come home." He stepped away to speak to a rotund, bearded man who seemed anxious for a chat.

I patted my head covering and tried to fluff the white fabric, then I redid the rubber band holding my ponytail and tucked my loose hair under the back of the cap. "Will you give me a ride home, Armin?"

"Yah." Armin winked. "I won't leave you stranded, Sally."

"Thanks, I'll grab a quick bite and then be ready. Ginger might need to go out."

"She woke me up last night wanting to relieve herself."

"Off leash?"

"Yah, but I kept a good eye on her."

I envisioned a coyote lurking around the property or Ginger wandering off in search of me, and I felt a cloud of anger darkening my mood.

"You worry too much." Armin's statement rubbed me the wrong way, like gritty sandpaper or a cat's tongue.

"Well, it seems you don't worry enough." My hands moved to my hips; a straight pin jabbed my back, but I kept my face from wincing.

Armin's gaze landed on my prayer cap, then took in my features. He seemed to be bestowing a look of endearment upon me.

CHAPTER 22

In an act of bravery—and because I figured all eyes were surveying me, anyway—I wandered over to Lizzie's table and was met with grins and giggles. Two young women slid over to give me a spot across from Lizzie, who introduced me as her cousin. I assumed she'd already filled them in, at least on the cousin part of the story and why I was dressed Plain, as she called it.

A young woman around Lizzie's age greeted me. "Gut ta meetcha."

One woman cradled a baby, and another tended to her toddler, an angelic little boy with long golden bangs.

Rhoda stepped behind me balancing a dinner plate mounded high with food; she placed it and flatware before me. "Eat yourself full, Sally," she said. I felt her hands adjusting my head covering, gentle movements that reassured me. "Bring Lizzie home with you and Armin, won't ya?" she said.

"I'll do my best."

"I doubt anyone will be playing volleyball today," Rhoda said.

"But, Mamm," Lizzie said, "we might play board games, and it's ever so much fun to sit and talk. And we haven't had dessert and coffee—"

"Don't say another word, Daughter. The subject's closed." Rhoda spun away and dashed back into the kitchen for her own meal.

Two of the young women at the table tilted their heads together and spoke in Pennsylvania Dutch. Lizzie glowered at them. I wondered if any of Lizzie's friends knew Lizzie's intentions. If they knew Joe. Or was Lizzie duplicitous with everyone?

"So, you've come for a visit," one of the young women said to me. Her forehead was wide, her hairline high. "How long will you be staying?"

"I have no idea. Not long."

"I'm trying to talk Sally into working for Mrs. Martin tomorrow. Did you hear she hurt her ankle?"

"Yah, we heard," another young woman said. "And we also heard you gave notice, that your dat won't allow you to go back."

"He doesn't have the last word on everything I do," Lizzie said, garnering their attention.

"I surely hope you don't do anything against the Ordnung," the woman with the infant said.

"Don't you want a husband and *Kinner*—children—of your own?" the woman with a toddler asked. The little boy wriggled and tipped his glass of milk. "How about you, Sally?" She mopped up the milk with a paper napkin. "Are ya married?"

"No, and no kids." I assembled a sandwich and chomped into it so I wouldn't have to explain how close to marriage I'd been or how much

I desired children. I wondered if the young women sitting at the table looked at me as an old spinster compared to them. A woman only had so many years to bear children and be attractive to the opposite sex. Yet I looked around the room and saw the sea of smiling women—none wearing makeup, but each beautiful in her own way.

"As you've all probably guessed, I'm not Amish," I said, and the young women smiled, their lips pressed together.

"But you look lovely dressed that away," the woman cradling the infant said.

Seeing her and her baby, I envisioned my mother as a young woman. Even if Mom weren't Amish, could there be older people in this room who knew about her or her family? I got the crazy notion to stand up and say, "Does anyone here know a woman named Mavis?"

Lizzie interrupted my thoughts. "Please, won't you get Armin to drive us to the Singing tonight?" she implored me.

"No, and you should respect and obey your parents." But I was curious. "What kinds of songs do you sing?"

"We start with German hymns."

I recalled Pops singing German hymns and carols, especially around Christmas and Easter. All his oddities and quirks were gelling.

A cute freckle-faced redheaded young man came and stood behind Lizzie. He tapped her on the shoulder once, so lightly I was surprised she noticed. But she turned her head at a flirtatious angle and said, "Hello, there, Ethan."

"Could I talk to you for just one moment?"

Lizzie swiveled around. "Yah? What is it?"

He bent down, his mouth nearing her ear, but I could make out his words above the din.

"Would ya ride with me to the Singing tonight?" His cheeks turned redder than his hair.

The other women hushed. I wondered if they all wanted her to go out with Ethan and drop Joe, if they even knew about him.

Lizzie looked at the ceiling for a second, then back to Ethan. "I do want to go tonight, but my mamm won't let me." She swiveled in her chair to face me. "Oh, please, Sally. Won't ya talk Mamm into letting Armin drive the both of us?"

Armin sauntered over to the table, said hello to Ethan and the young women, then spoke to me and Lizzie. "We'd best be on our way. The snow's coming down hard again."

"I just got asked to go to the Singing tonight," Lizzie said to Armin, "but I said no, because Mamm won't let me go unless you drive."

Armin glanced out the window. "I'm guessing we're in for three or four inches by tonight."

"Then you could bring out the sleigh." Lizzie's voice grew exuberant.

"But it's so late in the year and it's put away."

"Would you like a ride in a real sleigh?" she asked me.

"I don't know; I never have." In fact, it sounded delightful. "If I bundled up warmly enough." I asked Armin, "Has Thunder ever pulled a sleigh?"

"Yah, once, and it went well enough. He cut through a neighbor's field, but it turned out fine."

Nathaniel strode over to us. "Armin, I'd like to invite you to come for supper tomorrow," he said. "On Monday."

Armin stiffened. "Nee, I can't."

"Mei *Fraa*—my wife—wants me to invite you. You'd refuse Esther's invitation? Is her cooking no longer good enough for you?"

"Don't go twisting my words. I know she's a gut cook. Ya see, we have a guest."

"Then bring her along." Nathaniel glanced at me out of the corner of his eye. "Aren't ya going to introduce us?"

"Sally, this is my brother, Nathaniel." Armin's tightened tone hinted of animosity—or a serious case of nervousness. Maybe every family was messed up. But not as badly as mine.

Nathaniel rotated in my direction but made no move to shake my hand, which was just as well. I didn't want to become entangled in their dispute.

"You're welcome to join us for supper, Sally." His voice softened and his dark brown eyes hinted of kindness.

"Anyone else invited?" Armin cocked his head.

"Not that I know of. Just you. And Sally, if she likes." His face drew closer. "Really, Sally, you're most welcome. My Esther would enjoy having another woman in the house."

"Sure, thanks," I said. "If I'm still here tomorrow night." I was more than a little curious.

"Then 'tis all set." Nathaniel canvassed the room. "Seems the bishop is fixing to leave but not with his wife. I'll bet he's paying a call on someone. With all the snow falling, I'm thinking people will head home early. Esther and I can give the bishop's Fraa a ride. You want to meet her, Sally?"

"No, thanks. I've already had the pleasure." From a distance, the bishop's wife seemed amiable as she chatted with the elderly woman, Nathaniel's mother-in-law. Maybe the bishop's wife wasn't as surly as I'd first thought.

CHAPTER 23

I'd felt a blissful sense of serenity and belonging on the ride back to the Zooks'—until we rolled into their lane and I saw Pops's SUV by the house and a covered buggy, which Armin said was the bishop's, because it was open in the front.

Minutes later, Rhoda met me as I entered the kitchen. Her face was pasty white. "Ach, I never should have left Ezekiel with our parents this morning." She helped me remove the borrowed coat and bonnet. "While we were gone, your father fainted."

Glancing down at my apron and dress, I felt a wave of confusion encompass me. I recalled my cozy ride home from church. I'd sat in the middle, snuggled between Armin and Lizzie. Lizzie had leaned against me, nudging me toward Armin—which I hadn't minded. I'd enjoyed the sound of Thunder's hooves on the compacted snow as well as inhaling the brisk clean air.

"Fortunately, they managed to get Ezekiel back into bed," Rhoda said. "They're in the Daadi Haus resting now."

My hands covered my cheeks as I pictured my father crumpling. Remorse overwhelmed me. "I should have stayed home to look after him. He actually collapsed?"

"Yah, leaving the bathroom. They said he was so dizzy his legs gave out and he melted to the floor. Apparently he'd gotten up and lost his dinner, and then couldn't fall asleep again."

I wondered how many nights he'd repeated the same episode. No wonder he'd dropped so much weight. My first impulse was to rush in and check on him. "Is he conscious? Is he breathing all right?" I stepped into slippers.

"Yah. He's sleeping and I didn't want to wake him."

She raised on her toes and looked over my shoulder. "Ach, where's our Lizzie?"

"We brought her home. She's walking Ginger while Armin's looking after Thunder."

"Denki." Her voice sounded strained. I wondered if she knew about Joe. The Amish certainly had unique customs when it came to courtship, but I couldn't fault them. It appeared they gave their children opportunities to stretch their wings and come to conclusions on their own before joining the church.

I exited the kitchen, tiptoed to his bedroom, and peeked through the cracked door. The sheet, blanket, and a quilt were pulled up to Pops's chin. The air smelled stale, oppressive.

I felt as if a gorilla were strangling me from behind, keeping my lungs from expanding. How could I have been so blind? What if he died without our reconciling? For the rest of my life, a yoke of guilt would burden me, dragging me into the past.

I noticed Pops's arm twitch, and he rolled onto his side. I

wondered if I should call 911 or at least take him to the nearest ER. Not that we had much insurance coverage—catastrophic only. And the way the snow was coming down, saturating the air and accumulating more inches, even an emergency vehicle would have trouble making its way here. Then Pops would tell them to scram and leave him alone. Unless reality had finally sunk in.

I headed for the front hall as my grandparents came out of the Daadi Haus looking distraught.

"Sally, *liebe*." My grandmother's arms clasped me tightly, then she stepped back and my grandfather gave me an embrace. Grandma Leah beckoned us to follow them into the kitchen where Rhoda stood at the sink, rinsing off several plates. My grandmother must have assembled a meal for my father. Maybe a mother never gave up on her child. No, not true. My mother had tossed me away.

"What should we do for Ezekiel?" Grandma Leah asked me. "How sick is he?"

"It's his kidneys—pretty much all I know. He's avoided the doctor other than to get a diagnosis."

"Surely, he'd listen to you." Rhoda dried her hands on her apron.

"He never has before," I said. "Begging him to seek treatment hasn't worked."

The morning's sermons wormed their way through my brain. I recalled one Bible verse; Jesus had told a group of men poised to stone a woman to death: "Let anyone who is without sin be the first to throw the first stone." They'd meant to kill her, but everyone laid their rocks aside and left, the oldest and wisest first. I wasn't perfect. I couldn't toss the first stone, although I was hankering to pitch a boulder—which was wrong.

"Sally, is that you?" Pops called in a weak voice from the bedroom.

All eyes in the kitchen turned to me and waited for my response. I paused, trying to gather my wits.

"You want me to go with you?" Rhoda touched my arm.

"Thanks, but no, thanks." I hadn't a clue what I'd say to Pops. I went to his bedroom door and pushed it open. He was staring at the ceiling. A pillow supported his head. His hair was greasy and flattened on one side.

A battle raged inside my brain—and in my heart. My father was dying. The only person in the world who'd ever loved me could be gone by the end of the day. I'd be an orphan. And I'd miss him terribly, more than I could imagine. To never hear him crack a joke, call me his darling Mustang Sally, tell me he loved me.

"Am I hallucinating?" His eyes widened when he noticed me. "Why on earth are you dressed like that?" he asked gruffly. "Go change your clothes immediately."

I felt as if I'd walked into a glass door, smashing my nose against the transparent obstacle. Not since I was a teenager had he spoken to me so harshly. My hand reached up and patted my head. The covering hadn't slipped to the side too badly. I was tempted to pull it off but decided instead to find the strings and knot them under my chin, the way the bishop's wife wore hers.

"I still don't understand how you ended up here." With his elbows, he maneuvered himself into a semi-sitting position. It took everything in me not to rush over and help him.

A montage of images scattered through my mind: Pops buying me my first dog, his watching me at my piano recital and then letting me quit after I begged him, his teaching me to drive a car when I was only thirteen, on his lot. Pops had always been my hero, making my wishes come true, giving me everything I wanted within his financial power. I could think of a thousand acts of kindness he'd shown me, but he'd always kept me from my real prize: my birthright—my mother.

"Why did you come?" I asked. "Why didn't you just tell me the truth when you figured out I was staying with your sister?"

"I should have. I should have told you the truth many times, and I can't give you an excuse that will make things right except that I was trying to spare you pain."

"But I deserved an explanation. I had a right to find Mom."

"Sally, meeting her would be entering a dragon's den."

"How do you know? Have you kept in touch with her?" If he were hiding letters or not telling me about telephone calls, I didn't know what I'd do, other than let my anger explode like an erupting volcano.

"No, she hasn't tried to reach me."

"And you haven't made it easy, have you? In fact, you've made it near impossible for anyone to find you." An act of cowardice from a man I'd always considered invincible. "And don't give me that baloney about her wanting to steal me away. I'm a grown woman, not a helpless underage child. She couldn't legally gain custody of me." The taste of acid rose in my throat. Here I was arguing with a man who could be on his deathbed when I should be bridging the troubled waters, not agitating them.

Rhoda poked her head into the room. "Is everything all right?" She must have heard my voice, its volume raised.

"Rhodie, why are you dressing my daughter like this?" His voice was filled with antagonism.

"It was my choice," I said. "I can't believe you'd speak that way to your sister, a woman who's waited to see you over twenty years."

Rhoda wrung her hands, held them under her chin. "Maybe I should let you two be alone."

"Never mind. I'm leaving." I spun on my heels before I let my thoughts materialize into a heated confrontation. Partly because I cared what Rhoda thought of me; partly because I knew better than to disrespect my father, no matter what he'd done.

Passing through the living room, I shambled back into the kitchen. My grandparents, both sitting at the table, waited for me to fill them in. All I could do was shake my head. I wouldn't burden this sweet old couple with the long sordid story of my dad's deceit. Or maybe I was the only person on earth who didn't know. I recalled that Lizzie said a Mennonite driver had recognized him and told her and Rhoda. I wondered if God had orchestrated that chance meeting. According to Rhoda, my grandparents had been praying long enough. I'd heard of God fulfilling prayers, even if I hadn't received answers to mine.

Grandma Leah reached out her arms as if she'd been longing to do so my whole life, and I sank onto the chair beside her. To deprive me of my grandparents made every Christmas present Pops had ever given me seem like a trifle. I wondered if he'd known Leah and Leonard were still living. Did Pops have a contact here in Lancaster County who filled him in on his parents' well-being, or was he a man without convictions?

My heart beat erratically, as if it might refuse to pump my blood anymore.

"How can we help you?" Grandma Leah said. Imagine, they

were trying to assist me when they were the ones who deserved compensation for all those years of their son's neglect.

"You are." I turned to Grandpa Leonard and tried to smile without success. "Thank you for accepting me." I didn't have the heart to tell them they may not be my real grandparents. My mother was a tramp, according to Pops. I might have a father and a boatload of siblings somewhere—more than I could deal with now. Possibly my grandparents had already considered that scenario.

But I couldn't let this opportunity slide by. "Do you know where my mother is?" Both shook their heads. "Do you remember a girl named Mavis?" Speaking her name closed my throat as if I'd swallowed a glass of saltwater.

"I recall your father mentioning her, but we never met," Grandma Leah said.

"Yah, after our Ezekiel left, her parents came one day asking about her. The only thing we could figure was that the two of them were together. Her parents were furious and blamed our son. All we could do was apologize. We suspected Mavis lured Ezekiel away, but we never said a thing."

"Do her parents still live near here?"

They looked toward each other, then back to me. "I don't rightly know," Grandpa Leonard said.

My mind swarmed with detective-type methods of tracking her down—but I'd need a computer and Internet access. "Did they live far from here?"

He smoothed his beard. "I haven't seen her parents for over ten years. They could have moved."

"Do you remember their last name?" I persisted.

"I don't recall." My grandpa turned to Grandma Leah, who lifted her narrow shoulders.

"Nee, me neither. I think her father worked at a college."

"Did Mavis have siblings who could still live in the area?"

"Rhoda might know. They'd be about her age."

I popped to my feet and met Rhoda as she entered the kitchen. Her face was ashen and her eyes frightened, like a cat that had just dashed in front of a car and barely missed the tires' deadly tread.

"Your father says he doesn't want us to call 911. He claims he feels this way all the time and will snap out of it." Rhoda glanced out the window at the falling snow.

So peaceful and quiet, each flake unique and perfect. The opposite of my life.

I heard the back door open and close. Lizzie waltzed into the kitchen through the utility room. Her complexion was rosy and her eyes sparkling: the same exhilaration of being in the snow I'd felt only twenty minutes ago. She removed her woolen bonnet.

"Mamm, I still want to go to the Singing tonight," she told Rhoda in a whiny voice. "Such a beautiful afternoon."

"You'll have to speak to your dat," Rhoda said. "I don't know how you can think of such trivialities when Sally's father is so ill."

"I didn't know." She flipped her palms up. "How would I?"

I glanced out the window and could barely see the barn through the curtain of snow. "Will Reuben set foot in the house again with my father here?"

"When he's good and ready." Rhoda placed water on the stove to boil, then set a small ceramic bowl containing teabags on the table. "He's probably looking after the livestock."

"Nee, he's speaking to Bishop Troyer," Lizzie said.

"Ach, the bishop's still here?"

Lizzie wandered over to Grandma Leah and kissed her cheek. "Isn't that thoughtful for such a busy man to pay us another call?" Lizzie seemed nonchalant, maybe an act for our grandparents' sake. I wondered if the bishop would come into the house to see for himself that my father had returned. Or to ask about me.

Rhoda set mugs and teacups on the table. Then she arranged a plate of cookies and brought them to me. "Sally, would you like an oatmeal cookie or a coconut macaroon?"

As I inhaled the scent of coconut and sugar, my hand moved toward the plate. But if I kept eating everything in sight, I'd need to go on a diet. "They look delicious, but I'd better not."

"How about coffee, tea, or hot apple cider?"

"Maybe later, thank you. Right now I want to check on Ginger." I considered changing back into my normal clothes but decided to wait until after dashing out to the cabin. I glanced down at my dress's hem and noticed it was damp. Why get myself soggier? "May I continue using your dress and coat?" I asked Rhoda.

"Yah, of course. And any of the boots by the back door. But, here, let me lend you a darker apron."

I switched into a black apron and pushed my arms into the coat's sleeves. My father called my name, but I plunked the bonnet back on my head and hurried outside. Off in the distance, the sky seemed brighter, giving me hope that the clouds were parting. I saw Armin exiting the barn and moving toward his cabin. Good timing. Or would the bishop see our being together as immoral? I asked myself why I cared what Bishop Troyer thought, but I did.

Kate Lloyd

I closed in on Armin as he mounted the few stairs to his small front porch. He acknowledged me but seemed disturbed, judging from his furrowed brow.

"What's going on?" I asked. "Is the bishop planning to come into the house?"

"He's in Reuben's workshop. I couldn't hear them. It's best I stay out of the conversation."

Armin opened the cabin door and Ginger sprinted out, wanting to play in the snow. I let her frolic for a few minutes, then dusted the white chunks off her coat and commanded her to follow me inside.

I bent to run my hands along her loins. Sure enough, her ribs were extended. How could I have been so blind? In every arena of my life, I'd been wandering in a fog of denial.

The cabin was toasty and inviting, as only a wood fire could be. The chairs stood by the table, and I noticed Armin's bed was haphazardly made.

"Do you mind if I come in for a few minutes?" I asked.

"Make yourself at home." He helped me remove my coat, took off his long black jacket, then shook both outside the door before hanging them up.

As I relaxed on the couch with Ginger at my feet, I realized he probably wanted to change into casual clothes. And go to the Singing? I was still unclear what that occasion was all about.

Knuckles rapping on the door made both Armin and me start. Ginger growled; her hackles raised.

"Coming." Armin seemed reluctant to answer it.

But someone turned the knob from the outside and pushed the door open.

CHAPTER 24

I was perched on the couch when Bishop Troyer stepped inside. His eyes zeroed in on me—I was in the wrong place at the wrong time.

I shot to my feet the same way I had when I was fourteen and Pops had caught me watching TV with a boy. My father had forbidden boys in the house without his chaperoning. I'd been grounded for a month.

"Hello, again," I said. "I came to check on my corgi." Her ears pricked, Ginger cocked her head and stood looking up at the bishop as if he were judging Best of Group at the Westminster Dog Show in Madison Square Garden.

"Yah," Armin said. "Reuben doesn't want dogs in the house."

"Reuben doesn't want a lot of things," the bishop said.

Armin's gaze lowered in a subservient manner. At least that was what my pups had always done to show submission: the dominant alpha male stared the other one down. But then Armin raised his chin and looked the bishop in the face.

Was Armin about to get lectured for entertaining me? As far as I could tell, the bishop's proclamations were the law of the land for the Amish in this district. And knowing Armin, even for a short amount of time, I had the impression he would demand the last word. I guessed he could be lippy and strong-willed, character traits I found attractive for some odd reason.

I heard a weighty clump of snow slide off the roof and land with a thud at the side of the cabin. It occurred to me that I hadn't thought about Donald most of the day—one small victory. I didn't miss him and I was glad, because I'd be heartbroken if I did. Well, maybe I was more hurt than I'd realized, since he'd found my replacement so quickly. Perhaps the reality of his betrayal would swirl around and sting me the way an angry hornet circles its target before attacking from behind.

On the other hand, maybe I'd found Donald's replacement. No. What was I thinking? Armin and me an item? Only if we were beached on a deserted island. Or in a snug little cabin during a snowstorm.

The bishop cleared his throat. This could be a crucial day in Armin's life, and I had no right to interfere.

"Would you like privacy?" I asked the men.

"Nee," both answered.

"It's gut seeing you again, Sally." Bishop Troyer seemed sincere, but I worried that he'd think I was mocking the Amish by my dress and apron. I hoped not, because in the last twenty-four hours my esteem for them had bloomed. Yet if life in the tight-knit, structured community were idyllic, why would Lizzie wish to elope and why had Armin taken off for such a long time?

"It's good to see you, too," I said. Our chance meeting was my opportunity to find out more about my parents. "Did you know that my father's still here?"

"Yah, Reuben told me."

"Did he also tell you how my father kept my Amish heritage a secret and that he refuses to reveal my mother's last name?" I wouldn't delve further into the cesspool.

"Reuben didn't mention your mother," he said. "I can see you're greatly distressed, Sally."

"Frantic is more like it." My words faltered in my throat, stumbling over each other. The enormity of my emotions caught me by surprise. I felt like the runt in the litter, overlooked and cast aside by its own mother. Because there was something wrong with the puppy. With me.

"I feel like I'm losing my marbles," I said, trying to sound lighthearted but hearing a tremor in my voice.

Bishop Troyer sent me a kind smile. "I can imagine you must be disoriented."

"You don't know the half of it." I was tempted to tell him about Donald's escapade, but I would have been too humiliated to mention it in front of Armin. "Let's just say, my life has taken a radical U-turn."

"It seems you and Armin both have decisions to make," Bishop Troyer said, glancing over at Armin.

"If you have something to say to me, go ahead." Armin's voice filled the small space. "I don't mind if Sally hears."

I was touched that Armin trusted me. I guessed he alone would know how topsy-turvy my life was.

"Nathaniel told me you're going to his house for dinner tomorrow and that you might bring Sally," the bishop said to Armin. "I hope this is a step toward reconciliation with your brother. To become baptized, you must hold no bitterness or resentment."

"If I become baptized." Armin tossed wood in the hearth.

The bishop's shaved upper lip barely moved when he spoke. "Do you want to remain a rambler for the rest of your life, living in the periphery of the community and missing out on all the Lord's blessings?"

"You can see I'm dressing and living an Amish life." Armin stoked the fire until it roared. "And attending church."

"And surely you wish to get married and start a family before it's too late." Bishop Troyer's gaze fastened onto Armin. "You should attend the Sunday Singings," the bishop said. "Or have you already met a *Maedel* who's caught your eye?"

"The only woman who's captured my attention recently is Sally here."

"Me?" In my shock, I squawked like a parrot. My hand flapped up to cover my mouth.

"Armin, you know what happened the last time you took a shine to an Englisch girl," Bishop Troyer said.

"She's happily married now, and it all turned out for the best." Armin tilted his head; his thick bangs shifted across his eyebrows. "She wasn't meant for me from the get-go. She was in love with another man." Armin's eyes locked onto mine. "How about you, Sally? Are you in love with someone else?" he asked me.

"No, I'm not." I did owe Armin an explanation when we were alone; I would eventually fill him in on my fizzled engagement.

Unless I left when Pops did. But my chest felt as parched as the Sahara Desert when I considered never seeing Armin again.

"That's fine gut news." Armin rubbed his palms together. "When I first met you, I saw an engagement ring on your hand. And you were awaiting a man's telephone call."

"That's part of my old life, in the past." Yet I still needed to officially break off my engagement to Donald. I should have done it when I'd had him on the phone. I could text him. No, that would be the coward's way out. And I owed his mother an explanation, out of common courtesy.

"In that case, what do you have planned?" the bishop asked me.

"I don't know. Depending on what my father does, I might work at the Sunflower Secondhand Store this next week if Reuben and Rhoda will let me stay." The job would keep my mind occupied since I had no control over Pops. And I didn't know if he would be up to the long drive home. Staying would give me time to consider Armin's declaration too.

"Would you go dressed thusly?" the bishop asked, scanning my apron and dress. "You mustn't pretend to be Amish to make money."

"I've never heard that," Armin said. "What about all those actors in movies pretending to be Amish?"

"Because Englischers do *greislich* things doesn't make it right." The corners of his mouth angled down. "Those actors are not baptized Amish."

"Neither is Sally."

"Well, that's true. Unless she desires to join the church."

"You mean I could?" I ached to be a member of a genuine community.

"It's possible but not likely." The bishop furrowed his brow. "Some Englischers think they might like to live our life only to become disappointed and give it up."

"But I could?" I asked. "I could actually join the church?" My life in Connecticut was a charade, like a puppet show I'd seen as a child.

"I certainly wouldn't wish to persuade you," he said. "The fact that you were just engaged to another man tells me you're unstable. And you know little of our ways."

"I could learn. And I'm usually not wishy-washy."

"Well, at loose ends, then," he said, and he was right. He turned to Armin. "You're not thinking of running off with Sally, are ya?"

"Nee, nothing like that. I'm hoping she'll stay here."

Was he kidding? I'd have to wait for Bishop Troyer to leave to talk to him—

"Perhaps the Almighty is tapping Sally on the shoulder," the bishop said. "Maybe he wants to bring her home where she belongs."

Armin fell silent; he was no doubt pondering what I'd told him earlier, that I wondered if Pops were my father, making me no blood relative to the Zooks. I wanted Rhoda to be my aunt, Leah and Leonard to be my grandparents, and even Reuben to be my uncle. This farm, their house, and Armin's cabin, felt like home— although it was preposterous to become so attached in such a short time. I prayed God would lead me on the right path.

The bishop moved closer to Armin. "It wonders me that you'd refuse the Lord's blessings. Just how long are you planning to dangle one leg in the Englisch world? I hope you're fixing to stop your adolescent behavior. It won't be tolerated much longer."

"Okay, you're right." Armin inhaled deeply, then exhaled through puffed-out cheeks. "I'll attend baptism classes and get baptized in the fall."

The bishop shook his head; his beard swayed back and forth. "You don't look very happy, Armin. When you're baptized, it should be the happiest day of your life."

"Even better than the day you marry your wife?" Armin's confident boldness was a quality I found appealing, but I figured he was wading into quicksand.

"Are you ridiculing me and the sanctity of marriage?" By Bishop Troyer's stiff countenance, I could tell Armin had over-stepped his boundaries. "If you're not truly ready to submit to the Ordnung, then you'll have to wait another year. I won't baptize a man with such an arrogant attitude."

"Sorry, I meant no offense." Armin ran his thumb up and down his suspender. "I'm looking to get married, really I am. I've been a bachelor long enough."

"How does a person become baptized?" I asked, in part to take Armin out of the spotlight and also because I wanted to know.

"You mean a person such as you?" Bishop Troyer's eyes seemed to gaze right into my wounded soul. "She must demonstrate she's willing to follow the teachings of the Bible emphatically, and also our Ordnung as taught by me, the ministers, and the deacon."

I wasn't a member of the church I attended back in Connecticut, and I wondered why I'd never felt prompted to join it. If I were to become Amish, really Amish, I'd have to stop using electricity and driving a car. Right now, those options seemed reasonable, but how long would my carefree attitude last? And could I submit to the bishop, ministers, and deacon?

"I might look into it," I told the bishop. My whole world seemed to be condensed to this farm. And I liked it. "Or is that crazy thinking?"

"All things are possible with God if a person is truly determined to follow him."

"How will I know what God wants for me?" I asked in all sincerity.

"Should you like, we can talk further, say in a few days." He moved toward the door.

"Are you going to see my father?" I asked.

"Yes. Do you think he'll appreciate my visit?"

"No. But I would." The bishop might be the perfect person to knock some sense into Pops.

CHAPTER 25

I watched the bishop's large gloved hand turn the doorknob.

"I'd better stay out here," I said. I'd be content in the cabin with Armin and Ginger while Bishop Troyer made his house call. But then I considered how vexed I'd be if I woke up in the morning and found my father had stolen away during the night. I got to thinking about what I'd miss if I didn't accompany the bishop—possibly clues about my mother.

A block of chilly air barged in as he headed outside. The door shut behind him.

"Wait, I changed my mind," I said. "I'll walk over to the house too." I grabbed my coat, stuffed my arms into the sleeves. "Rhoda might need help preparing dinner."

"On Sunday, we have leftovers," Armin said. "Rhoda did her cooking yesterday."

"You all take this day-of-rest business seriously, and yet the bishop's working."

"As did Jesus when he healed the man with the shriveled hand in the book of Mark." Armin gave Ginger a back rub and the dog stretched out her short rear legs. "I'll come into the house later." I guessed he meant after the bishop left. Armin probably didn't want to be further enmeshed in the family's tumult. But I had no choice.

I stepped into the boots and hurried outdoors. Dusk had begun to spread her tinny-gray wings; tissue-paper–thin clouds drifted overhead. The air felt a smidgeon warmer. The snow beneath my feet was softening.

"Wait up," I said, trailing Bishop Troyer across the slushy barnyard.

I figured he was about fifteen years older than Pops, but in spite of his slim frame and somewhat stilted gait, the bishop possessed ten times the vitality; his strides were taken with purpose. From what I'd seen, he was a righteous man. I recalled the other night; he'd had every reason to glower at me when I'd nearly pulled my car out onto the road in front of his carriage. I'd been negligent, yet he hadn't brought the incident up to shame me.

I caught up with him. "Just a minute," I said, my heel skidding on the snow.

He kept heading toward the back steps. Someone had shoveled and swept them off—I assumed Peter or Jeremy. "You don't have to come in with me," he said, "if it's too painful for you."

"I can't hide out at Armin's all night. And I'd like to see Rhoda." Bitterness continued to eat me, like termites chiseling into decaying wood. I eagerly awaited Pops's bewildered expression when he saw the bishop. Then I recalled the Ten Commandments. Honor thy father. I prayed in silence: Please, God, remove this hostility. Let me start with a clean slate.

The bishop climbed the stairs, scuffed and stamped the snow off his boots, and made his way through the utility room in a confident manner that told me he'd been here many times before. Entering the kitchen, he shed his black hat and coat.

Rhoda stood at the counter. "What a fine gut surprise." But her facial expression seemed filled with dread: her lips pulled tight. And yet for all I knew, Rhoda herself had asked Bishop Troyer to come see Pops. Maybe she hoped the bishop would convince Pops to stay a few days. I liked Rhoda so much; I hated to see her disappointed. She took the bishop's coat and hat.

"I'd like to speak to Ezekiel, if I may."

"Yah, that would be gut."

"Where might I find him?"

"He was up for a short while, but he's back in bed in our small room on the first floor. I'll show you the way."

I followed the two of them through the living room. They were speaking in Pennsylvania Dutch so I wouldn't understand them. Or maybe it was just out of habit. I realized when they spoke English, they were doing it as a courtesy to me. I could make out several words; they were talking about Reuben and how furious he was having my father in the house. Reuben had threatened to bodily remove Pops. The bishop said it would be unfitting for an Amishman to physically evict a person, no matter the weather or circumstance.

I didn't know what I expected as we neared the bedroom. I got this crazy notion Pops might be gratified to see the bishop, to confess his wrongdoings. But why would my father spontaneously reverse his thinking the moment he saw Bishop Troyer?

Pops was wearing reading glasses and sitting in bed drinking tea—his cup sat on a tray on the bedside table. A propane lamp stood nearby. A magazine—*The Connection*—lay open in his lap. He looked better, his face less gaunt and his eyes clearer.

"Hello, Ezekiel." Bishop Troyer pulled the door completely open and stepped into the room with Rhoda and me shadowing him. "Do you remember me from when we were younger?"

"I guess." Pops flipped the magazine's page. "Rhoda tells me you're a bishop now." Pops didn't seem to be showing much respect. I wanted to jump in and say something, but I remained silent. The bishop would get nowhere if I interfered.

"Once again, God has worked all things together for good," Bishop Troyer said.

"How's that?" It seemed Pops was trying to antagonize the bishop, but Bishop Troyer remained calm.

I recognized the reference to Romans that our pastor had quoted, something about God working for the good of those who love him, to those who were called according to his purpose. Which left Pops out, I assumed. And me, too, if I were honest with myself. Did I really love God? More than caramel ice cream and lattes? More than anything on earth? Even the dream of finding my mother?

As my thoughts did loop-the-loops, I compressed my lips together so I wouldn't interrupt the conversation.

Bishop Troyer moved to the foot of the bed. "Do you think your being here is a coincidence, Ezekiel?"

Pops folded his glasses. "I go by Ed."

"You can call yourself whatever name you please, but don't forget that God is in control."

"I'm in no mood for a theological debate." His hand wobbly, Pops set the magazine off to the side. "In fact, I'm ready to hit the road. I have a thriving business that can't run itself."

"Nee, please don't go." Rhoda pulled up a chair next to the bed and sat by him, laid her hand on his arm. "If you want to be called Ed, we can do that. But I can't let you leave the house to drive on icy roads all the way to Connecticut. It isn't safe." She paused and looked him in the eyes. "Dear Bruder, it will never be your true home. In some way or another you will be forever Amish."

"Bah." Pops sounded like Scrooge. I was disappointed and embarrassed by his boorish behavior. "Rhoda, you were always such a sweet girl," Pops said. "I don't deserve your sympathy. You should listen to your husband and toss me out on my ear."

"Even if you leave," the bishop said, "God will pursue you."

Pops endeavored to get out of bed, but it was obvious by his trembling arms he didn't have the strength. He wilted back again.

"What on earth are you thinking?" Rhoda plumped the quilt around Pops's legs.

"That I won't stay in a house where I'm obviously not welcome."

At the thought of Pops leaving, I could no longer contain my concerns about his health. "Bishop Troyer, if Pops doesn't receive medical help soon, he'll need a kidney transplant. I was planning to have the blood work done to see if I'm a donor candidate." I didn't want to explain why Pops and I might not be compatible.

"You're so young, Sally," Rhoda said. "I'd be a better donor. We have a cousin with kidney problems, but mine are in fine shape. And your father and I are siblings."

"I don't know," the bishop said, scratching his chin. "A transplant? I don't believe that's permitted in our Ordnung."

"Don't say that, please." Rhoda stood. "I can't let my brother die."

"Where he'll spend eternity is more important than his time on earth," the bishop said.

"All his medical records are in Connecticut," I said, and all heads rotated toward me. "Tomorrow I'll call his doctor's office and find out what to do." In the back of my mind, I got an itchy feeling. Was Pops still manipulating me? But no matter what he'd done or might do, I loved him more than anyone.

"I can't imagine any doctor wanting to perform a transplant if there are other medical remedies available." Bishop Troyer turned to Pops. "Have you tried everything possible?"

"I can answer that." My hands clamped my hips. "No. He's ignored most of his doctor's suggestions."

"And how would you know that?" Pops demanded.

"I called your doctor's office."

"Without my permission?" Grim lines bracketed his mouth.

Thinking about his many falsehoods, my thoughts reverted to Mom. "You've got your nerve, scolding me for keeping information to myself when all this time you've lied." Unable to restrain myself any longer, I turned to Rhoda and said, "There's got to be a way for me to find out who my mother is. I wouldn't be surprised if Pops knows exactly where she lives."

"But isn't your father's health more important right now?" Rhoda said.

Of course, she was right, but my tongue seemed to have a will of its own. "What if he dies and never tells me?" I said.

"You care more about her than me, the man who raised you?"

It felt like a noose was cutting off my air supply. He'd lied to me for so long, I didn't know what to believe. "Do you remember a girl named Mavis?" I asked Rhoda. "At least that's what he says my mother's name is." Pops could've been fibbing about that, too.

"Yah, I do, vaguely," Rhoda said. "Around here, Mavis is an unusual name. I think she was Mennonite, but her parents were modern and liberal. Not politically, mind you, but the way they dressed, and they owned the latest appliances, cars, and gizmos. Of course, that was a long time ago."

"What was she like? Do I look like her?" I glanced past Rhoda and saw Pops shifting away from us.

"Well, now, it's been so many years, I don't recall." Rhoda patted her prayer cap. "What was her last name?" she asked Pops.

His head shook. "I don't rightly know."

"I'm not buying that," the bishop said. "Surely, you'd recall the name of the woman who birthed your daughter."

I could have run over and hugged the bishop, but I didn't want to do anything to break the spell. We three stood staring at Pops, who gazed out the window into the darkening sky. Finally, he said, "I guess it could've been Miller."

My heart leaped inside my chest. "Rhoda, do you know anyone with that last name?"

"Yah, Sally, there are many Millers in this county." She turned to Pops, who seemed bent on ignoring our conversation. "Can you not tell your daughter more than that?"

Bishop Troyer folded his arms. "We're asking you for the truth, Ezekiel."

But my father kept silent.

I felt my compassion for Pops shrinking. To think, I'd idolized this man my whole life.

Plodding footsteps came from the hall. A moment later, Reuben bobbed his bearded face through the doorway. "Are ya having a tea party?" When he strode into the room, the floorboards creaked.

Rhoda moved to his side. "You can see we have the bishop here—"

"I'm aware of his presence. And I'll not let your brother deceive him."

My father glanced up at Reuben, and I couldn't help but notice the difference in their builds. Pops, weak and sickly. Reuben, strong and bursting with vitality. Fortunately, the Amish were nonresistant and were taught to never strike an enemy. Yet Reuben had not shown a meek disposition—quite the opposite.

"Please, Reuben, let the bishop reason with Ezekiel." Rhoda massaged her fingers. "I mean Ed."

"There's no use." Pops crossed his arms, tucking his hands out of sight.

"If you confess and repent from your sins, you will be forgiven and welcomed back home," the bishop said. "You could have returned at any time."

"Not everyone chooses to come back and you know it." Pops's voice turned surly. "How about me? How about my daughter? Sally's mother has never asked us for forgiveness."

"She may never apologize," the bishop said, "but that doesn't mean you can't forgive her."

I stepped forward. "How could she ask for forgiveness if you didn't want to be found?" I turned to Rhoda. "Has no woman ever come around asking about me?"

"Nee." She let out a sigh. "I'm sorry."

The lamp hissed. I chided myself for my gargantuan disappointment. Ridiculous to think my mother would have been searching for me. Yet Lizzie had located me. Did the Lord not want me to have a mother?

"I tell you, I want this man out of my house." Reuben aimed a finger at Pops.

"This is what I want," Bishop Troyer said, "to see you on your knees confessing before the congregation in two weeks." He shot Reuben a stern look, more like a warning. "Can I count on you being there?"

Reuben shifted his weight, seemed to be teetering. "Yah, okay, I'll do it." He glared at my father. "But I still want this man out of my home."

"To refuse to forgive is a sin," Bishop Troyer said. "I expect you will resolve this dispute and confess your unforgiving attitude."

Reuben scratched his belly. "Yah, okay."

Rhoda and my grandparents had chosen to pardon my father for running out on them. If Lizzie hadn't found him, his life would be chugging along as usual. No, not really, because his health was deteriorating. I figured his driving here at night had compromised his immune system further, weakening him. If only I hadn't left for the weekend. But then I wouldn't have met Armin—a realization that caught me off guard.

The air in the small room grew moist and heavy. I recalled Pops saying, "Don't worry about what you'd do if you lived your life all over. Get busy with what's left." It occurred to me that it might be an Amish proverb, as could many of his snippets of advice.

I left the room, and moments later Rhoda followed me into the kitchen. "Are you all right?" she asked.

"Too many people in there." I reached around my waist to check the straight pins and was glad they were in place. What was I doing still wearing this getup? As I watched Rhoda slicing ham, I realized I enjoyed dressing like her, a woman who had never judged me on my looks. Unlike the rest of the world, none of the Amish cared if I wore designer jeans or the latest fashions. Hadn't I stood out from the crowd enough for one lifetime? And I'd grown accustomed to the feel of the dress's soft fabric against my legs.

Rhoda assembled ham, leftover meat loaf, pickles, and cheeses on a platter, and positioned it on the table. Yes, I'd like to emulate her, including wearing what she called her Kapp—prayer cap.

"Should I call everyone for supper?" I asked. Unsure how many were dining, I brought out nine plates and placed them around the table.

"We best let Bishop Troyer have his say first." She handed me flatware. "I pray he'll steer both men on the right course."

"Good luck when it comes to my father. I doubt he can distinguish the truth anymore." I laid out the plates as she delivered napkins.

"Yah, he can. I saw it in his eyes."

"You mean he knows where my mother is?"

"That's a different story." Her hands cupped her cheeks. "But he feels the conviction of the Holy Spirit. I can sense it."

"I'm blown away that you'd offer my father a kidney."

"He's my Bruder, so I assume I'd be a good fit. But I know little about DNA and transplants. And I'd have to receive the bishop's permission."

"It sounds like Bishop Troyer might forbid it."

"If he does, then of course, I'd have to follow his direction." She seemed older; for the first time I noticed crow's-feet etched at the corners of her eyes.

"I was planning to get my blood tested this week," I said.

"But now you're not going to?"

"I don't know." I couldn't bring myself to tell her my fears. If I asked to have a paternity test at the same time, it might settle two questions. Yet the thought of me being another man's child sent a shudder through my torso.

CHAPTER 26

With Rhoda directing me, I laid flatware on the table. Lizzie sashayed into the kitchen and took over, her movements graceful and automatic from a lifetime in this room. I wondered if she planned to make this her last meal here. Should I mention to Rhoda my suspicions that Lizzie was planning to run away? Maybe Rhoda already suspected.

"I could hear Bishop Troyer's and Dat's voices." Lizzie cut wholewheat bread without looking down to measure her even slices.

"They were talking to my father," I said.

"I hope Dat got everything squared away with the bishop."

"Yah, I think so," Rhoda said, "but I don't know the details."

Would I be here in two weeks when Reuben confessed his sins? Unlikely, and I wasn't a church member, so I doubted I'd be allowed to stay to listen to him anyway. The image of a humble Reuben on his knees refused to gel in my mind. How about my father? He was nowhere near ready to lay out all his sins. And even if he did, could I forgive him? I recalled reciting the Lord's Prayer in church: forgive us our trespasses as we forgive those who trespass against us.

I couldn't think of anything I needed to be forgiven for, which was probably a sin in itself.

Humming, Lizzie splayed the slices of bread on a plate and placed it on the table next to the butter and an assortment of jams and jellies. "How's about going to the Singing tonight, Sally?" she said to me.

"Only if Armin really wants to, and I don't think he does. Would you like to hear my opinion?"

"Nee, denki. I'm sure you have good enough reasons." Lizzie straightened the flatware I'd put out like soldiers in formation.

Reuben lumbered into the room and stood near the table. He looked dazed, oblivious to Lizzie, Rhoda, and me.

Minutes later, Bishop Troyer came into the kitchen wearing a dour expression.

"Would you like to stay for supper?" Rhoda asked him in monotone. "Nothing special, but we'd be happy to have you."

"Thank you, but I must get home. My sons do the milking, but my Lillian will start fretting about me."

Rhoda gazed up into his somber face and asked, "Would you let me know about donating a kidney?"

"It seems you're getting ahead of yourself, Rhoda. But I'll not discourage Ezekiel from seeking medical help. I doubt I have much influence over him. Although, I did sense a mellowing in him."

"It was kind of you to pay us a visit," Rhoda said. "Ich bedank mich."

"Yah, thank you," Reuben muttered. "I'll come outside with you to make sure my sons get your horse from the barn."

"No, thank you. I can do it myself." He put on his coat and hat, and left. As soon as the bishop was outside, the house seemed to let out its breath, some of the tense air leaving with him.

"Does Armin eat with you every night?" I asked.

"Usually." The corners of Reuben's mouth tipped down—a look of disapproval souring his face. "But he has Amish friends." It was obvious that he wanted my father and me out of this house immediately. We were nothing but a bad influence on his family; that was a truth. And yet he must've known his daughter had enticed me in to coming here. That tangle of oblique happenstance still rocketed through my mind.

"Sally is going to work in the store tomorrow," Lizzie said, her voice aflutter.

"I suppose I'd rather have her working there than you, Lizzie," Reuben said.

I glanced down at my apron. "But what will I wear?"

"Ach, Sally, I'm sorry I forgot to wash your clothing yesterday," Rhoda told me. "How could I let myself get so verhoodled? Tomorrow is laundry day."

"But she looks so pretty dressed this away." Lizzie clasped her hands together at chest level. "Those tourists won't know the difference."

Reuben harrumphed.

"If I dress Amish, the bishop's wife is sure to stop by again and then report me to her husband," I told Lizzie. "He informed me it was wrong to pretend to be Amish to make money."

"But surely she can work at the shop." Lizzie laced her fingers together, rested her chin on them. "Sally said she needs the money."

I had? Maybe I did mention my financial crisis when admiring the books.

Reuben rotated his head toward Rhoda. "I'm going to read *Family Life*, unless you gave that magazine to your Bruder too."

"Nee, it's right on the table." Rhoda followed him into the living room.

Lizzie grinned. "Then it's all set," she said to me. "We'll ask Armin or one of my brothers to give you a ride tomorrow morning."

"But I have a car again," I said. "As long as the streets aren't too slick."

"They'll still be icy. And don't you prefer the buggy?"

"I guess." It might be my last chance. "But what should I wear? Bishop Troyer said I shouldn't dress Amish at work."

Lizzie sidled over to me and spoke into my ear, "Never ya mind. I have a stash upstairs."

"Of clothing my size?"

"Yah, that I picked up here and there."

"I know all about them." Rhoda strode back into the room. "It's time to get rid of those fancy Englisch outfits. Your running-around days are officially over."

Lizzie shrank back. "Yes, Mamm."

If Rhoda knew half the story, she'd be appalled. I weighed my options. To whom did I hold my allegiance? To crafty Lizzie or faithful Rhoda, who'd demonstrated loyalty to Pops and to me?

"Mrs. Martin is going to be so grateful you'll be working for her," Lizzie told me, sidestepping her mother's queries.

"Are you sure your clothes will fit me?" I asked.

"Yah, upstairs I've got a green mid-calf length skirt with an elastic waist, a blouse, and a knit top that are all too big for me."

Rhoda shook her head. "You're putting Sally in an awkward position."

I juggled the pros and cons. Pops would be here in the morning when I woke up. If I worked at the secondhand store, I'd have something to fill my day other than trying to cajole him into seeing a doctor and fretting. And maybe I'd get to know some of the locals who would remember Mavis Miller—if that were indeed her name. If her parents were still alive, I imagined myself going to their home and having them turn me away in disbelief. But I was determined to persevere until I exhumed the truth.

"Do I have time to take Sally up and show her the clothes?" Lizzie asked. "Nee, I should call Mrs. Martin first."

"Use the phone shanty on a night like this?" Rhoda brought napkins to the table.

"Want to use my cell phone?" I asked.

"Not in the house." She jabbed her arms into her coat sleeves and grabbed her hat. "I can find the way. I did all winter. I'll take the flashlight with the new batteries." Her voice sounded joyous, as if she had the best news in the world to impart.

"Should I bring Ginger with me?" I wondered aloud. "Or is she better off here?"

"Armin wouldn't mind, Sally," Lizzie said. "You want to come out with me and ask him?"

Rhoda linked her arm through the crook of my elbow. "Sally should stay here with me. But hurry, will ya, Lizzie, so you don't keep your father waiting on his meal when Jeremy and Peter are done milking."

Lizzie skittered out the back door. I felt as though I'd been set up like a pawn in an ill-fated chess game. But I actually looked forward to working in the store again.

"I'll make up a plate of supper for Ezekiel and bring it in to him." Rhoda winked. "And whilst I'm in there, I'll take the keys to his automobile for safekeeping so he doesn't try leaving during the night."

CHAPTER 27

Thirty minutes later, I sat at the kitchen table nibbling my supper. With Pops still sprawled in bed, I felt vulnerable, as if an impending plague was festering on the other side of the house and would soon seep under the door and contaminate us. What was I thinking? I was already contaminated.

I was glad to have Armin sitting next to me and Rhoda across the table. My grandparents had opted to eat their supper with Pops, balancing their plates on trays they would set on their laps. The rest of us consumed our food silently, except for Rhoda occasionally offering pickled beets or sliced cheese to one of us. No one seemed to have an appetite, except Peter and Jeremy, who'd come in from milking. I certainly didn't. Every once in a while, Reuben rubbed his eyes and forehead. I wondered where his thoughts lay.

Lizzie perched across from me, between Rhoda and Peter. Lizzie craned her neck to see the wall clock, then turned back and spoke to

Jeremy, who sat next to me. "Are ya going to the Singing tonight?" she asked him.

"Yah, I was planning to."

"Would there be room in the buggy for me?"

"Nee. I'm giving someone a ride." He shoveled into his coleslaw, filling his mouth.

"Anyone we know?" Lizzie wiggled her eyebrows.

"Hush, now," Rhoda said. "I'm happy he's going."

"But how about me?" Lizzie said, her voice shrill.

"You're stayin' home where we can keep an eye on you," Reuben said.

"But, Dat—"

Rhoda clucked. "You've refused to go to a Singing for two months, and now on this icy evening, you suddenly wish to?"

"Mamm, I'm doing everything you and Dat want me to. I don't have a job to look forward to tomorrow, so what does it matter if I stay up late? Can't I have any fun at all? How do you expect me to meet my future husband?"

"You've decided you're ready to get married?" Reuben tossed her a look of skepticism, his eyes rolling. "It's about time."

I felt like a traitor sitting in their midst, knowing what I knew about Joe and not saying anything.

"Who was that young man who stopped in the store yesterday?" Rhoda asked. Lizzie winced. "Yah, news travels quickly, Daughter."

"Just somebody I knew from school." Lizzie dabbed her mouth with her napkin.

"Someone who drives a car?" Her upper lip curled. "Please tell me it isn't that *rilpsich*—rude—Joe Stoltzfus. He's nothing but trouble, Lizzie."

A lopsided smile took over Jeremy's face, and Peter snickered.

"You wouldn't up and do something crazy, would you?" Reuben's callused hand balled into a fist on the table.

"Dat, if you'd like to come with me to the Singing you're welcome." Lizzie sent him a furtive glance. "Actually the solution is right here." She tilted her head in Armin's direction. "Ask Armin and Sally to be my chaperones."

I felt Armin's elbow nudge mine. "I suppose I could drive you there," he said, "but I won't be held responsible for your actions, Liz." Armin turned my way. "How about it, Sally? Are you curious enough to come along?"

I considered my alternatives. "Could I go dressed like this?"

"Are ya kidding?" Lizzie's demeanor turned festive, her fingertips tapping each other. "There will be young men and women from all over the county, and none of them will pay mind to how you're dressed. You went to church that away."

"But I told you what the bishop said."

"You won't be selling anything, will ya?" Lizzie's hand covered her mouth and she giggled. She really was a conniver. I wondered if I should put the brakes on this whole escapade.

"I don't want to be Lizzie's babysitter either," I said to Rhoda, "but if it would help you out, I could go." I was curious about the get-together and wanted to spend time with Armin.

Reuben set his elbows on the table. "All right, Lizzie, you may stay for two hours, then come home. No excuses."

"I can't imagine what you're all so riled up about." Lizzie got to her feet and commenced to clear the table with a flourish.

"My, you sure are in a hurry," Peter said, and gobbled a mouthful of meat-loaf sandwich.

"If you don't like the way I clear the table, you may do it."

"Yah, then you come out to the barn tomorrow morning and milk the cows."

"Dat, you see how he teases me?" A pout took over her mouth. "It's no wonder I want time away from the house."

An hour later, the evening sun cast shadows into the barnyard as the sun slid behind the hills to the west. After a ten-minute ride—Thunder's hooves crunching through layers of ice—Armin and I remained in the family buggy outside the barn at the same house where we'd attended church earlier that morning. The interior of the lofty structure was illuminated by what must've been gas or propane lamps casting a yellowish light. Aromas of hay and manure floated in the chilly air, but I didn't mind them in the least. I'd borrowed Rhoda's long wool coat and her bonnet.

Holding the reins through the open rectangle with one hand, Armin passed me a lap blanket, and I tucked it around my legs.

"Thanks. It feels like it's below freezing." I could see poofs of my breath when I spoke. "Why would they sing in a barn?"

"More freedom. They don't want their parents watching their every move. But adults wander in now and again."

I heard a German hymn gathering volume—sung a cappella—one I recalled from my youth, which filled my heart with gladness. Contentment eased over me. With Armin at my side, I felt protected. He seemed a man able to accomplish any task he put his mind to. He understood what I'd been through. What I was still going through. No other man I'd ever dated, Donald included, would have braved a snowstorm in a horse and buggy. Not that any other man I knew owned one. But that made Armin's deed all the more valiant.

"Do young Amish men and women really find their future spouses at these affairs, even at age sixteen?"

"Many do, and it's not such a bad idea if you think about it."

I gazed out the buggy's window and saw stars inhabiting the indigo sky. I considered all the ways young men and women met each other in the outside world. I'd encountered Donald on Lake Candlewood in Connecticut. A startling thought volleyed through my mind: Was this my new reality?

"Do you want to go inside?" I asked.

"Nee, I've already found the woman I want to spend the evening with."

I turned toward him and tried to discern if he was joking, but it was too dark. "Me?" I said.

"Yah, I'm serious." He leaned closer.

My heartbeat, the earth's revolving, everything slowed down as my world narrowed into nothing but him.

"You told the bishop you were going to get baptized in the fall," I said.

"Yes, and right after that is the wedding season."

My jaw dropped open in an unladylike fashion. "Are you getting married?"

"I don't know yet."

I'd heard the term *on the rebound*, which made me think of a bouncy ball ricocheting off the walls and ceiling. Was I the first single woman to happen by? No, not from what Lizzie told me of the many young women who were trying to entice Armin into marriage.

He brought my fingers to his lips. "Will ya think about spending time together getting to know each other better?" His voice flowed smooth and steady.

When I didn't answer, he said, "Would you at least consider it?"

Speechless, I nodded. I couldn't help but be flattered. Never had I met a more captivating man.

CHAPTER 28

The next day I enjoyed working in the secondhand shop more than I thought I would, even if I were fretting about Pops. When I'd left the house in the foggy morning, he was still bedridden. Or so he'd said. Rhoda had promised to call from the shanty phone if his condition worsened.

I helped customers and learned the art of running a consignment shop. An Amish woman who said she often brought Mrs. Martin merchandise arrived with several vintage quilts already priced, but beyond that, I was helpless to stock anything. Mrs. Martin finally called and attempted to answer my questions about pricing a box of used books. She told me to do my best and thanked me profusely, but I warned her she'd need to find my replacement in the near future.

As the hours meandered by, I wasn't surprised when the bishop's wife strolled in and looked the place over. I assumed she was scouting for Lizzie, but she made pleasant conversation and remembered my name, making me wonder if Bishop Troyer had discussed my father. "You may call me Lillian," she said.

"Thank you, Lillian." She was the only customer at the time, so I gathered my courage and said, "I don't suppose you know anything about my mother, Mavis Miller?"

Her frame went rigid. "I recall your dat, but—"

The bell on the door clanked and several women entered the store, zeroed in on the new quilts, and inquired about their prices and history. "They should be marked," I said, hoping the women would be on their way so I could speak to Lillian again. But the next time I looked up, she'd departed.

Throughout the day the fog lifted, exposing an azure sky with small tufts of feather-like clouds, reminding me of an impressionist painting. Warm air was moving in from the south, melting most of the snow that had nearly paralyzed the county yesterday. Yet I had no desire to hop in the Mustang and head home. While nibbling the sandwich Rhoda had packed for me, I pondered whether I could be content living in this world of horse and buggy, where life moved at half time.

Hours later, at five, I closed the shop. I locked the persnickety front door and gave it an extra tug. I recalled my first evening here, helping Lizzie coax the lock, and was glad she'd come home from the Singing the previous night with Armin and me. Apparently, her dreamboat hadn't been there.

At that moment, I spied a blue Chevy compact motoring in my direction. As it passed I noticed a missing hubcap and recognized the dent on its fender. I could make out Joe's profile and a non-Amish brunette cuddled next to him. He must not have seen me, because he slowed and lifted a bottle to his mouth, then kissed her before speeding away.

Now what? Should I tell Lizzie? If I did, would she believe me? She was not a young woman easily deterred, and might even find Joe more desirable if someone else also wanted him.

Jeremy should have been waiting for me in the parking lot as Reuben had dictated to him this morning. But I was delighted when I rounded the building and spotted Armin standing by his open buggy and Thunder.

Ginger belted out a bark. I'd left her at Armin's. He and Lizzie had promised to look after her, and the veterinarian was scheduled to come by in the afternoon. Armin assured me Zach would check her over thoroughly.

Armin proffered his hand and helped me climb in next to Ginger and a boisterous mutt—a handsome collie mix with a black muzzle.

"I'd like you to meet my Rascal." The large dog waved his plumed tail. "He came around my brother's today looking for me. I knew Rascal would come home eventually."

"That's wonderful." I flattened my palm for the dog to sniff.

"He and Ginger have been playing together like they've been buddies their whole lives." Armin untied Thunder and the horse tossed its luxurious mane. His glossy coat looked to be recently brushed.

"So, Rascal, you came home to your master." The dog seemed congenial.

"Yah, here to stay." Armin gripped the reins to steady Thunder.

"What's to keep him from running way again?"

"He never will. Not with Ginger and you here to keep him company." Rascal jumped behind us and draped his neck over the seat's back. Ginger remained snuggled next to me.

"Did the vet show up today?" I asked.

"Yah." Armin's lips curved into a smile.

"What did he say about Ginger?" She nosed into me for attention, and I stroked her under the chin.

"Zach Fleming is full of himself, but he knows his stuff. He said Ginger is expecting a small litter in two weeks."

"I can't believe it. That means the puppies' sire must be Mr. Big." I felt like weeping for joy.

"What kind of Hund was your Mr. Big?" Armin asked. "A Great Dane?"

"No, a Pembroke Welsh corgi like Ginger."

Armin muffled a belly laugh. "Yet you called him Mr. Big?"

"Yup." I couldn't wipe the grin off my face. "I named him Mr. Big for fun."

"It's been a fine gut day all 'round." Armin climbed into the buggy. "Mei Bruder, Nathaniel, and I got to talking, and we worked the whole thing out. His wife Esther's—well, her mother Anna's old vacant home—is legally mine. 'Tis in writing. I now own the house and barn and forty acres, without strings."

"Congratulations," I said. "That's fantastic."

"And I've been thinking about you all day, Sally."

"Did you worry I'd blow it at the secondhand shop?"

"Nee." He took up the reins as Thunder pranced in place. "I was worried you'd like working there so much you'd never want to quit and stay home to become a housewife."

"What—?" My words caught in my throat. "What are you talking about?"

"Isn't that what Englisch call a woman who stays home to cook and mind the children?"

This discussion was whizzing along too quickly. He couldn't be referring to the two of us.

"Are you having fun at my expense?" I tried to see what lay behind his coffee-brown eyes, into the depths of his soul.

He stared back without blinking. "I'm as serious as can be. I want to court you. I have since the moment I first laid eyes on you."

"As in dating?"

"Yah. Serious dating." His words were as sweet as cotton candy, but our relationship would never work for a myriad of reasons. His gaze fastened on to mine, practically devouring me. He leaned closer until I thought he might kiss me. I couldn't help but notice he had beautiful full lips, straight white teeth, a perfect mouth. But I must not become involved with him, I warned myself.

Thunder's hoof pawed the ground, splintering the fragile moment. "Whoa, now." Armin jerked away to steady the horse. Then he steered the buggy out of the parking lot and onto the road.

With Armin working the reins, we rolled over asphalt still covered with patches of snow and ice. My thoughts leaped about like acrobats. Listening to the clip-clop, clip-clop, I inhaled the scent of impending spring: damp, fertilized soil, sprouts burrowing toward the light, farm animals—an intoxicating fragrance like no other. As it had been the night of my arrival. I wondered if the newly planted alfalfa had survived the snow. The trees' bare limbs seemed to bulge with new growth. Was it possible for leaves to push their way through the bark in one day? I'd always discounted love at first sight. Was it possible to fall in love with someone so quickly? No, I couldn't be falling for Armin, a near-stranger.

"Are you still planning to have supper with your brother and his wife tonight?" I hoped to change the subject.

"Yah, and I want you to come meet his Esther."

"Are you sure that's a good idea?" Esther and Nathaniel would probably disapprove of anyone not Amish—not that I'd blame them.

"And wait until you see my new house after we eat supper," Armin said. "Well, now, it's not new. It was in Esther's family for many a year. But it's as fine gut a house as you'll ever see."

"When are you moving out of the cabin?"

"Tomorrow."

"What will I do with Ginger?"

"Reuben said she could join the family in the house. It appears he's finally met a dog he's not allergic to."

"Really? Are you sure?"

"Yah, he told me so himself."

Ten minutes later, we arrived at the Zooks' farm and entered the barnyard. I was blown away to see my father lounging on a chair at the bottom of the steps, soaking up the last rays of the lingering sunlight. A quilt wrapped his shoulders and a blanket covered his legs. Pops raised a hand, and Armin slowed the buggy for me to jump out.

"You wait here with me, peewee," Armin said to Ginger, and my dog obeyed.

I stood for a moment in indecision. I had no idea how to react to my father. All day, the bishop's words about forgiveness had wafted through my thoughts, but deep in my heart lingered a dormant seed of resentment like a wad of chewing gum in my stomach.

"Hi, Pops." I noticed a folding chair next to him.

"Hey there, Sally girl." His cheeks wore a healthy glow and his voice was strong—not the man I'd left this morning. "Sorry about the Mustang," he said. "I replaced the battery."

"But I gave the key to Armin."

"I brought a spare one with me."

"The roads are so slippery."

"But not for a horse and buggy?"

I glared down at him; I would not be sidetracked by his banter.

He patted the other seat. "Rhoda insisted I come outside for a bit. She's in the kitchen. She's been stuffing me with food all day."

I lowered myself next to him. "I'm surprised you're still here. Why didn't you head home?"

"My parents—Leah and Leonard—insisted I let Rhoda nurse me back to health. If anyone can, it's my *Schweschder*." The fact my father was speaking Pennsylvania Dutch hit me like a rainsquall on a cloudless day.

"Rhodie called my doctor in Danbury and is having my medical records sent to a local clinic in Lancaster." His eyes pooled with moisture. "I'll go see him later this week."

"I could drive you," I said.

"She's already arranged for a van to take us. A Mennonite driver."

"That's good. Do you want me to come with you?"

"Naw, I'll be fine. And while Rhoda was in the phone shanty, I used my cell phone to call Ralph." His voice cracked. "Ralph said he and his wife and sons will run the car lot for as long as I need." He pinched between his eyes. "I asked Ralph to be my business partner, and he agreed. I should have done it years ago."

From a distance, I watched Armin detach the buggy's wooden shafts from Thunder. Ginger seemed content to hang out with Rascal, who tailed Armin and Thunder into the barn. "I'm planning to stick around here until the end of the week if the Zooks will have me," I said. "Or I'll sleep in the back room at the store where I work."

"What's your real motive for staying?" He cocooned into the quilt. "Trying to track down your mother?"

"I guess, partly." I still held hopes Pops knew where she lived. I waited for a few moments, wishing he'd come clean. But no such luck.

"Armin says he wants to spend time with me," I finally said. "Hard to do long-distance dating when the man drives a horse and buggy."

"Knock me over with a feather." He slapped at his knee. "You prefer an Amishman over big-shot Donald? Now I've heard everything."

I crossed my legs, then uncrossed them. "Would you be opposed?"

"I suppose I like Armin better. But if you married Armin, you'd have to join the church. Unless he doesn't join."

"I think he will."

Pops clasped the quilt to his rib cage. "I'm the last man on earth who has a right to give out spiritual counsel, but you're jumping into this too quickly. Think of all you'd be giving up."

"If you could do it all over again, would you have left?" I asked.

"No use fretting about the past when we can't change it. You, on the other hand, have your whole future ahead of you. Don't commit to a man and a lifestyle you know nothing about."

"I'm not planning to marry him tomorrow." As the sun lowered behind the forested hills, I gazed at the remnants of the sun's radiance. "I like Rhoda so much." And Armin. He'd captured my heart. The jury was still out when it came to Lizzie. No, I liked her in spite of what Pops would label her monkey business. She and Pops shared several dubious character traits. Somehow, she'd reeled me into her home, landed me a job, and introduced me to Armin, a man few women could resist.

As I watched Armin exit the barn, I felt a knot coiling at the back of my throat. I'd almost married the wrong man. I shouldn't walk off a cliff blindfolded unless I knew for certain a safety net was at the bottom to catch me. I hadn't even broken off Donald's and my engagement. I needed to return his ring in person.

But I couldn't leave Pops. "Maybe I should drive us both home," I said to him.

"No, I'm sticking around, since it's all arranged."

"You're comfortable living under Reuben's roof?"

He crossed his legs at the ankles. "After tomorrow, if I'm strong enough, I'll sleep in Armin's cabin."

"No way. It's too cold." I hugged myself to ward off the chill air.

"Nee, it isn't. He has a woodstove. Besides, spring's right around the corner. Remember, I grew up without electricity."

"How can I remember something I never knew?" The prickly feeling I'd lived with most of my life besieged me like a case of poison ivy. I needed space. "Fine, you do what you want. I need to drive home next weekend to take care of some unfinished business."

"How will you get there?" Pops cocked his head. "That Mustang belongs to me."

"But you gave me permission to use it."

"That was then and this is now."

As Armin strode toward Pops and me, I felt a magnetic pull. He came to a stop several yards away, Ginger and Rascal at his side.

"Ed, gut ta see you," Armin said to Pops and reached out to shake his hand. My father obliged with an apathetic shake.

"Are you the man who wants to steal my daughter away?"

"I suggested we spend time together."

My father guffawed. "What are you talking about? You barely know each other."

"I know her well enough."

"You don't know nothing," Pops said in a mocking voice, reminding me of the quarrelsome crows out in the field.

Armin widened his stance. "I know more than you think I do."

"Stop it, you two." I sprang to my feet. "I'll choose where I go and with whom."

"Yah, okay," Armin said. "Sorry, Ed, if I offended you." Armin turned to me. "Are you still coming to my brother's tonight for supper? And after, to see my new house?"

"Yes. I'd like that."

"Gut, I'll be back for you in an hour."

As he strode toward his cabin, Ginger wandered over to Rascal, who bowed before her, bringing his head to her level to initiate play. She'd certainly adapted to life on the farm as if she'd spent her life here. But I was not a Welsh corgi. I was a woman who needed to make rational, practical choices. Perhaps Pops was right: I was acting irrationally. I recalled the saying "Follow your heart" and decided I'd already done enough of that to last me a lifetime, without results.

Look at me: single, no kids, no career. I'd always relied on a man to be my fallback cushion—Pops, and then Donald. Maybe I should live by myself with Ginger. But if I stayed single in my twenties and thirties, my chance for children might pass me by. I'd seen it happen. A neighbor in New Milford had dated a guy for nine years; by the time they split up and she found someone new, she was unable to bear children. A cruel twist of fate, yet one of her doing—according to her.

But was dating Armin as loco as Pops made it sound? Yet I had to admit I was terribly attracted to Armin. Would I prefer him wearing a Wall Street pinstriped suit and an Ivy League tie like Donald, and driving an Audi instead of his horse and buggy?

Not really.

CHAPTER 29

An hour later, Armin and I set off on foot to his brother's home for supper. Except for occasional slivers of moonlight piercing the clouds, the sky was gunmetal gray, making it hard to see the patches of icy snow still littering the ground.

I was glad I'd borrowed Rhoda's long black woolen coat and worn my clothes from work—my laundered jeans hadn't dried thoroughly. But chilly air billowed up my skirt, prompting me to keep pace with Armin's long strides. I was fatigued from standing all day and waiting on customers, but I kept plodding along, all the while wishing I'd brought a flashlight.

I thought Armin might engage me in conversation, but he stuffed his hands into his pockets, hunched his shoulders, and stared straight ahead as if ready to face a firing squad. Was he fuming over my going back to Connecticut for the weekend?

We took a left into a lane alongside a stately white house as the moon glimmered through the clouds; a magnificent barn, silos, and a windmill stood like sentinels behind it.

"Here it is." Armin slowed his pace. We entered the barnyard and climbed the back stairs. Armin opened a door, guided me into the dimly lit utility room housing a brigade of work boots, tools, and an old-fashioned washing machine.

He stepped aside and I passed him. "I used to live here," he said. "With Nathaniel before he wed Esther."

"So I hear." Lizzie had briefly explained that Esther, a widow, recently married Nathaniel, a widower. Two lovebirds was how she'd described them.

Armin made no move to knock on the door, which I assumed led to the main house. Before I could ask him why he was hesitating, the door swung open and an Amish woman about Pops's age said, "Willkumm. Gut ta meet ya." She stood a couple of inches taller than I did and was clad in a turquoise-blue dress and black apron; her white prayer cap was neatly pressed and her hair parted down the center the same as Rhoda's. "I'm Esther King, Armin's sister-in-law." She didn't carry the same lilting accent as Rhoda and Lizzie. But Armin had mentioned Esther once lived on the West Coast. Somehow, she and her daughter, Holly, had ventured to the area to visit long-lost relatives after decades of absence, and stayed.

"Kumm rei," Esther said. "I mean, come in, won't ya, please." She shook my hand, her grasp firm but gentle, then peered around me to see Armin examining a propane lamp—lollygagging was what he was doing.

"Armin," she said, "don't you go changing your mind about staying for supper after I've been cooking all afternoon." Esther back-stepped into a spacious kitchen housing an oval table, ample cupboards, and counter space. A refrigerator and stove looked brand new. Quite impressive. My nostrils inhaled a myriad of scrumptious fragrances. A loaf of wheat bread and muffins still emitting steam sat on the counter.

Armin wandered in, removed his hat, and left it on a peg next to another straw hat—I assumed Nathaniel's.

"Have you met my husband?" Esther asked me as Nathaniel strolled into the room carrying a newspaper. She sent him a look that was nothing less than adoration. Her lashes fluttered and her green eyes shone with loveliness.

"Yes," I said. "Hi, Nathaniel."

"Good evening." He smiled, then narrowed his eyes at Armin. "Did ya bring that mutt along?" Nathaniel folded the newspaper in half and whacked the lip of the counter with it.

"Quit your worrying. He's in the cabin with Sally's little dog."

"Wait until your Rascal gets into Reuben's chicken coop. Sparks will fly." Nathaniel set the newspaper aside and lowered himself onto the chair at the head of the table.

"That won't happen, because I'll be moving into my new home," Armin said, hand on hip. "Unless you've changed your mind."

Nathaniel's brown beard swayed as he shook his head. "Nee, I'd never go back on my word. The house and property are yours."

Armin demonstrated not a pittance of gratitude. He glanced down at the table set for five. "Did you invite another guest?"

"Just Anna." Esther turned to me. "My mother lives in the Daadi Haus." Esther moved to the gas stove and switched off the heat. She opened the oven door and exhumed a bubbling casserole of cheese-covered noodles, filling the room with the aroma of melted cheddar, mushrooms, caramelized onions, and ground beef. She placed it on a cooling rack.

"Please, have a seat." Esther motioned to me toward a chair midway down the table. I marveled at the plethora of salads and relishes gracing the table's green-and-white–checked oilcloth.

A moment later, an aged Amish woman tottered into the kitchen.

"Sally, this is my mamm, Anna." Anna must have been well into her eighties, judging by her wrinkled face, silvery hair, and stooped posture. A white heart-shaped cap covered her head, its strings tied beneath her chin. Armin had explained that Anna had been ill in the past, but she looked fit, her eyes lively and riveted on me.

"Hello." Her glasses perched on her nose, she scanned my hair and clothing, then asked Esther, "Ya need help, Essie?"

"Nee, everything's ready. I hope you all have good appetites."

"Yes, I'm starving," I said with too much exuberance. Guess I had a case of the jitters.

Anna positioned herself across from me and gave me another looking over through her thick spectacles. Armin stood behind her and helped her walk her chair in to the table, then sat next to her. She patted his hand. "Denki," she said.

As the others chatted with me about the snow, Armin remained uncharacteristically taciturn. Lizzie had mentioned it was not the Amish way to show affection in front of others. But if he wasn't going to acknowledge my presence, why bring me? Maybe Armin was nervous around his big brother. Although he acted at ease with Esther and Anna.

"Armin, ya need help moving?" Nathaniel said.

"I don't think so, thanks all the same."

"I could ask some of my friends to come over."

"Then I suppose you'd want me to grovel and thank you profusely."

"Nee, you don't owe me a thing. If anything, I'm the one who needs forgiveness." Nathaniel turned to me. "From you, Sally. I should have come clean days ago." He gazed into my face with what seemed to be contrition and blinked several times. "I went poking around your red car the night you arrived. I only opened the door, then I heard you and Armin coming outside, so I decided I'd best skedaddle home. I didn't realize it had caused such a ruckus until yesterday when Esther heard about it from Rhoda. I thought Armin might be entertaining someone." Nathaniel flattened his napkin across his lap.

"You're the culprit?" Armin slapped the table. "Ya mean to tell me my big brother isn't perfect?"

"Now, Armin, he never said he was," Esther said. Although I could see in her eyes she thought he was as near to perfect as a mortal could be.

Nathaniel swiped his hand across his mouth. "I'm sorry and hope you can forgive me, Sally."

"No big deal," I said, as I recalled the relentless downpour and my ruined shoes. "I overreacted. In hindsight, I should have borrowed a pair of boots."

He turned to Armin. "And you, too, Armin. I'm sorry. I had no business snooping into your personal affairs."

"That's the truth." Armin chortled. "Old habits die hard. Yah?"

"Come on, Armin," Anna said with a playful grin. "Your brother told you he was sorry."

"He says he's sorry for something, like grousing at me when he found out his precious standardbred Galahad ran away, then he turns around and does it again."

Anna tsked. "I can think of a few pranks you've pulled and have yet to admit, Armin."

"And we love you just the same," Esther said. "Let's not ruin our time together by rehashing the past." She set the casserole on a trivet in the middle of the table and slid a serving spoon into the casserole's browned-to-perfection surface.

Nathaniel cleared his throat. "Shall we thank the good Lord from whom all blessings flow?" He bowed his head, and we all did the same. I peeked up to see Armin had also bent his head.

Nathaniel led us in a minute of silent prayer before he said, "Amen." I had a multitude of requests for the Lord, but all I could think about was making it through this meal without embarrassing myself. Or Armin, who was ignoring me as if I'd turned invisible. Did he regret bringing me?

"What's on your calendar?" Esther asked Armin as she served Nathaniel, then Anna, casserole.

"After I move, I'll buy draft horses."

"No one knows horses better than Armin," Anna said to me, the skin around her faded sage-green eyes creasing.

"Are you sure you wouldn't be better off with mules?" Nathaniel said. "They eat less and work harder."

"Doling out advice already, big brother?" Armin spooned up some coleslaw.

"I'm planning to bring one of my milking cows over to your barn tomorrow." Nathaniel served himself several pickles. "You'd best not forget to milk her."

"Can you wait on that for a few days?" Armin asked. "I'll have my hands full."

"Yah, you come over and get her when you want. I could lend you my extra bridles and plowing equipment. Come out to the barn after supper." He forked into a pickle and took a chomp. "I could lend you money, too."

"You think I'm destitute?"

"Nee, just trying to help."

"With this late spring, I can still prepare the land for planting corn as well as the next man," Armin said.

"Yah, this snow will set my alfalfa back weeks." Nathaniel dabbed the corner of his mouth with a napkin. "You should go organic, the way I do."

"I'll think about it," Armin said.

He declined dessert, but after consuming two servings of casserole and steamed vegetables, and a scoop of each salad—three-bean, coleslaw, and beet—I accepted a medley of whoopie pie, custard, and gingersnap cookies. So much for my waistline.

"Lizzie and I can help you set up your kitchen in your new house, if you like," Esther said to Armin as she topped off his coffee. "We left some essentials." She glanced my way. "Zach's and Nathaniel's homes were already stocked—both being bachelors so long. And Zach and my daughter, Holly, received so many wedding presents."

Armin shifted in his seat.

"Were you afraid we'd invited Holly tonight?" Anna asked him.

"Why would I care?" Armin's cheeks reddened.

Anna tsked. "Ach, no need to become tetchy."

"Zach says they're having a child," Armin said. "Are ya excited, Esther?"

"Oh, my, yes." A grin crept across her face.

Anna covered her mouth with her fingers, their joints knotted. "We shouldn't speak of such personal and private matters."

"With my Holly dressed Englisch, the whole world can see her full figure." Esther's countenance radiated happiness. "Finally, I'll cuddle a grandchild in my arms. I'm knitting a blanket for the bassinet."

"What color is it?" I asked.

"Yellow."

"It must've been the Lord's will that they wed," Anna said with a shrug, "although I'll never understand why."

"Zach is a gut man." Esther set more plates of gingersnap cookies, and chocolate and pumpkin whoopie pies on the table. "He's a fine husband to my daughter."

"I've been missing her ever so much," Anna said, and it occurred to me Armin did too. How could I have been so blind? Armin was pining over Esther's daughter. Was that why he wanted me here? To put on a false show of bravado for his family? To prove he'd moved on?

In spite of my turbulent thoughts, I finished my bounteous array of desserts, then helped Esther clear the table. She deposited scraps into a bucket for the hogs. "Nothing's wasted around here," she told me.

She moved to the sink and commenced washing the dishes and pots while Armin and Nathaniel trekked out to the barn to inspect the extra bridles he'd offered to give Armin. He seemed to be more than generous with Armin, but I could tell by their stilted conversation that bad blood rivered between the brothers. I wondered if Armin were the type of man who ran hot and cold.

I stood and asked Esther for a towel to dry the dishes while Anna sat at the table nursing her coffee. Now was my chance to ask about my mother. I told myself to go ahead and plunge into the frothy water the way Esther was immersing the dirty flatware.

"Esther?" I said. "I assume you and Anna have heard about my father returning."

Esther nodded as she scrubbed the serving spoon.

"Did either of you know him when he was young?" I asked.

"Yah, I remember him," Anna said, and added a tablespoon of sugar to her coffee.

"Now, Mamm." Esther pivoted to her mother. "Ya know your memory is sometimes fuzzy."

"Not anymore. Not since my surgery. Ask me anything. I could answer all the doctor's questions at my last appointment. My memory's as good as new. Let me see ..." She straightened her prayer cap with speckled hands. "Yah, I recall Leah and Leonard's Ezekiel."

Esther seemed ill at ease as she scrubbed the bottom of a pan. "We heard from Reuben that your father's staying with them," she said to me.

"But he wouldn't attend church yesterday," Anna said. "According to Leah, the bishop visited Ezekiel in the afternoon, but he gave the bishop the brush-off."

"Mamm, remember what the minister preached about last month? Exodus 20:16. 'Thou shalt not bear false witness against your neighbor.'"

Anna's mouth narrowed. "Telling the facts isn't bearing false witness, Essie. In fact, we are admonished to speak truthfully. Leah told me about Ezekiel today."

I couldn't let this stellar opportunity bypass me. I parked myself on the chair next to Anna. "If you know anything about my mother, please tell me."

"Your mamm?" Anna wagged her head. "I don't believe I knew who she was. But it's not unusual for our young people to go about their own way during their running-around years."

"But we must not hold past indiscretions against those who return to the fold," Esther said. She unplugged the basin; the water gurgled down the drain.

"Yah, you're living proof of that." Anna sipped her coffee. "When they return and ask for forgiveness."

"But do you remember a girl named Mavis Miller?" Speaking her name made the inside of my mouth burn as if I'd consumed chili-pepper paste.

"Nee." Anna shook her head. "But I'd be lying if I told you your father's name hasn't come up. There's speculation that he—"

A rap-rap on the kitchen door startled me. The knob turned, the door swung open, and an attractive brunette dressed in a loose-fitting flowered dress and a jacket strolled into the room as if well acquainted with the house. She carried a paper bag.

"Hi, Mom." Her jacket wouldn't close in the front—her tummy curved as only a pregnant woman's can. At the beautiful sight, a welling deep inside me for a child of my own expanded.

"We didn't hear your car," Esther said, taking the bag. "Aren't the roads slippery? Ach, you shouldn't be out on such a night." Esther set the bag on a vacant chair.

"It's four-wheel-drive, and I inched along like a turtle."

"Holly, liebe." Anna beamed up at her granddaughter. "I've been missing you so."

"Hi, Mommy Anna. Here's the fabric you wanted." Holly kissed Anna's cheek. Then Holly noticed me. "Sorry, I didn't know you had a guest."

"Sally, this is my daughter, Holly Fleming," Esther said. "Holly, this is Armin's friend, Sally."

"Oh?" Holly gave me a skeptical looking over. I suddenly felt inferior in her eyes.

At that moment, footsteps tromped through the utility room.

"Actually, we have two guests," Esther said, and Holly's mouth flattened.

I heard Armin's and Nathaniel's voices intermingling. Armin stopped when he crossed the threshold to the kitchen. For a moment he and Holly stared at each other as if a palpable current ran between them.

"Long time no see," Armin finally said, not removing his hat.

"How're ya doing?" Holly smoothed her hand over her round belly. "Couldn't be better."

As if coming to their rescue, Nathaniel edged over to them and said, "Yah, Armin is moving into Anna's. Gonna make a go of it as a farmer."

"I'm glad," Holly said. "I hope you're very happy, Armin."

"Yah, I will be. Don't ya worry." He spoke to Esther. "Thanks for the *appeditlich*—delicious—meal. We'd best be on our way."

"Leaving so soon?" Esther said. "Thank you both for coming." As she handed me my coat, her gaze lingered on mine. "Nice to meet you, Sally."

"Thanks for having me." I had many unanswered questions clamoring to make themselves heard but decided to come back by myself when neither Armin nor Nathaniel were here.

"Good-bye," Holly said, not looking up from a swatch of eggplant-colored fabric she was unfolding for Anna to view. Holly seemed to have everything I longed for—a husband, a baby on the way, an extended family, and a mother who adored her.

Armin and I stepped into the night. The sky had cleared, the waning moon illuminating our path. The temperature had dipped. Our footsteps crunched and the soles of my shoes slipped. I slid my hand through the crook of Armin's elbow to maintain my balance.

"Maybe this isn't the best night to see my new place," Armin said. "The house will be dark and cold as a tomb."

I glanced up at the halcyon moon and the star-studded galaxy. "I don't care. Just a peek?"

"The house will look better in daylight. And I left Rascal in the cabin."

"Lizzie said she'd let Ginger out. I'm sure she'll look after Rascal, too."

He steered us back to the Zooks'. "Nee, Rascal will track me down and then Nathaniel will have a fit."

I didn't buy his excuse. Why the abrupt turnaround when he'd been so eager to show me his new abode? Did Holly still own his heart? My hunch was that comparing me to her had catapulted him back into what Pops would call the lovesick blues.

We advanced along the side of the road. A truck whizzed by and Armin draped his arm around my shoulder, turning me away from the glaring headlamps.

I looked up into his face. "So, you had a thing going with Esther's daughter?" I asked. More a statement than a question.

"She had a fondness for me," Armin said. "But it never would've worked out. She wouldn't have been satisfied living on a farm."

"In other words, she broke it off."

"Nee, I did. And I don't appreciate your insinuating otherwise."

A car sped by, spraying up an arc of slush. He made no move to shield me.

"Why didn't you tell me ahead of time?" I said.

"How was I to know Holly would show up tonight?"

"What does that have to do with it? You're obviously still carrying a torch for her."

"I am not." He started toward the Zooks' and my hand slid from his elbow. "Don't say another word about it," he said.

On the walk home, I tried to center my concentration on staying upright and not being furious at Armin or jealous of Holly. Their relationship was ancient history; she was married and awaiting her first child. I shouldn't have been envious, but I was. What had happened to my joyful anticipation of spring?

CHAPTER 30

On Saturday morning, after an early breakfast, I told Rhoda I was driving back to Connecticut to pick up some clothes and check the mail. Truth was, I was so discouraged I didn't intend to return. Not unless Armin vaulted over here and begged me to stay this very instant.

He'd moved out of the cabin Tuesday morning. I'd worked all week and didn't see or hear from him, except passing him once in the Zooks' barnyard. He and Reuben had been speaking Pennsylvania Dutch and didn't switch to English.

I'd driven myself to work each day but received no pleasure from sitting behind the Mustang's wheel. Over suppers, Reuben and Rhoda had mentioned Armin had attended a livestock auction to buy draft horses. He was feeding them and settling new chicks in the coop, plus milking the cow Nathaniel had given him. Apparently Lizzie and Esther had gone to the grocery store and stocked up Armin's refrigerator and also dropped off several prepared meals, enough to last him through the week. Plus a cupboard full of canned vegetables and fruit. Armin was all set. He had no use for me. I doubted he'd given me two thoughts.

I packed my few belongings, scooped up Ginger, and headed out to the Mustang. I couldn't wait to escape all the uncertainty and heartache Armin was causing me.

Pops sat on the back stoop, his elbows on his knees, his hands cupping his chin. As I passed him I kissed his stubbly cheek. "Are you sure you're okay?" I asked.

"With Rhoda looking after me? Absolutely."

Lizzie and Rhoda escorted me to the Mustang. "I do hope you'll come back soon," Rhoda said. She placed a wicker basket containing sandwiches, fruit, and cookies on the passenger seat.

"Please tell us you will," Lizzie said, then hugged me.

"I honestly don't know. I could work at the car lot and earn twice the money I earn at the Sunflower Secondhand Store." Not that I hadn't enjoyed the store's ambience and its customers. But in New Milford I'd have quiet solitude to puzzle my life back together and care for Ginger's pups. And I needed to speak to Donald face-to-face instead of taking the coward's way out—no matter how he'd acted. As for Armin, I'd given up on him.

The sky grew ominous as a battalion of clouds moved in. But I didn't care.

"See ya," I said to Pops, and he raised a hand—not much of a farewell. And where was Armin? Maybe to him I was a wisp of a cloud that had dissipated into oblivion. An image of Armin atop Thunder charging over here to try to stop me entered my mind. But he didn't.

I slid the key into the Mustang's ignition. The engine rumbled to life, thank goodness. If the battery had been dead again, I might have screamed. I'd never been in such an irksome, awkward position. I felt as though I were on a boat without sails or motor, floating in the doldrums, a windless ocean of self-pity.

I tried to elevate my mood by singing. "Just can't wait to get on the road again," I crooned as I rolled out of the lane. One of Pops's favorite oldies, so I switched to singing the first verse of "Amazing Grace." Again? What was wrong with me?

My thoughts circled back to the Zooks' home, and to Armin. I missed him.

Several hours later, after crossing into Connecticut, I passed Honest Ed's Used Cars. The lot was buzzing with activity. Ralph had brought his two teenage sons to help him, and I saw his wife's silhouette in the small business office. I kept going until I reached our driveway and parked outside the kitchen. I helped Ginger exit the Mustang with the greatest of care. I wouldn't allow anything to injure her pups. I put her in the fenced run, gave her fresh water, then headed to the house for her food.

I brought my key to the kitchen door's lock, then noticed the door wasn't completely shut. Had Pops left in such a hurry he hadn't bothered to close it properly? I wondered if he were one click shy of dementia. I'd read that decreased mental sharpness was a symptom of kidney disease.

I stepped into the house and saw the square kitchen table and its two chairs sprawled on their sides, helter-skelter. The vinyl floor was littered with shards of glass and broken dishes. The place had been ransacked!

I glanced into the living room: the couch was also tipped and its cushions sprawled. Our plasma TV's screen had been bludgeoned, one of Mr. Big's Best in Group trophies lay on the floor in front of it, and the computer had been knocked off Pops's small desk. All my other trophies and our books, once housed in the cases on either side of the fireplace, had been toppled to the floor. Some fiend had gone on a rampage.

A spike of adrenaline gushed through me as I tried to imagine who would commit such a monstrous act. Had Pops left the door unlocked? No, I glanced into our laundry room, just off the kitchen, and saw the wooden door to the outside hanging at a tilt, the top hinge broken, as if a heavy shoulder or foot had kicked it in. Perhaps a group of teenage boys? Unlikely: Pops's bottle of scotch was still on the top shelf in the laundry room. And they surely would have taken the TV and computer.

Stunned by the wreckage, my lungs froze. My hand shaking, I fished out my cell phone. My hand shaking, I fished out my cell phone, turned it on, and called 911.

The operator asked me if anyone were still in the house. "I don't think so," I said, hearing a tremble in my voice.

"Are you alone?"

"Yes."

"I'll send a patrolman around. You wait outside."

Figuring the police would take a few minutes to get there, I called Ralph, who dashed over from the car lot. As he and I waited for a squad car, he filled me in on how the lot had fared in the past week. "Business has been hopping," Ralph said. "I've sold six cars." His wife, a certified CPA, was keeping the books. I'd heard that nature abhorred a vacuum; from what I could tell, the empty space we'd left had been filled. I didn't feel needed at Honest Ed's anymore.

"Have you seen anyone over here?" I asked him.

"Just your fiancé. I noticed his car several days ago but didn't think anything of it." He ran his fingers through his thinning hair. "I should have kept a better eye on the place, not just sent my son over to bring your mail to the lot."

Moments later, a patrolman arrived and did a walk-through. Ralph and I followed him. In my bedroom, my undergarments were strewn across the carpet. I felt queasy as I envisioned grubby hands pawing through my lingerie drawer. Its lid wrenched off, my jewelry box lay upside down on the floor. Not that I had anything of monetary value, but several pieces, like my charm bracelet and the locket Pops had given me on graduation day, held sentimental value. I'd always secretly hoped my mother had bought them for me.

Do any of these possessions matter anymore? I asked myself in an attempt to calm my racing thoughts and steady my galloping heart. Life was fleeting. On my deathbed, none of these items would matter. The reality of my dwelling here alone, even with my darling Ginger and her puppies, brought a shroud of doom.

The patrolman wrote out his report. When I told him my father and I hadn't been home for days, he shook his head. "Better make out a list of your lost possessions for your insurance company."

"I don't think we have that kind of insurance." I felt deflated, a balloon pinpricked.

"Can you think of anyone who would have done this?"

"I saw her fiancé's car over here a few days ago," Ralph said.

The officer took Donald's name and asked for the make of his automobile. "A disgruntled boyfriend?" the patrolman muttered. I'd dismissed the notion. Surely Donald wouldn't have done this.

"Are you all right, miss?" As the policeman spoke, his radio buzzed to life. He was being summoned elsewhere.

"I'm fine." Not true; there was nothing fine about me.

"In that case, I'll be on my way." He left for his squad car and rolled out of the drive.

My cell phone chimed. Glancing at the screen I saw Donald's name. I couldn't take more drama, but I needed to speak to him. "Hello, Donald."

"Finally." The word oozed with scorn.

I almost apologized, but how dumb was that? He owed me an apology.

"Were you at our house recently?" I asked.

"Yeah, I came by."

"And?"

"You mean the mess? Yes, I saw it."

"Why didn't you let me know?"

"Duh. I've been trying to call you." Derision darkened his voice. "Where have you been?"

"I don't owe you an explanation. Not after your tryst." I wondered how many other women had slipped between his sheets.

"Look, I came by to say I'm sorry. I made a mistake. I brought you roses."

I scanned the counter and saw no trace of them. "Why didn't you call the police?" I asked. "You could have at least tried to repair the broken door."

"And have your father get on my case? For all I knew, he'd locked himself out and kicked the door in, himself."

"And broken the TV and knocked the furniture over?"

"It's possible for a man to go nutsoid if he's pushed far enough." Donald spoke with such certainty a chill slithered up my spine. Was Donald that kind of man?

"I can't talk anymore," I told him. "I need to put this house back together." He started to say something, but I pushed the End button. I'd heard enough.

After I'd set the phone aside, I led Ginger into the laundry room where she turned a tight circle and plopped into her basket. "I need to get you fed, baby girl." I brought out canned food, added prenatal vitamins I had on hand, and filled her metal dish. I propped the back door closed with a box of Tide. For her own safety, I closed the sliding door between the kitchen and the laundry room, then sorted through my scattered clothes and stuffed the light-colored items into the washing machine. I added extra detergent, bleach, and hot water. They'd never be clean again—not really.

As I gathered clothing for the next load, Ralph and his son brought over a replacement door they'd picked up from Home Depot. They hung it and installed a deadbolt. I was grateful but felt no sense of peace. Whoever had done this was still out there.

Ralph handed me the new key. Then he and his son stood the kitchen table and couch upright. "Anything else we can do for you?" Ralph asked. "Want me to call your father?"

"That would be great." Or would it make Pops too anxious? He'd seemed so peaceful when I left. "Never mind, Ralph. I will." The woman speaking barely sounded like me—more like a bag lady twice my age—her words slurred. "Thanks, guys. I can't tell you how much I appreciate your help."

"I feel terrible this happened," Ralph said. "I should've come over here every day, but I didn't think to. Do you want me to stay here with you tonight?"

"No, I have Ginger to protect me."

"Maybe you should borrow a Doberman pinscher," he said with a shrug.

"Not such a bad idea. But I have pepper spray around here somewhere. At least I used to."

CHAPTER 31

As I swept shards of glass and debris from the kitchen floor, I couldn't shake the feeling I'd been violated. The image of a stranger's grubby hands pilfering through my personal belongings and trashing what he considered of no value filled me with revulsion. Was this a one-man crime? I'd heard of teenagers taking over temporarily vacant houses to party while the owners were out of town, but I saw no evidence of cigarette butts or booze.

I heard an automobile coast up and park behind the Mustang. I figured maybe it was the patrolman or that Ralph had returned. Ignoring Ginger's whining from the laundry room, I set the broom aside and went to the kitchen door. It occurred to me that Pops and I rarely used the front door, just like the Amish. Well, why should that surprise me? My father was Amish. That topsy-turvy reality still made me feel as if I'd just stepped off a merry-go-round.

I opened the door and saw Donald exiting his sleek black Audi S8 sedan. He wore a white Polo shirt and tan khakis. He strutted over to the back step, putting me at eye level with him. All the better for him to glare at me, but I was determined not to look away.

"My mother's having a hissy fit since I told her the wedding's off," Donald said, eyeing the pile of debris on the dustpan in my hand. "Her blood pressure's sky-high. If she has a stroke, I'll hold you responsible."

"Excuse me? You want me to fill your mother in that you've been sleeping with who knows how many women? Give me a break." I brought the dustpan to the plastic garbage receptacle under the sink; bits of broken glass and the handle of my favorite china teacup fell in, filling it.

"She won't believe you."

"I don't doubt that. You had me fooled." I set the dustpan on the floor, then tugged the plastic bag from the garbage container and tied the ends. I lugged it to the back door, and Donald took it to the large garbage can sitting outside. He stuffed the bag in, then replaced the cover. Judging from his smooth hands and manicured nails—the opposite of Armin's—he hadn't taken the garbage out in many years, if ever. But I wasn't being fair. I knew he'd been pampered; his parents had a live-in housekeeper and someone came to his apartment twice a week to clean.

"Thanks." I looked into his symmetrical face and recalled why I'd found him so appealing. He was what most unmarried women sought in a husband—wealthy, gregarious, a go-getter. But my attraction to him had dissipated like the melting gray snow back in Lancaster County.

He stepped into the room and scanned the kitchen with a look of disdain. "This place was a dump before this happened. I should

have made a U-turn the first night I came to pick you up for a date."
He scrubbed his hands with liquid soap next to the sink and dried
them on a paper towel, which he dropped on the counter.

At least the perpetrator hadn't unplugged the refrigerator, but
the door hadn't been closed all the way, allowing warm air inside.
I'd better face the fact: anything perishable was rotten. I opened the
refrigerator door and a wave of rancid air wafted out. A carton of
eggs, the milk, and a container of leftover chili were tipped on their
sides, their contents dribbling to the bottom of the fridge. Thinking
about someone taking the time to destroy our food filled me with
disgust. I recalled Esther's saving scraps for their hogs. Nothing
wasted.

"Yuck." Donald recoiled, revulsion distorting his features. "That
old fridge should be hauled off to the junkyard. It's a breeding ground
for bacteria, probably teeming with salmonella."

I shoved my hands into rubber gloves. Pops and I couldn't afford
a new refrigerator.

I stretched another plastic liner into the garbage bin and scooted
the rectangular container over to the refrigerator. Trying not to
inhale, I removed everything—either threw the food away or set it
on the counter. Then I brought out a bucket, squirted in Mr. Clean,
and filled it with hot water—the way I thought Rhoda would. The
sharp odor of scouring solvent filled the room.

Donald lingered close by. "While I was here the evening you
took off, I demanded to know the real reason why your mother
wasn't coming to our wedding."

"I told you she left when I was a baby. I haven't seen or heard
from her since."

"When I kept prodding, old Honest Ed let the truth slip, that he never married her."

Feeling the veins in my neck bulge, I swung around to face him. He smirked. "You know what that makes you?"

"Don't say it." I wanted to cover my ears, but my hands were encased in gloves.

"You're illegitimate." He aimed his index finger into my chest. "You, Miss High-and-Mighty, have been acting like a perfect little princess, as if you're too good to marry into my family." His words skewered into me.

"That wasn't my intention." I felt an ache under my breastbone · and moisture accumulating on my forehead.

"My family has a reputation to preserve." Donald poked my shoulder with his index finger. "Thank God our engagement wasn't announced in the paper," he said.

Hoping he'd vamoose, I turned to the sink, poured in an opened pint of half-and-half, and watched the putrid liquid slither down the pipe.

"It looks like your past is catching up with you," he said, goading me. Why didn't he leave?

"I did not knowingly deceive you, Donald." I noticed a couple bottles of beer Pops kept on hand for guests; they were tipped on their sides in the refrigerator but unopened. A teenager would've swigged one down. No, an adult had done this. A revolting thought.

"Why exactly were you here a few days ago?" I glanced over my shoulder and saw Donald's face—white and rigid—an ugly mask of anger, an expression I'd rarely witnessed before.

He edged closer. "Are you accusing me?"

"No, but I thought you might have seen something, like fresh tire tracks."

"Did you tell the police I'd been here?"

"Yes." I sniffed a cube of butter and decided I'd better discard it.

"You have your nerve," he said. I pivoted toward him. His eyes bulged as he grabbed hold of my upper arms, clamping them, hurting me. The butter jettisoned from my hand and skidded across the floor.

Fury rose up inside me. I tried to wriggle out of his grasp, but he lifted me off the ground. I was paralyzed, couldn't catch my breath. I should knee him or scream, Pops would tell me. But I felt helpless, like a snared rabbit. And who would hear my cry?

"Let me go!" I managed.

Finally, Donald loosened his grasp. Off balance, I stumbled backward, whacking my spine against the counter and landing on my rump.

"Leave this minute," I got out, afraid his anger would escalate.

Ginger barked from the laundry room. I heard her nails digging under the door, trying to work her way into the kitchen.

Donald turned toward the laundry room. "Shut up, you miserable mutt." Spittle flew from his mouth; he swiped his hand across it. I was horrified at the brutality that lay hidden behind his typically composed surface of charm.

"Don't speak to her that way," I said from the floor. "She's expecting a litter."

"Another one of your secrets?"

"I've never lied to you, Donald." A dull ache permeated my lower back and shoulders. I unfolded my legs, got to my knees, and hoisted myself to my feet. Then I passed him on wobbly legs and opened the door to the laundry room.

Ginger propelled herself into the kitchen—her short legs scrambling—and nipped Donald's ankle. I'd never seen one of my dogs bite a person before.

"Why you little—" Donald's leg swung out to kick her but missed, his foot hitting a cupboard door, cracking the wood.

"Don't you dare!" I said.

"Are you threatening me? I suppose you're going to call the police and attempt to have me arrested." Balancing on one leg, he bent his other and pulled down his argyle sock to examine his ankle. No evidence of broken skin or blood, for which I was thankful. "I should report your vicious dog." He hopped on one leg. "Have her put to sleep."

I didn't believe he was in pain. I, on the other hand, felt as though I'd been slammed against a wall. If only Pops were here.

Donald seemed to regain his usual I'm-cool-and-in-control deportment. He put his weight back on his supposedly hurt ankle. "Sorry I lost it, Sally. The strain—"

"You'd better go." I gathered up Ginger, held her to my chest. Both our hearts were beating triple time. I prayed she wouldn't go into early labor.

His lip lifted in a sneer. "You should have heard your father the other day." Donald snorted. "Good old Honest Ed isn't so happy-go-lucky when you're not around."

I wouldn't admit I'd seen Pops lose his temper a few times. On the car lot last year, on a rainy day after an ornery customer had haggled for an hour then walked away hurling insults, Pops had thrown a hubcap so hard it hydroplaned halfway across the lot. But I didn't believe for an instant he'd ruin our home.

"He's trailer trash," Donald said. "That's what he is."

Barbed missiles skated at the end of my tongue, but I feared he would retaliate. And I recalled the Amish minister last week speaking about turning the other cheek. I longed to be back in Lancaster County among the gentle Plain people.

"I'm done wasting my breath on you." His face blotched, he moved to the open door.

Much as I wanted him out of the house, I said, "Wait a second." I closeted Ginger in the laundry room and unzipped my purse. I fished to the bottom until I found my engagement ring. "Here, take this."

His hand snatched it away like a frog's tongue snagging a gnat and jammed it in his hip pocket, then he jogged out the door. A moment later, his tires spun out of the driveway.

CHAPTER 32

That evening, after spending hours scouring and mopping the kitchen, I remade my bed with clean sheets and started an Amish novel I'd brought home from the store. I had a fitful night's sleep, even with the bed lamp on and the pepper spray in the nightstand drawer. I'd located the small vial and my locket—flattened and its chain broken—under my bed's dust ruffle, along with a ritzy Montblanc fountain pen that looked like the one Donald owned.

Around 2:00 a.m., Ginger's cool nose touched my fingertips, rousing me from slumber. My first thought was that she was ready to whelp her litter. My legs tangled in the sheets, I freed myself and sat straight up in bed. "What's wrong, girl?"

She gazed into my face. Normally, when ready to give birth, my mama dogs were restless, nested, and panted, just for starters. But Ginger showed no signs of impending delivery.

"You okay?" I asked.

She stared back at me with soulful eyes. Ginger normally announced the arrival of strangers, but her ears were pricked and her breathing calm. I wished Mr. Big were still alive. Well, I wished a lot of things.

Ginger glanced around the room. It occurred to me: her keen nostrils could detect the odor of the person who'd pillaged our house. Dogs' sense of smell was far superior to people's. Was that one reason why she'd bitten Donald?

A sickening thought flooded me. The intruder—Donald?—had returned. I leaped to my feet and locked the bedroom door, then made sure the windows were closed securely. Not that a man couldn't break down my puny door or punch a rock through the glass. Whoever had vandalized the house must've known there was nothing of value. I felt a fresh round of anxiety invade me as I envisioned Donald marauding through my bureau drawers.

"Something wrong?" I asked Ginger. She yawned, padded over to her bed—a blanket-lined basket—and flopped on her side, her ribs expanded.

After stubbing my big toe, I climbed into bed and pulled the covers around my chin. To ease myself back to sleep, I pretended I was in the Zooks' upstairs bedroom. Reuben was in the living room reading the Bible: "Do not be anxious about anything … present your requests to God."

The next morning as I emerged from the groggy sheaths of slumber, I forgot where I was. Pretty lame, since I'd slept in this bedroom my whole life. My ears strained for the sounds of cows leaving the milk house, Rhoda's jovial voice in the kitchen, songbirds volleying up and down the octaves. And my nostrils strained for the fragrance of cooking bacon and dark coffee. Instead, I heard the steady stream of cars motoring by on the highway out front. On a Sunday morning, were all these people going to church?

I wished I were spending the day with the Zooks. Rhoda had explained that the congregation met for a service every other Sunday. Today would be a restful time of visiting friends and entertaining neighbors and relatives. I wondered how many would gather at the Zooks' home. How would Armin spend his day?

I peeked at the clock and realized it was already nine o'clock. I'd slept eight hours, but I didn't feel restored. My neck, back, and arms were stiff and bruised from Donald's rough treatment. He could have easily thrown me to the floor. I supposed I should've been grateful he hadn't suppressed his anger; I might have been sucked back in and married an abusive man.

Ginger stretched to her feet and nosed the bedroom door. "Time to go out?" I asked. "You must be hungry." I left her in the enclosed yard for a few minutes, then put her in the laundry room and erected a low portable partition. I gave her fresh water and spooned canned dog food I ordinarily saved for special occasions into her dish.

The kitchen looked clean, better than it had in ages, but I didn't want to be here. I drank black coffee and gobbled dry cereal. Who but a deranged sicko would smash eggs and allow milk to spoil, and break the house apart with such violence? I'd heard most burglaries took under ten minutes. Intruders entered the home, found pillowcases to carry the loot, and took off. But as far as I could tell, nothing was missing. I figured Donald was the perpetrator, but I doubted I could prove it. If I pressed charges he'd probably hire a hotshot attorney and report Ginger.

I'd heard the Amish turned the other cheek and never retaliated. I mulled over the biblical principle and decided to abide by their practices even if I weren't one of them. There was no point in holding on to anger; nothing good came from seeking revenge.

Wandering into the living room, my shoulders slumped as I saw the disarray still awaiting me. If Rhoda were here, she'd have already straightened the house and scrubbed every inch of it. I decided my best approach was to tidy up, then vacuum. I brought out the old stand-up Hoover, plugged it in, and flipped on the switch to make sure it worked. The whirring rattled my eardrums like pebbles in a soda can. After staying in the Zooks' quiet house, I'd forgotten how much the noise grated on my ears. I'd spent a lifetime ignoring the obvious, sidestepping to make others happy. I turned off the vacuum.

I noticed my framed photo from high school graduation on the floor, its glass cracked. I stared at the image and hardly recognized myself. My hair had turned darker since high school, and I wondered if I'd fabricated my smile even back then. Had I ever been happy? My vision blurred in and out of sharpness, until I set the photo aside.

A mishmash of papers and envelopes lay on the floor on the worn shag carpet around Pops's small desk. I knelt down to retrieve them. It was going to be a long day, I told myself, so I sat on the swivel chair and took the time to straighten the envelopes and papers according to size.

The largest letter was from a local bank on Route 7, which I figured was a sales pitch to buy CDs. But the words *Payment Due!* in bold red ink grabbed my attention. Some stupid advertising ploy. Using my thumbnail, I ripped open the envelope and slid out a letter, which in essence said Pops was two months behind on his mortgage payments. Huh? Pops had informed me he'd paid off the house in full several years ago.

"You won't believe this," I said to Ginger. Since it was Sunday, I couldn't call the bank to straighten them out. My fingers shuffled through more envelopes addressed to Mr. Edward Bingham, and I found several more from the bank. They contained payment stubs and return envelopes.

"Would Pops take out a mortgage without informing me?" Scrolling back in my memory, I recalled a couple years ago when sales at the car lot had been paltry as the economy plunged. His business had been scraping by; he'd barely accumulated enough cash to purchase inventory and make quarterly tax payments and property taxes.

I rifled through the remaining envelopes, tore open anything from the bank, and was relieved to see no mention of Honest Ed's Used Cars. But the address of this house certainly was. My father had borrowed money, using our home as collateral, without telling me.

This calamity was in part my fault. Besides working part-time on the car lot, I should have taken a second job. And not spent so much money entering and traveling to dog shows. I would have quit if I'd known he was short on funds. My breathing grew shallow and my throat tightened. The room seemed to shrink, smothering me. My heart sped up, hammering against my breastbone.

As I chucked superfluous mail into a wicker wastebasket, Lizzie's words zigzagged through my mind like guppies in a fish tank. She'd promised to ask around about my mother. Apparently Amish work frolics, be they get-togethers for quilting or to clean a house in preparation for a church service or wedding, served as a venue for gossip—not that Lizzie used that word. "Ya know how women enjoy chatting," Lizzie had said. I hoped she'd keep an eye on Armin, too, but I hadn't asked her to.

Then a zany thought entered my mind: a note from my mother could be hiding among this pile of papers. I shuffled through the letters again, then overturned the basket, its contents spilling onto the carpet. On my hands and knees, I pawed through the papers. Most were postcards offering discounts on pizzas or dry-cleaning, and an invitation to attend a local church. The last thing I wanted. If God would allow the very foundation of my life to crumble, why would I want anything to do with him?

What prayers had God ever answered? As a child, I'd begged the Lord to bring my mother home. Last month, I'd pleaded with him to save Mr. Big's life, and now this: more proof that Pops was a liar and God didn't care about me.

I searched every scrap, hoping to find evidence of Mom, but nothing. Then I got to my feet and strode toward Pops's bedroom. I'd have a look around in his private world, which I should have done years ago but hadn't out of respect.

I rounded the corner to see the bed unmade and several of the bureau drawers half open. Nothing new about that; Pops wasn't a meticulous housekeeper. I often picked up his dirty laundry on washday, part of my contribution to living here. His room had not been vandalized like the rest of the house. Which made sense. Donald wouldn't have demeaned himself by entering Pops's bedroom.

If I were Pops, where would I hide my most treasured possessions—like letters from Mom? Most likely in the large safe at the car lot. But I'd looked through that metal cubicle for work in the past, and had seen only business-related documents. If in this house, where? I tried to think like a thief on a mission. I dug through every drawer, plunging my fingers between socks and T-shirts. I checked behind the framed prints adorning the wall, between the mattress and springs. Nothing.

I moved to his closet and pulled the string hanging from the lightbulb, illuminating the small space. Pops didn't own many clothes or shoes, mostly casual stuff. Three out-of-style jackets, the fabric shiny from years of use, a couple pairs of slacks, a few narrow ties, and a half-dozen collared shirts.

I lifted my chin and saw two wooden cigar boxes and a cardboard carton on the shelf. I stood on tiptoes and used a hanger to jiggle them down. They fell to the floor with a thud and a thunk. I stooped, undid a metal latch, and found one was filled with old baseball cards, and the other with a coin collection: Indian Head nickels, a few silver dollars, and a bundle of two-dollar bills. I doubted any of it was worth much beyond its original value. In my rankled state, I scorned my father's meager possessions. If the coins or cards had any monetary value, surely he would have sold them instead of taking out a mortgage on the house. The hairs on the nape of my neck lifted as a surge of antagonism swashed through my veins.

The remaining carton—slightly larger than a shoebox—crouched on the shelf out of my reach. I fetched a stool and climbed up. The box was light. Then I felt something shift inside. I admonished myself to expect nothing. The Rolling Stones' song "You Can't Always Get What You Want"—a refrain Pops sang back in the days when he was healthy—looped through my mind. I was living proof of Mick Jagger's statement.

Like an archaeologist lifting the lid off an ancient sarcophagus, I held my breath, opened the carton, and saw a stack of papers: a title for a '48 Ford that might've been Pops's first vehicle for all I knew, a letter from Grandma Leah begging him to come home—I wondered where she'd sent it, but there was no envelope—and two yellowing legal-size pieces of paper. The first was a birth certificate. Mine! Both my parents' names were cited: Mother: Mavis Miller. Father: Edward Bingham.

I reached for the next paper, praying it was their marriage license in spite of what Pops had told me. But it was a mimeographed copy of the purchase agreement for this house—not the title—of no value. I dropped it back into the box.

I felt like a dunce for feeling devastated by what I already knew was true. I was illegitimate, just like Donald said.

My face contorted like melting wax. I bent at the waist and allowed my tears to flood into my open palms. Sobs heaved out, their grotesque sounds echoing off the walls as I wallowed in despair. Pops had always told me to keep a stiff upper lip, but I couldn't anymore. I hobbled to the living room, then collapsed onto the couch.

The doorbell ding-donged. I looked out the kitchen window to make sure Donald's car was nowhere in sight. Then I opened the door to find Ralph and his pleasantly plump wife, Sheila, with her overpermed hair.

"I never should have let you spend the night here," Ralph said. Sheila bobbed her small head. They were dressed as if on their way to church. She handed me a Starbucks cup covered with a plastic lid.

"Thanks." My hands wrapped around the warm paper cup. "Just what I needed."

"You must have been up until midnight cleaning this kitchen." Ralph eyed the cracked door Donald had kicked in and grimaced. "I'm glad your father wasn't here to see it yesterday."

"Me too." Pops had maintained the house's interior, done all the painting, and built the bookshelves on either side of the small fireplace. His and my books still lay in disarray on the floor among my dog-show trophies.

"You need help?" Ralph's wife asked me.

"I'll be fine," I said with as much moxie as I could rally. I wouldn't admit that a bone-deep fear had overwhelmed me. I'd never felt so alone.

From what Rhoda had told me, I assumed if I were Amish, men and women would be arriving at our home with food and to help me clean. Although it was Sunday, the day of rest. So maybe they'd wait until tomorrow. In any case, the community would restore the home and make sure I was safe and well fed.

After Ralph and Sheila left, my cell phone chimed. I viewed the caller ID to see a Pennsylvania prefix: 717. No name. I hesitated to answer. If it were Pops calling from the phone shanty, should I risk telling him the truth in his fragile state? But it could be Rhoda with bad news about Pops's health. Or Armin. I longed to hear his voice.

"Sally, is that you?" Lizzie said when I answered. "You've gotta come home right away."

"I can't go anywhere." I was tempted to reveal the mayhem.

"Please," she said, her voice nasal, as if her nose were stuffed up, "we need ya here. Your father is fixing to take off. Mamm says he has a doctor's appointment on Thursday, but he won't wait. Mamm says it's not safe for him to drive. He's too weak."

"Why did he decide to leave? Is Reuben harassing him?"

"Nee, he's worried about you. Your father and Dat have made their peace. Dat says Uncle Ed's the only man in the county who's not judging him." Starlings cackling in the background told me she was in the phone shanty. "Dat's fixing to burn his fancy jewelry boxes tomorrow."

I envisioned the inlaid roses on the covers of the boxes, the meticulous craftsmanship. "Can't Mrs. Martin sell them at the Sunflower Secondhand Store?" I asked.

"Nee, not after the bishop ordered them to be destroyed."

"In any case, please don't let my father drive all the way here in his condition."

"Mamm's doing her best to stop him. And, Sally, Armin was hanging around yesterday afternoon, finding every excuse to come over here."

"He didn't bother while I was there."

"He was too busy, I'm sure of it. Can you imagine moving into a new farm and house? He was securing his stock and purchasing equipment and feed." She sniffed twice. "Tell me you're coming back today."

"No, I need to stay here." As soon as the bank opened the next day, I had to call and perhaps go in person. I hoped the banker would deal directly with me even though my name wasn't on the loan.

"What about the Sunflower Secondhand Store?" Lizzie sounded close to tears. "You'd leave Mrs. Martin in the lurch tomorrow?"

"You must have other friends who can take the job."

"None that can ... uh ... use a cash register."

"Come on, I don't believe it. Put a Help Wanted sign in the window. Won't Reuben let you fill in?"

"Well, yah, okay, I'll ask—" Lizzie paused, as if weighing her words.

"Lizzie, please tell me you're not planning to elope with Joe. I saw him—"

"Ach, I never want to hear his name again." She let out a sob, then blew her nose. "He drove by our house yesterday afternoon with an Englisch girl in his car. She was nibbling on his earlobe."

CHAPTER 33

Even when cleaned up, Pops's and my home held little appeal anymore. What had once felt like a cozy sanctuary now looked shabby and drab. I noticed cracks in the ceiling and chips on the painted molding. The house had been defiled.

I was startled by every sound, even the refrigerator motor clicking on. And I'd lost all desire to work at the car lot; I preferred the Sunflower Secondhand Store. If I hadn't been replaced by one of Lizzie's friends. I decided—after I settled things at the bank—I'd drive back to Lancaster County for a look-see, as Pops would say. I might as well face it; his voice and quips inhabited the crevices of my brain. I wondered how many of his idiosyncrasies I unknowingly carried. When the kids taunted me as a child, they'd been right: I was damaged goods. Maybe we all were, maybe that was why we needed God's intervention.

Those jumbled thoughts inundated my brain as I tried to sleep that night—without much success. The next morning, on Monday,

I called the bank and transferred what I had in savings into Pops's checking account to pay off the late payments; my name was on his account so I could make deposits from the car lot. Then with Ralph's help, I exchanged the flamboyant Mustang for a modest 1997 Ford Escort wagon and brought it back to the house. Plenty of room for my clothes and Ginger. I was surprised at how willingly she hopped into the vehicle; she seemed eager to get back to the farm.

My thoughts retraced my initial sojourn to Lancaster County. I hadn't mentioned to Lizzie over the phone that our house had been vandalized, but perhaps Ralph had told Pops about it; I assumed the two men kept in touch. Yesterday, I'd tackled the mountain of books and dog-show trophies sprawled willy-nilly on the living room rug, making vacuuming possible, but the house still seemed grimy to me.

I prayed Pops wasn't on his way here—that we wouldn't pass each other on the highway. I recalled my ire when I'd first examined the letters from the bank. I'd have to confront him, but his health trumped all my other concerns.

Leaving several lights on, I locked the house, climbed into the Escort, and set my purse on the passenger seat. I slid the key into the ignition, set the car in reverse, and rolled a few feet, backing out of our drive. I heard a dull honk. I jammed on the brakes, glanced in the rearview mirror, and saw a midsize passenger van. The vehicle blocked my way. I felt trapped. In my scattered and unbalanced state of mind, I resented anything in my path. I craned my neck and saw its driver—a middle-aged guy with long sideburns—and a passenger: a tall man exiting the van. Armin?

My heart skipped a beat at the sight of him dressed in black pants; vest; and a white, collared shirt. I lowered my window as he ambled over. "You're the last person I expected to see," I said. And the one I wanted to the most.

He rested his elbows on my windowsill. "Hullo, Sally."

I wanted to say something clever and witty, but with his face so close to mine I couldn't speak. He opened the Escort's door.

I shut off the engine, slipped the key in my pocket, and got out. I wondered what he thought of my life here, of Honest Ed's Used Cars. Of me.

"I should have called first."

"It doesn't matter. But you almost missed me." I weighed the pros and cons of telling Armin I was about to drive back to Lancaster County. Would I sound desperate, like I was running after him or plain-old running away?

He glanced into my borrowed car. "Why did ya leave without telling me?"

"Are you kidding? I dropped off your radar screen the night we had supper with your brother."

"Nee, you've been on my mind every minute."

"You haven't acted like it." In spite of the truth of my words, I wanted to fling myself into his arms and hold on to him with all my strength. But I maintained my composure.

He removed his hat and set it on the driver's seat. "I shouldn't have let Nathaniel's spouting off advice get under my skin that night."

I slipped my hand in my pocket and extracted the Escort's key. "What are you doing here, anyway?"

"I came to fetch you."

"I'm supposed to drop everything and come with you just like that?" The key fob dangled between us. "I'm beginning to understand why Rascal ran away." I found him so attractive I could barely look into his face without grinning.

"Ach, that's not fair. He probably caught scent of something."

"And what's to stop you from disappearing again?"

"My farm. My commitment to join the church. And my devotion to you." He moved closer. "I came to tell you I'm sorry I wasn't more attentive these last few days," he said. "I won't burden you with a list of reasons when you're more important to me than any of them."

"Lizzie said you were busy."

"But I should have stopped over. *Es dutt mir leid*—I'm sorry." He moved closer. I could feel his breath. "Will you accept my apology?" he said.

"Yes." Everything about him was impossible to resist. But I supposed the bishop would tell me I should seek God's guidance. So I said a quick silent prayer: I need help!

"Hey, how did you find me?" I asked.

He motioned to the van. "The driver's been here before. That's Arthur, the man who stumbled upon your father and recognized him from childhood. Your dat gave me your home address." His hand traced my cheek as if I were a priceless jewel. "Come back with me. We've got plenty of room in the van for you and Ginger."

"Are you sure my father's still there?" I asked.

"He was getting ready to leave, but Reuben convinced him to stay and help him with a project this afternoon. They've come to a truce. Ach, poor Reuben's past has caught up with him." Armin gave his head a slight shake. "One lie leads to another. Yah? Not that I haven't been guilty of that myself. I've lied plenty."

"Why are you telling me all this?"

"Because from this moment forth I promise you complete honesty. My reason for coming here is to ask you again if I may court you."

I recalled our dinner at his brother's and felt my legs stiffen. "But you're infatuated with another woman. I saw it written all over your face. You're in love with Esther's daughter, Holly." Or had I imagined it? If he really did love Holly, my chest might cave in.

"Nee, I'm not and never was. Old Anna—Holly's grandmother—had hoped for something that wasn't meant to be. And now Holly's happily married and with child."

"Even so, I can tell you resent Zach, the way you talk about him."

"Yah, I admit for many years I've harbored a grudge because he's held in such high esteem. That has nothing to do with Holly. It was false pride and I regret it."

He cocked his head. "And how about you? You were all set to get married not long ago, were you not?"

"Yes, but I guarantee that won't happen. I never want to see him again and I'm sure the feeling's mutual." I opened my mouth to list the reasons Armin's and my relationship wouldn't work either, but his firm lips found mine for a brief but impeccable kiss.

When we parted, I felt dizzy—in a good way, like a child who'd twirled in circles and was waiting for the world to stop spinning. But I reminded myself to keep a clear head and regain my footing. My future was at stake.

I said, "The first night I was at the Zooks' I saw you slip Rhoda a note."

"From an Englisch neighbor who'd seen Reuben ordering a drink. Ach, the bartender knew Reuben by name. I delivered the note, that's all." The corner of his mouth quirked up. "Did ya think there was something going on between Rhoda and me?"

"No." I expelled a puff of air, then sucked it back in. "Well, I didn't know what to think."

"Several people have reported seeing Reuben. But I best let ya hear it from him or Rhoda. There's been enough tongue wagging in our district to last us a lifetime." A smile fanned across his face. "Wait until you see my new home. I repainted the kitchen the color of your eyes and laid new vinyl flooring. Please come back so I can court you."

"Yes, okay, I will," I said, as if my tongue were forming the words before I could even think them.

He stepped between me and the van, providing a shield of privacy. Armin bent down, his mouth seeking mine. Not a polite, demure kiss but the kind of lips-melting-together kiss that moved worlds. The kind of kiss I'd always longed for.

The van's driver tapped on the horn. When Armin and I parted, I glanced over and saw Arthur raise his hand and point at his wristwatch. While Armin and Arthur transferred my belongings and Ginger into the van, I ran the Escort's keys back to the car lot and explained the situation to Ralph. Then Armin helped me climb into the backseat of the van. He circled his hand around my waist and gathered me close. My head on his shoulder, I watched the scenery float by out the side windows for several hours. In the span of a couple of days, springtime had reclaimed the land. The trees by the road displayed the vibrant greens I'd noticed last week, but conflicts still wrestled within me. How would I approach Pops when I saw him?

The van finally rolled into the Zooks' barnyard. Through the windows I saw Pops and Reuben carrying armloads of jewelry boxes and other wooden objects out of Reuben's workshop and dumping them in a pile.

Arthur opened the doors and helped us out. The sun shone brilliantly; the sky was hard cobalt, like lapis lazuli. All traces of snow were gone.

Rhoda and Lizzie trotted down the back steps and hugged me. "Willkumm!" Rhoda said.

"Please, won't ya let me take Ginger for a walk?" Lizzie asked.

"Sure, she needs to stretch her legs." I snapped on Ginger's lead and handed it to Lizzie. The two of them headed off down the lane with Rascal prancing alongside them.

I waved at Pops, but he didn't seem to notice. Nor did Reuben.

"I'm so happy to see you, Sally." Rhoda glanced to Reuben and Pops, then turned her back to them as if wishing the whole scene would disappear.

"Could ya bring our Sally's things inside?" Rhoda asked Armin.

"Yah, of course." He and Arthur emptied the van and ferried my belongings into the house. Then Armin paid Arthur, who sped away the moment the cash exchanged hands.

Bishop Troyer's buggy moseyed into the barnyard. Taking his time, the bishop got out and tethered his horse.

I turned to watch Pops and Reuben. His movements jerky, Reuben heaved up a metal gasoline can and spurted a stream of liquid over the mountain of music boxes.

"Hey, wait up, Reuben." Armin strode toward him. "Are ya crazy?"

But before Armin reached him, Reuben pulled out a box of wooden matches, struck one, and dropped the flame atop the gasoline-soaked boxes. With a roar, a blazing ball of sparks exploded, followed by a black cloud of smoke. Reuben whirled around, covered his face with one arm, and patted his singed beard with his free hand.

"Do you have a fire extinguisher?" Pops called above the crackling fire.

"In my workshop." Reuben pointed as a burning scrap of paper sailed toward the building. It landed on a thicket of dried grasses and ignited them, then spread to a stack of wood alongside the structure. Like ravenous dragons' tongues, the flames licked the side of the workshop, darkening its white walls. The partially open window on the workshop allowed the fire to scramble in.

Pops dashed past Reuben and shouldered open the workshop's door. A billow of smoke belched out, smelling of turpentine and paint. He vanished inside for a minute. An explosion shattered the air.

Rhoda shrieked—a primal screech.

"My propane tank." Reuben's face twisted.

"Pops!" I envisioned my father collapsing to the ground and being consumed by the flames. Or maybe he'd already died of asphyxiation.

I headed after him, but Rhoda grabbed my hand. "You'd better stay here."

"Please, God, if you never answer another prayer," I said. "Save him."

As Armin raced to the shop's door, Pops staggered from the noxious cloud carrying a fire extinguisher. Coughing, he fell to his knees, then used the red canister to prop himself up. He turned to face the scorching inferno, but his legs were too weak for him to stand. Armin seized the fire extinguisher and blasted the flames nearest the barn.

"The workshop's a lost cause," Armin said. He shouted to Bishop Troyer. "Use the garden hose to spray the barn!"

The bishop yanked a hose over to Armin as Reuben turned it on. Water shot from the hose, but it couldn't reach high enough to do more than dampen the lower half of the barn. Sparks were pulsating from the workshop's roof.

Lizzie dashed into the barnyard with the dogs.

"Hurry to the phone shanty," Rhoda told her. "Call 911."

"Here, take my cell phone." I tapped in the number and handed it to Lizzie, who rattled off the Zooks' address. Then I raced to the back stoop and tied Ginger to the railing.

Smoke hovered over the barnyard. When I looked at the small gap separating the workshop from the barn, my throat closed in on itself. The majestic structure must have been over a hundred years old, dry as kindling. One gust of wind and the flames would leap to it.

A tabby cat streaked out of the barn door, followed by another. I was glad Armin had taken Thunder to his new farm.

"The buggy horses!" Rhoda said.

I heard one scream—a shocking cry of panic.

Reuben stood staring at the barn as if paralyzed—a helpless spectator watching his world dissolve. Armin continued to spray water as Jeremy and Peter sprinted into the barn to free the horses, the animals' eyes bulging.

"Thank the Lord the cows are in the pasture," Rhoda said.

A moan of sirens in the distance expanded like a howling pack of wolves. The blaring increased, deafening. Two fire trucks, their lights flashing, ground down the lane, then into the barnyard. A crew of a dozen uniformed men leaped from the vehicles and turned on their pumps. Minutes later, rivers of water blasted the barn, saturating its siding.

I stood engulfed in smoke, my eyes burning. A crowd gathered as Nathaniel and other men dressed in black arrived on foot or in buggies to offer assistance. Battling for supremacy the fire fighters soaked the hissing furnace and finally subdued the flames. The smoke turned white. A wet stench permeated the air.

"My ... shop," Reuben sputtered to a fireman who added more flame retardant to what was now a blackened empty shell, a tangle of metal, charred plywood, and filing cabinets, their contents burned.

"You're lucky your barn is still standing." The fireman, sporting a mustache, glanced at the gasoline can on the ground and raised an eyebrow. Then he and his crew inspected the barn, which remained unscathed on the inside. Only the closest wall was singed—a reminder of how bad it could've been.

CHAPTER 34

Reuben slogged over to the spigot and turned off the hose. Then he, Armin, Pops, the bishop, and Nathaniel huddled in a circle and spoke in hushed tones. If I'd been one of them, I'd be elated the barn was still standing, but I figured Reuben was embarrassed—his face was streaked black and the lower third of his beard was missing. The bishop and Pops might be admonishing themselves for allowing Reuben to use gasoline. Even I knew it was a foolhardy method to start a fire.

"Praise God." Rhoda's hand wrapped her throat. She and Lizzie thanked the fire fighters as they gathered their hoses and prepared to leave. "May we serve you anything?" Rhoda asked. "Surely you're thirsty and hungry."

"Thanks, ma'am, but no time. Just got an aid call—not a fire, I'm glad to say." They climbed aboard their gigantic trucks, backed out of the barnyard and lane, and rumbled away. Lizzie waved at them and one responded with a wave of his own. If the barn had caught fire, the men might've been here half the night trying to tame the inferno.

My emotions were scrambled, my adrenaline spent. Sitting on the bottom step next to Ginger, I must have looked like a ghost. Bishop Troyer ambled over to me.

"*Was fehlt dir den*, Sally? Are you all right?" He lowered himself next to me. "You look sad in your face."

I watched Pops poke the pile of burnt jewelry boxes with a rake; I assumed he was checking for live embers. Reuben came alongside him and patted Pops on the shoulder—what seemed an act of gratitude and admiration. Pops had committed a daredevil feat, and I was thankful beyond measure he'd emerged from the workshop unscathed.

"I'm grateful everyone's okay and that the barn didn't burn," I said to the bishop.

"It was the Lord's will or it would have."

"How can you be so sure?"

"Do you think it was a coincidence that Ezekiel came back and that you're here?"

"I don't know what to think about anything." I gathered my courage, as if I were about to leap across a stream. "Did you know my mother ditched me when I was a toddler? I don't even know for sure that Pops is my father."

"Do you think the Lord holds that against ya?"

Elbows on knees, I clasped my hands. "I've read about the sins of the father being passed on for three generations."

"That was before the Lord atoned for our transgressions by sacrificing his Son."

"Do you really believe that's true?"

"Yah, absolutely. Do you not know how Nathaniel's Esther left for the majority of her adult life, then was welcomed back by her family and the community? Think about the apostle Peter, who denied Christ three times. And the apostle Paul, who claimed to be the worst sinner of all after persecuting early Christians. Both went on to be church leaders and write most of the New Testament."

I envisioned the letters from the bank and felt my anger toward Pops rekindling. "My father has lied to me over and over. I just learned he took out a mortgage on our house and wasn't paying the bank."

"'Tis not my place to judge another man. The Lord will do that. But it is my position to admonish willful disobedience and to encourage repentance. Your father could ask the Almighty to forgive him."

Using shovels and pitchforks, several bearded Amishmen helped Pops unearth the charred rubble. Steam continued to rise from what used to be Reuben's workshop. Amish women, among them Esther and Anna, unfolded a card table and covered it with baked goods and paper plates—for the men, I guessed. Lizzie and Rhoda brought out cups and lemonade. I watched people, both Amish and English, continue to arrive to help, a community of goodwill and solidarity.

I zeroed in on Armin—his wide shoulders and rugged good looks.

"I've heard you and Armin are growing close," the bishop said, following my stare. "He told me he was going to see you today with hopes of bringing you back."

"That's true." Ginger's moist nose nudged the back of my hand. Her maternal condition demanded I settle down somewhere for the next few months. "I'd like to stay in the area. Rhoda said I could live with them if Reuben agreed. Would you be opposed?"

"To your living with them? Not at all. But do you understand that Armin is planning to join the church?"

"Yes, he told me." I swung my knees toward Bishop Troyer. "Would you let me join too?"

"I suggest you try living a Plain life for six months—maybe a year—before you consider joining, to see if you can make the adjustments." His eyes softened. "'Tis a lifetime commitment, do ya understand that? Some Englischers look at us as a perfect society, but we have our share of troubles, trials, and temptations, just like anyone else." He glanced to my father, then back to me. "I know of a dozen people who've joined the Amish church and then eventually left. On the other hand, a few have joined us and stayed."

"I've felt alone my whole life," I blurted out.

"If God cares about the sparrows—according to a verse in Matthew—then he certainly cares about you. The hairs on your head are numbered."

My hand moved to my hair, straggling out of its ponytail. I doubted if God cared if I went bald. But here, I might finally feel whole.

"I would never proselytize—encourage an Englischer to join us," he said. "But come meet with me when and if you're ready. For starters we can talk about forgiveness. Something we all struggle with."

"Even you?"

"Yah, we're all sinners in our heart. 'Tis human nature. I've asked the Almighty to forgive me a dozen times today."

I wondered if he were referring to his reaction toward Pops and Reuben. "How can you forgive someone who's never asked for it? Like my mother."

"When we hold on to unforgiveness, it's like an iron chain around our neck dragging us into the past." He stroked his beard. "You come by, and we'll talk about it more."

"I might just do that," I said. "In fact, I will."

Smelling of smoke, Pops shambled over to us. Soot covered his clothes, and black streaks masked his sweaty cheeks. He held out his arms. "There's my girl."

I leaped to my feet and hugged him. "Thank God you're okay." In the short time he'd been here, I could tell he'd put on a couple pounds. "If anything happened to you I don't know what I'd do," I said. "Now we need to get your kidneys better."

"Rhodie's taking me to a specialist in a few days."

The bishop handed Pops a white handkerchief and he dabbed his face.

"She's already changed my diet—lowered my salt and protein intake. And she's praying to beat the band." He scuffed his toe into the ground and dislodged a pebble.

"Aren't you happy about that?" I asked, noticing his look of defeat.

He shook his head. "I've failed you as a father."

"No, you haven't. You've been two parents in one. The best." Tears pressed at the backs of my eyes. "I shouldn't have taken out my hostility on you."

"But I've made a mess of things," Pops said. "Even if I get better, I can't work on the car lot anymore. I need rest and Rhodie insists I recuperate here. Ralph wants to buy Honest Ed's from me lock, stock, and barrel, but I don't want to leave you high and dry." He dabbed around his eyes. "There's more I need to tell you."

"Pops, I saw the letters from the bank. I know you took out a second mortgage."

"Oh." He crammed the handkerchief into his pocket. "And to think I had the impudence to call myself Honest Ed. The only person I fooled was myself."

"If you'd told me you needed money, maybe I could have helped." I took his elbow and assisted him onto the step next to Bishop Troyer. "I could have taken on a part-time job and still worked on the lot when you needed me."

"I thought I could handle it—" His chin dipped. "I'm no use to anyone. But I could pay off the house with the money from Ralph and give it to you, Sally."

"Thanks, but I wouldn't want to live there without you."

"Would you rather I leave?" Bishop Troyer asked.

"No, please stay." Pops seemed comfortable sitting next to this righteous man. I wondered if they'd spoken in my absence. "No more secrets," Pops said. "Yah?"

"Including about Mom?" I said.

"I figured I was protecting you by keeping you from locating her."

"Then you know where she is?"

He brushed soot off his pants leg. "No, but I'll help you track her down if that's your wish."

I glanced over to the women—Rhoda, Lizzie, Esther, Anna, and more—offering snacks and drinks to everyone helping. I was tired, so very tired, of carrying around my anger, my disappointments, and my bitterness. My hand on the railing, I closed my eyes and listened to the women's laughter and conversation. Then all their joyful chatter quieted. I could hear only the breeze tickling my ears and a bird's trilling. I inhaled the farmland fragrances of anticipated springtime.

I prayed: Dear God, I'm not strong enough to make it on my own. I need you, now and forever.

A mantle as smooth and plush as velvet seemed to drape itself across my shoulders, comforting and soothing my weary soul. It was as if the God of the whole universe had materialized in this barnyard to tell me I'd never be alone again. He was a better father than Pops could ever be. He would never let me down. Would never abandon me as my mother had. I experienced peace and tranquility I'd never felt before.

I opened my eyes to see Pops watching me with a worried expression. "Well, of course you'd want to meet your mother," he said.

"Maybe next year. You're the guy who raised and loved me. And you were right, she could have found me if she'd wanted to." I took his hand, the one I'd held on to all my life. "I've got more important things to think about right now."

"But can you ever forgive me?" His voice cracked.

"Yes, of course." The art of forgiveness; it was time I learned it.

CHAPTER 35

Carrying a couple doughnuts, Armin sauntered over to us. "I've got to head to my place." He handed me one. "Would ya like to come with me, Sally?"

When I hesitated, Pops said, "Sure, go ahead, honey. I need to talk to the bishop."

Strolling with Armin along the side of the road, I sank my teeth into the most scrumptious chocolate-covered doughnut ever. I was surprised my taste buds still functioned after all I'd been through. Maybe everything was better with Armin at my side.

I'd left Ginger with Lizzie and Rhoda; Rascal tugged on his leash—a gift from Nathaniel—in front of Armin. After swallowing his doughnut down in two gulps, Armin seemed quiet. I considered the possibility he was pondering our relationship and having second thoughts.

My legs grew heavy. I reminded myself Armin had endured a long day and then helped subdue a fire. The Zooks' barn still stood intact. Pops was safe and the two of us reunited. And Lizzie had dumped her lowlife boyfriend. Answered prayers aplenty. The words to "Amazing Grace" filled my head: "I once was lost, but now am found; was blind, but now I see." No matter what happened between Armin and me, I would praise God.

My labored steps lightened. We passed Nathaniel and Esther's stately home and walked until we reached a two-story white clapboard house. Green shades covered the windows at half-staff. A small Daadi Haus clung to a corner, where Esther's mother, Anna, had once lived. A freshly painted white picket fence, a mailbox, and a curved trellis greeted us.

"I've never seen such an inviting entrance," I said.

He sent me a darting glance. "Do ya mean it?"

"Absolutely. Couldn't be prettier."

The color in his cheeks heightened; Armin looked younger. He unclipped Rascal, who bounded onto the wide porch.

"We're using the front door?" I mounted several steps.

"Yah, for today. I want to make a fine gut impression."

Aha, he was nervous.

He opened the unlocked door, and Rascal hastened ahead of us. Following the energetic canine, we crossed the front hall and strolled through the living room. I savored every detail: the polished wooden floorboards and throw rugs, a stone hearth. I envisioned myself nestling in front of it with Armin.

He must have noticed I was lagging. "Come on, Sally." He took my hand and led me into the kitchen, where Rascal sat waiting by the refrigerator. A table large enough to accommodate ten to twelve dominated the room. The counters looked newly varnished, as did the oak cabinet doors. I glanced at the walls: a light cerulean blue,

like a rippling creek on a sunny day—the color Armin said he saw
when he looked in my eyes. I hadn't realized my eyes were so beautiful. Which made me feel beautiful and feminine.

"Well, what do ya think?" he asked.

"It's *wunderbaar*," I said, taking my first stab at Pennsylvania
Dutch. But I knew his question was serious and the implications of
it lay as deep as the ocean floor.

My mind churned with insecurities. I was touched that he'd
gone to all the trouble for me. But was I really the woman to fulfill
his dreams and was he the right man?

I peeked out the window and admired the freshly painted white
barn—smaller than Nathaniel's, yet substantial. Not to mention
several outbuildings and a towering silo and corncrib.

"Can ya imagine yourself living here?" Armin said. "With me,
that is."

I faced him and felt a tingling of attraction. I reminded myself:
Armin was not asking me to go to a movie; he was proposing marriage and that I join the Amish church. I replayed the bishop's words
in my mind and deliberated all the doubts and burdens I carried.
Most self-imposed, if I were honest with myself. Our pastor in New
Milford had said we should give our troubles over to the Lord. But
it was hard to let go.

"My top priority needs to be my father," I said, knowing I was
sidestepping Armin's question.

"I heard him tell Reuben he'd help rebuild the workshop tomorrow. The two of them are starting a new business making rocking
chairs—after running the idea past Bishop Troyer, of course. I can't
imagine the bishop will disapprove."

"Pops means well, but he might not be able to fulfill his promises."

"Yah, I know he's ill. But today, he proved he's a brave man."

"Sometimes people dive into things without thinking them through."

"He had the courage to raise you, Sally. For that alone he's gained my admiration."

"He got stuck with me. That's how it happened."

"Maybe we could all say the same thing. But some people run away from their obligations. I did, for many a year after our parents died. But Nathaniel never gave up on me. Nor did the bishop." He extracted a meatless ham hock from the refrigerator, then opened the door to the utility room and gave the bone to Rascal, who carried his booty to a private spot.

Armin closed the door behind him and washed his hands. "By the way, I asked your dat to come live in my Daadi Haus after we get married, and he agreed."

"Pops living here?"

"Yah. We'll want him to move in, eventually." He gave me a slow smile. "Ya want to come out and see my new Percherons? Four perfectly matched beauties."

"Armin, what are you trying to do, change the subject?"

"Nee, I'm wanting to show my future wife her farm."

"But Bishop Troyer said I should try living the Plain life for at least six months, if not a year. Even then, he may not think I'm ready. And I might not be."

"Yah, I know you could change your mind and drive off into the sunset in a sporty red coupe. But I don't think ya will. Not with Thunder and me willing to take you anywhere ya need to go in the county and a passenger van at your disposal. Once we marry and start a family, you'll want to stick around. I'm sure of it."

I envisioned myself cradling a baby while a toddler crawled on this very floor. As much as I longed for a husband and children, was the whole notion of my becoming Amish insane, like a tightrope walker without a net? "But, Armin—"

"I know all I need to know, Sally. Except for one thing. Do ya love me as I love you?"

I recalled the night we'd met, the evening he'd driven Thunder and the buggy in the snowstorm, his arrival after the break-in, and battling the fire. At what point had I given him my heart? He owned it now hook, line, and sinker, as Pops would say.

"Well, do ya?" His brown eyes were intense, eating me up.

"Yes, I do love you, Armin King." My whole world centered around him. "I didn't know what love was until I met you."

"Me neither." I heard an unexpected hitch in his voice, as though he were holding back tears. He placed his hands at my waist. "I'll never leave nor forsake you, like your Mudder." As he said the words, her fuzzy image lingered like a phantom on the periphery of my mind. I would not allow her to rob me of my happiness again.

"Do ya look forward to becoming Mrs. Armin King and living on this farm?" Armin tilted his head and gave me an adorable grin.

"Yes. But will I ever fit in the community?" All my life I'd wanted to belong.

"You already do, my darling Sally."

He kissed me with such tenderness I could hardly breathe. I sank into his embrace, his strength supporting me.

EPILOGUE

Lizzie's mind spun like the blades of Dat's windmill on this breezy late-November day. She couldn't believe she was attending her cousin Sally's wedding to Armin King.

The fact Sally joined the Amish church eight months after arriving was akin to a miracle, according to Mamm, who'd said it was Sally's destiny to spend the rest of her life here among her people, her real family. With the man she adored.

Scarcely hearing the sermon, Lizzie sighed as she scanned her parents' home. The partitions had been removed and three hundred relatives and neighbors settled on backless wooden benches brought in yesterday—men on one side and women on the other. Among them Lizzie saw Anna, Esther and Nathaniel, and Zach and Holly Fleming, who cradled their baby girl.

The minister completed his sermon. Lizzie stood and pivoted to the wooden benches along with the rest of the congregation. She knelt during the silent prayer, then stood, still facing the bench. The deacon read a passage from Matthew 19, verses 1 to 12. She was only half listening until the deacon said, "What God hath joined together let no man put asunder." When he finished, she and all others rotated, and sat again. Lizzie tried to find a comfortable position without success.

Bishop Troyer rose and moved before them as if this were a most solemn occasion. Yet Lizzie noticed the corners of his mouth tipping up as he delivered the main sermon, listing biblical references to marriage. Mamm, Esther, Anna, and several other women dabbed the corners of their eyes. If Lizzie weren't mistaken, Dat and Uncle Ed had their handkerchiefs out too. Even Lizzie felt moisture creeping onto her cheeks when she contemplated the beautiful story of love and God's mercy.

"You may now come forth in the name of the Lord," the bishop said to Sally and Armin. They strolled together holding hands and stood before him. He first questioned Armin. "And you will not leave her until death separates you?"

"Yah." Armin looked especially handsome in his new black suit.

"And, Sally—" Bishop Troyer repeated the questions to Sally and she answered in an elated voice.

"Yes." Her cheeks flushed and her eyes glistened, as if she'd wandered in the desert for forty years and had stumbled upon an oasis.

"Do you promise to be loyal to her and care for her if she should have adversity, affliction, sickness, weakness, or faintheartedness?" the bishop asked Armin.

"Yah, I do." Armin's voice was saturated with confidence and determination.

Bishop Troyer asked Sally the same question.

"Yes." Sally glanced down at the sky-blue dress and white organza apron and cape Mamm had made for her. Mamm was giving her sewing lessons, but Sally said she wanted each article of clothing to be perfect—as perfect as everything else about this day.

Bishop Troyer placed Sally's right hand in Armin's and put his hands above and beneath theirs. Moments later, he pronounced, "Go forth in the name of the Lord. You are now man and wife."

Armin grinned and Sally's full lips parted. Lizzie bet she longed to kiss her new husband—and Armin looked equally eager—but they must wait until tonight when they were alone. They seemed to float on air as they returned to their seats.

Another minister addressed the congregation, followed by two others, giving Armin and Sally their blessing.

Ach, why didn't they hurry up? Lizzie couldn't tame her skittering thoughts. She mulled over the last few months. She and her mamm, with Esther's help, had had their hands full planning for Sally's wedding and cultivating celery, a Lancaster County tradition, to be eaten at the feast soon to follow this service. Lizzie captured a whiff of roasting chicken emanating from the kitchen.

Lizzie envisioned herself sitting with Sally and Armin at the corner table—the *Eck*—for the festive and bounteous meal soon to come. Sally had requested everyone sing "Amazing Grace" later, because there had been so much healing in her life. And in her father's.

To add to Sally's joy, her dog Ginger had given birth to four puppies, just as Zach predicted. Dat insisted he wanted a sassy female pup, shocking Lizzie and Mamm. A dog in the house eating scraps from the table? What next?

Bishop Troyer stood again and made a few closing comments. Lizzie fiddled with her Kapp strings as the assembly received the benediction, then sang the final hymn.

The moment the hymn ended Armin and Sally slipped out the door. In one fluid motion, Armin swept Sally up, twirled her around, then lowered her to the ground for a brief embrace. Lizzie and her friends were close on their heels. A crowd of well-wishers surrounded the couple.

Lizzie had never seen Sally look so radiant. Sally's and Lizzie's gazes met. The two extended their hands and clasped each other in a hug.

"I never thought I could be so happy," Sally said in her ear. "And all because of your emails."

Lizzie felt a bit prideful for setting this roller-coaster romance in motion, but she knew deep down she'd played but a small part in Sally and Ed's coming home.

Amazing Grace

Amazing grace! How sweet the sound
that saved a wretch like me!
I once was lost, but now am found;
was blind, but now I see.

'Twas grace that taught my heart to fear,
and grace my fears relieved;
how precious did that grace appear
the hour I first believed.

Through many dangers, toils, and snares,
I have already come;
'tis grace hath brought me safe thus far,
and grace will lead me home.

The Lord has promised good to me,
his word my hope secures;
he will my shield and portion be,
as long as life endures.

Yea, when this flesh and heart shall fail,
and mortal life shall cease,
I shall possess, within the veil,
a life of joy and peace.

When we've been there ten thousand years,
bright shining as the sun,
we've no less days to sing God's praise
than when we first begun.

By John Newton (1725–1807)

Acknowledgments

It is with deep gratitude that I thank my readers, each and every one of you. Thanks, Facebook friends, who have encouraged me, including Karla Hanns, who helped me often, and many, many more. I appreciate all of you!

I am greatly indebted to the folks at my publishing house, David C Cook, in no special order: Ingrid Beck, Amy Konyndyk, Michelle Webb, Karen Stoller, the hardworking sales team, and others. Don Pape, thank you for your faith in me.

Thanks, Traci Dupree, for your editing expertise. Kudos to librarians who have requested and recommended my books!

Thank you to the many Amish who helped me tremendously but prefer not to be mentioned by name. Thank you, Sam and Susie Lapp, and Old Order Amish quilter Emma Stoltzfus of E S Quilts in Lancaster County, Pennsylvania. Thank you, Lisa Ravenholt, for answering my equestrian questions, Connie Sidles, author and noted bird authority, Earlene Luke, dog breeder/handler/judge extraordinaire, and Donald Kraybill, author and expert of the Amish. Three cheers for Robert and Lisa-Ann at Web Designs by LAO, always ready to come to my aid.

A thunderous applause to my weekly writers group comprised of published authors: Judy Bodmer, Roberta Kehle, Kathleen Kohler, Gigi Murfitt, Thornton Ford, Paul Malm, and Marty Nystrom. Bravo to my steadfast literary agent, Sandra Bishop!

... a little more ...

When a delightful concert comes to an end,

the orchestra might offer an encore.

When a fine meal comes to an end,

it's always nice to savor a bit of dessert.

When a great story comes to an end,

we think you may want to linger.

And so, we offer ...

AfterWords—just a little something more after you

have finished a David C Cook novel.

We invite you to stay awhile in the story.

Thanks for reading!

Turn the page for ...

- **Discussion Questions**

Discussion Questions
for *Forever Amish*

1. Why is Sally so attracted to Armin, other than his good looks? Are they opposites, or do they have a lot in common? Do you think their marriage will last?

2. To marry Armin, Sally must give up her English/modern life and join the Amish church. Why do you think she is willing to do this? What will she lose and what will she gain?

3. In what ways has Sally lived a shallow life in the past, even with her many activities and sporadic church attendance?

4. Was Lizzie Zook justified in tracking down Sally and Ed, knowing her father and the bishop did not approve?

5. Why do you think Ed lied to Sally her whole life? Do you think he was trying to protect her or did he harbor other motives? Do you have empathy for him? What did he lose by leaving his Amish family and community? What will he gain by returning?

6. If you were in Sally's position, would you run a DNA test to certify that Pops was your biological dad or would you be satisfied that—in every way—he has been a father to you?

7. How was Sally's life affected knowing her mother has spurned her? Would you search for your mother although you may experience rejection?

8. How did Sally's father's illness alter the trajectory of her life? How does any ailing parent affect their child's life?

9. What are Reuben's good traits? Does he deserve acceptance and forgiveness as much as any other person?

10. How would you feel if you found out you were Old Order Amish? Would you seek your roots, wish to meet your relatives, and possibly adopt some of their traditions? Does anything attract you to their lifestyle?

11. What did Sally learn about forgiveness from the Amish? How about you?

About the Author

Author Kate Lloyd is a passionate observer of human relationships. A native of Baltimore, Kate spends time with family and friends in Lancaster County, Pennsylvania, the inspiration for her bestselling novels *Leaving Lancaster* and *Pennsylvania Patchwork*. She is a member of the Lancaster County Mennonite Historical Society. Kate and her husband live in the Pacific Northwest, the setting for Kate's first novel, *A Portrait of Marguerite*. Kate studied art and art history in college. She has worked a variety of jobs, including car salesperson and restaurateur. For many years she owned prize-winning show dogs.

Find out more about Kate Lloyd at
Website: www.katelloyd.net
Blog: http://katelloyd.net/blog
Facebook: www.facebook.com/katelloydbooks
Twitter: @KateLloydAuthor
Pinterest: @KateLloydAuthor

Or contact her by mail at
2301 NE Blakeley Street, #102, Seattle, WA 98105